Phoebe and Her Unicorn in Unicorn Theater

Dana Simpson

Andrews McMeel
PUBLISHING®

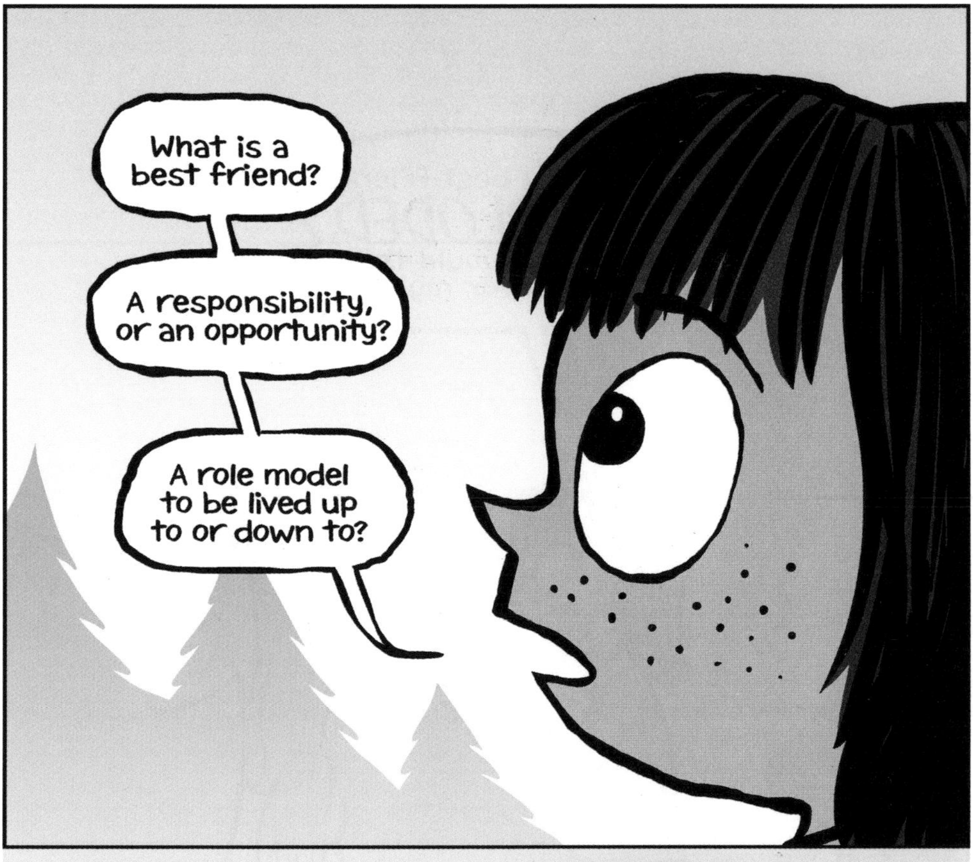
What is a best friend?
A responsibility, or an opportunity?
A role model to be lived up to or down to?

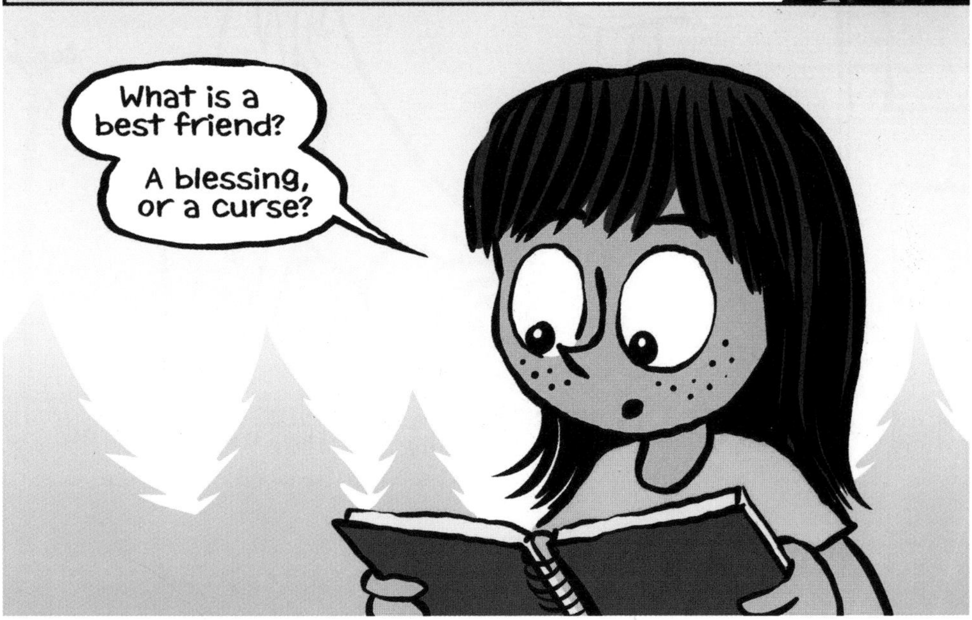
What is a best friend?
A blessing, or a curse?

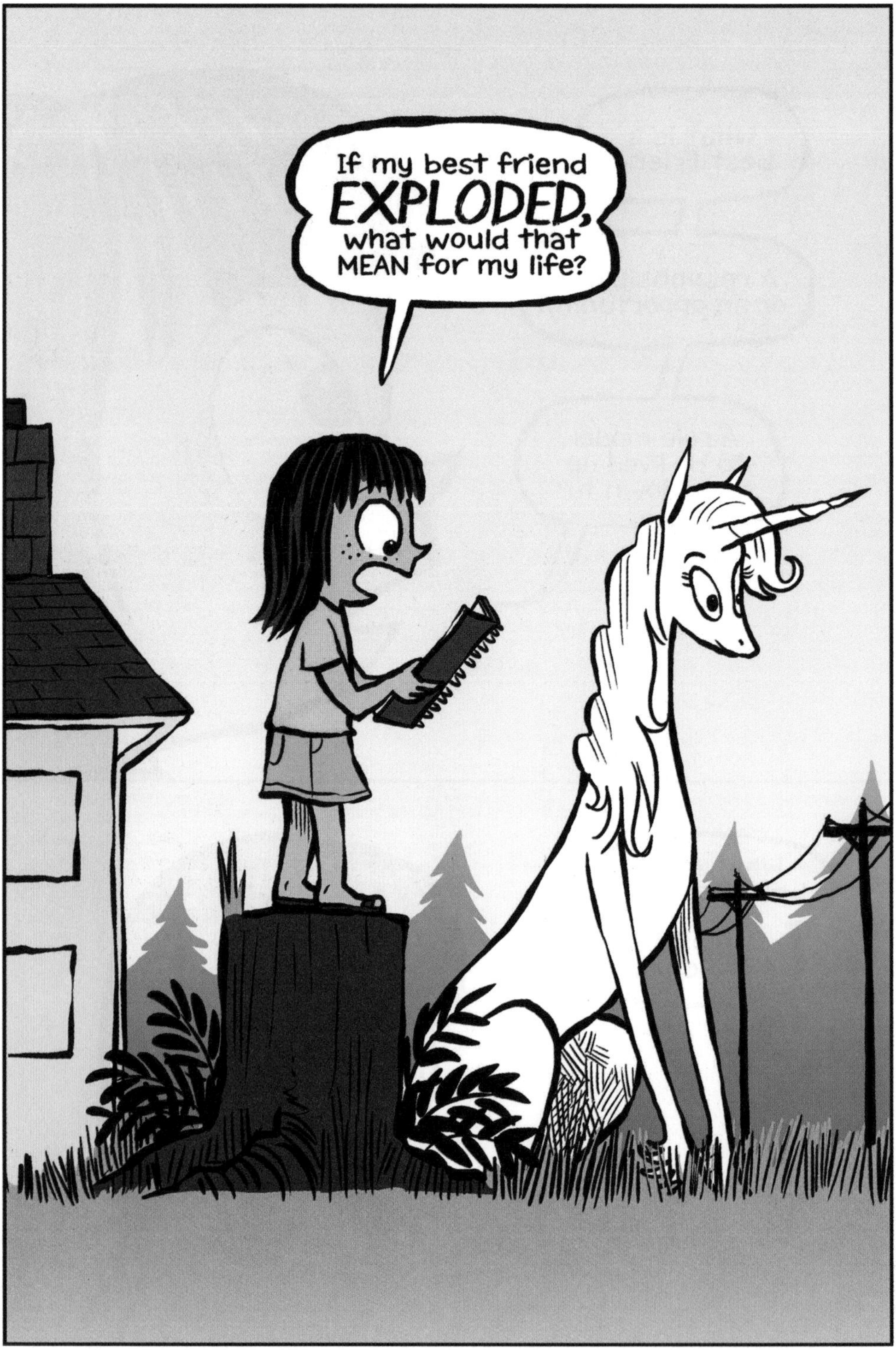
If my best friend EXPLODED, what would that MEAN for my life?

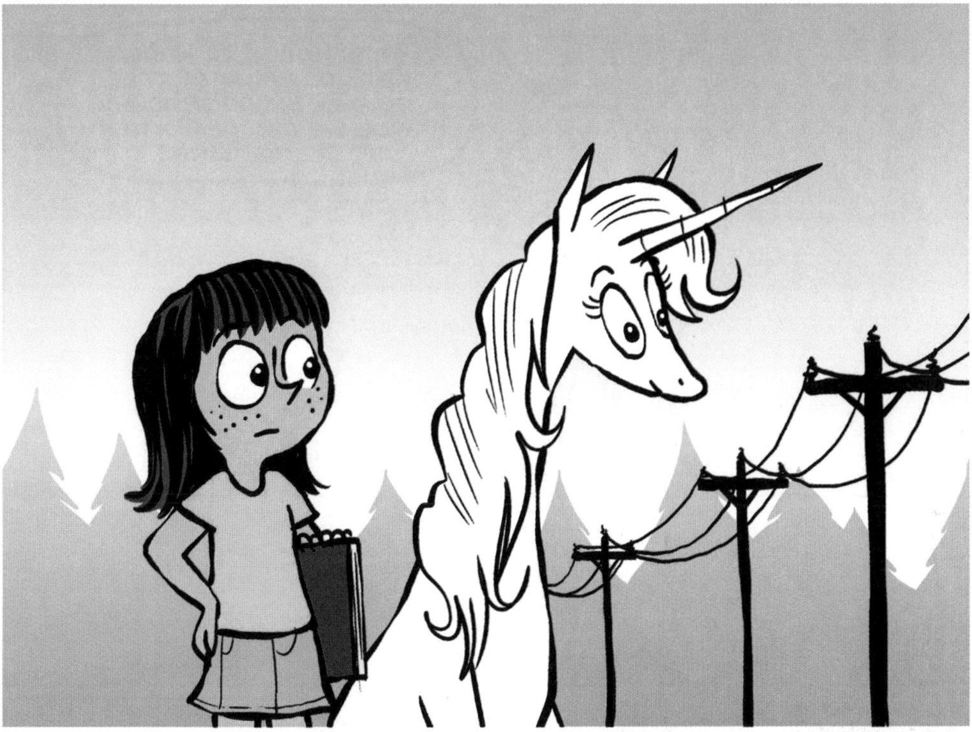

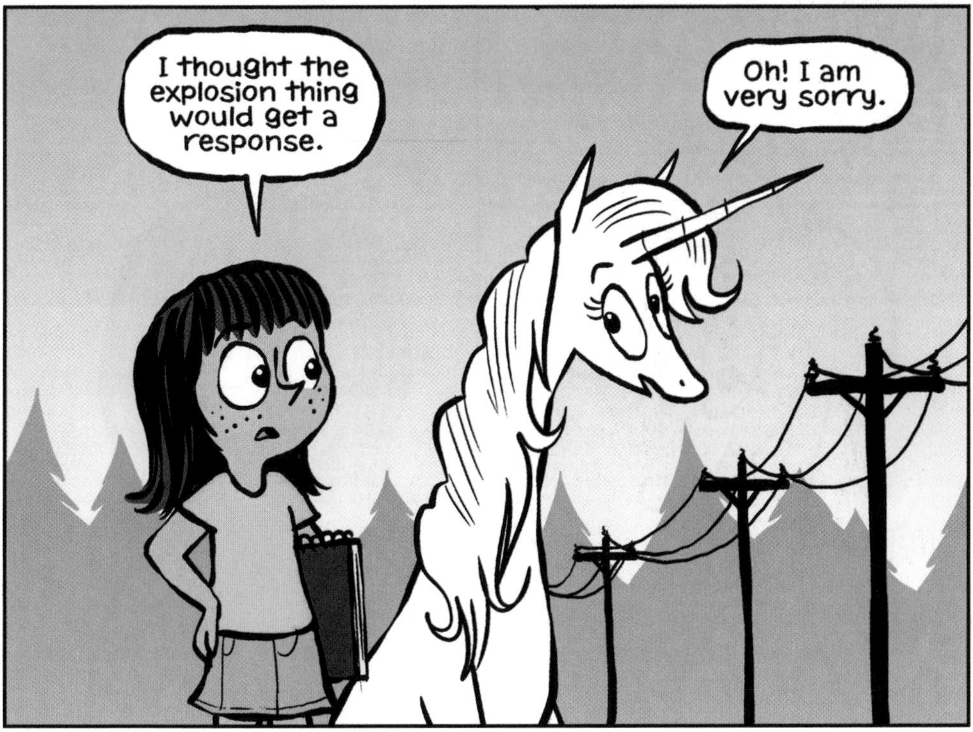
I thought the explosion thing would get a response.
Oh! I am very sorry.

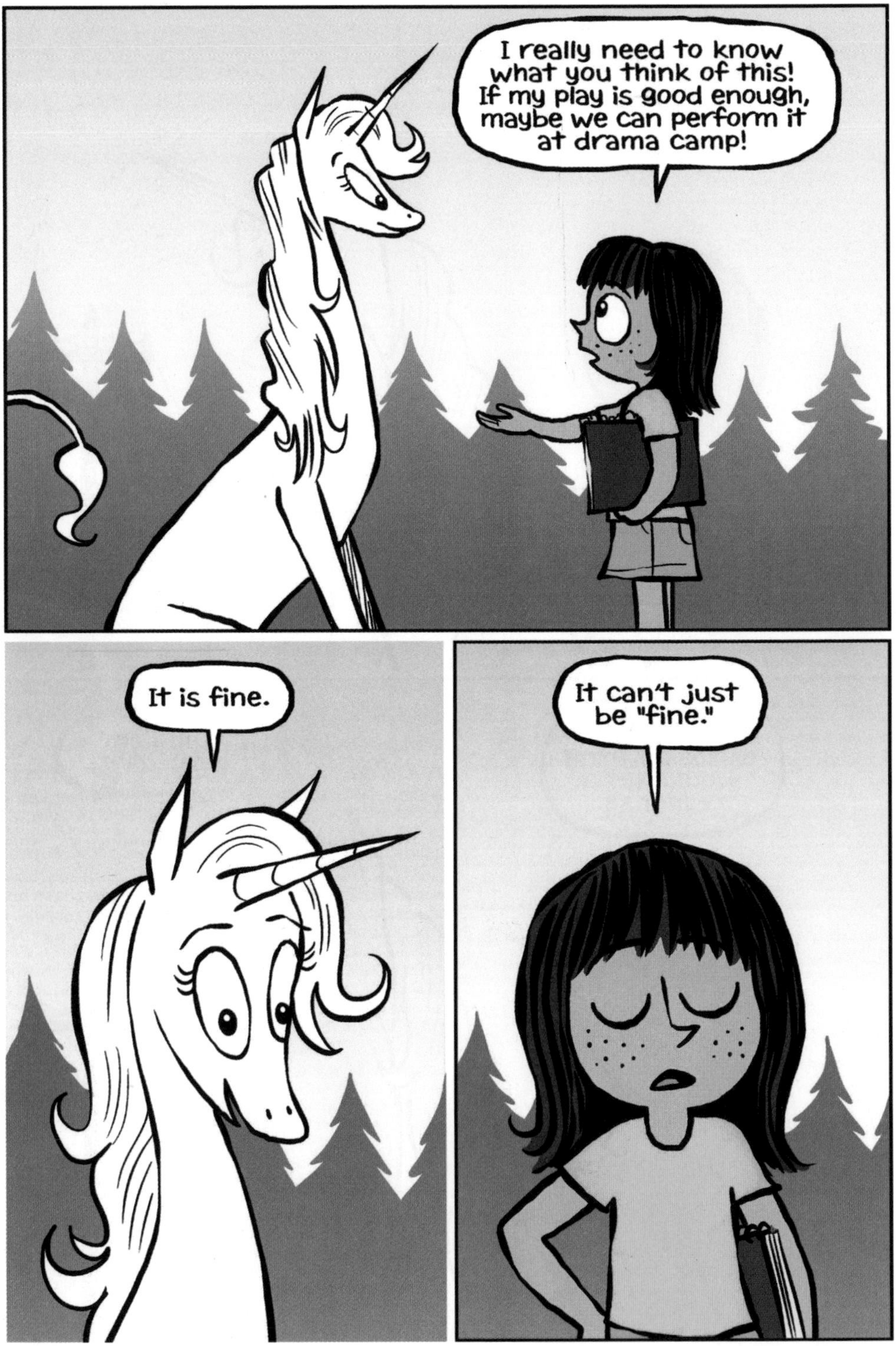
I really need to know what you think of this! If my play is good enough, maybe we can perform it at drama camp!
It is fine.
It can't just be "fine."

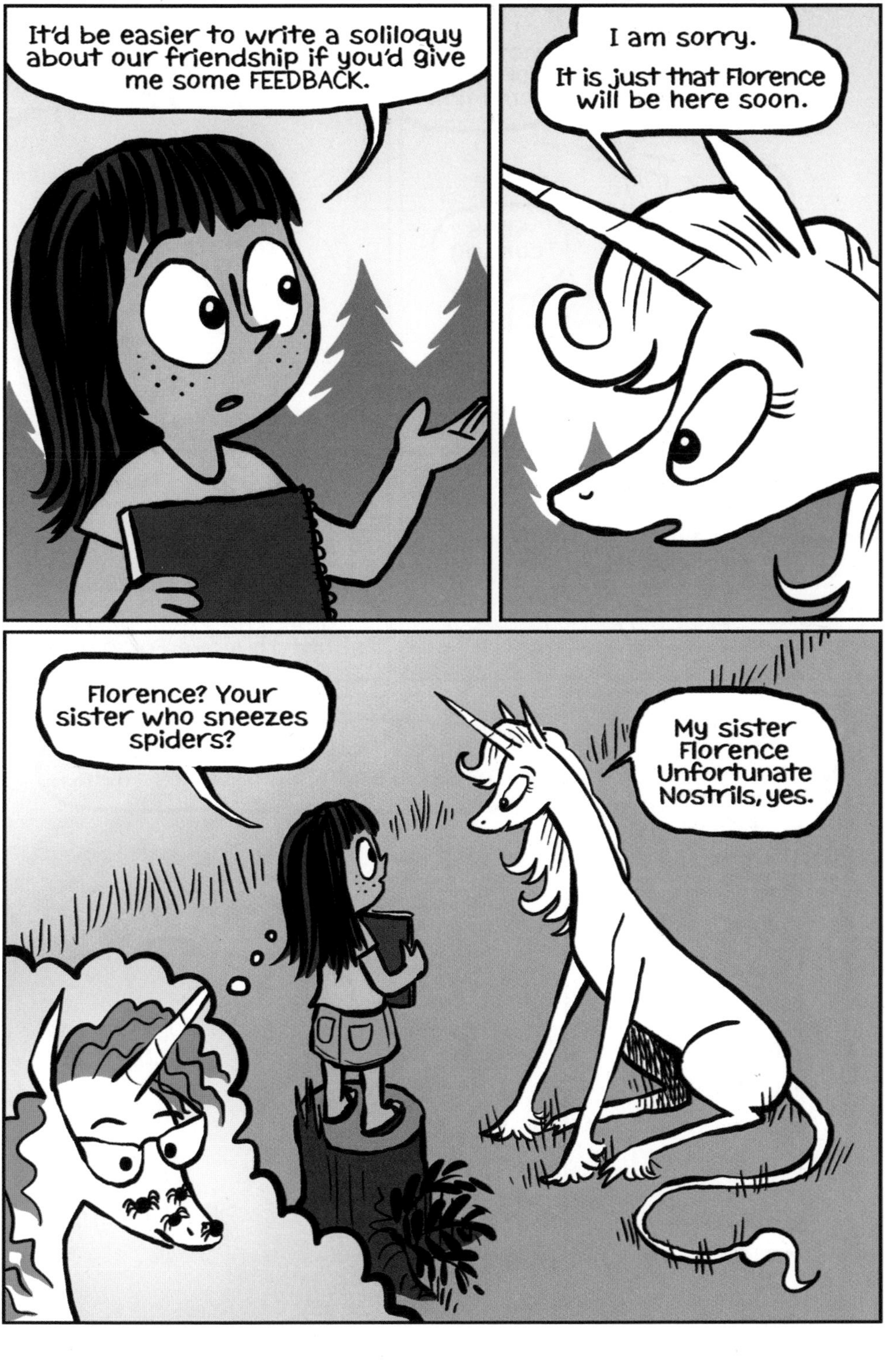
It'd be easier to write a soliloquy about our friendship if you'd give me some FEEDBACK.
I am sorry.
It is just that Florence will be here soon.
Florence? Your sister who sneezes spiders?
My sister Florence Unfortunate Nostrils, yes.

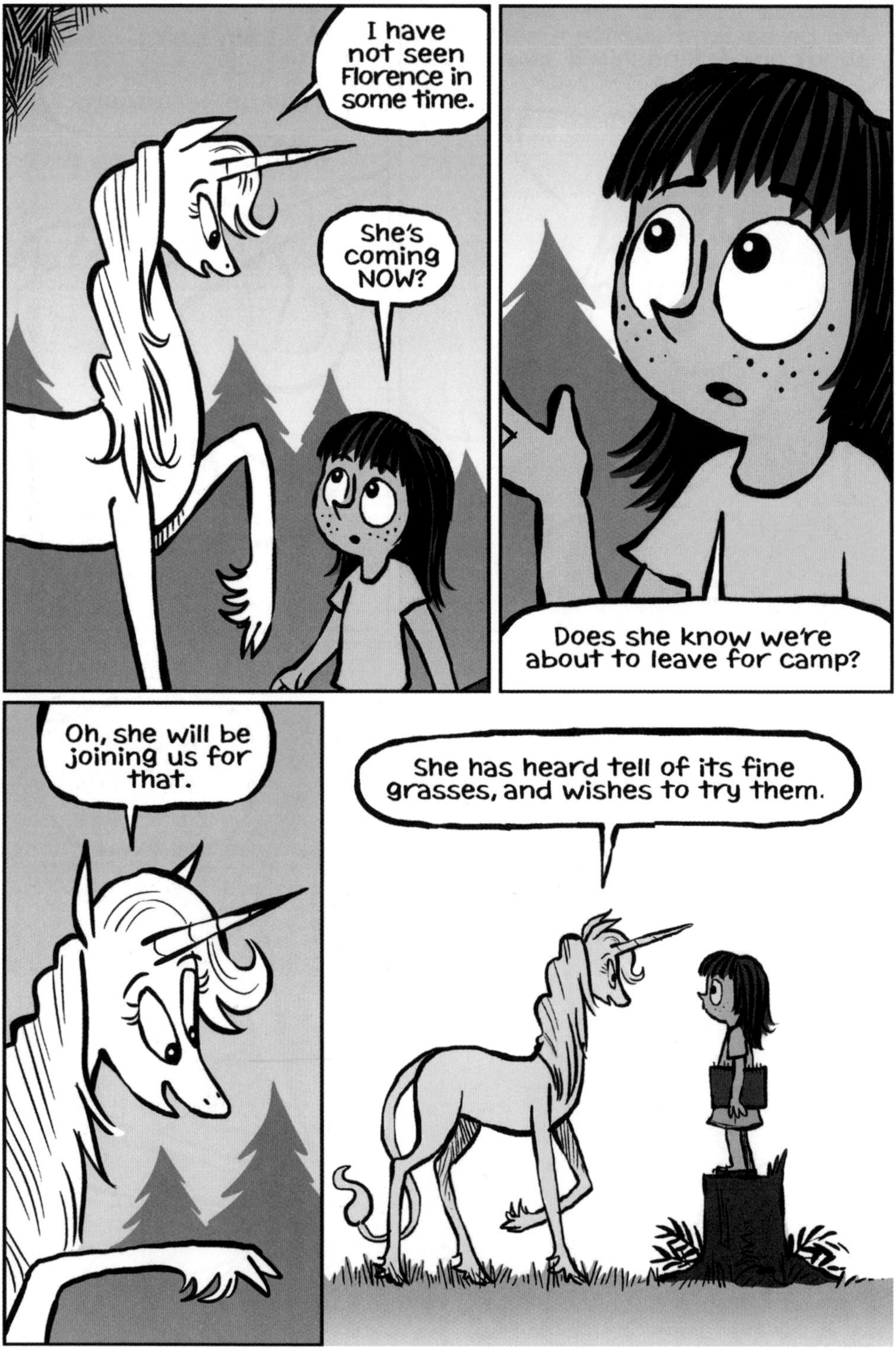
I have not seen Florence in some time.
She's coming NOW?
Does she know we're about to leave for camp?
Oh, she will be joining us for that.
She has heard tell of its fine grasses, and wishes to try them.

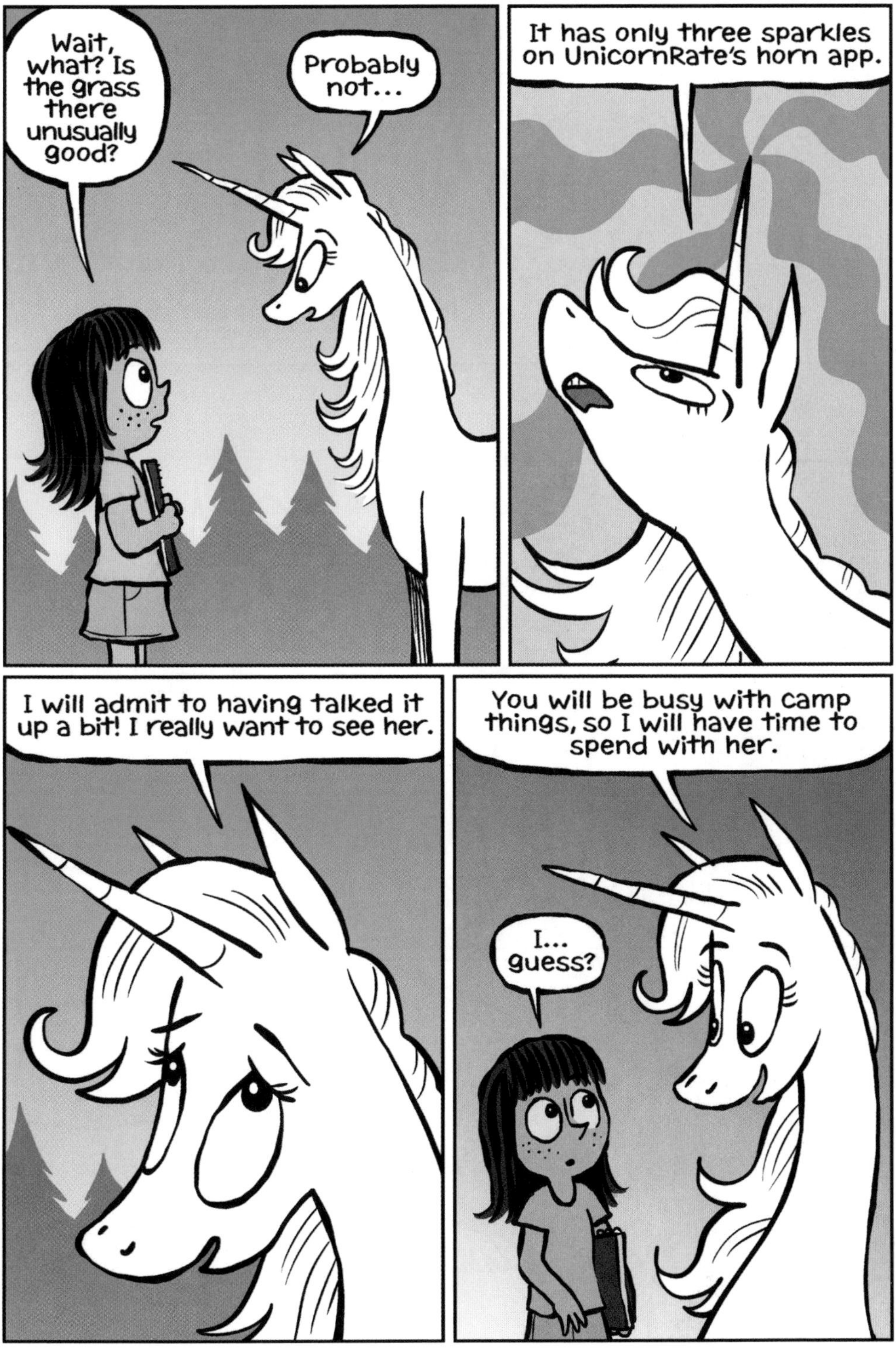
Wait, what? Is the grass there unusually good?
Probably not...
It has only three sparkles on UnicornRate's horn app.
I will admit to having talked it up a bit! I really want to see her.
You will be busy with camp things, so I will have time to spend with her.
I... guess?

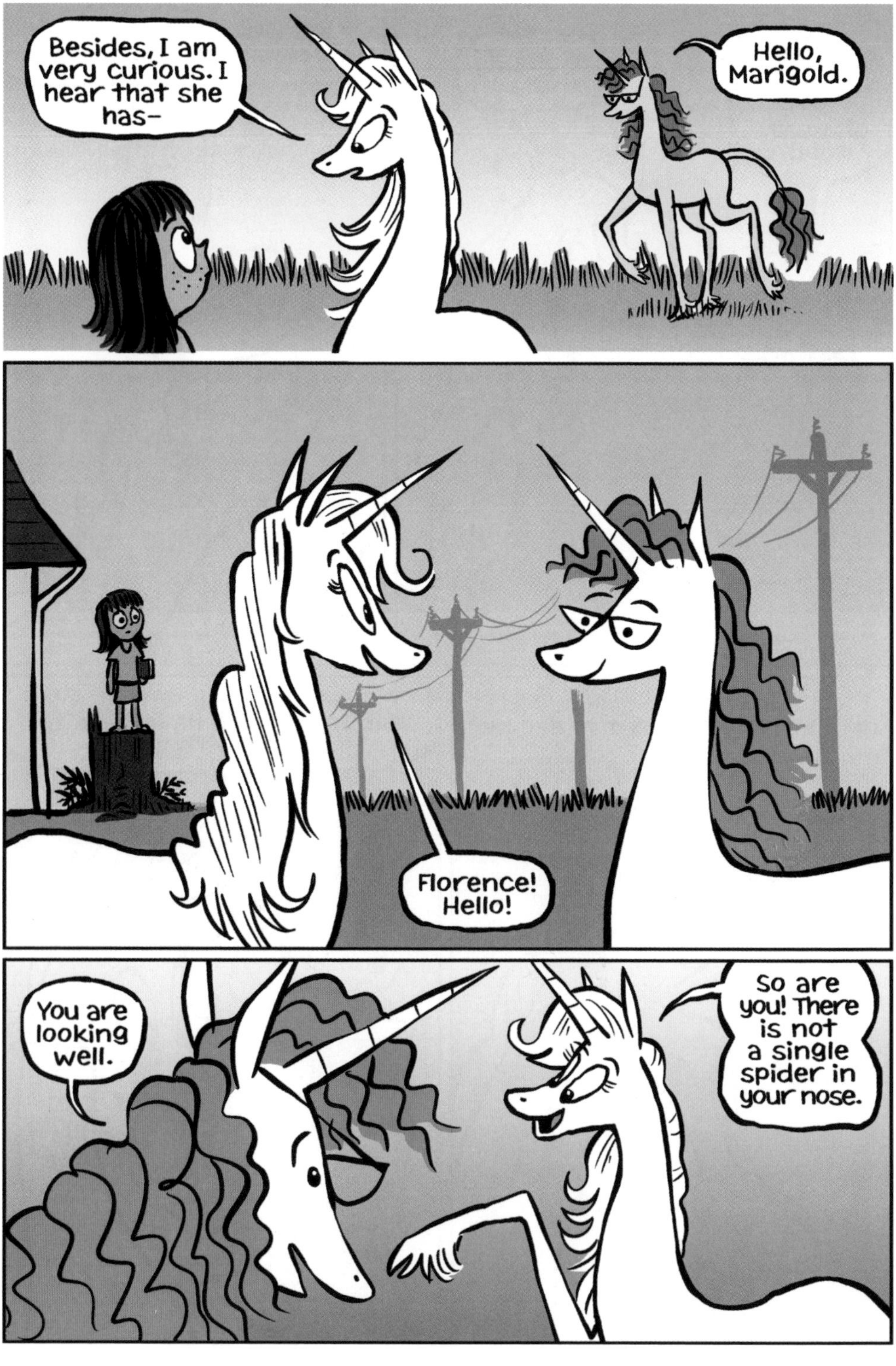

Besides, I am very curious. I hear that she has-
Hello, Marigold.
Florence! Hello!
You are looking well.
So are you! There is not a single spider in your nose.

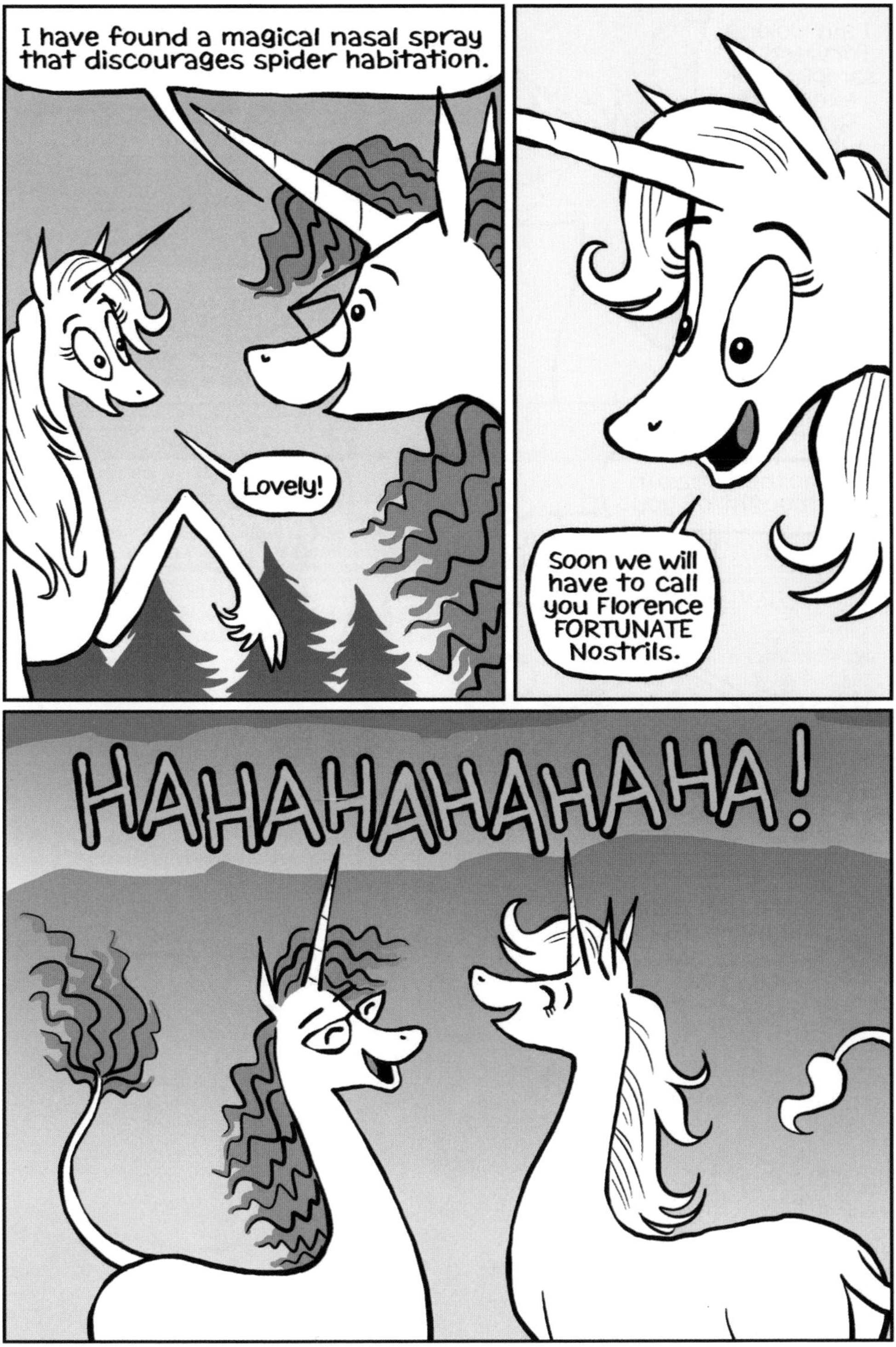
I have found a magical nasal spray that discourages spider habitation.
Lovely!
Soon we will have to call you Florence FORTUNATE Nostrils.
HAHAHAHAHAHAHA!

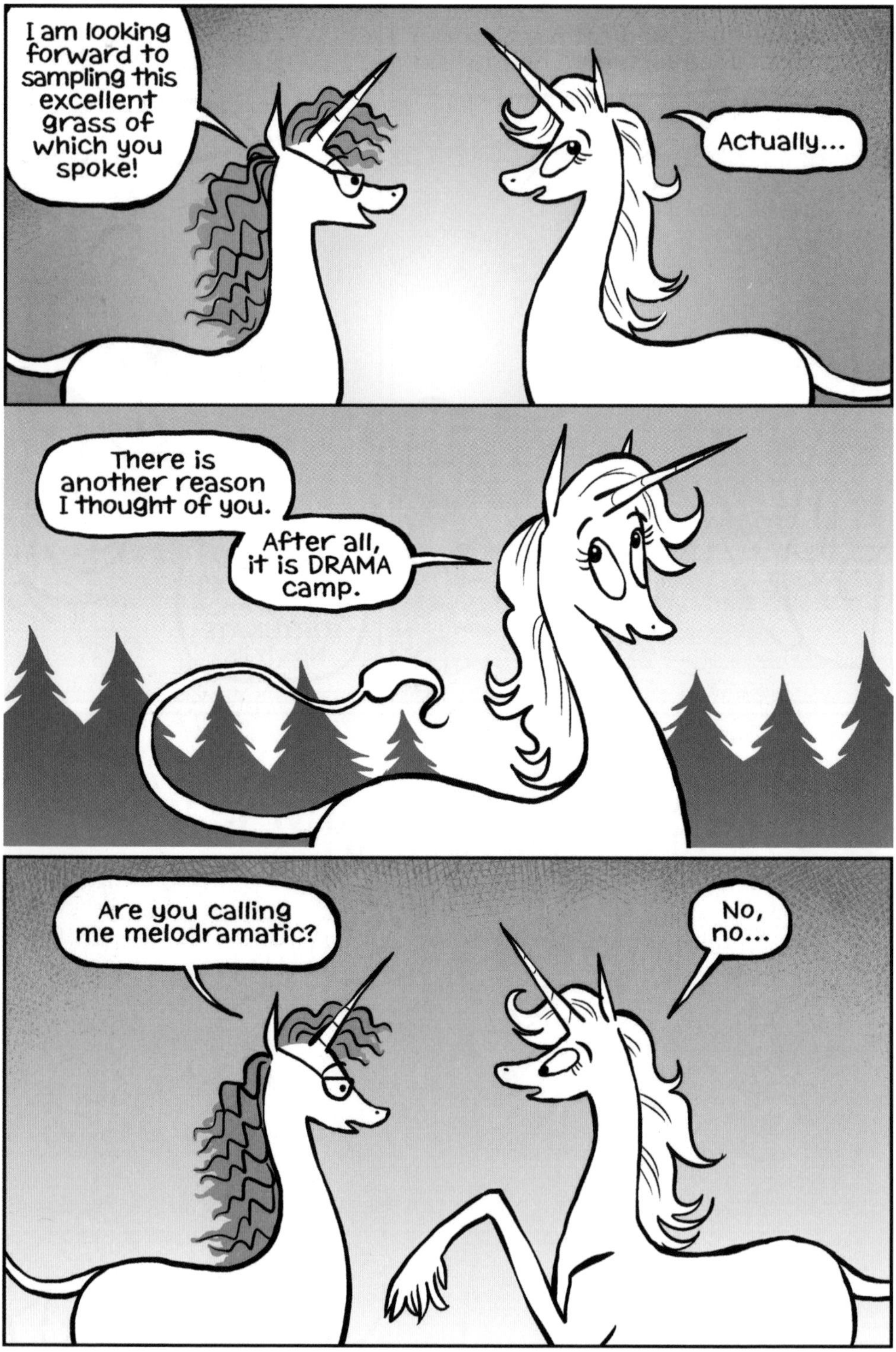
I am looking forward to sampling this excellent grass of which you spoke!
Actually...
There is another reason I thought of you.
After all, it is DRAMA camp.
Are you calling me melodramatic?
No, no...

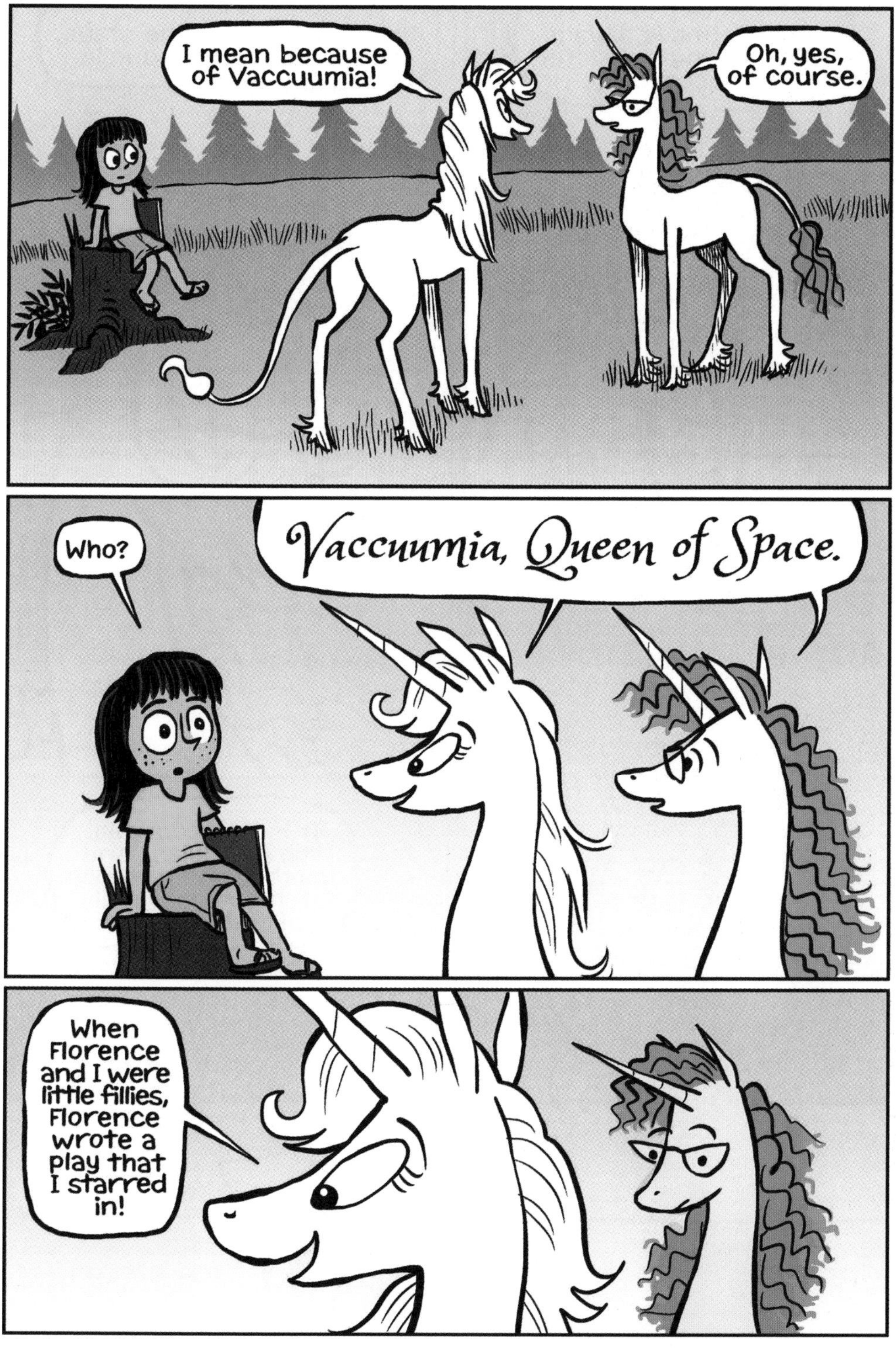
I mean because of Vaccuumia!
Oh, yes, of course.
Who?
Vaccuumia, Queen of Space.
When Florence and I were little fillies, Florence wrote a play that I starred in!

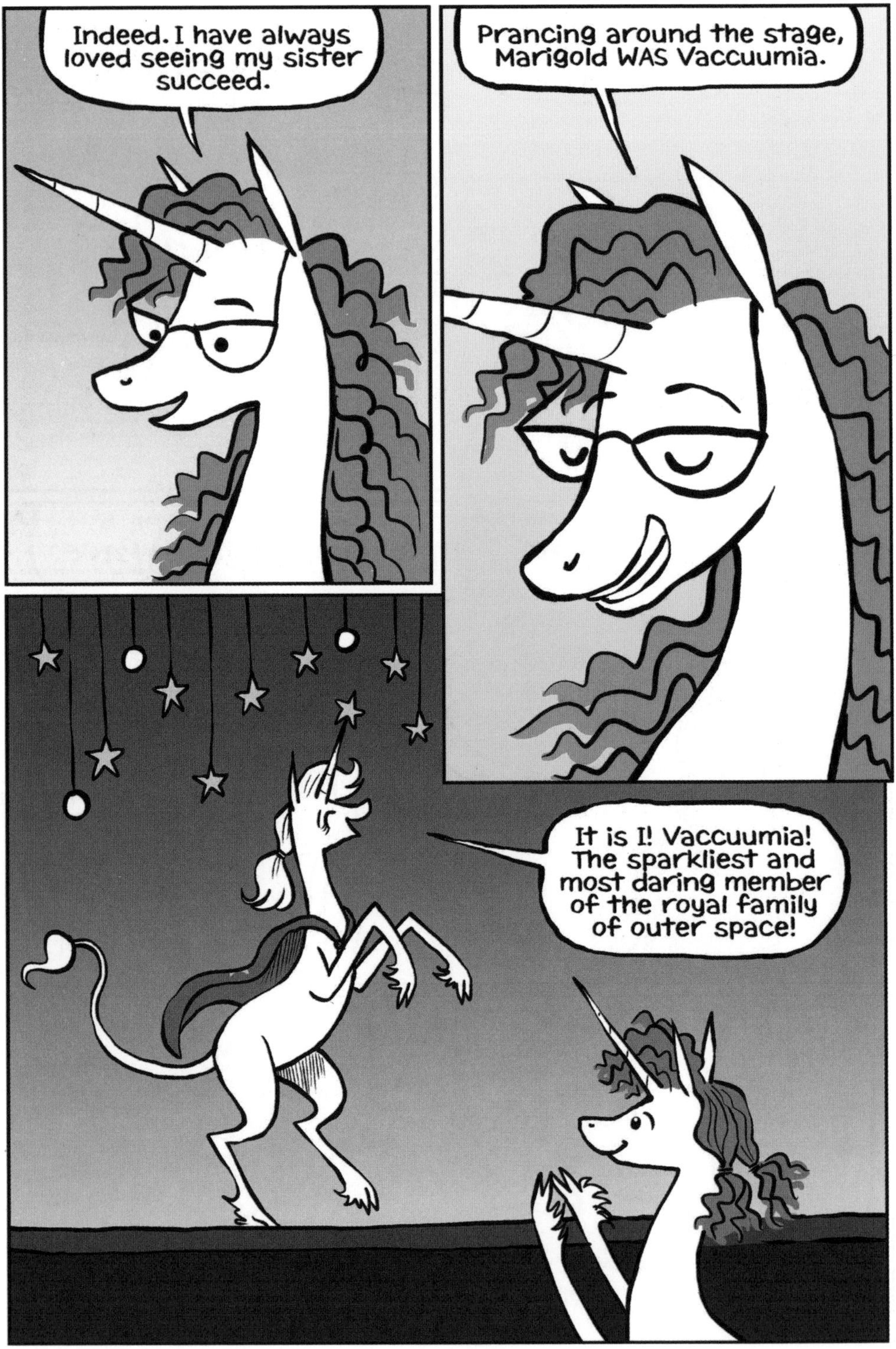
Indeed. I have always loved seeing my sister succeed.
Prancing around the stage, Marigold WAS Vaccuumia.
It is I! Vaccuumia! The sparkliest and most daring member of the royal family of outer space!

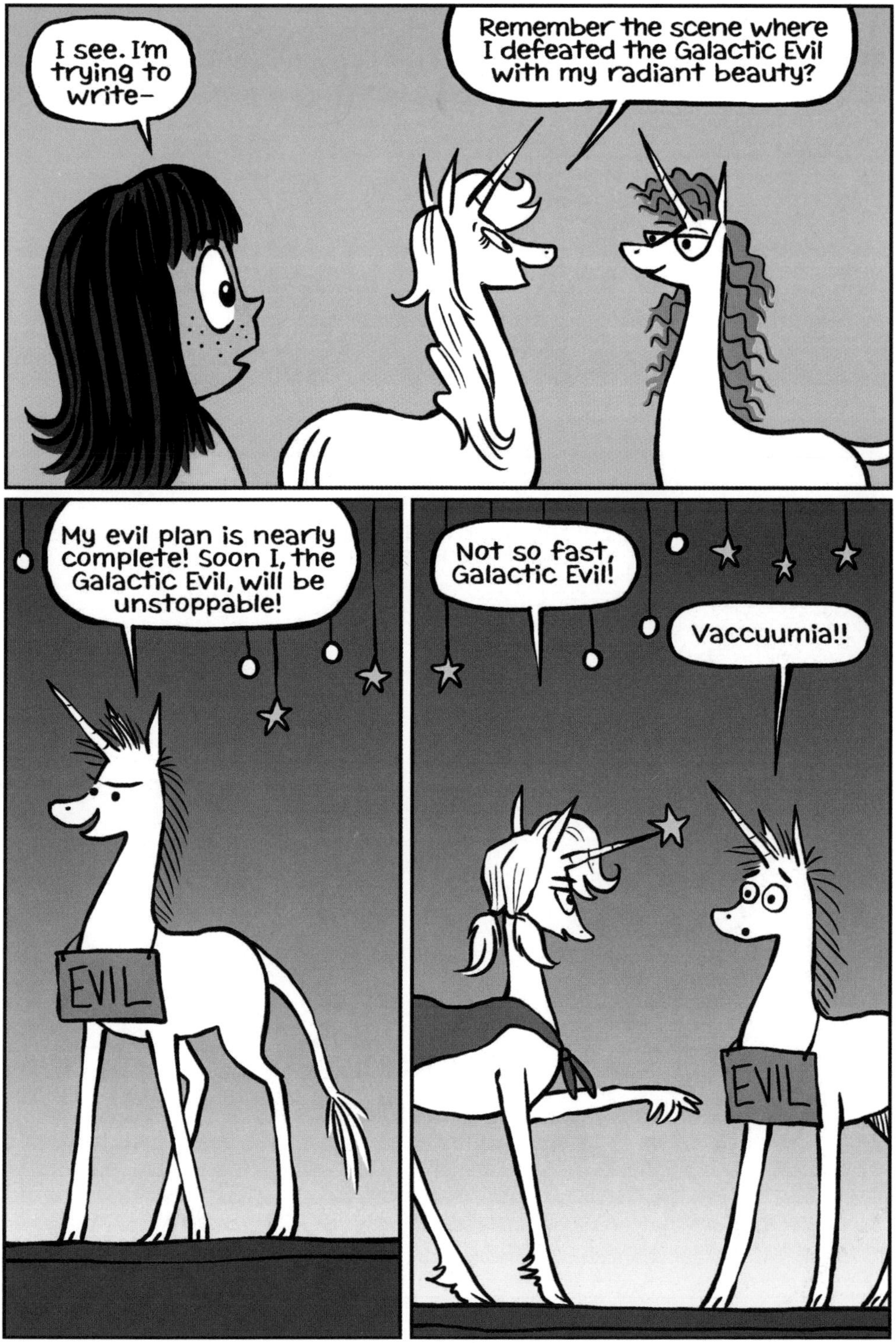

I see. I'm trying to write-
Remember the scene where I defeated the Galactic Evil with my radiant beauty?
My evil plan is nearly complete! Soon I, the Galactic Evil, will be unstoppable!
EVIL
Not so fast, Galactic Evil!
Vaccuumia!!
EVIL

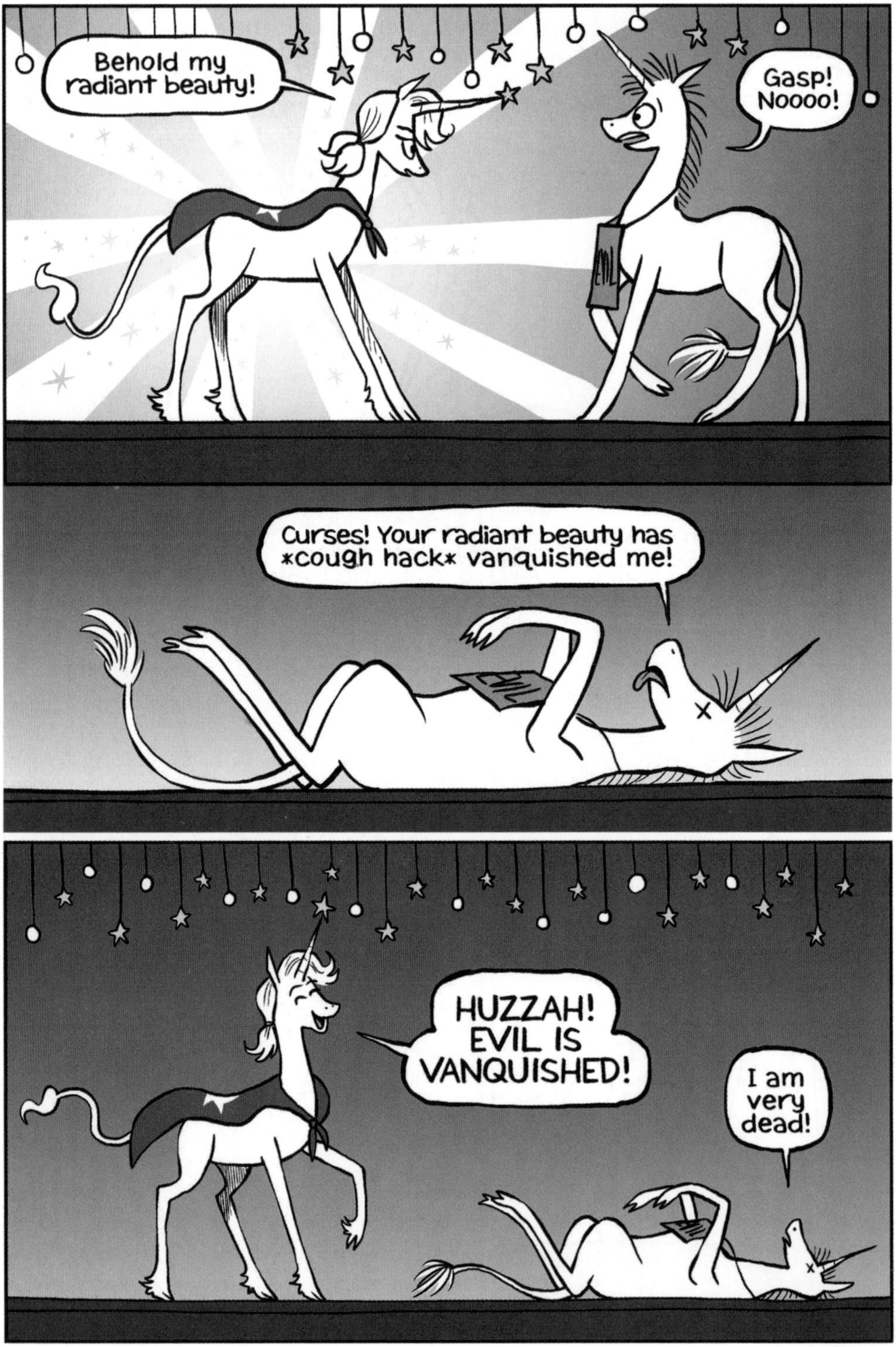
Behold my radiant beauty!
Gasp! Noooo!
EVIL
Curses! Your radiant beauty has *cough hack* vanquished me!
HUZZAH! EVIL IS VANQUISHED!
I am very dead!

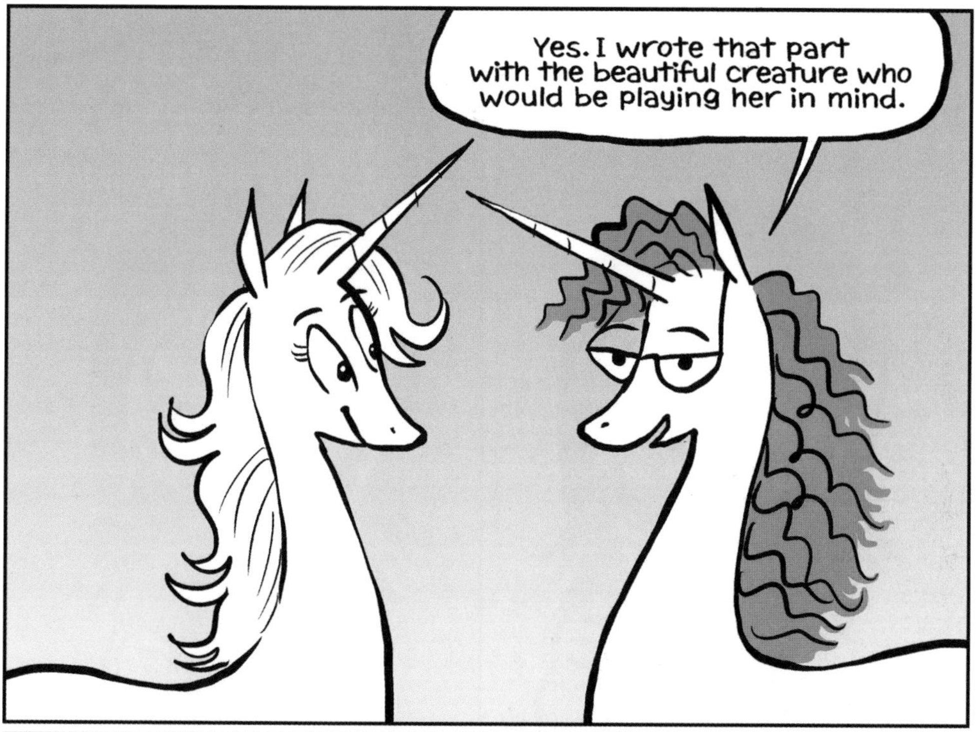
Yes. I wrote that part with the beautiful creature who would be playing her in mind.

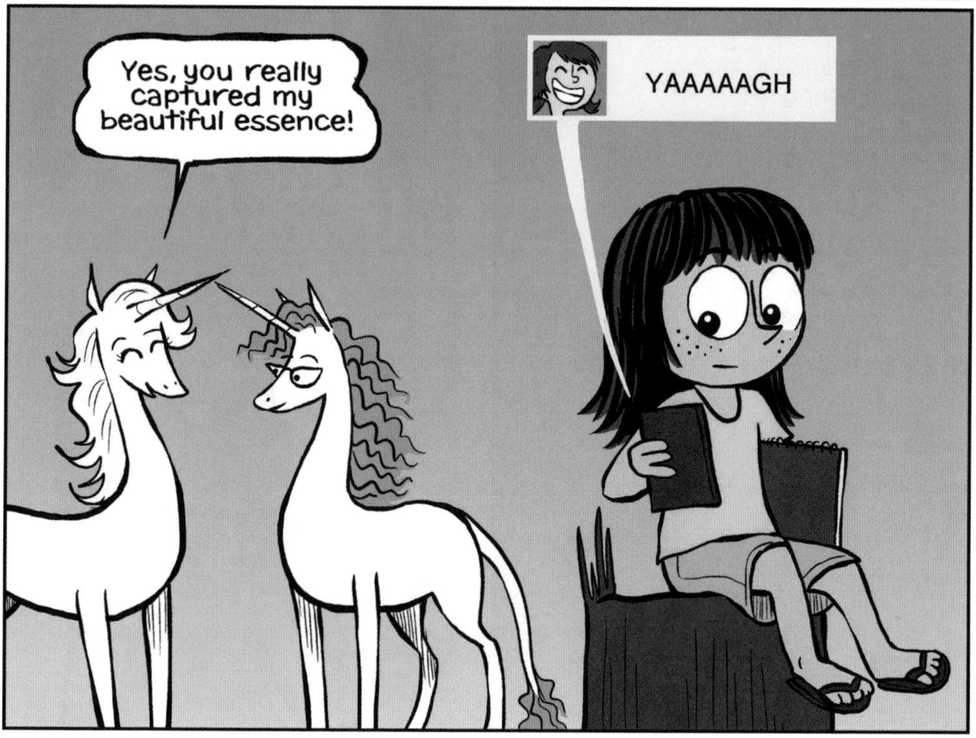
Yes, you really captured my beautiful essence!
YAAAAAGH

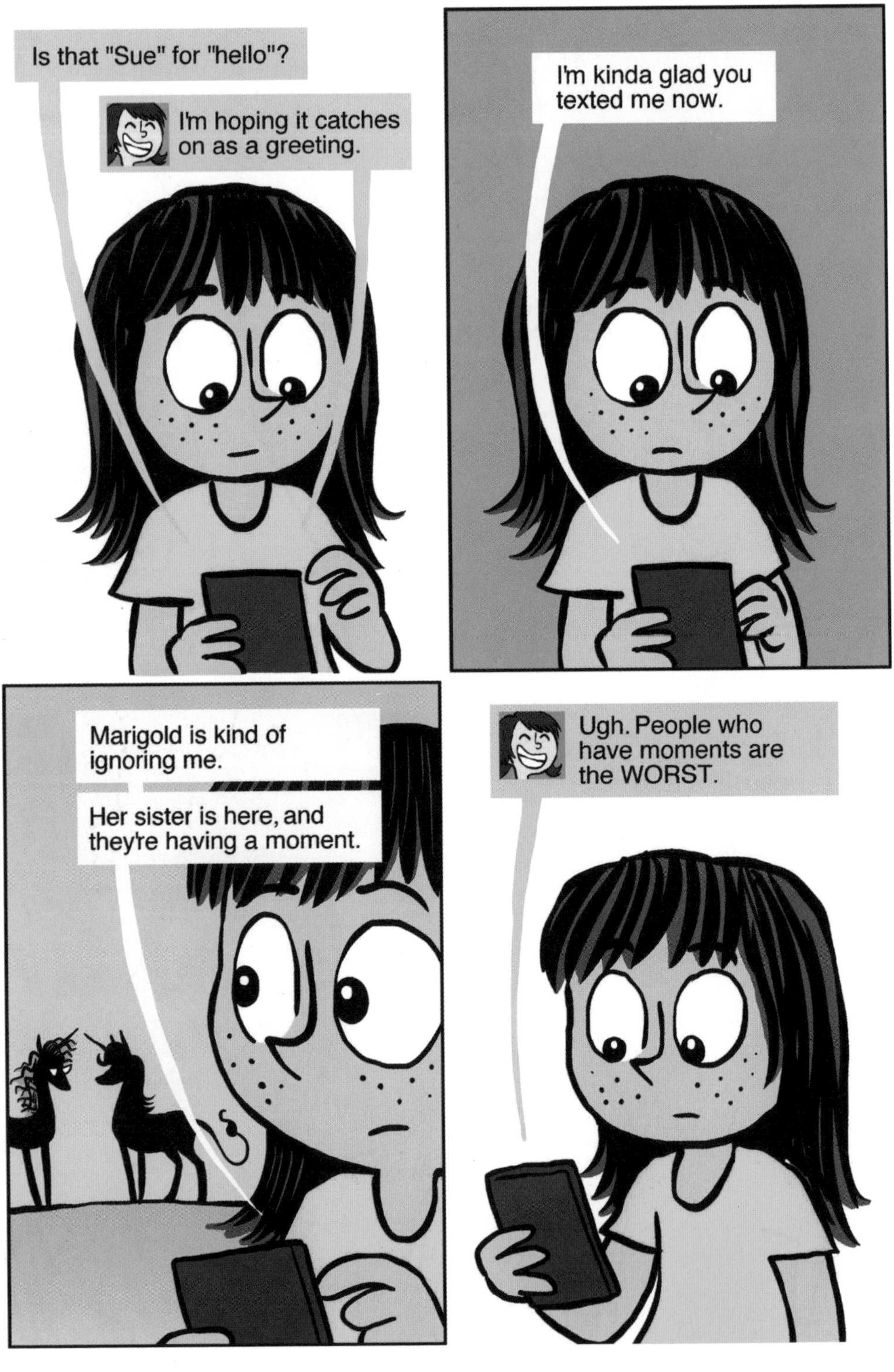
Is that "Sue" for "hello"?
I'm hoping it catches on as a greeting.
I'm kinda glad you texted me now.
Marigold is kind of ignoring me.
Her sister is here, and they're having a moment.
Ugh. People who have moments are the WORST.

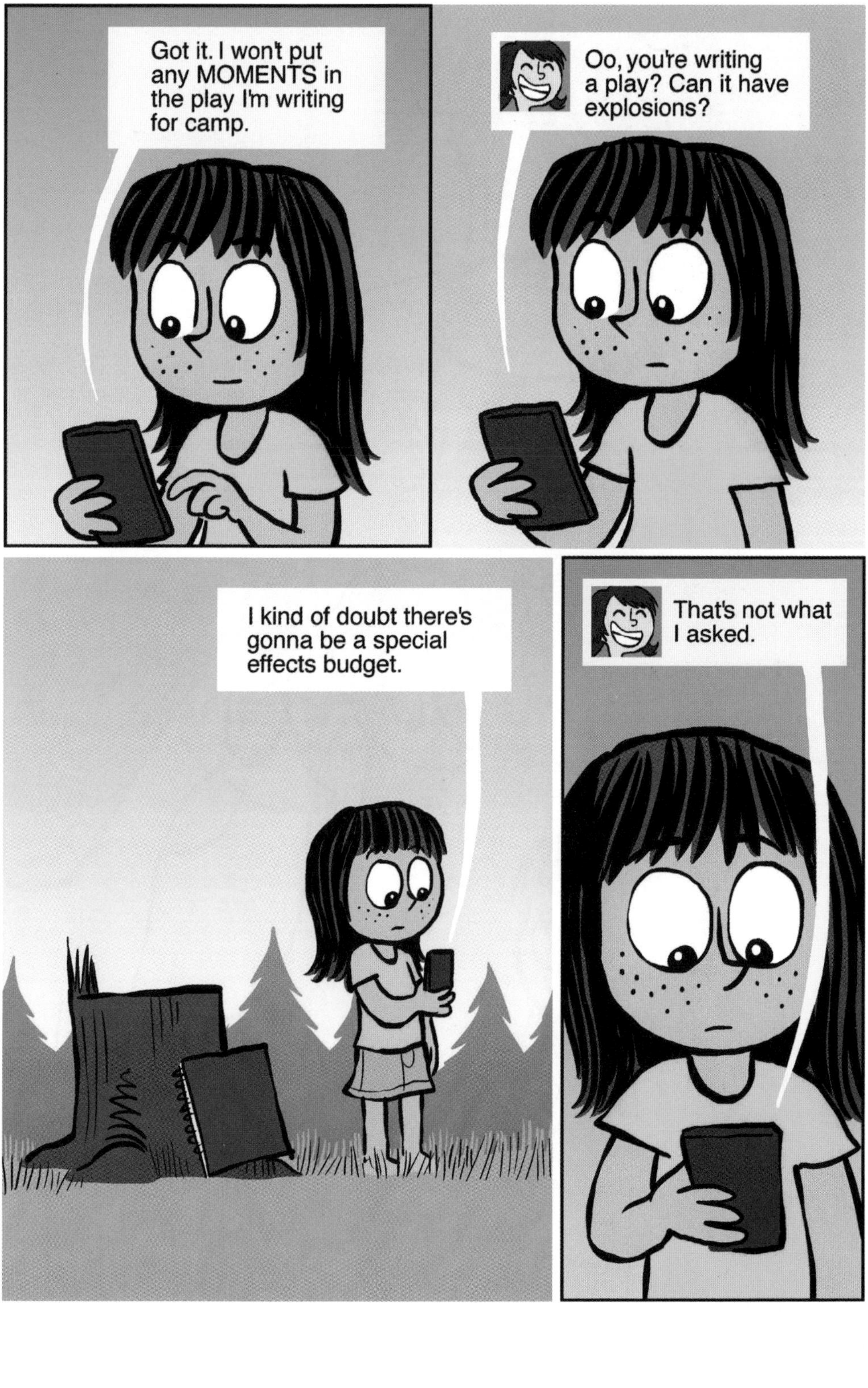
Got it. I won't put any MOMENTS in the play I'm writing for camp.
Oo, you're writing a play? Can it have explosions?
I kind of doubt there's gonna be a special effects budget.
That's not what I asked.

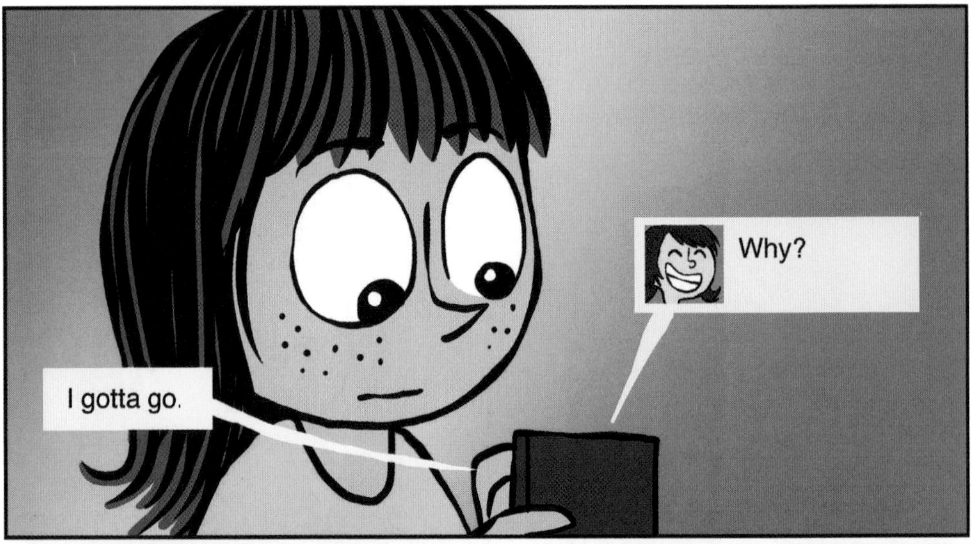
Why?
I gotta go.

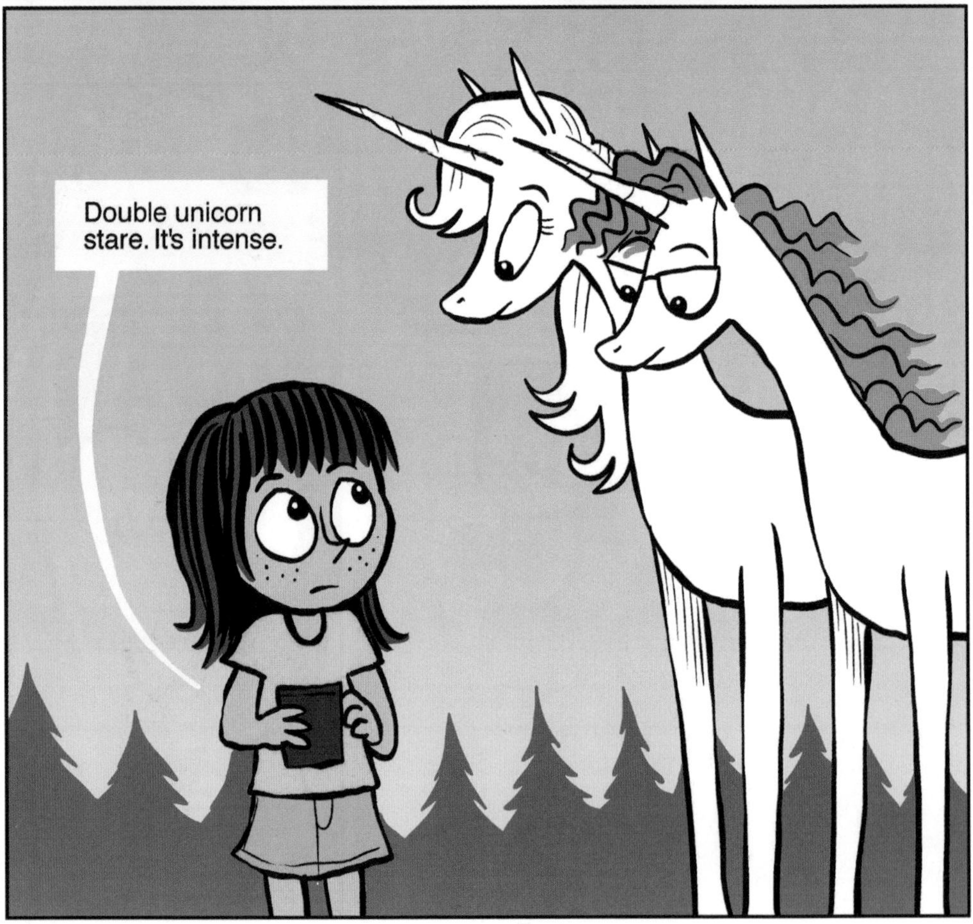
Double unicorn stare. It's intense.

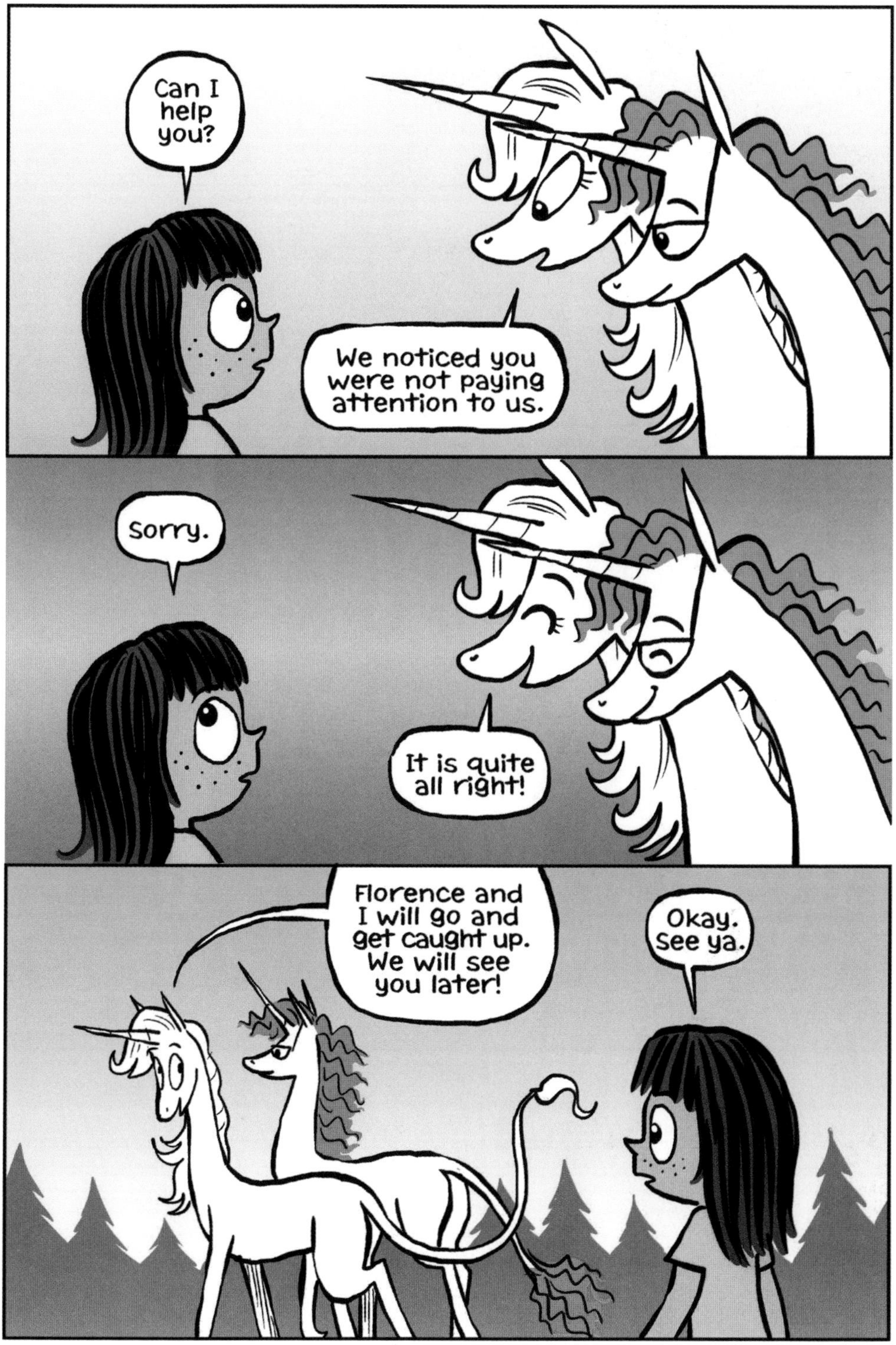
Can I help you?
We noticed you were not paying attention to us.
Sorry.
It is quite all right!
Florence and I will go and get caught up. We will see you later!
Okay. See ya.

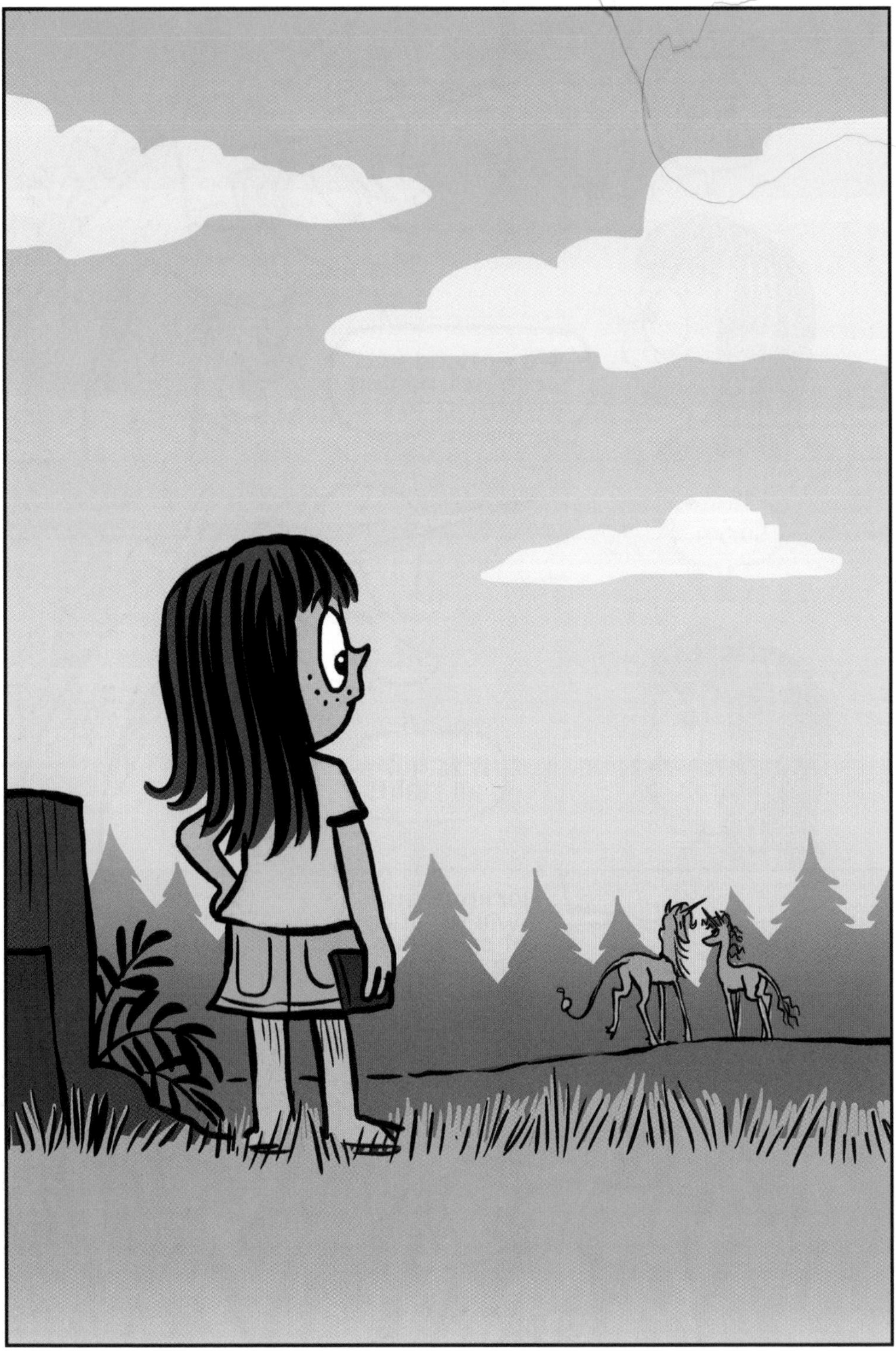

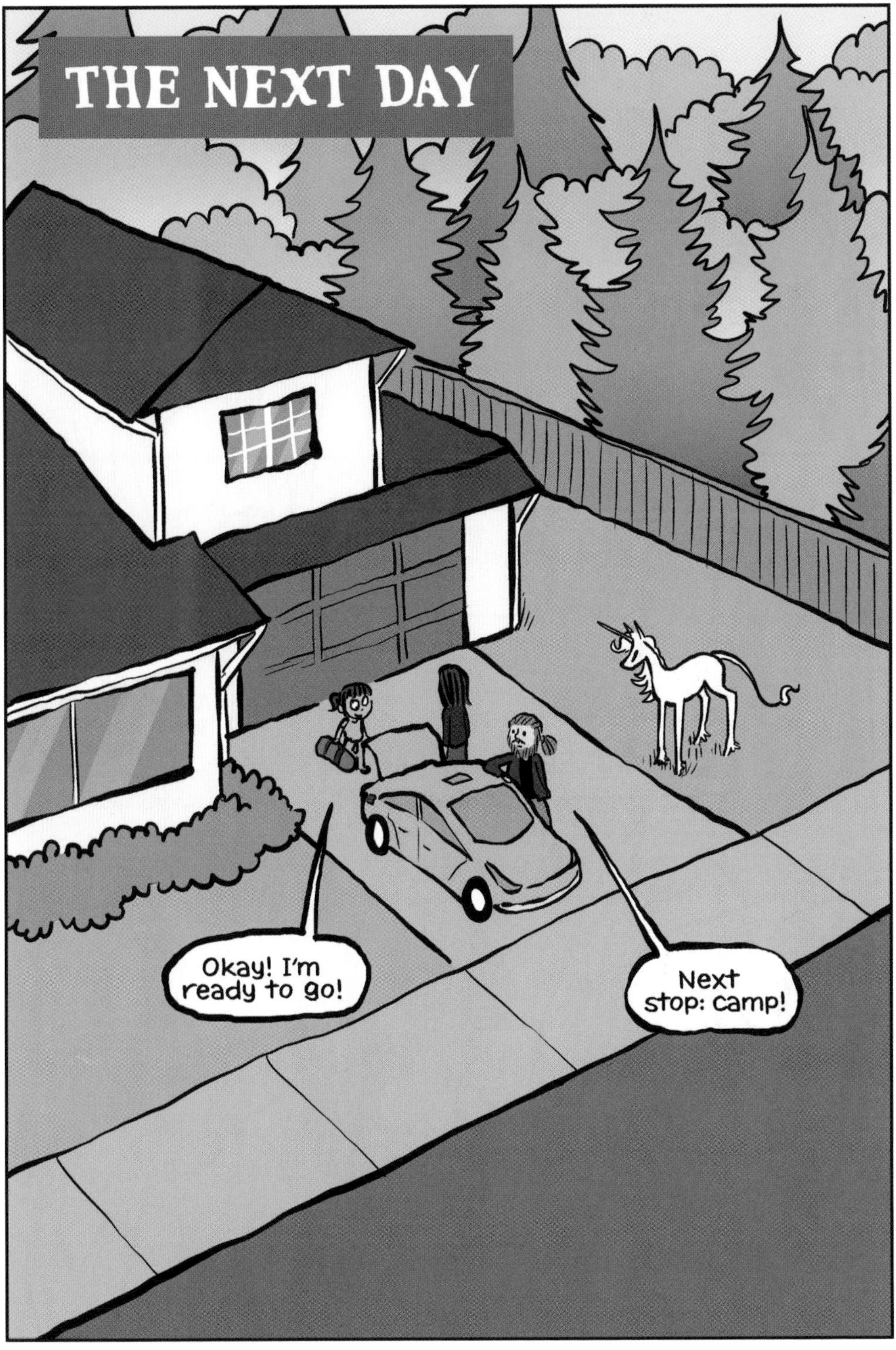
THE NEXT DAY
Okay! I'm ready to go!
Next stop: camp!

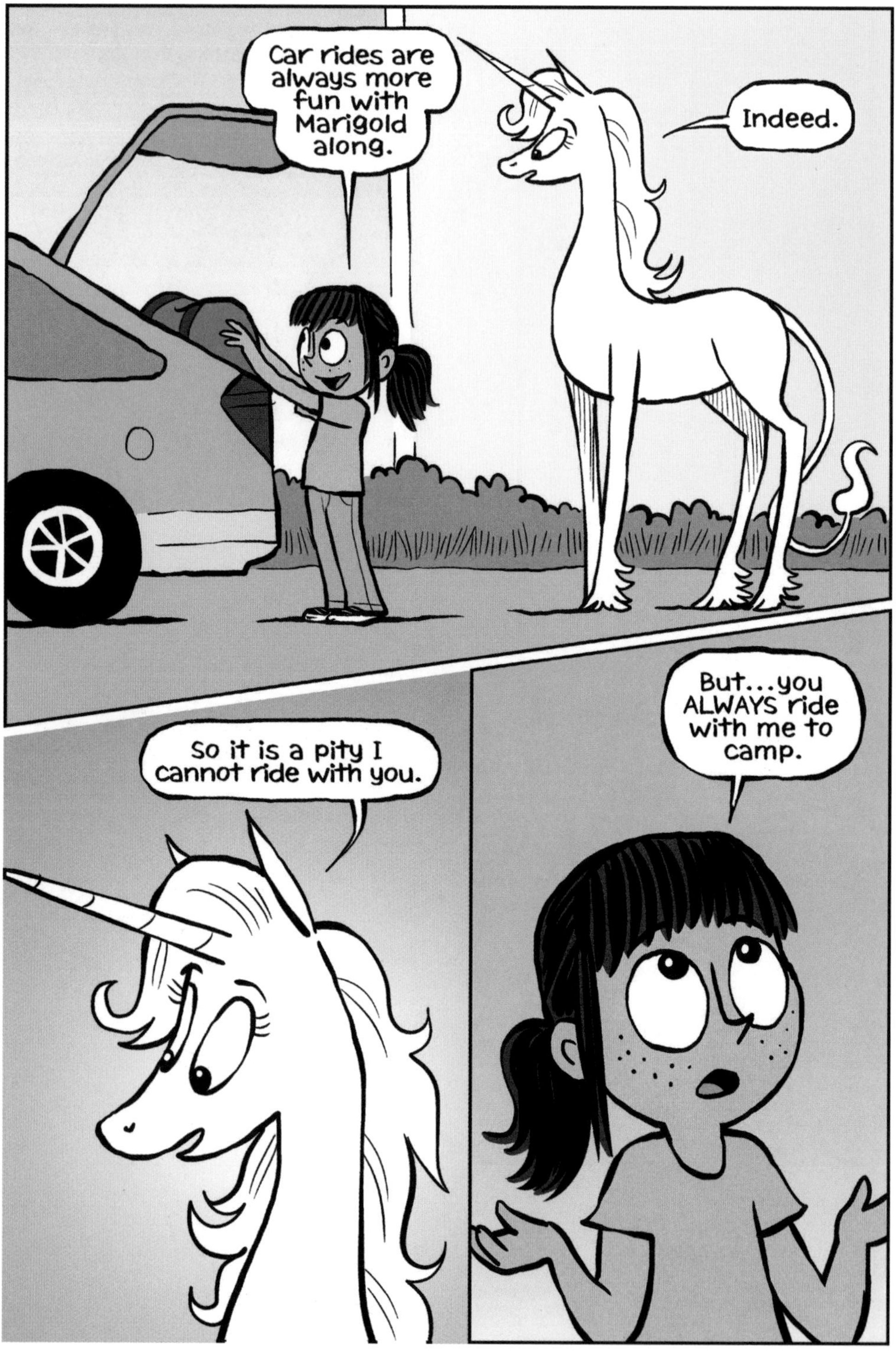
Car rides are always more fun with Marigold along.
Indeed.
So it is a pity I cannot ride with you.
But...you ALWAYS ride with me to camp.

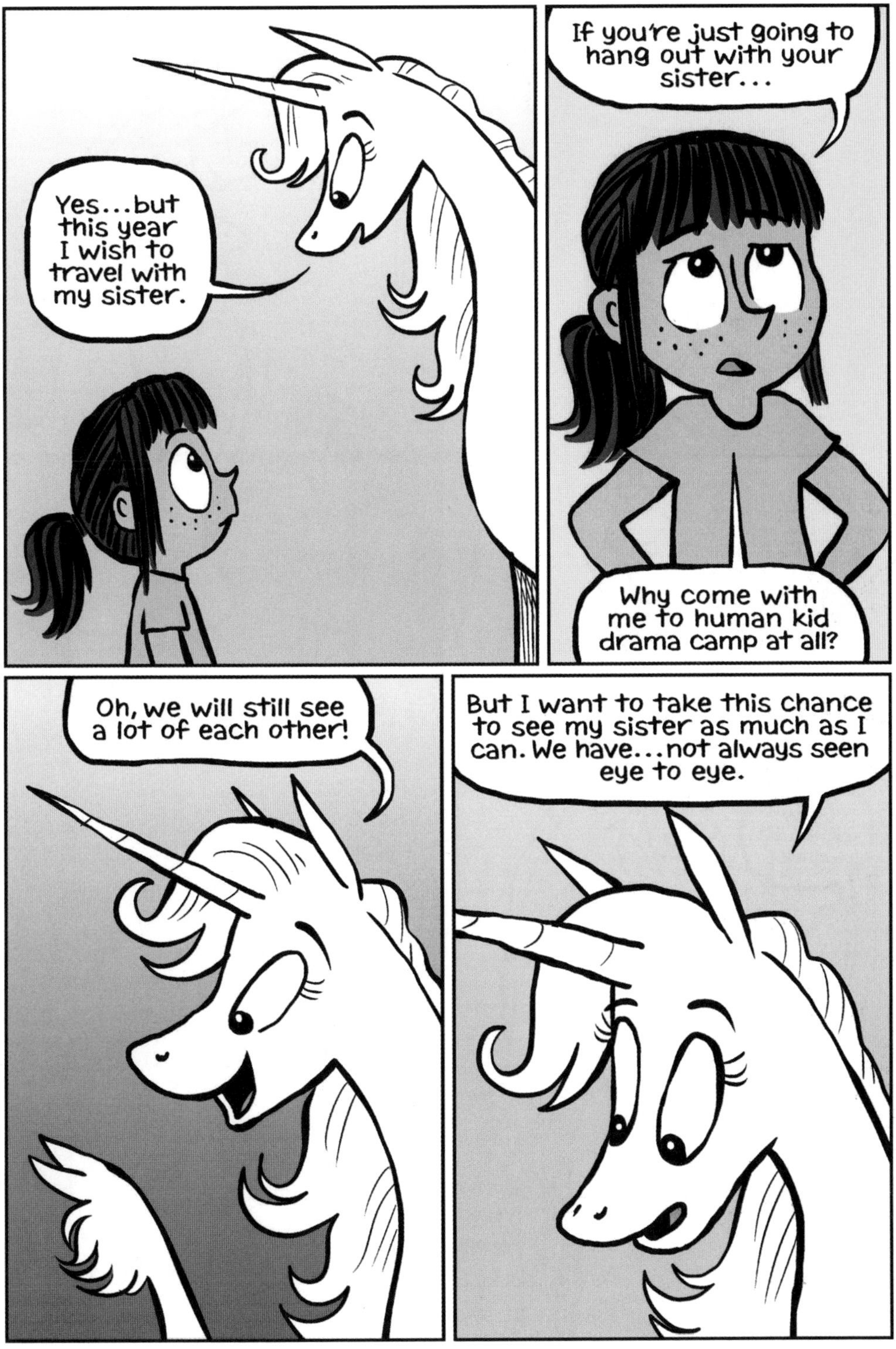
Yes...but this year I wish to travel with my sister.
If you're just going to hang out with your sister...
Why come with me to human kid drama camp at all?
Oh, we will still see a lot of each other!
But I want to take this chance to see my sister as much as I can. We have...not always seen eye to eye.

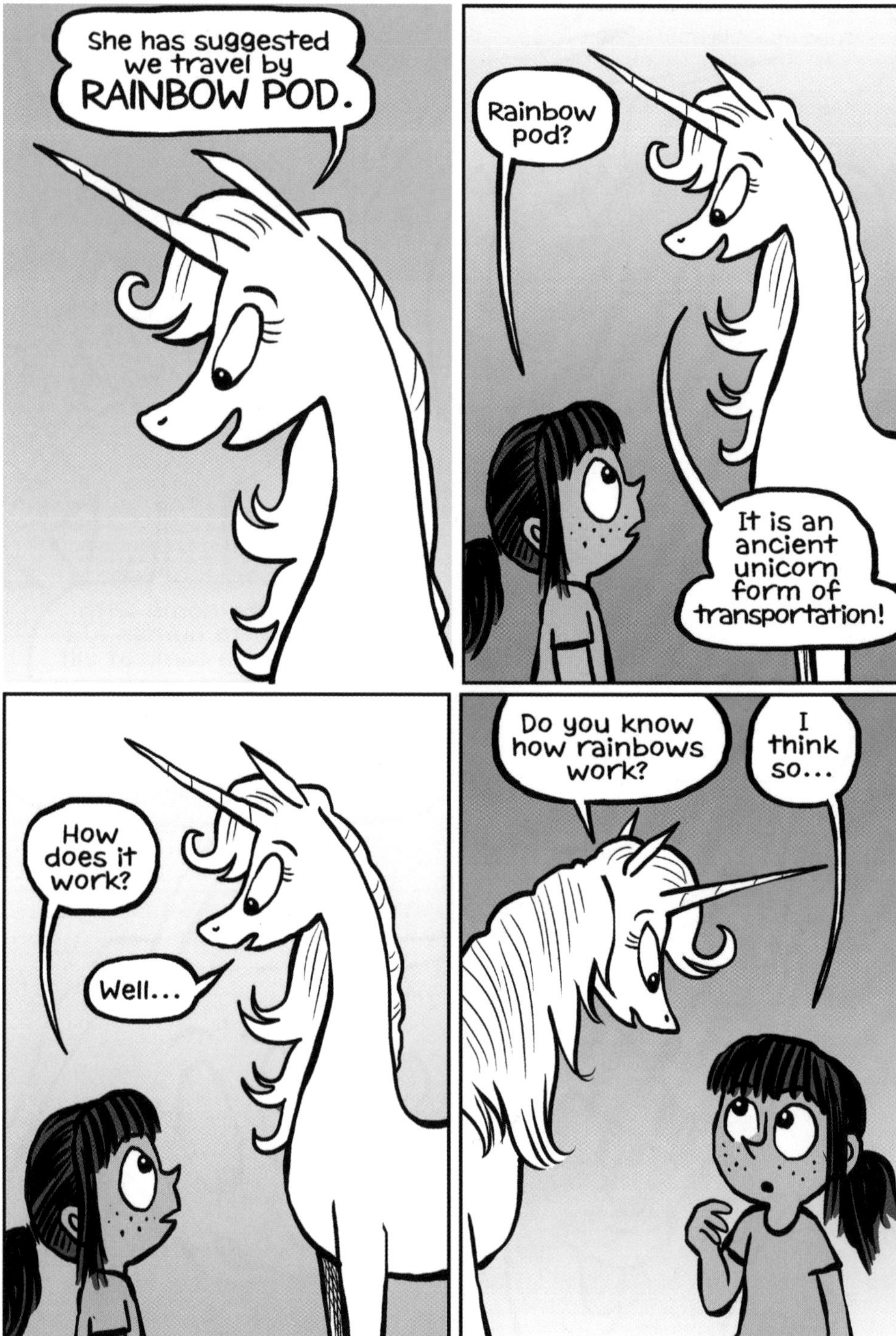
She has suggested we travel by RAINBOW POD.
Rainbow pod?
It is an ancient unicorn form of transportation!
How does it work?
Well...
Do you know how rainbows work?
I think so...

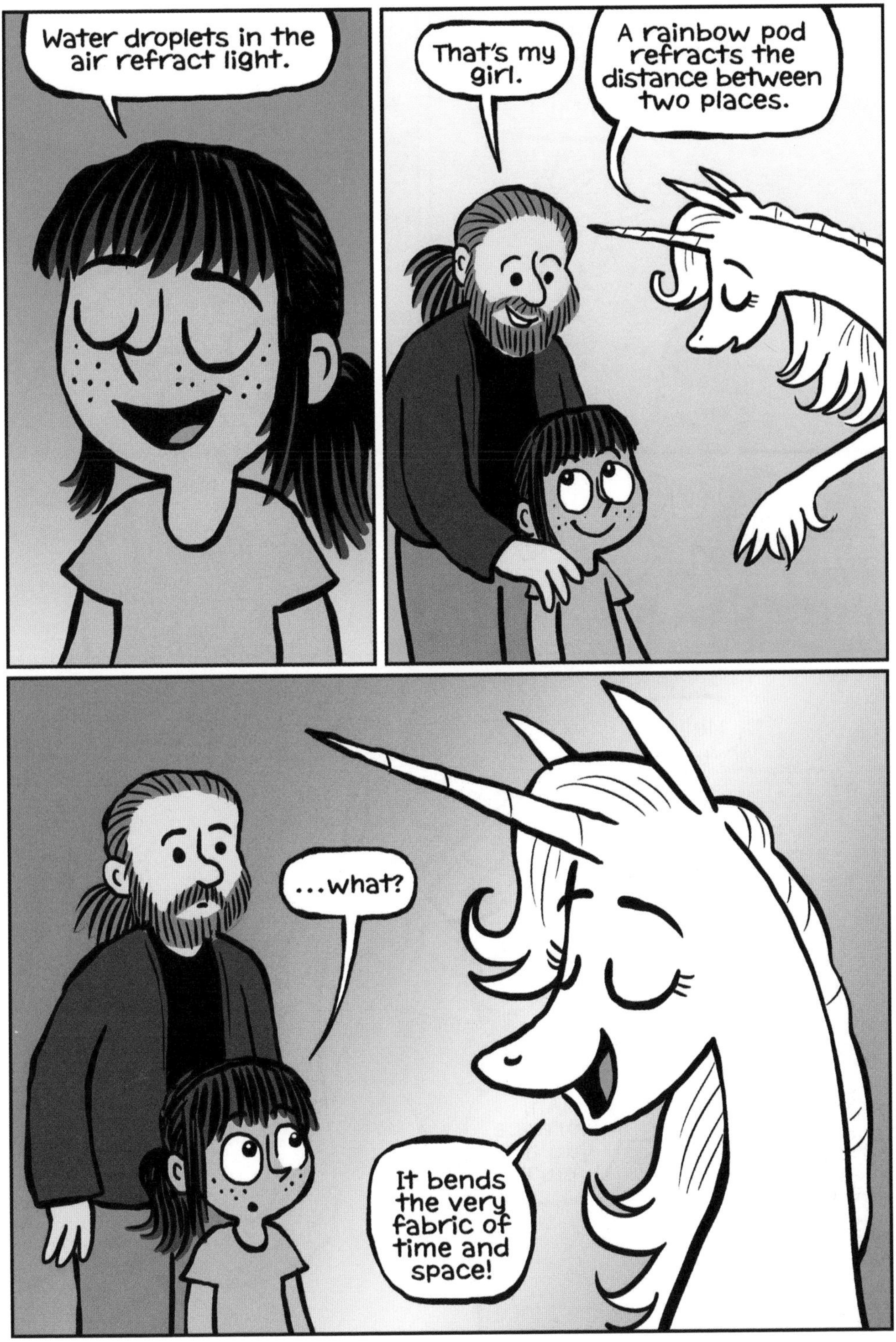
Water droplets in the air refract light.
That's my girl.
A rainbow pod refracts the distance between two places.
...what?
It bends the very fabric of time and space!

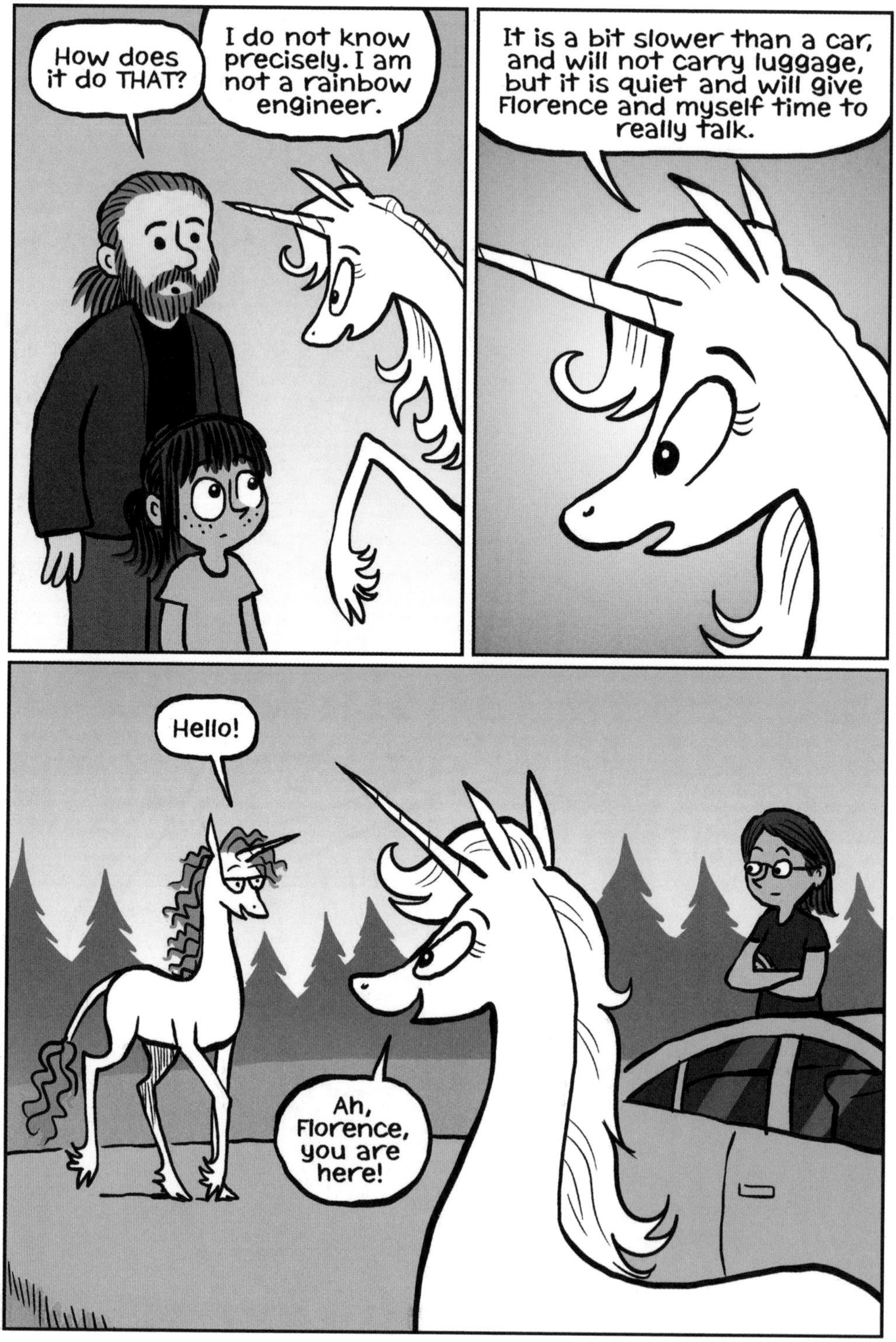
How does it do THAT?
I do not know precisely. I am not a rainbow engineer.
It is a bit slower than a car, and will not carry luggage, but it is quiet and will give Florence and myself time to really talk.
Hello!
Ah, Florence, you are here!

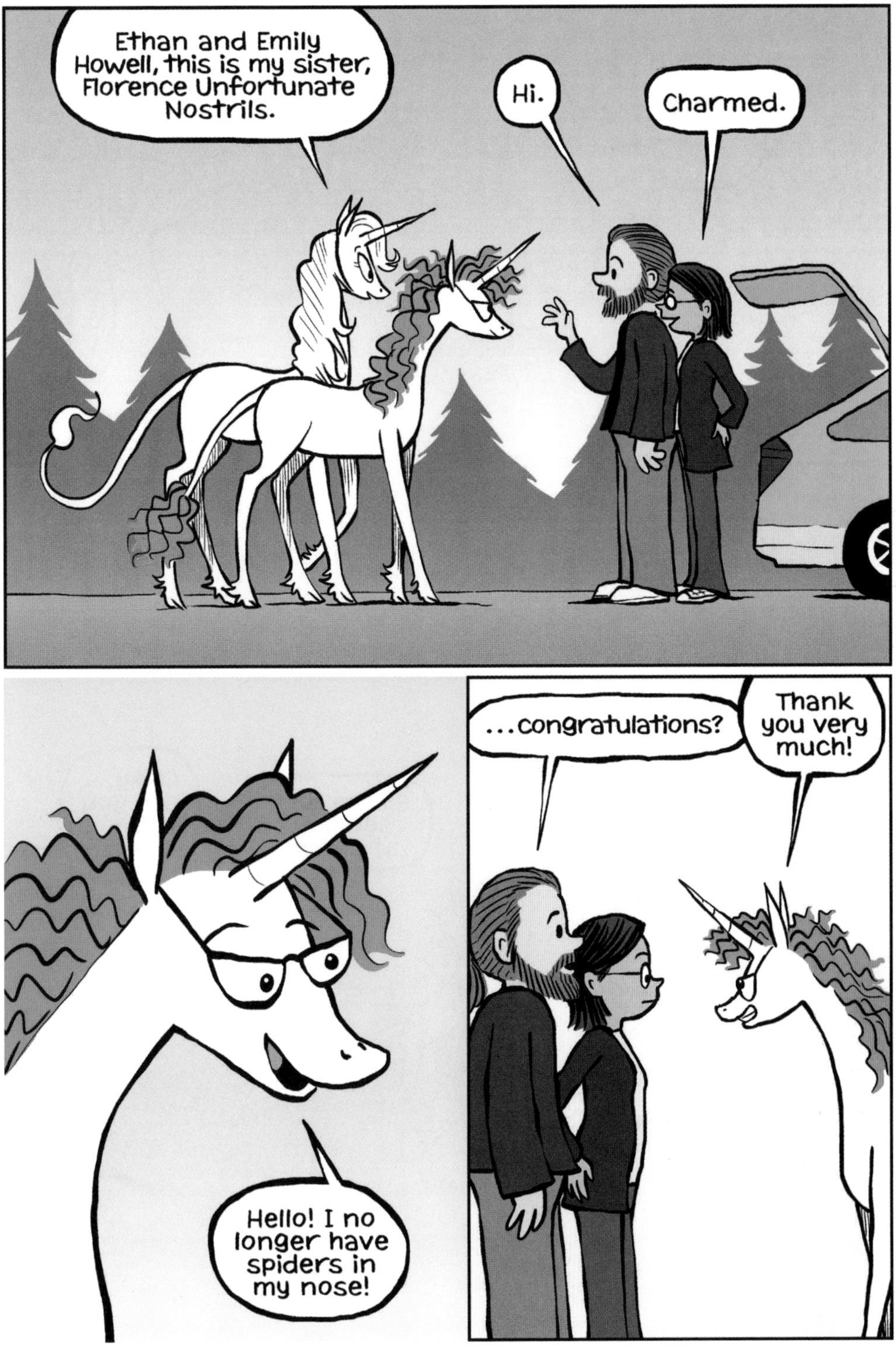
Ethan and Emily Howell, this is my sister, Florence Unfortunate Nostrils.
Hi.
Charmed.
Hello! I no longer have spiders in my nose!
...congratulations?
Thank you very much!

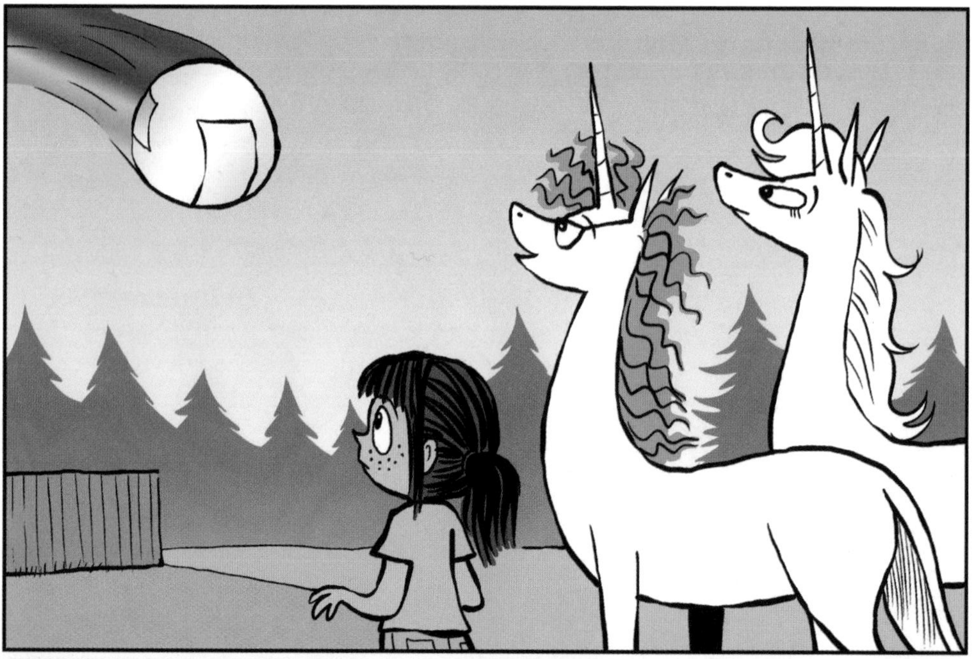

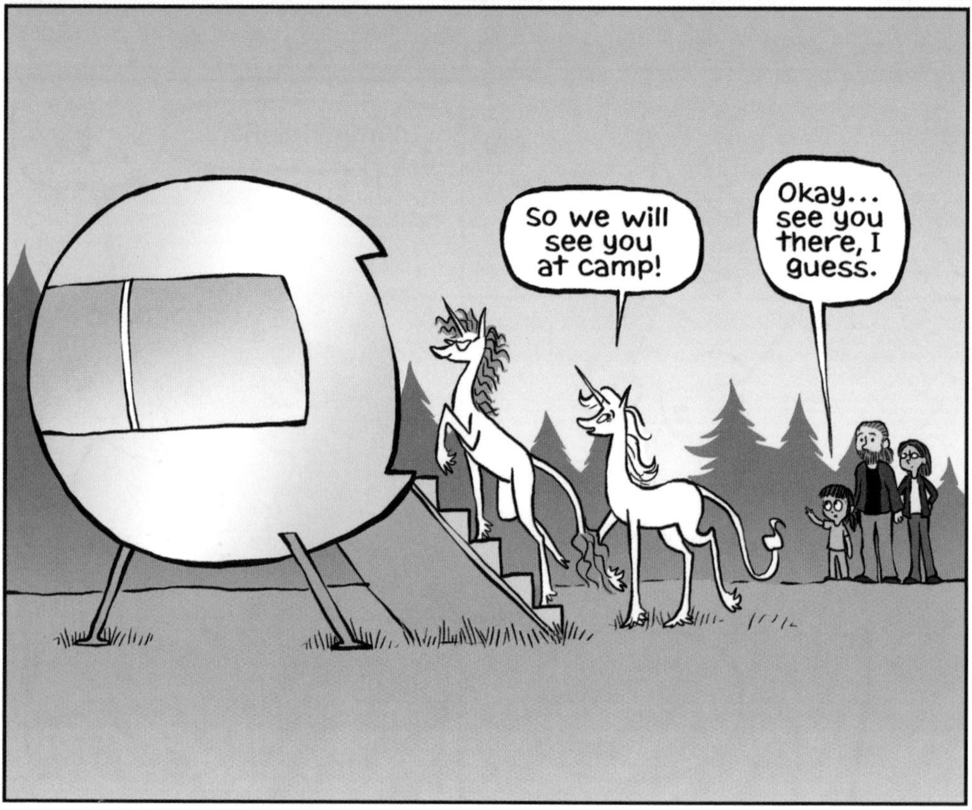
So we will see you at camp!
Okay... see you there, I guess.

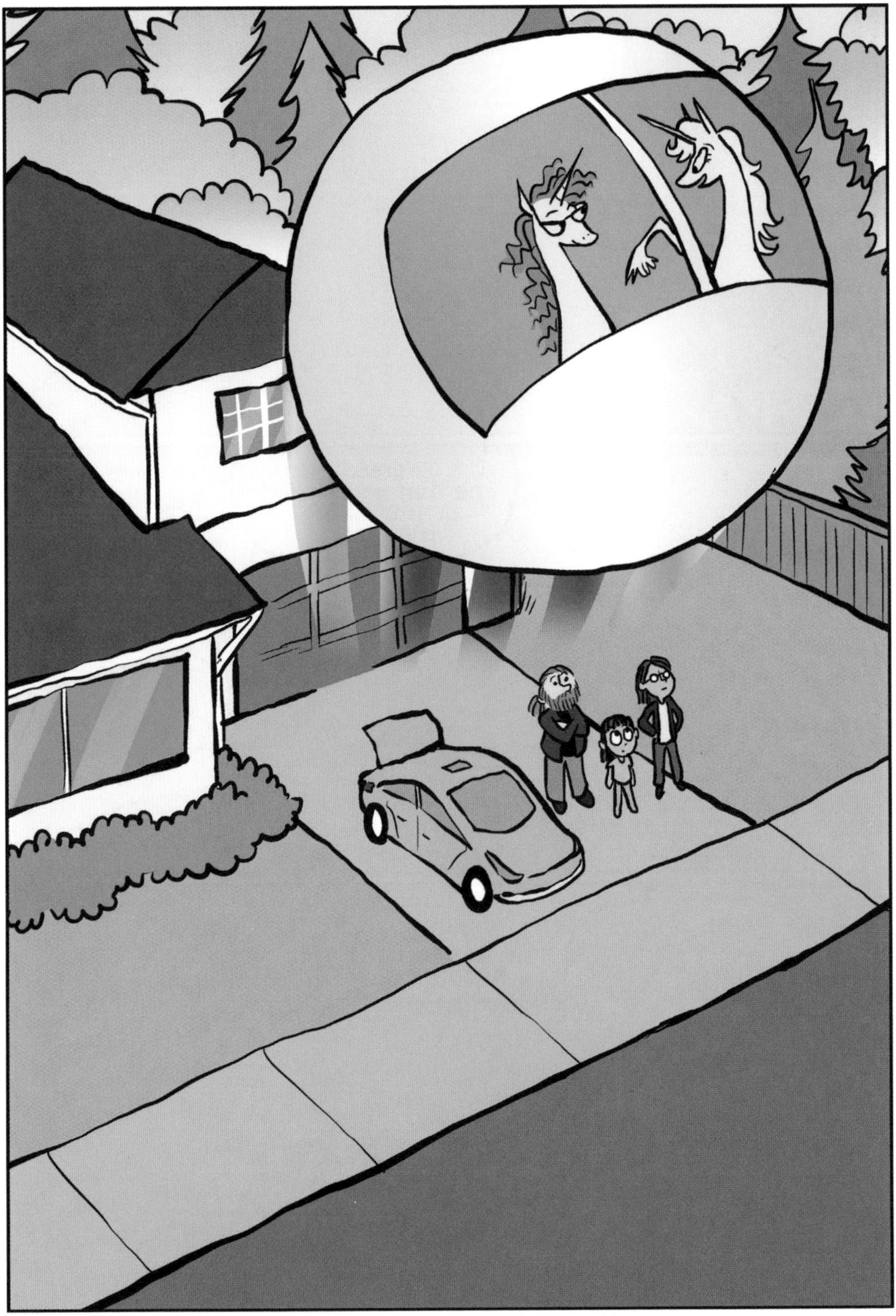

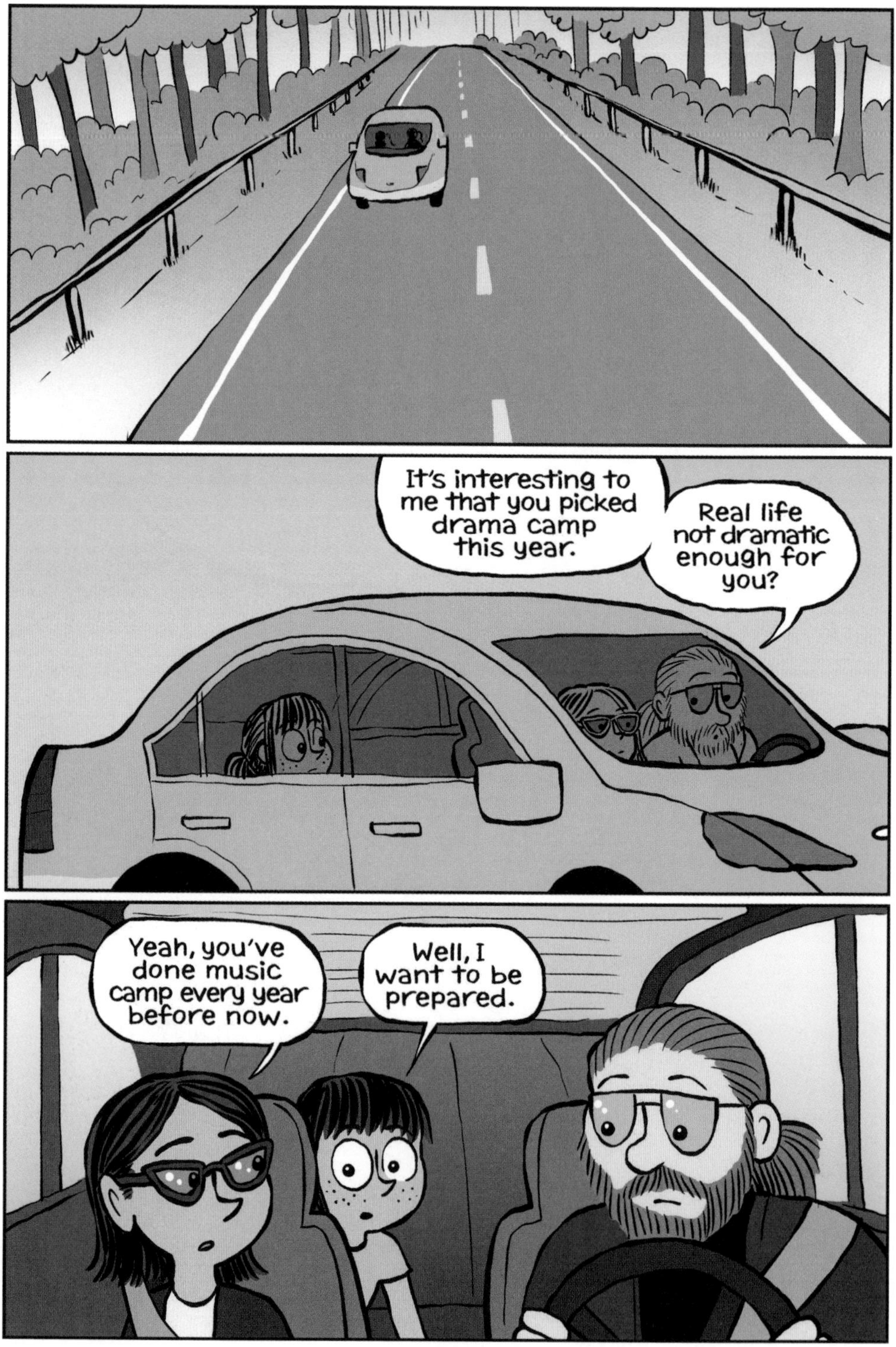
It's interesting to me that you picked drama camp this year.
Real life not dramatic enough for you?
Yeah, you've done music camp every year before now.
Well, I want to be prepared.

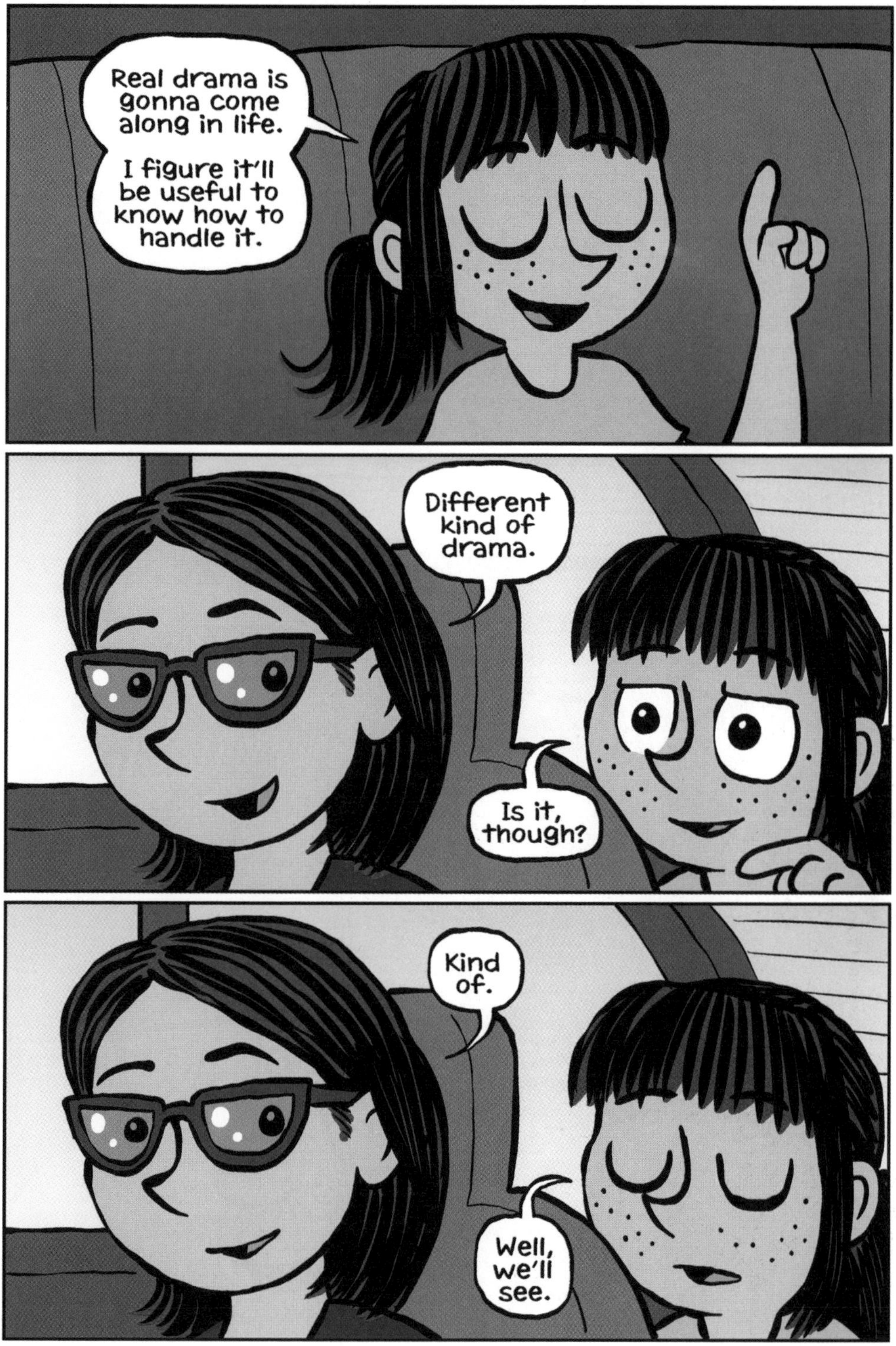
Real drama is gonna come along in life.
I figure it'll be useful to know how to handle it.
Different kind of drama.
Is it, though?
Kind of.
Well, we'll see.

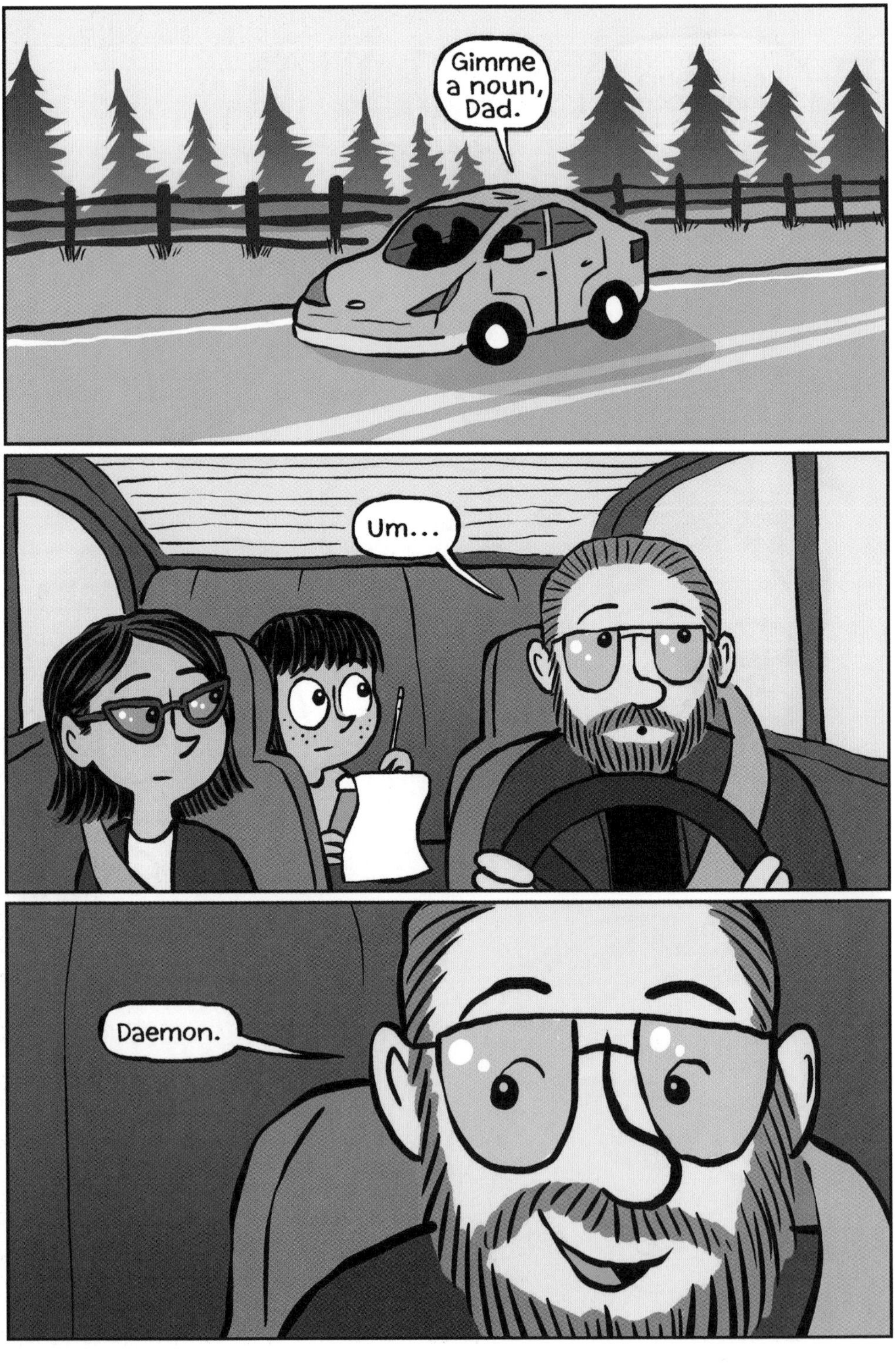
Gimme a noun, Dad.
Um...
Daemon.

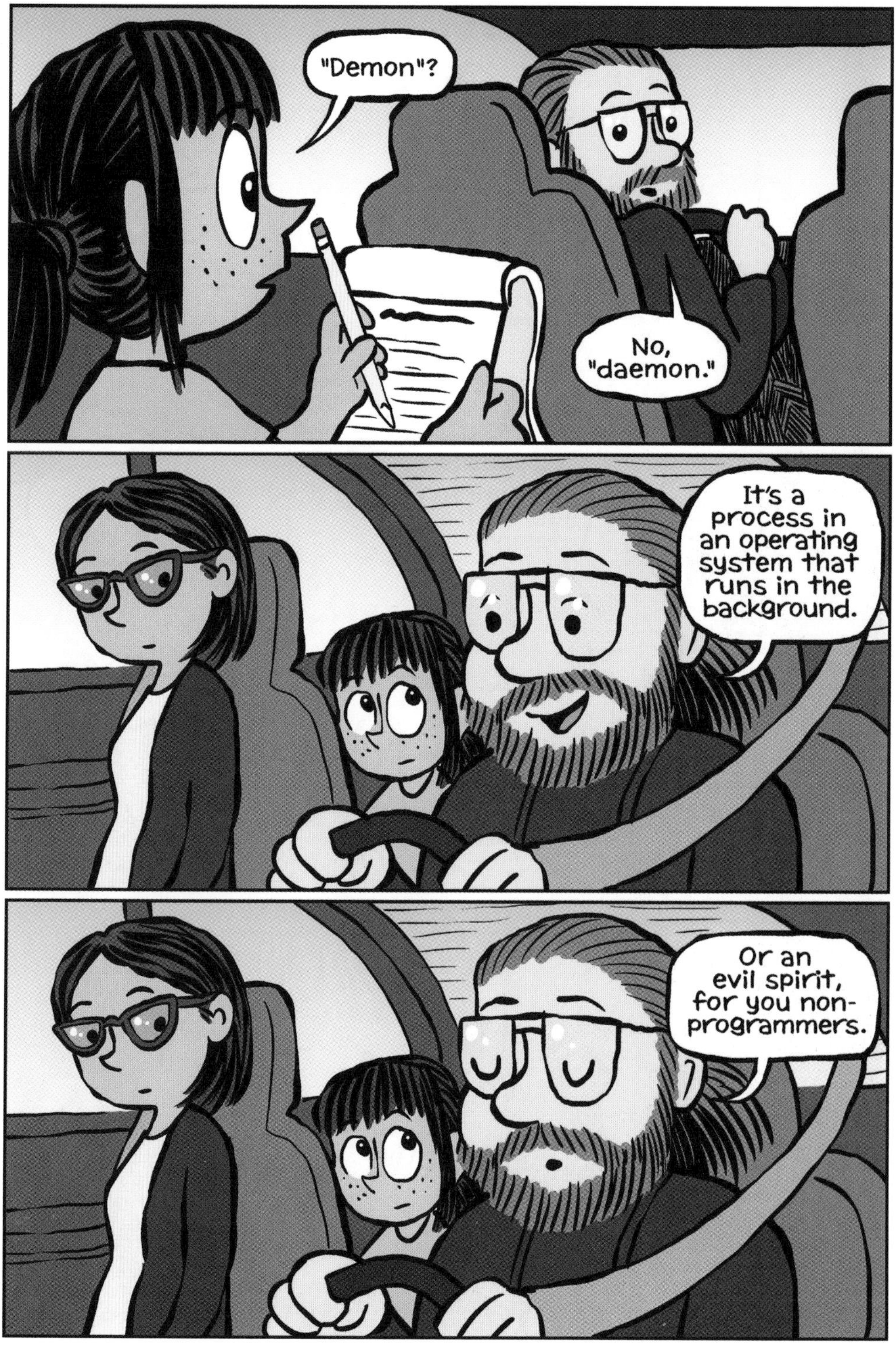
"Demon"?
No, "daemon."
It's a process in an operating system that runs in the background.
Or an evil spirit, for you non-programmers.

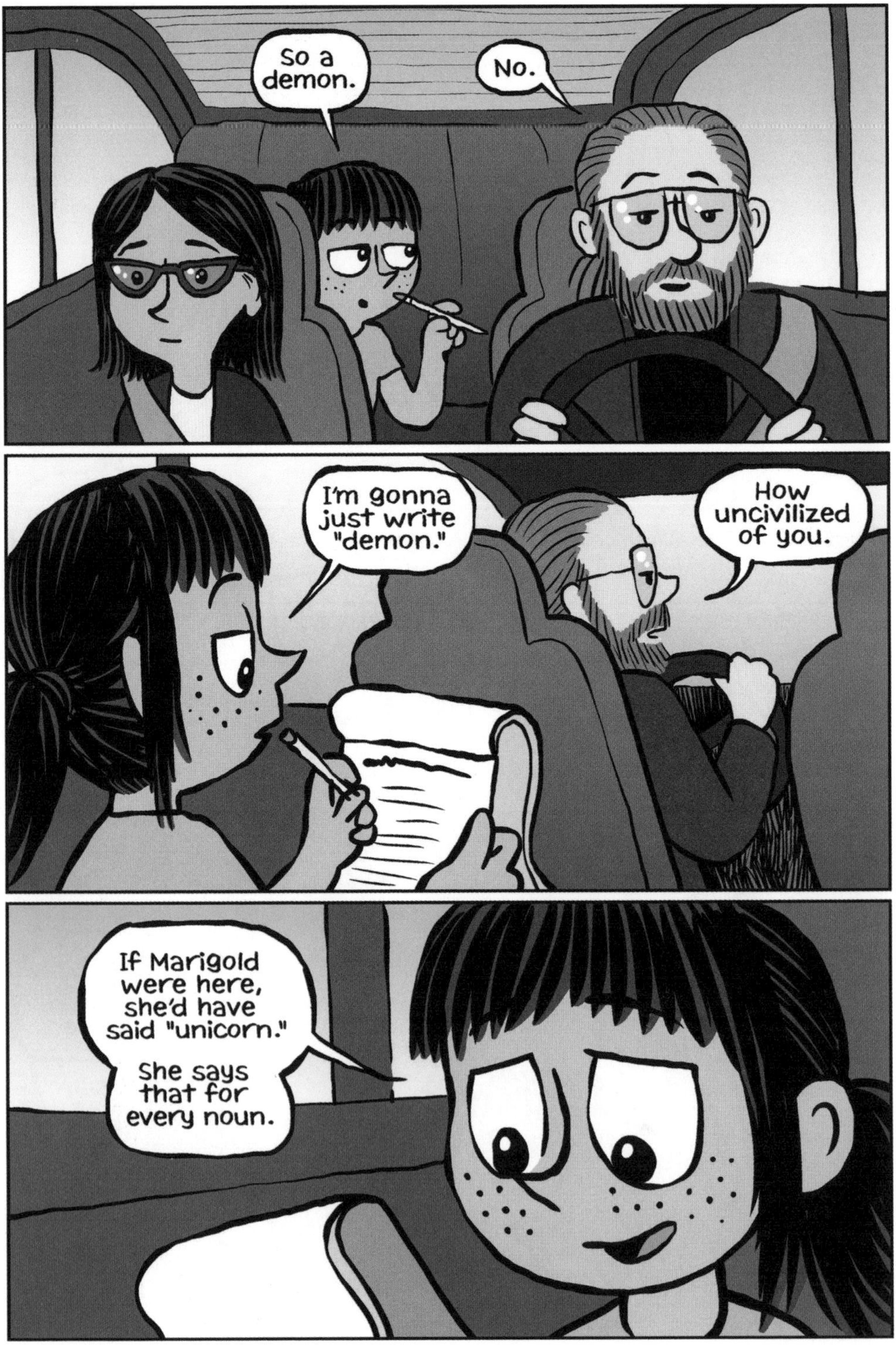
So a demon.
No.
I'm gonna just write "demon."
How uncivilized of you.
If Marigold were here, she'd have said "unicorn."
She says that for every noun.

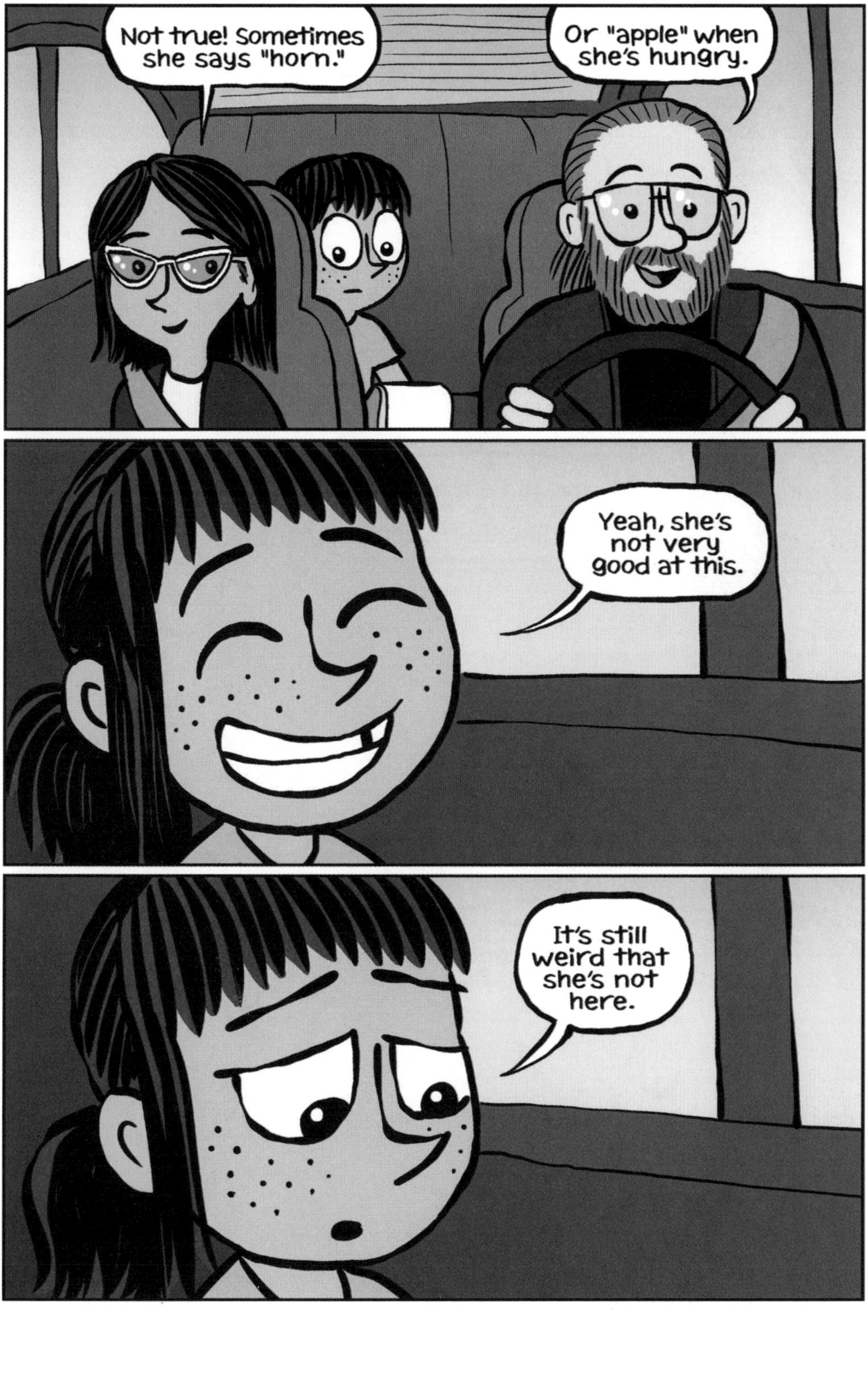
Not true! Sometimes she says "horn."
Or "apple" when she's hungry.
Yeah, she's not very good at this.
It's still weird that she's not here.

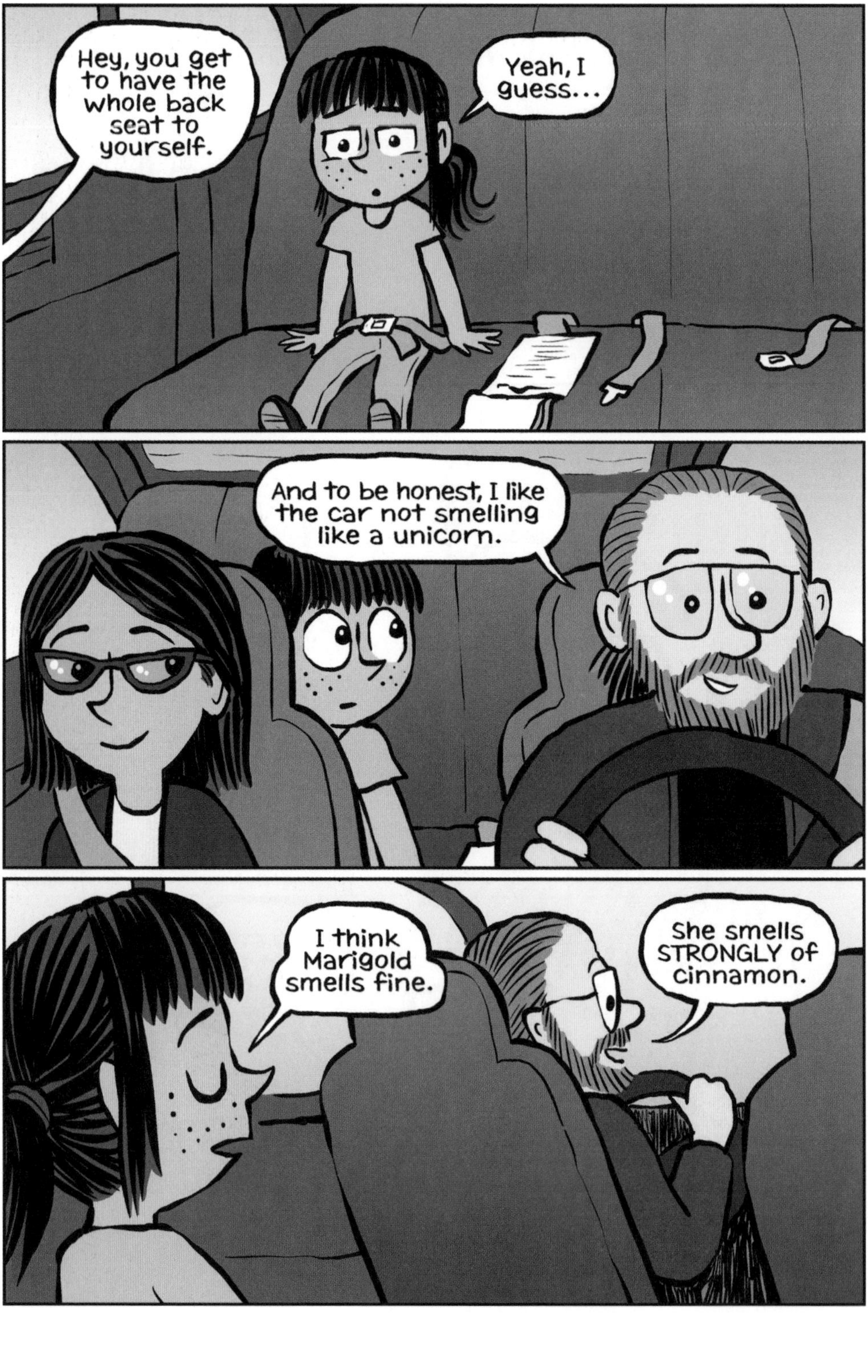
Hey, you get to have the whole back seat to yourself.
Yeah, I guess...
And to be honest, I like the car not smelling like a unicorn.
I think Marigold smells fine.
She smells STRONGLY of cinnamon.

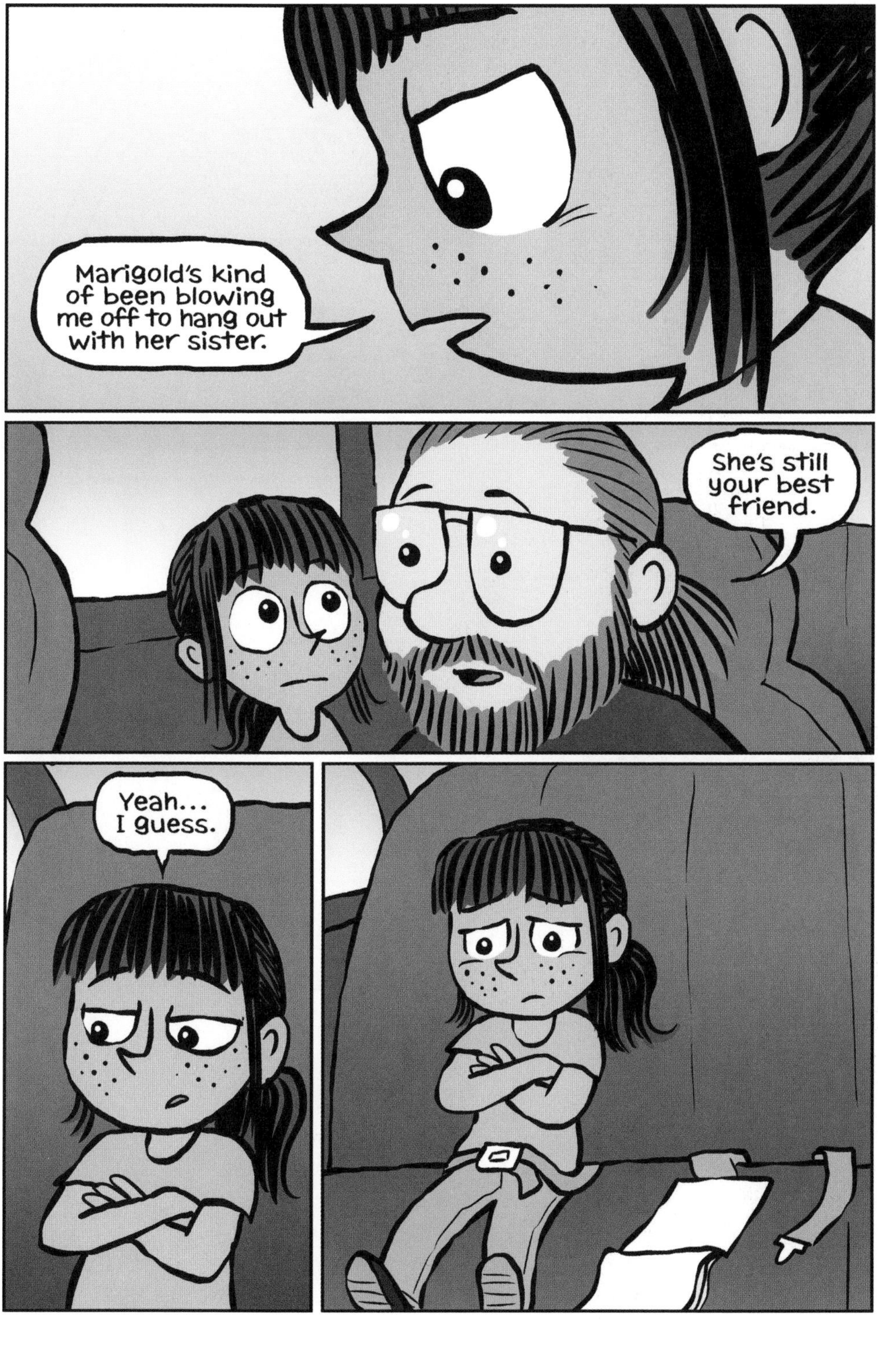
Marigold's kind of been blowing me off to hang out with her sister.
She's still your best friend.
Yeah... I guess.

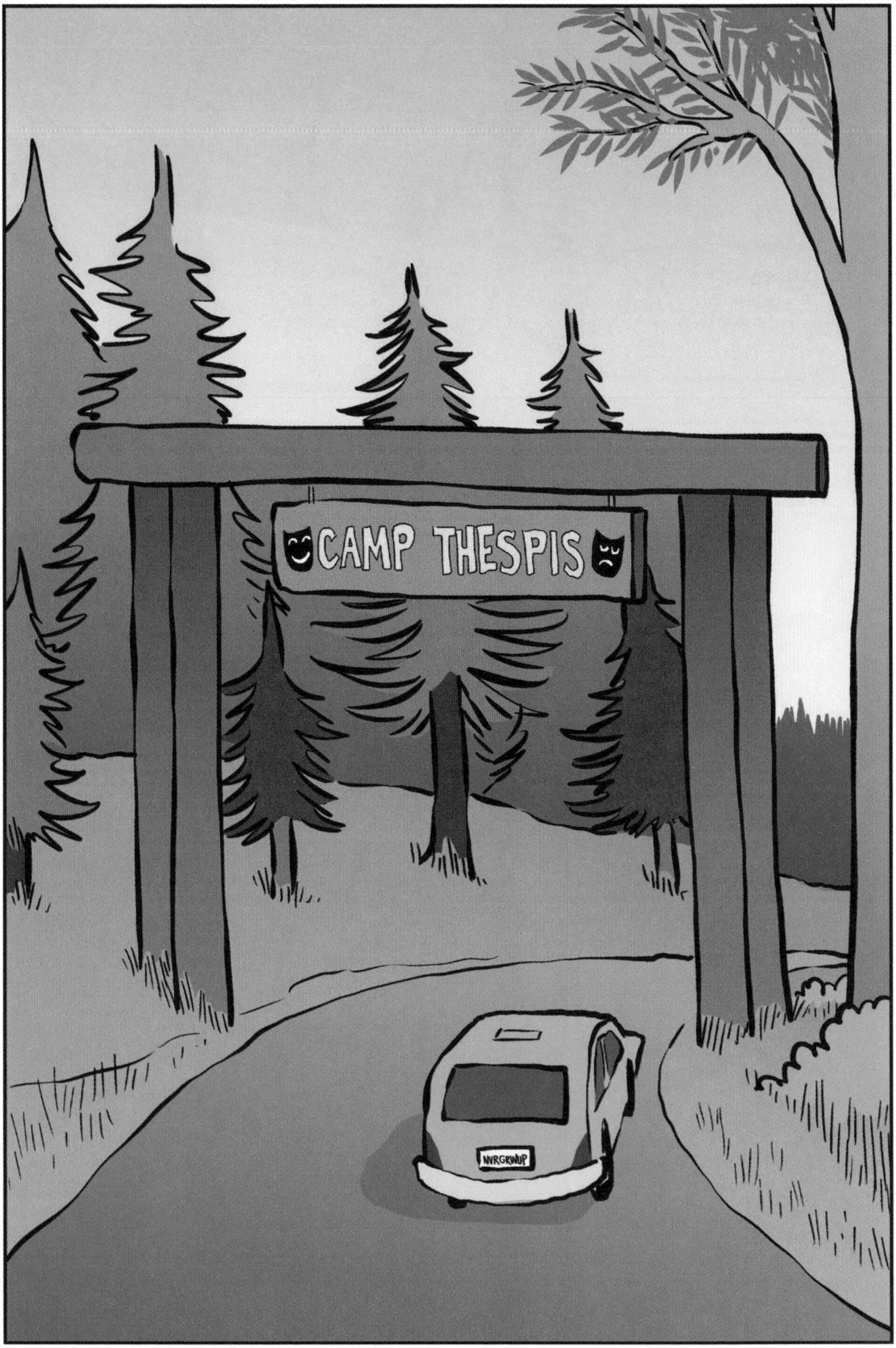
CAMP THESPIS
NVRGRWUP

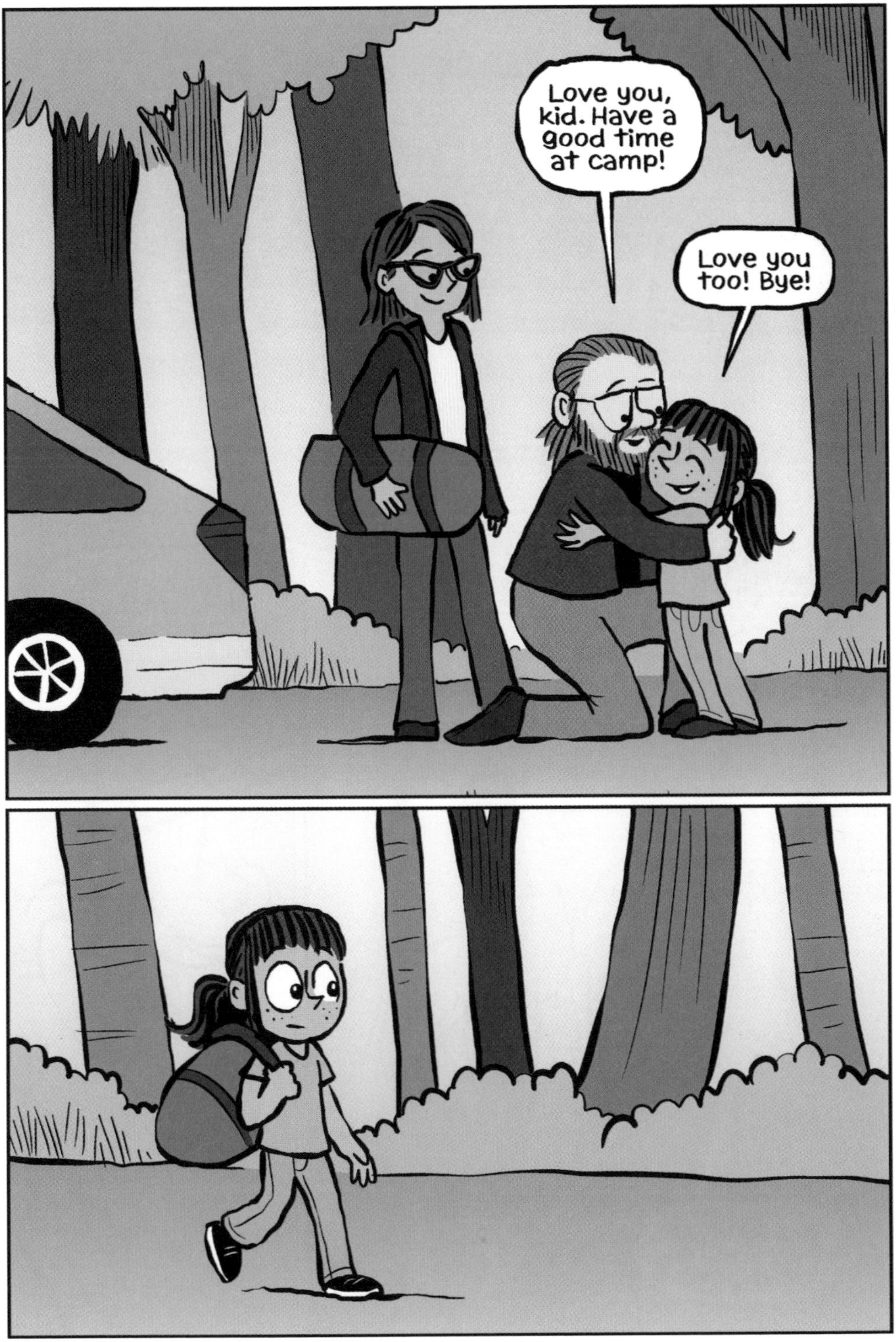
Love you, kid. Have a good time at camp!
Love you too! Bye!

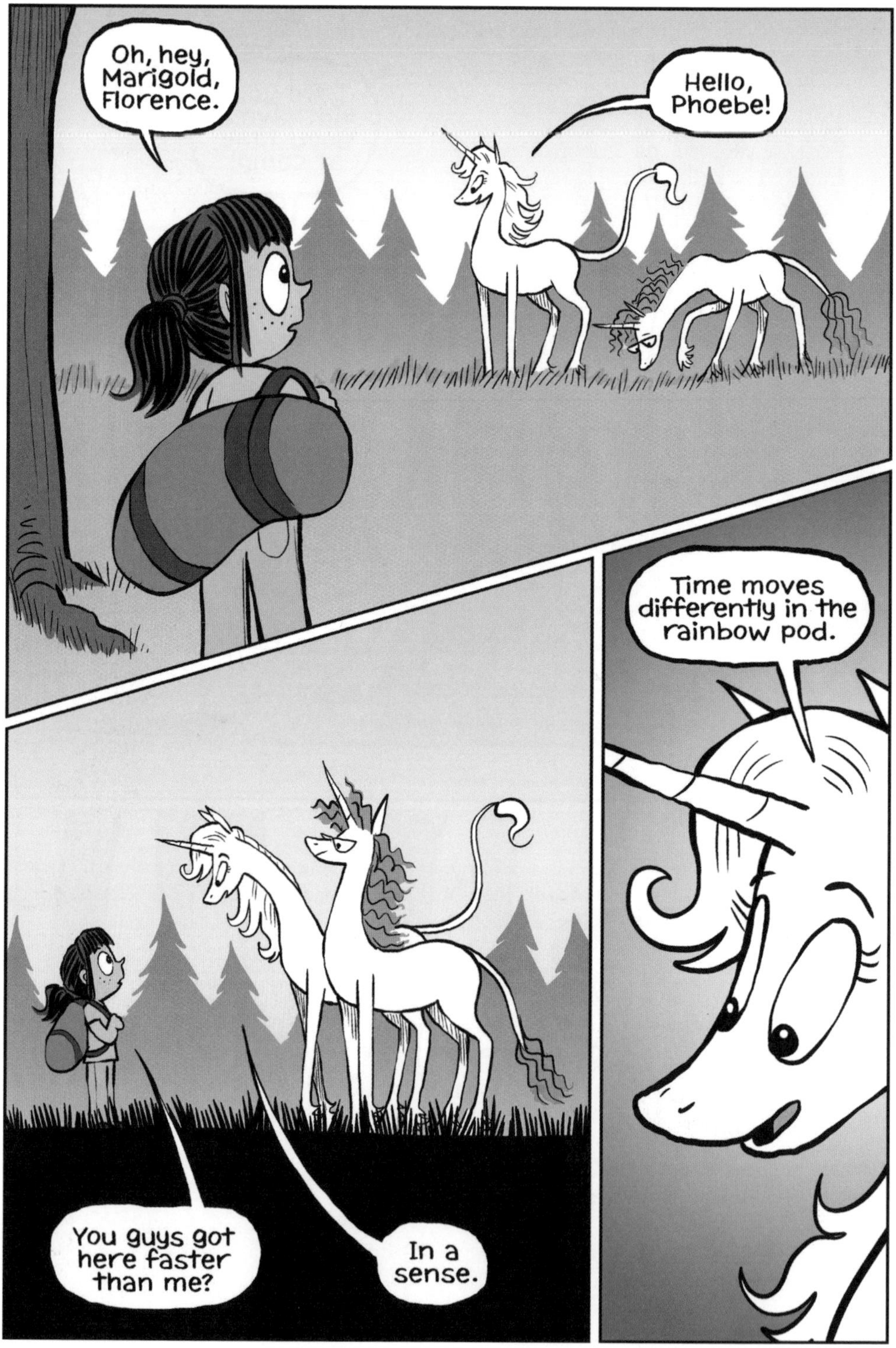
Oh, hey, Marigold, Florence.
Hello, Phoebe!
You guys got here faster than me?
In a sense.
Time moves differently in the rainbow pod.

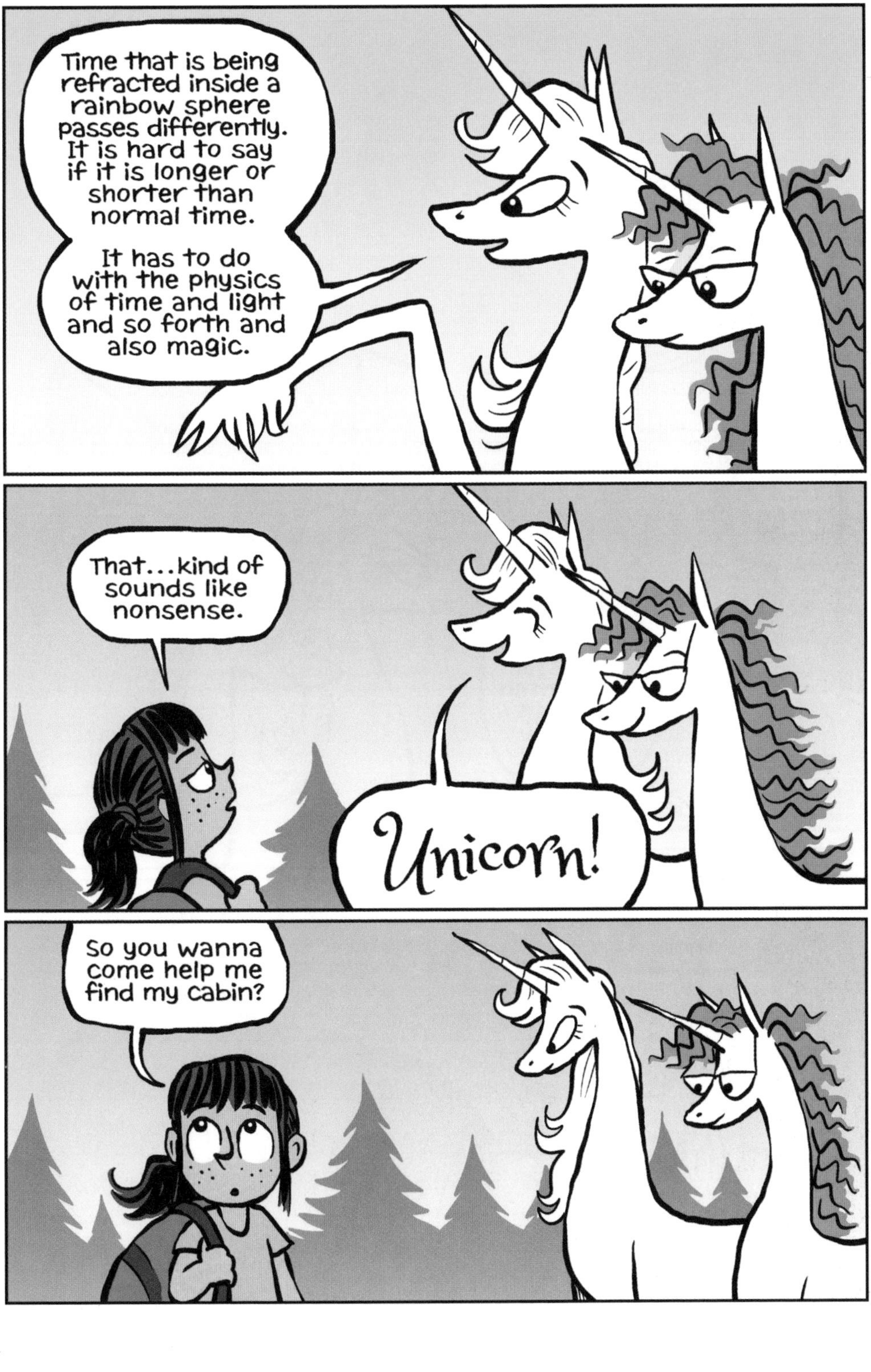
Time that is being refracted inside a rainbow sphere passes differently. It is hard to say if it is longer or shorter than normal time.
It has to do with the physics of time and light and so forth and also magic.
That...kind of sounds like nonsense.
Unicorn!
So you wanna come help me find my cabin?

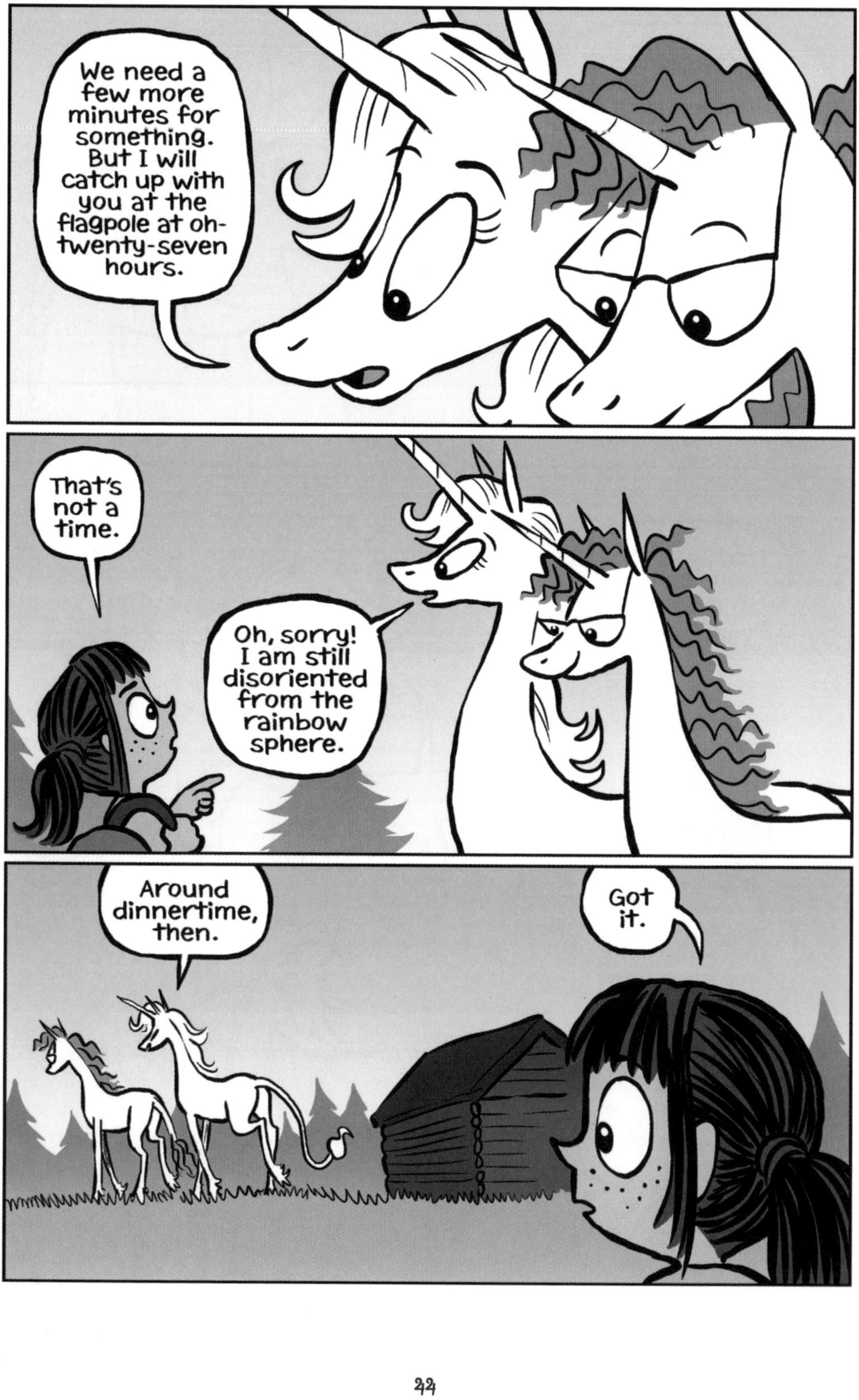
We need a few more minutes for something. But I will catch up with you at the flagpole at oh-twenty-seven hours.
That's not a time.
Oh, sorry! I am still disoriented from the rainbow sphere.
Around dinnertime, then.
Got it.

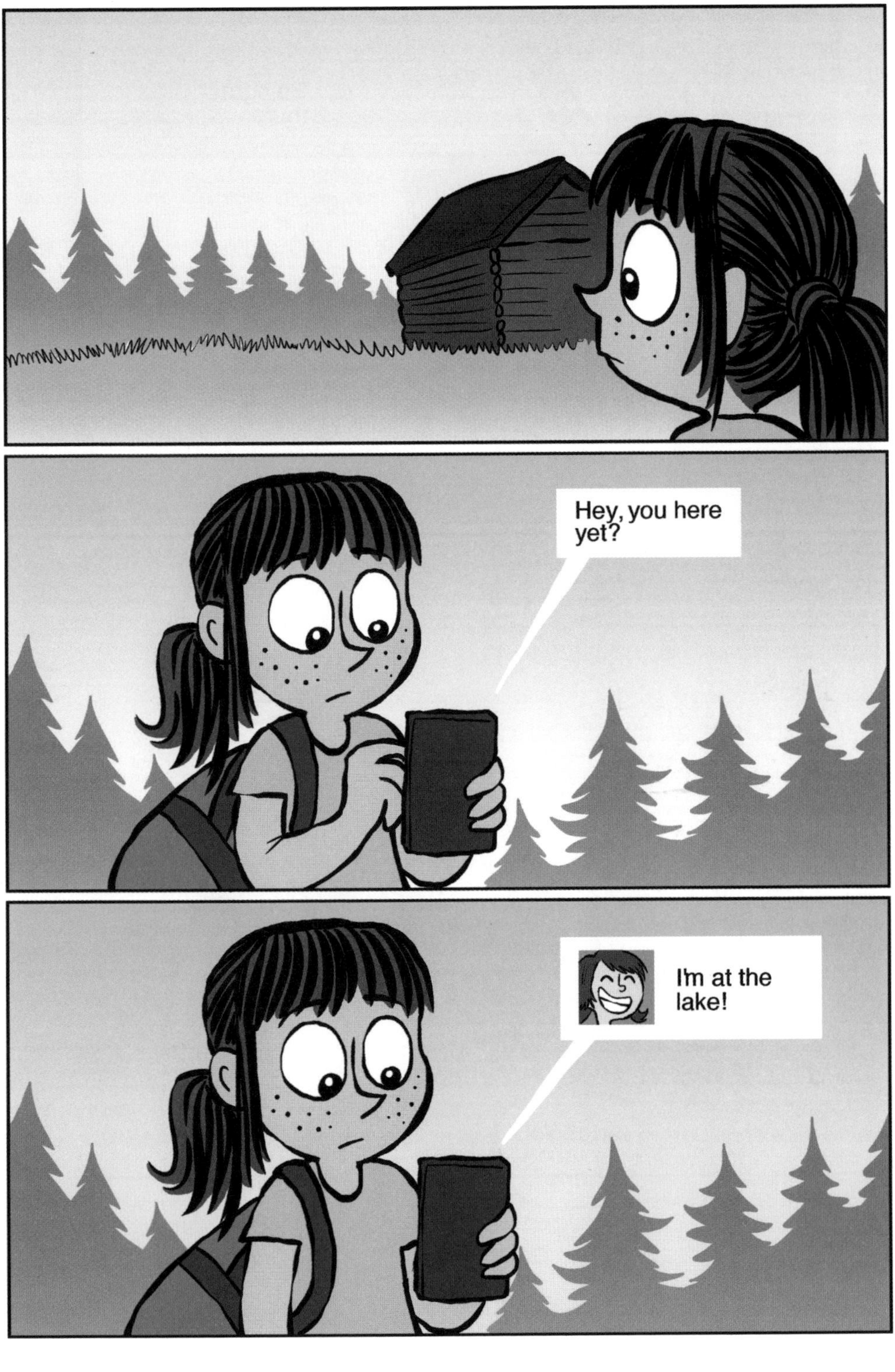
Hey, you here yet?
I'm at the lake!

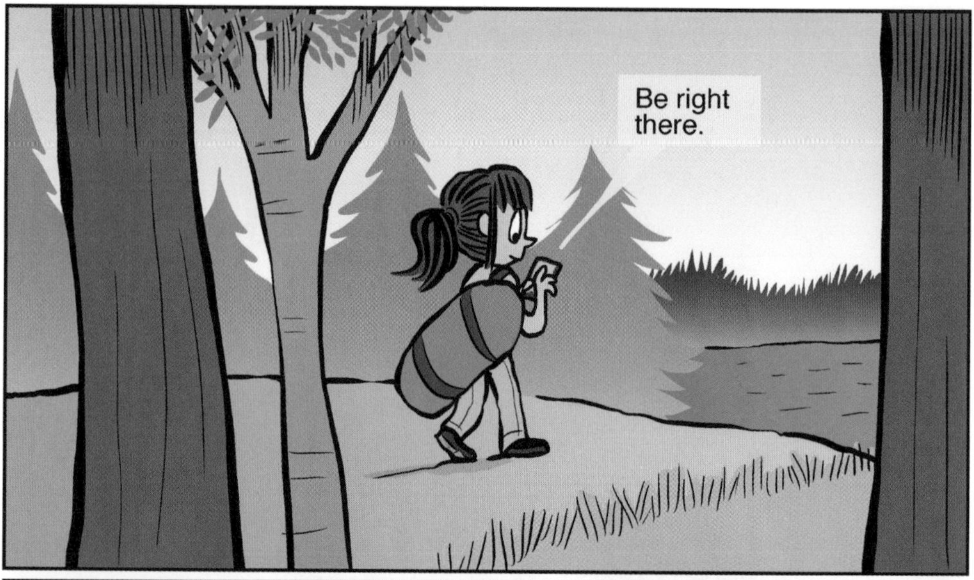
Be right there.

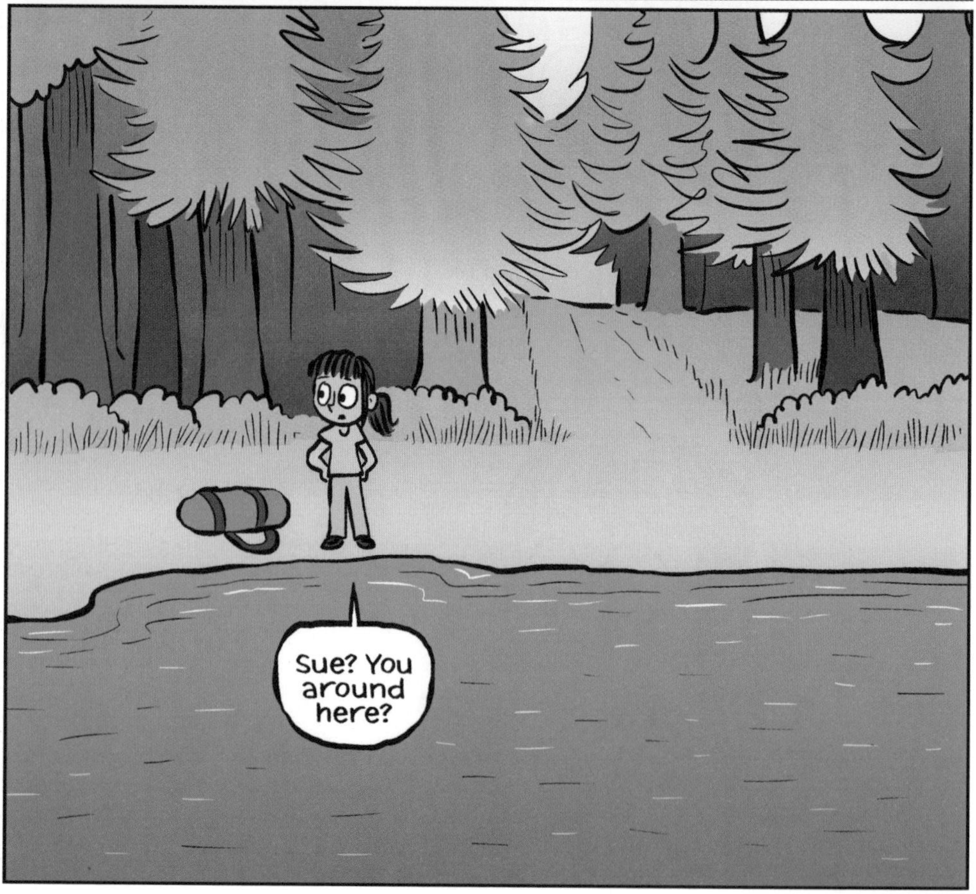
Sue? You around here?

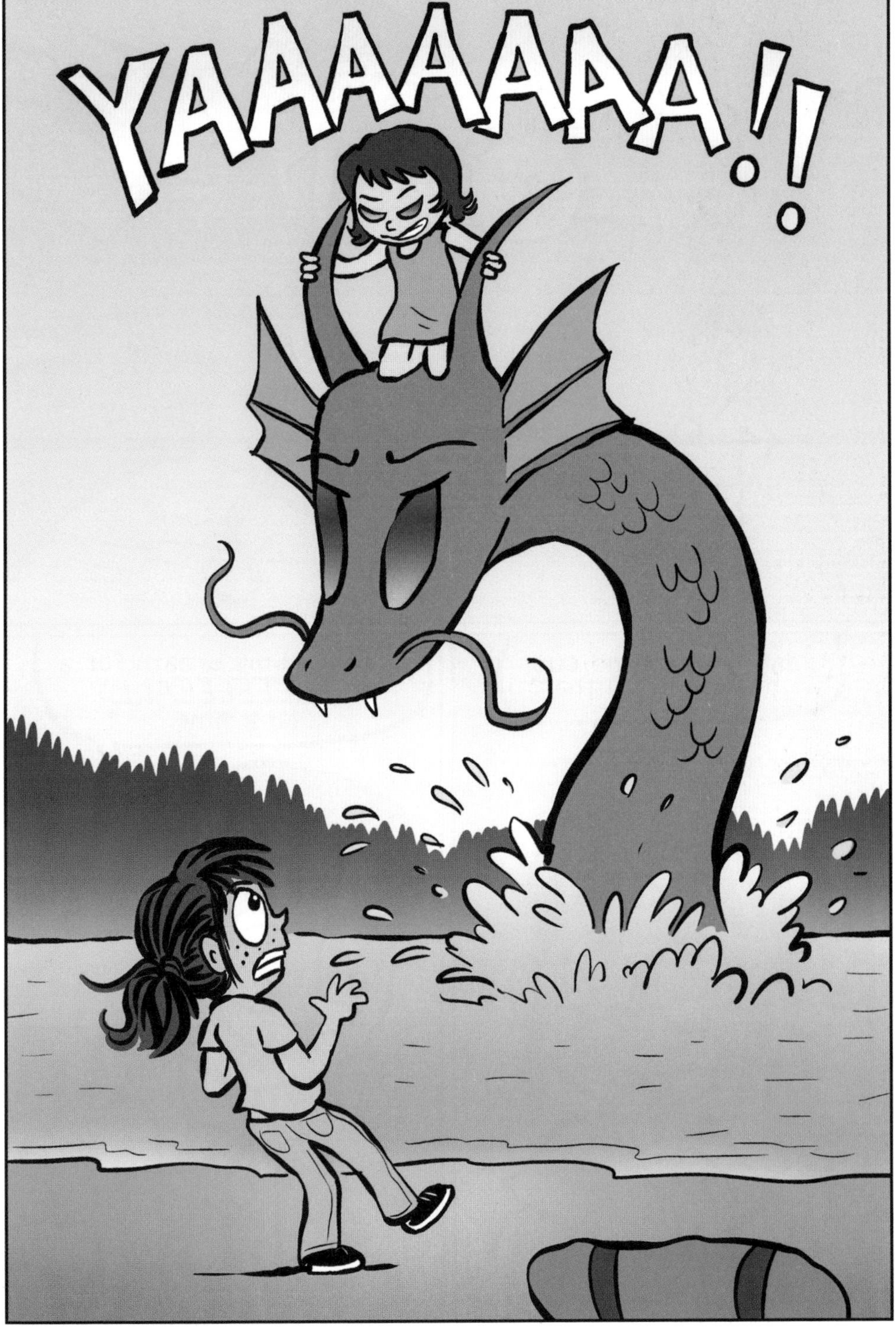
YAAAAAAA!!

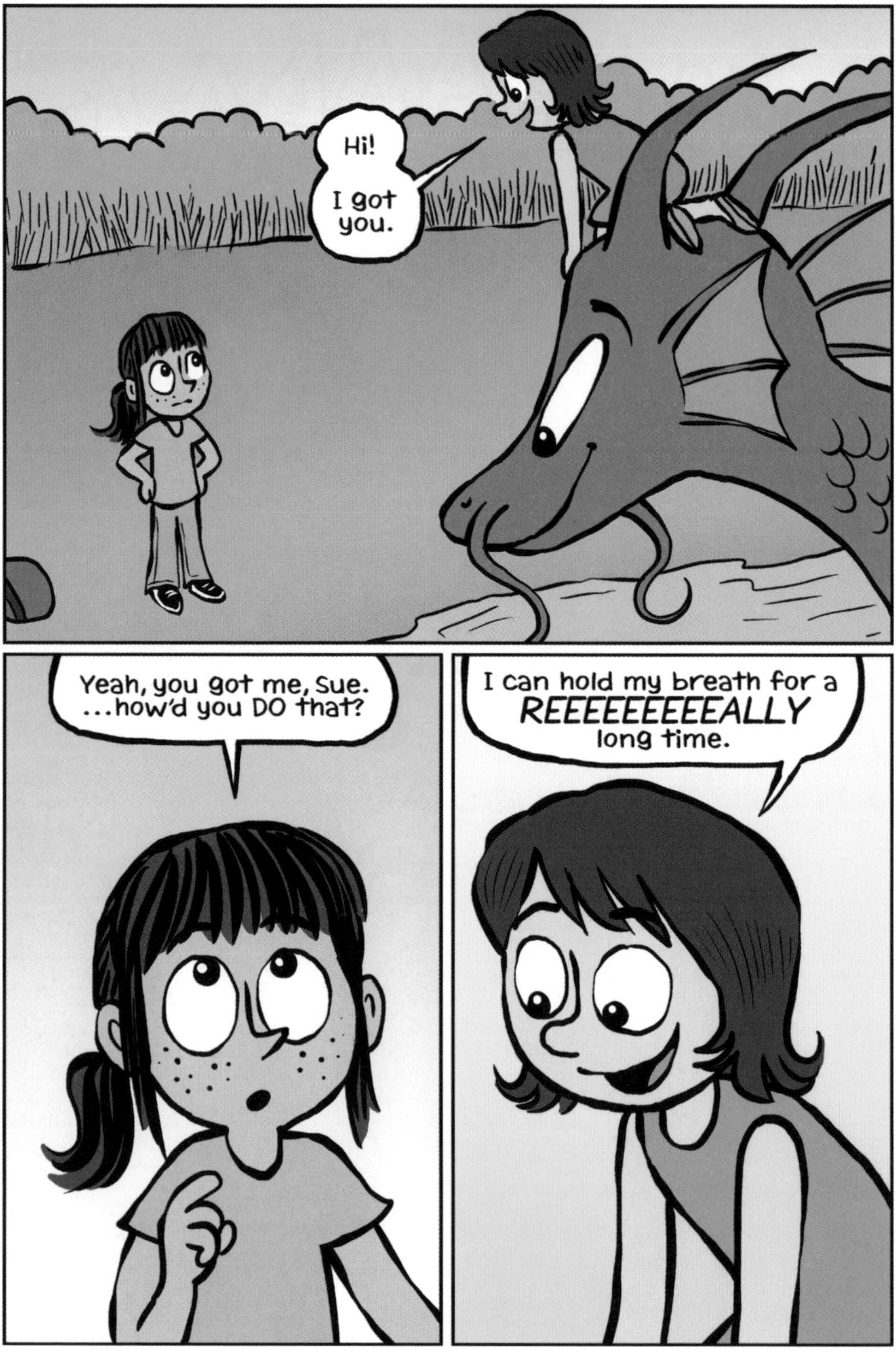
Hi!
I got you.
Yeah, you got me, Sue. ...how'd you DO that?
I can hold my breath for a REEEEEEEEEALLY long time.

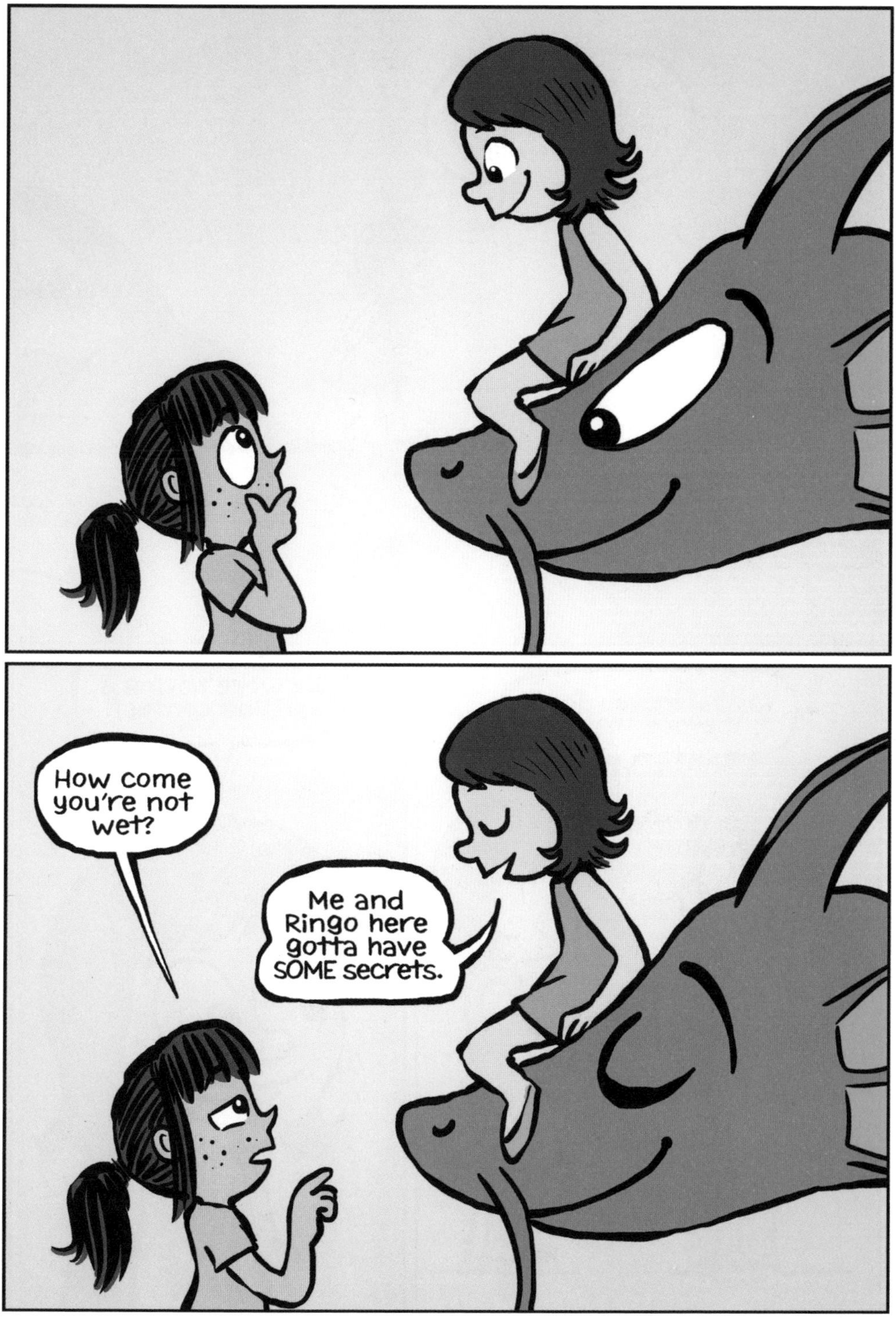
How come you're not wet?
Me and Ringo here gotta have SOME secrets.

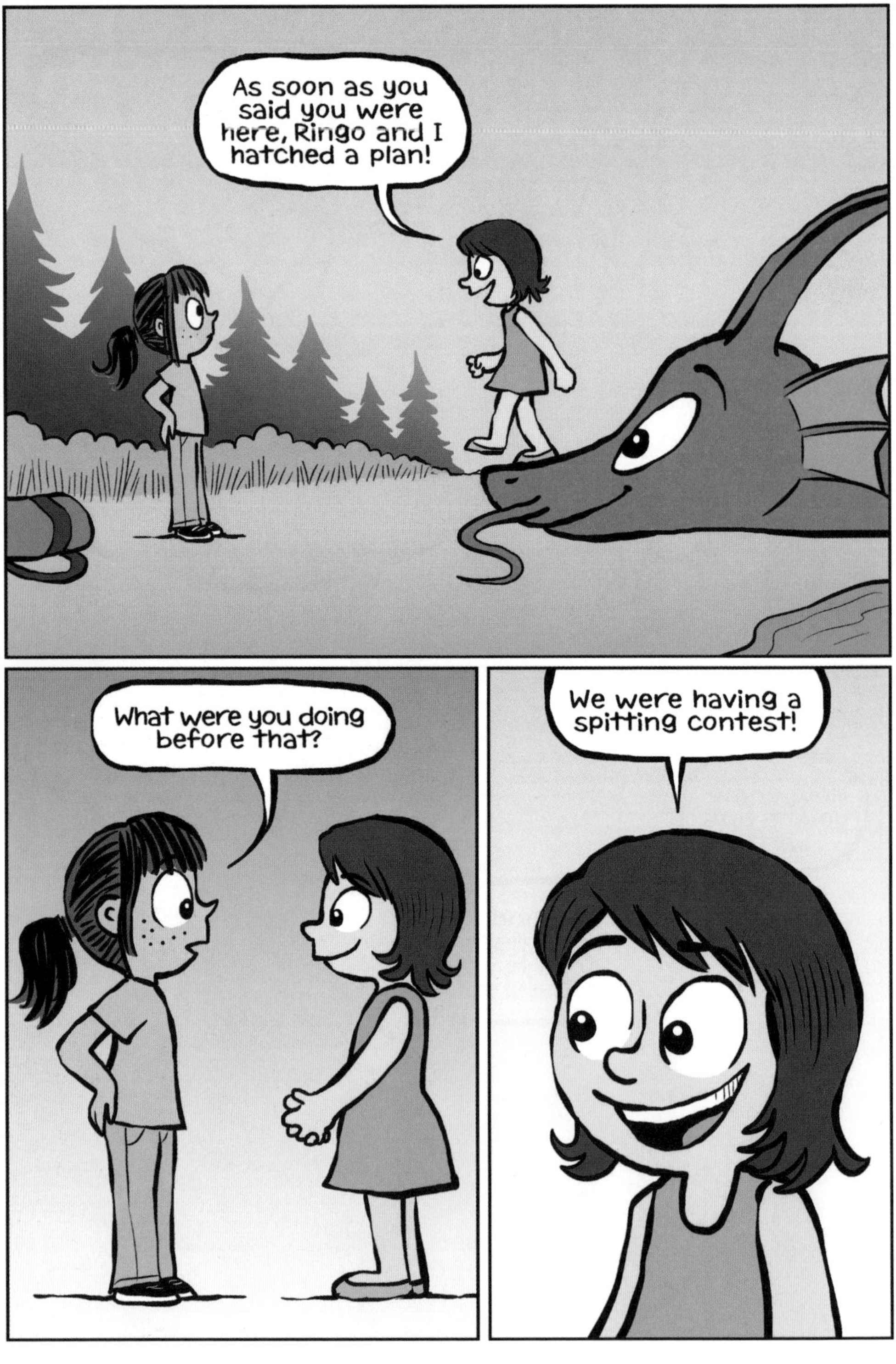
As soon as you said you were here, Ringo and I hatched a plan!
What were you doing before that?
We were having a spitting contest!

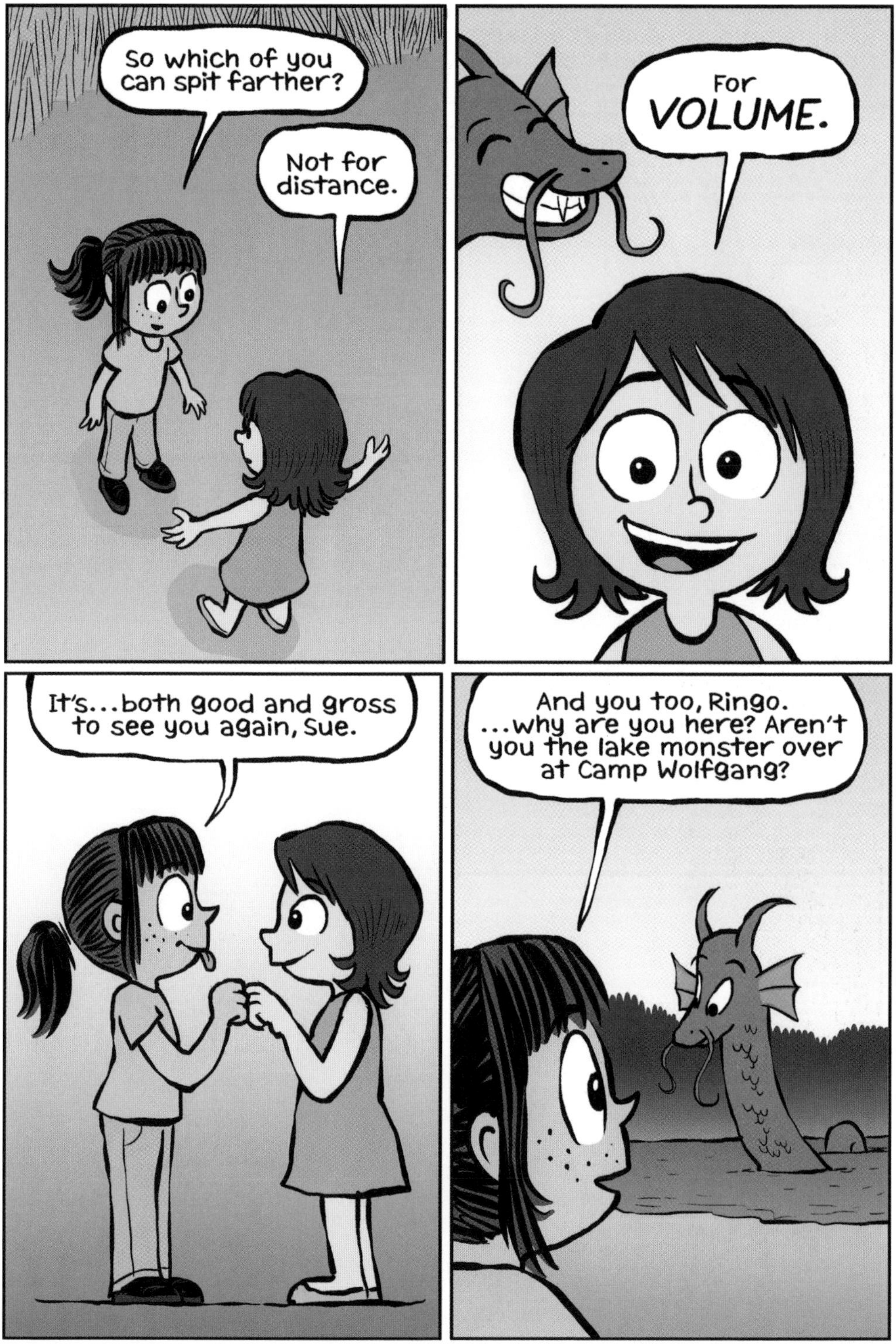
So which of you can spit farther?
Not for distance.
For VOLUME.
It's...both good and gross to see you again, Sue.
And you too, Ringo. ...why are you here? Aren't you the lake monster over at Camp Wolfgang?

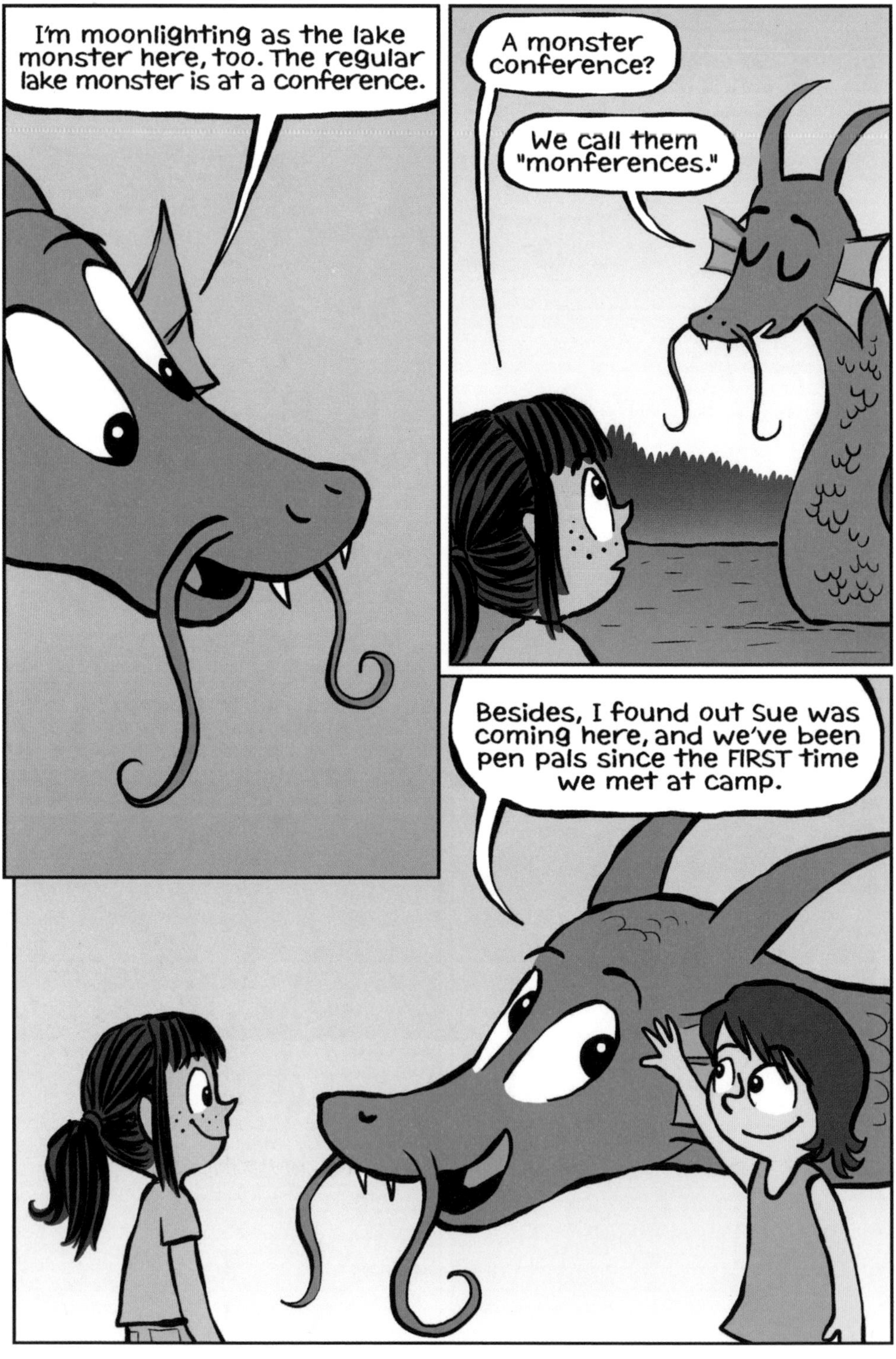
I'm moonlighting as the lake monster here, too. The regular lake monster is at a conference.
A monster conference?
We call them "monferences."
Besides, I found out Sue was coming here, and we've been pen pals since the FIRST time we met at camp.

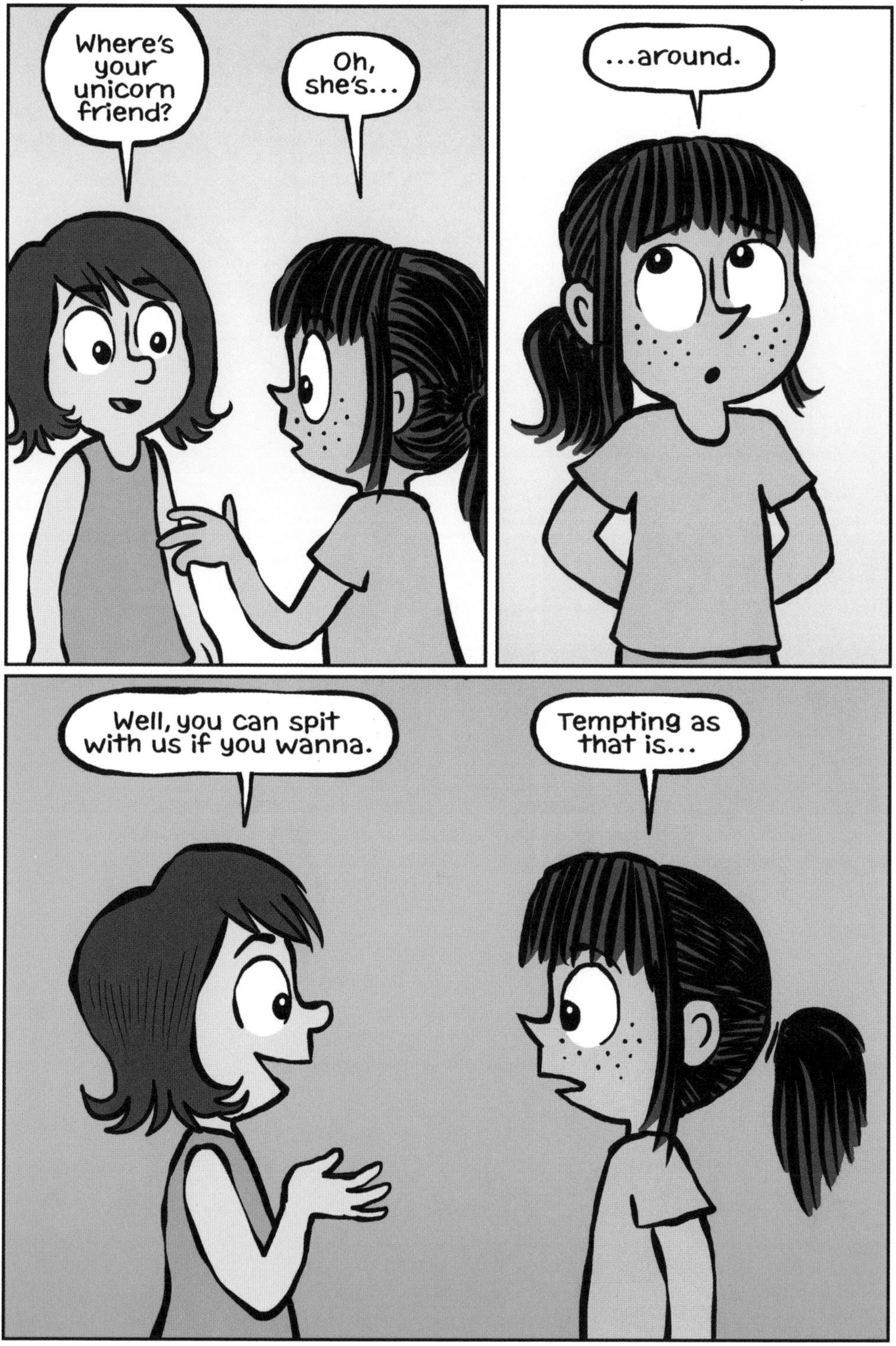
Where's your unicorn friend?
Oh, she's...
...around.
Well, you can spit with us if you wanna.
Tempting as that is...

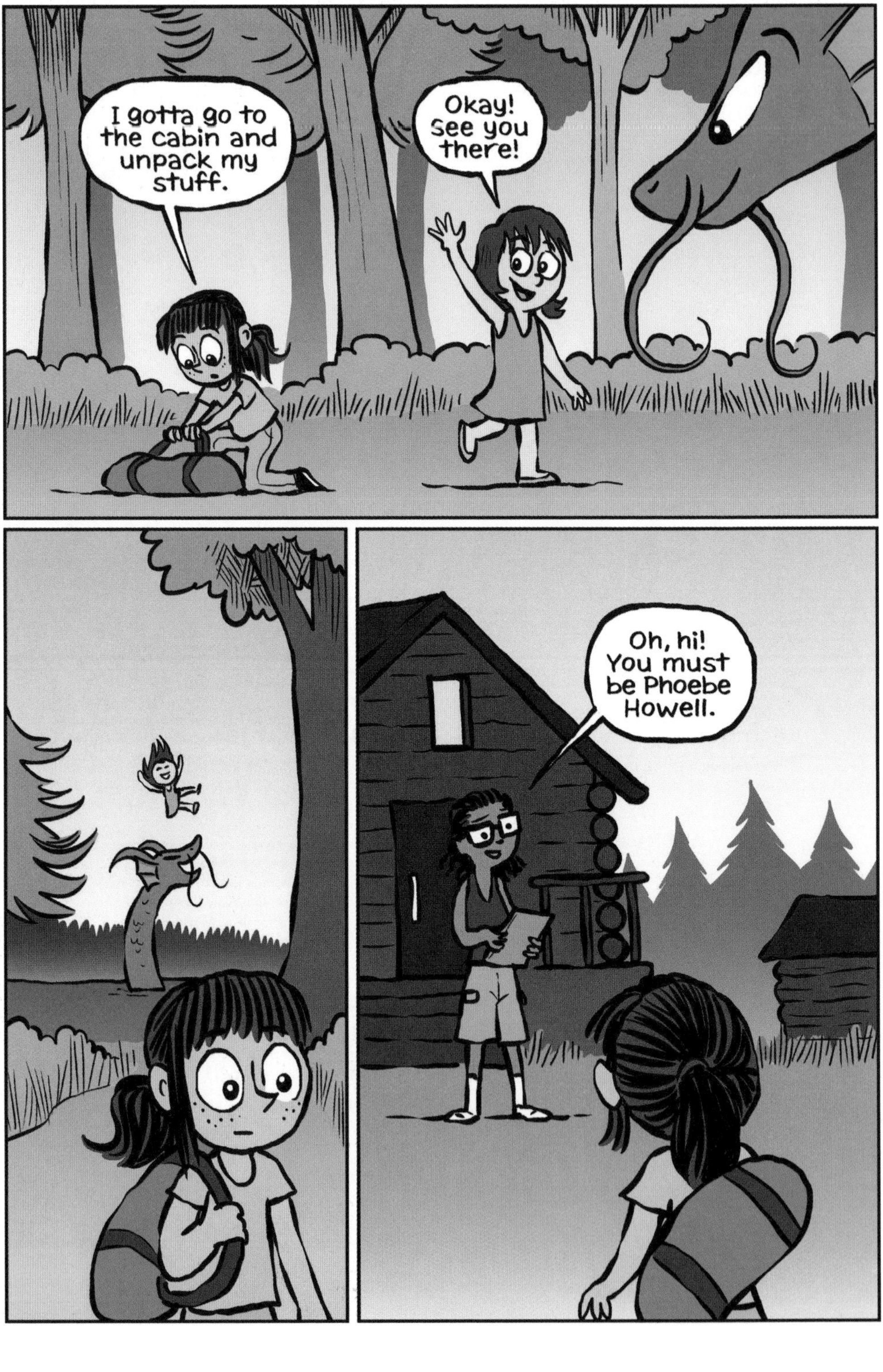
I gotta go to the cabin and unpack my stuff.
Okay! See you there!
Oh, hi! You must be Phoebe Howell.

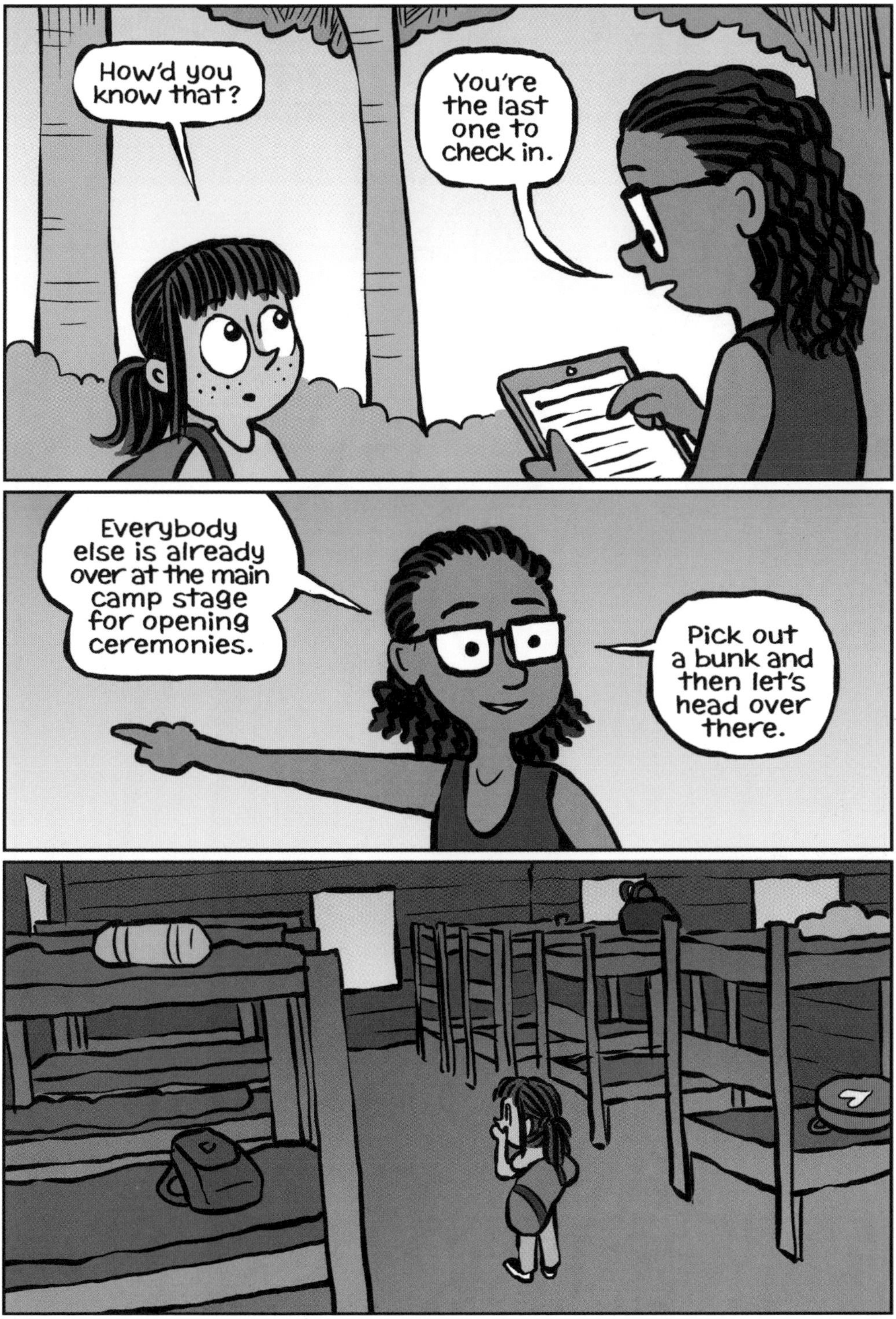
How'd you know that?
You're the last one to check in.
Everybody else is already over at the main camp stage for opening ceremonies.
Pick out a bunk and then let's head over there.

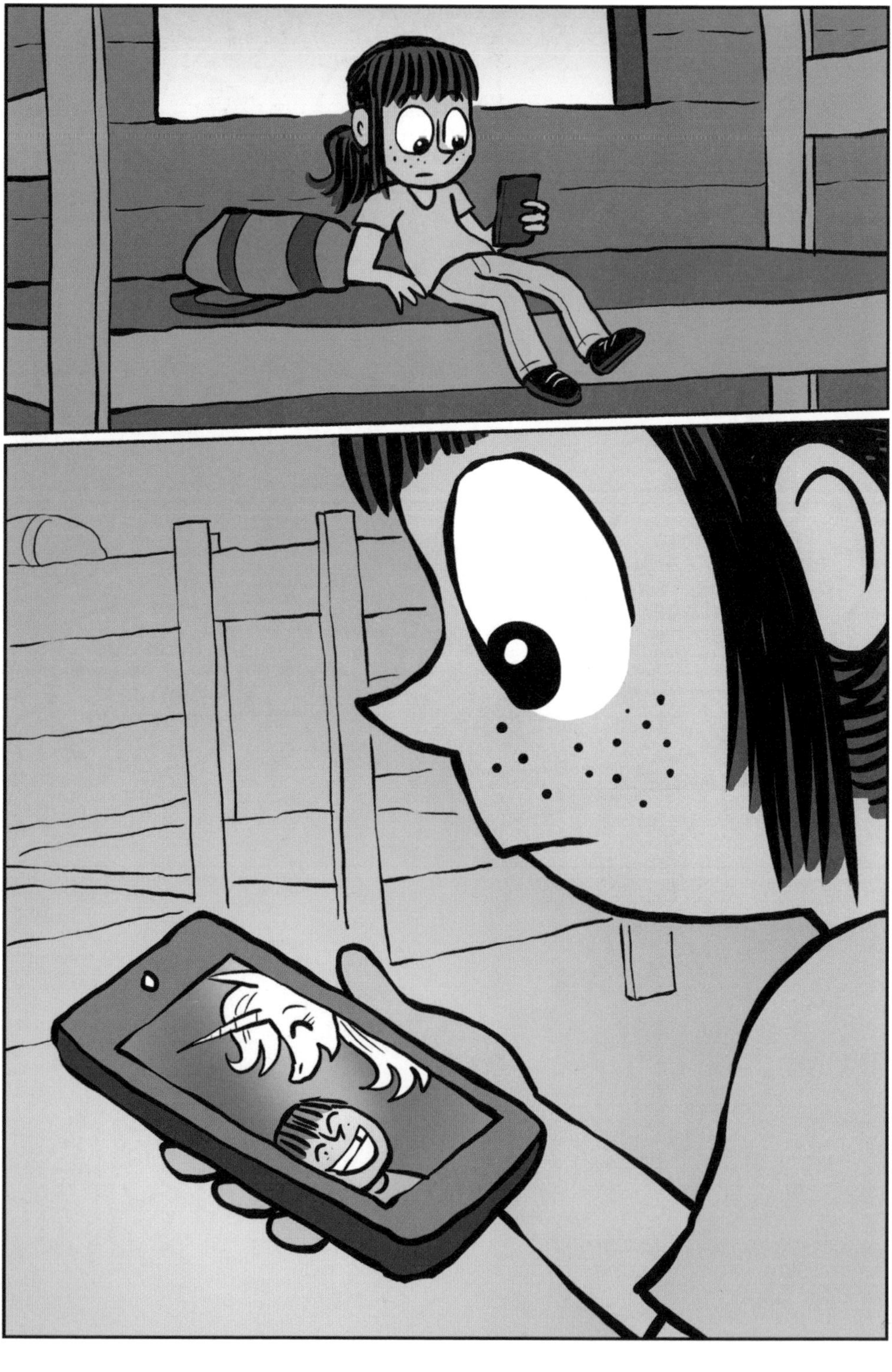

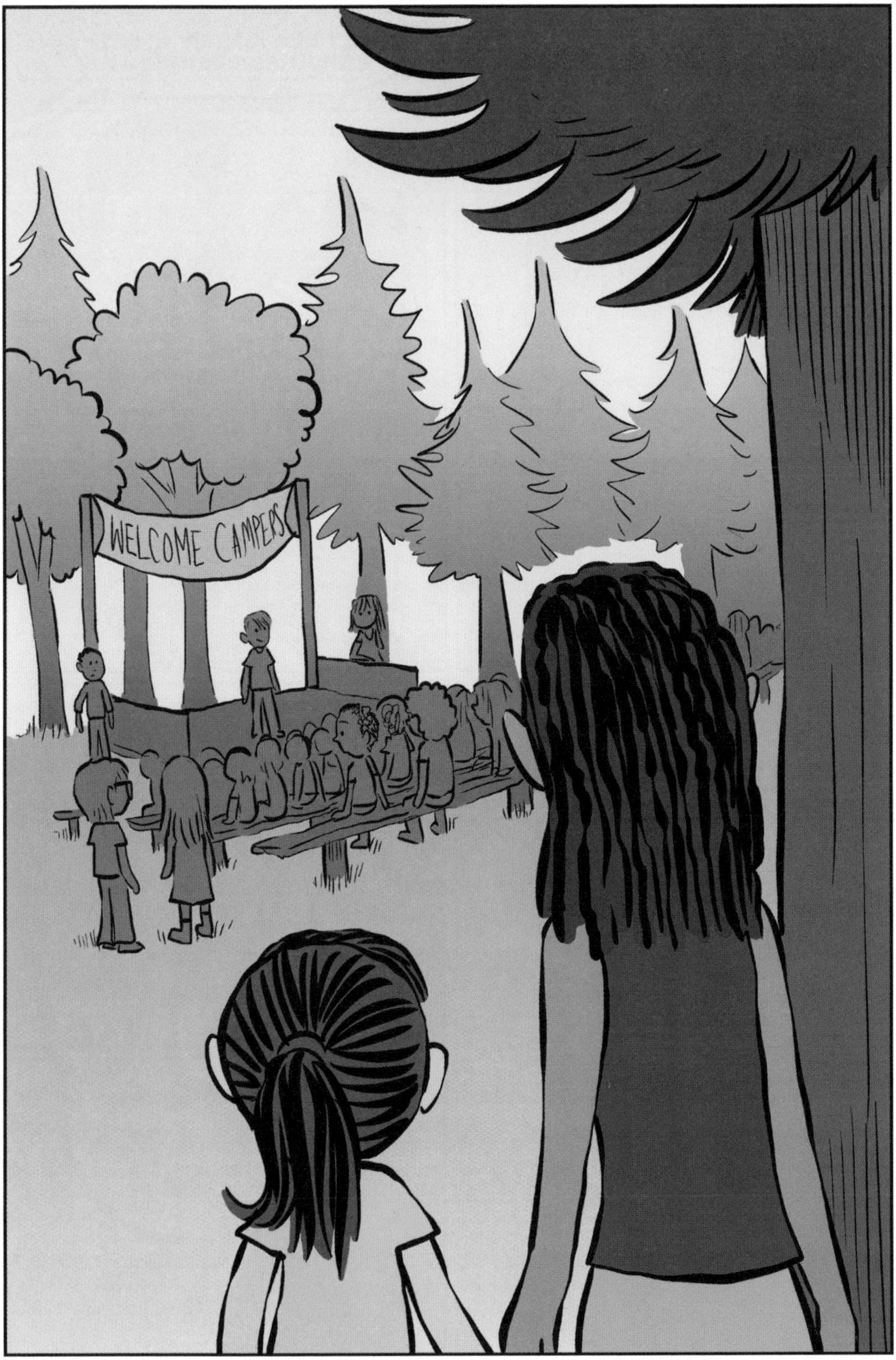
WELCOME CAMPERS

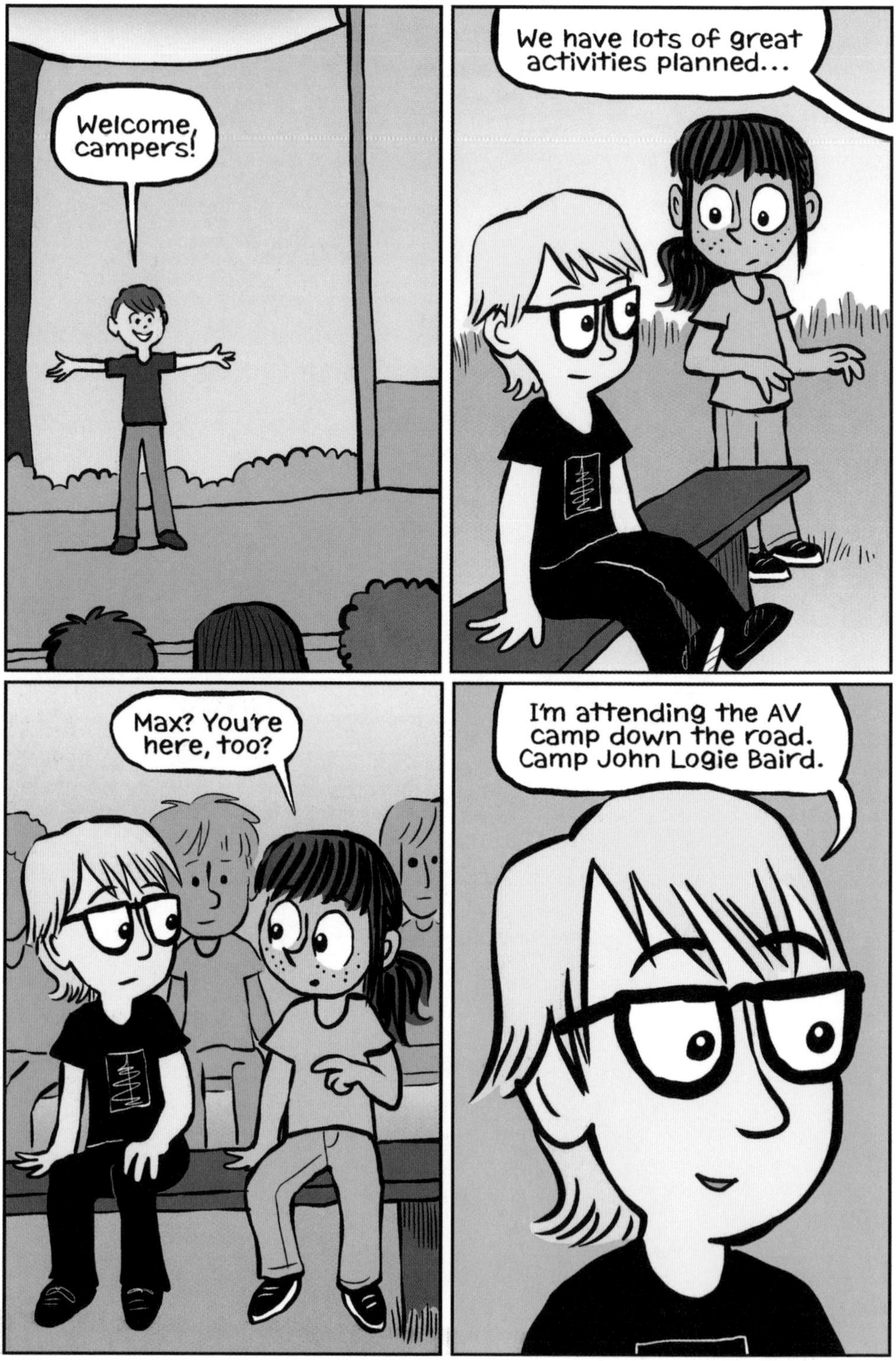
Welcome, campers!
We have lots of great activities planned...
Max? You're here, too?
I'm attending the AV camp down the road. Camp John Logie Baird.

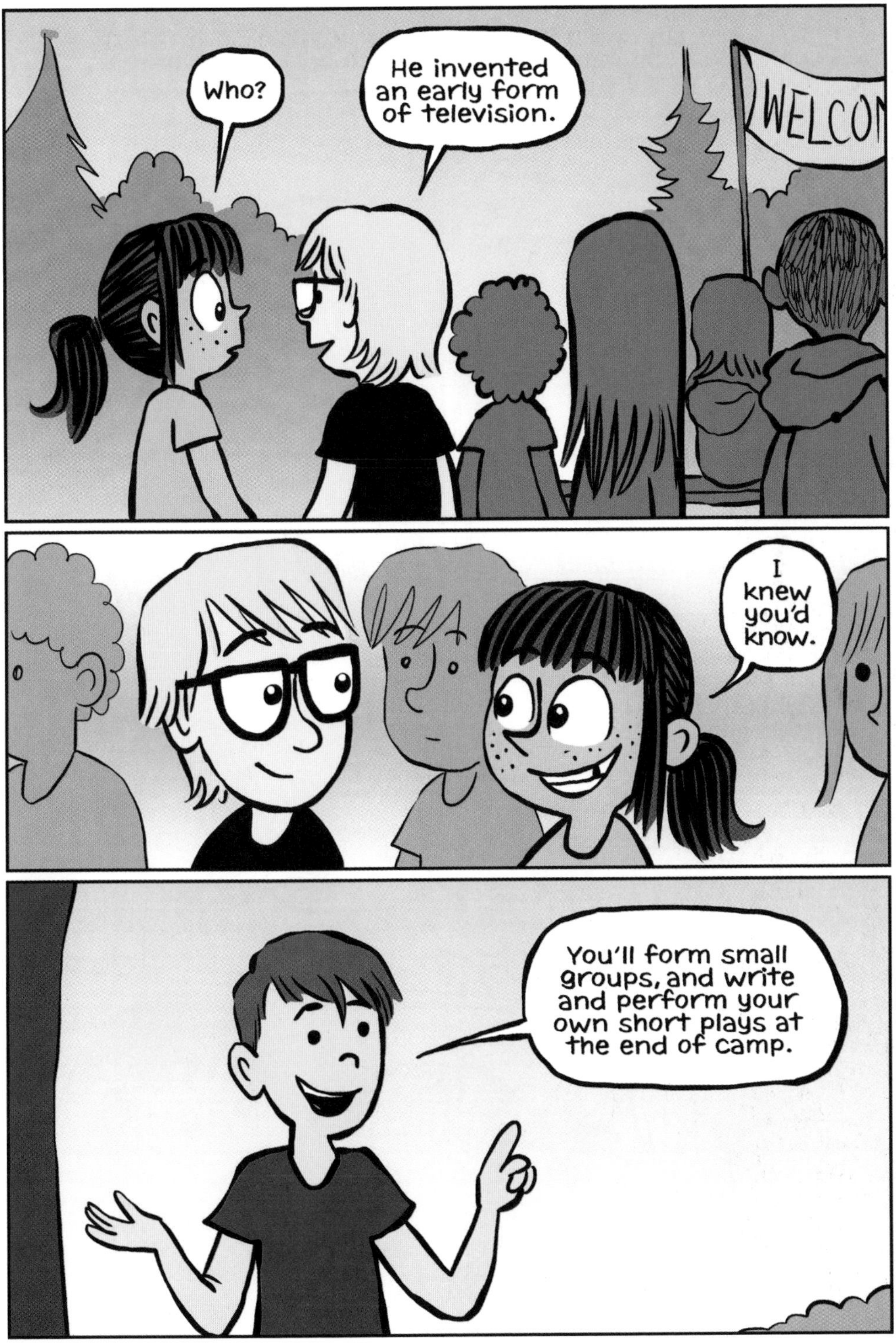
Who?
He invented an early form of television.
WELCOM
I knew you'd know.
You'll form small groups, and write and perform your own short plays at the end of camp.

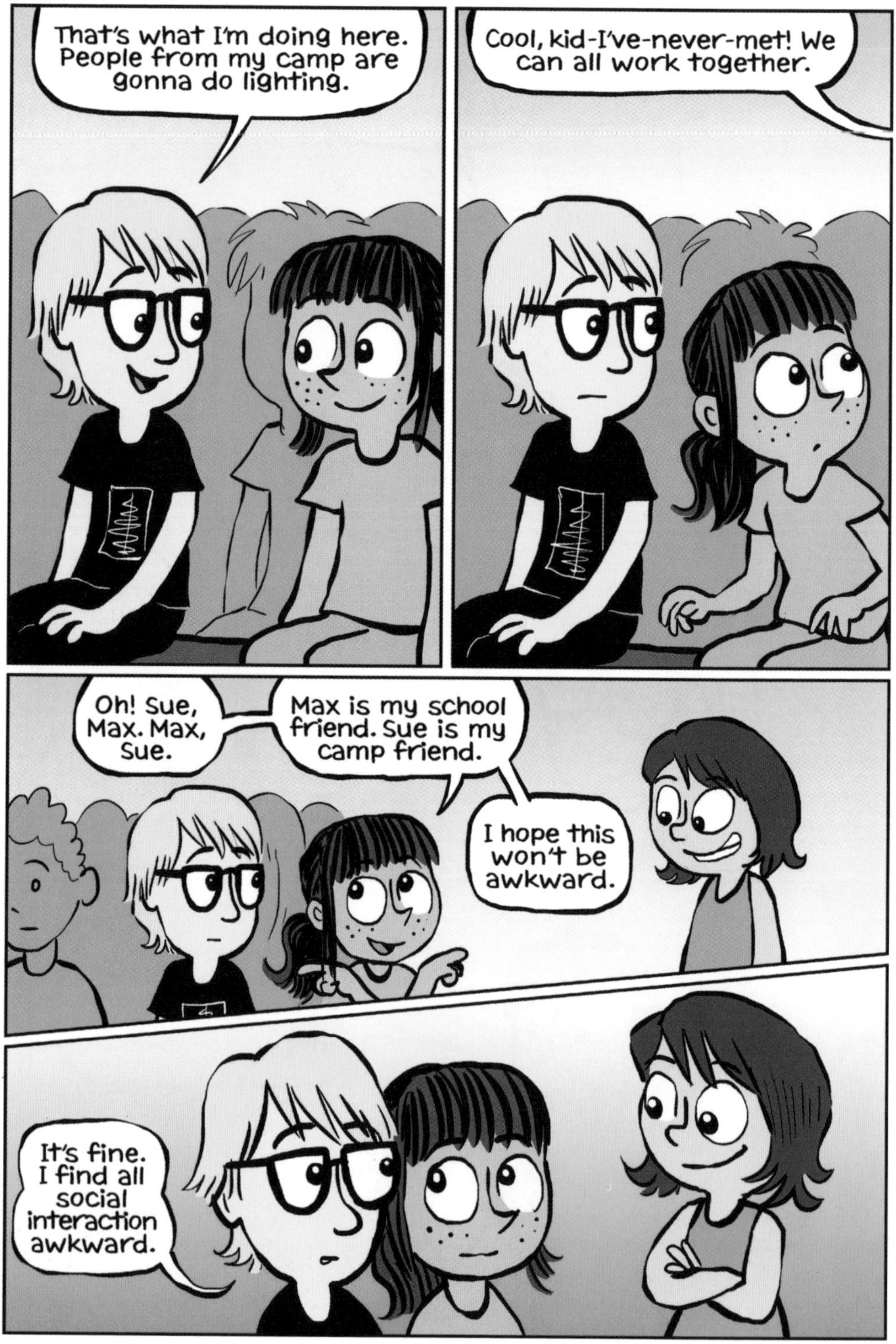

That's what I'm doing here. People from my camp are gonna do lighting.
Cool, kid-I've-never-met! We can all work together.
Oh! Sue, Max. Max, Sue.
Max is my school friend. Sue is my camp friend.
I hope this won't be awkward.
It's fine. I find all social interaction awkward.

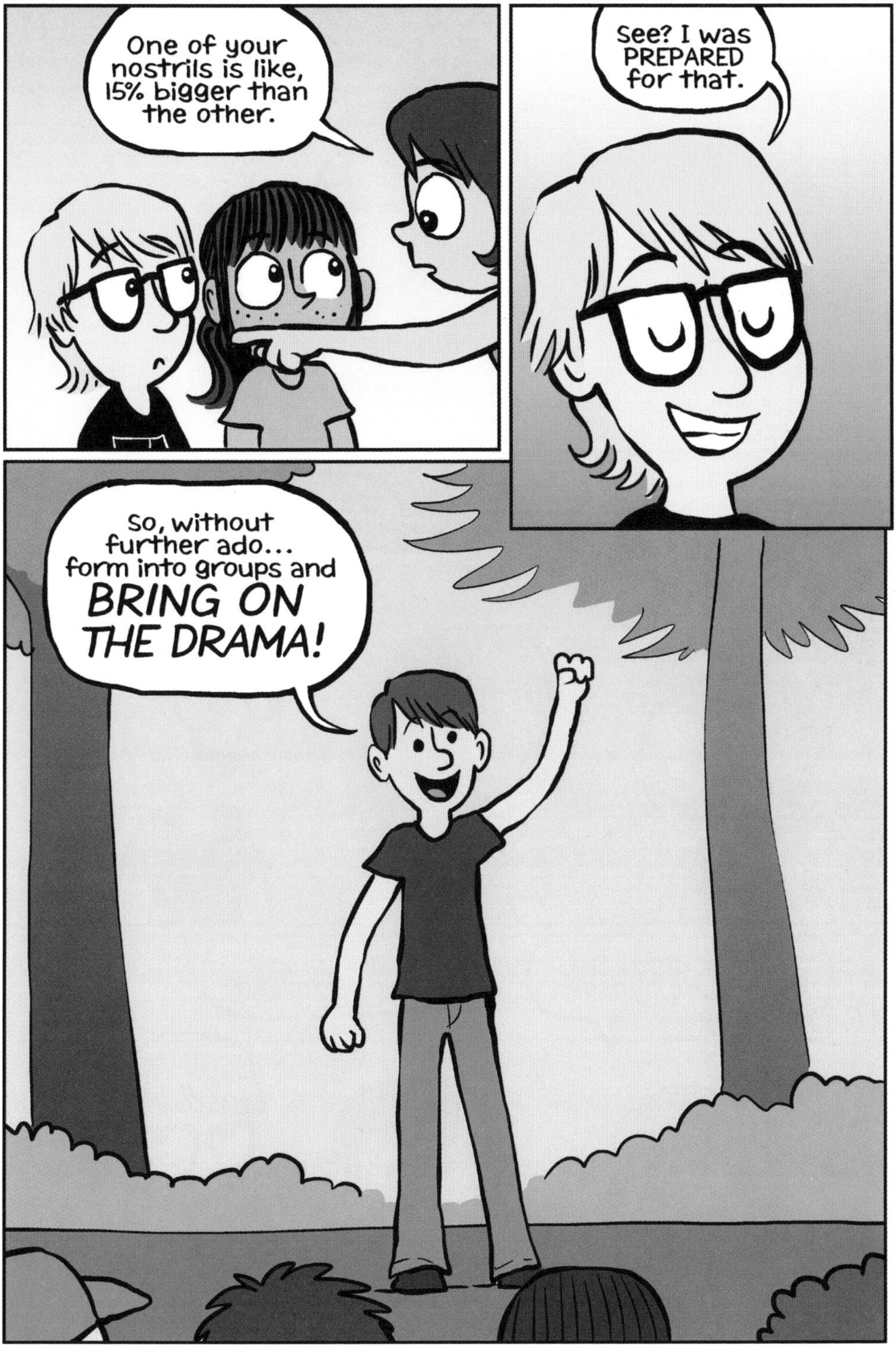
One of your nostrils is like, 15% bigger than the other.
See? I was PREPARED for that.
So, without further ado... form into groups and BRING ON THE DRAMA!

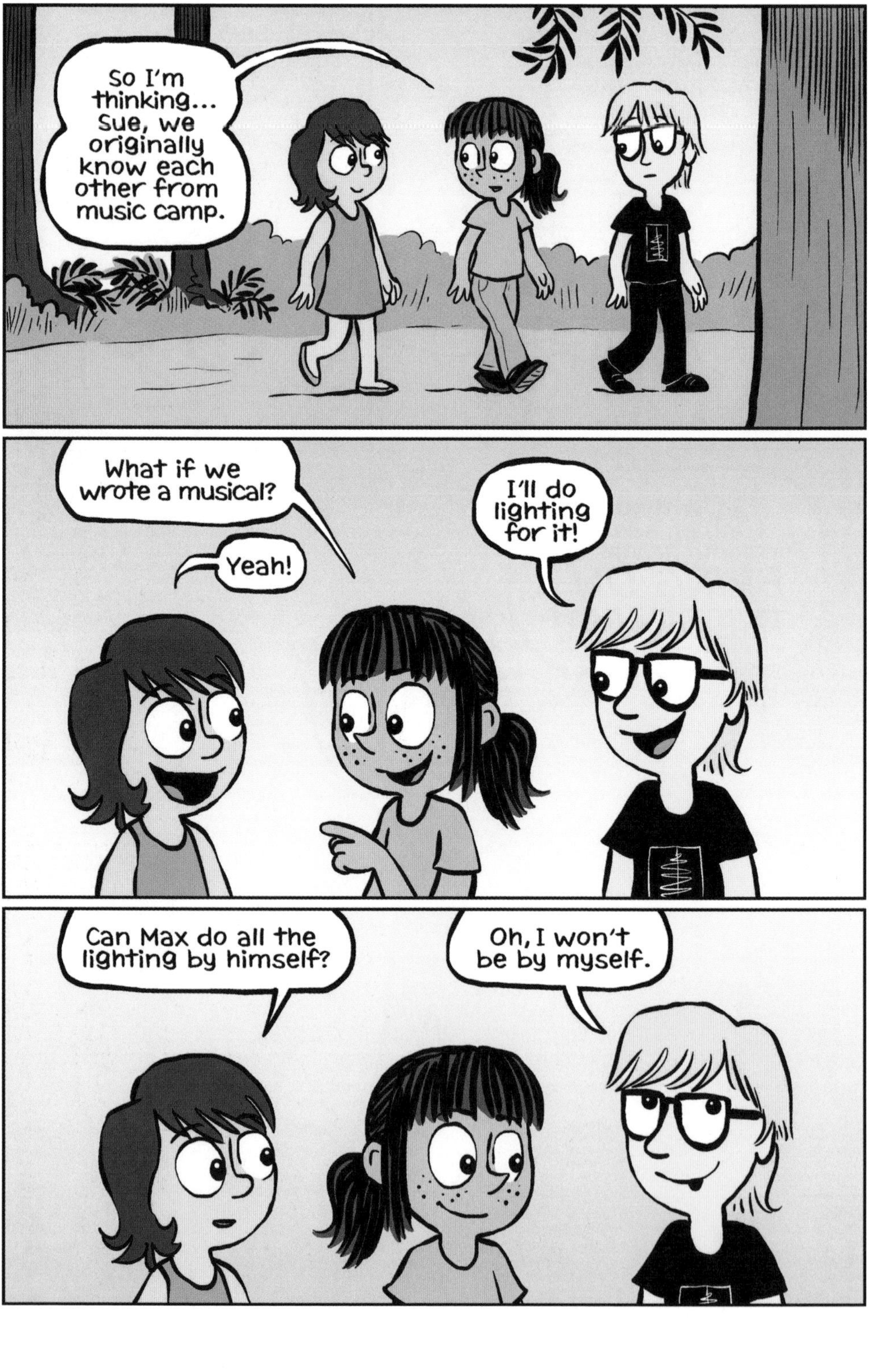
So I'm thinking... Sue, we originally know each other from music camp.
What if we wrote a musical?
Yeah!
I'll do lighting for it!
Can Max do all the lighting by himself?
Oh, I won't be by myself.

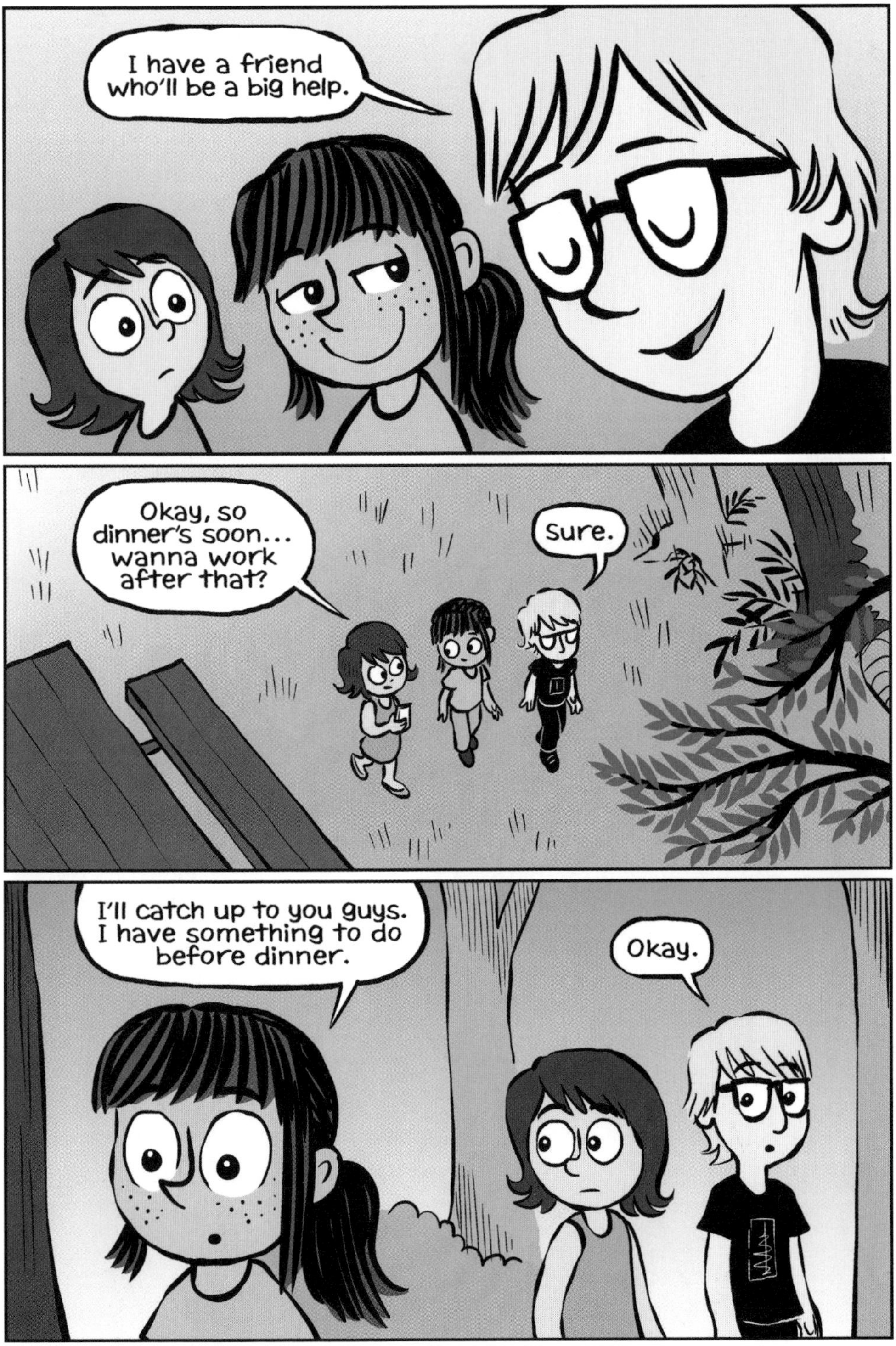

I have a friend who'll be a big help.
Okay, so dinner's soon... wanna work after that?
Sure.
I'll catch up to you guys. I have something to do before dinner.
Okay.

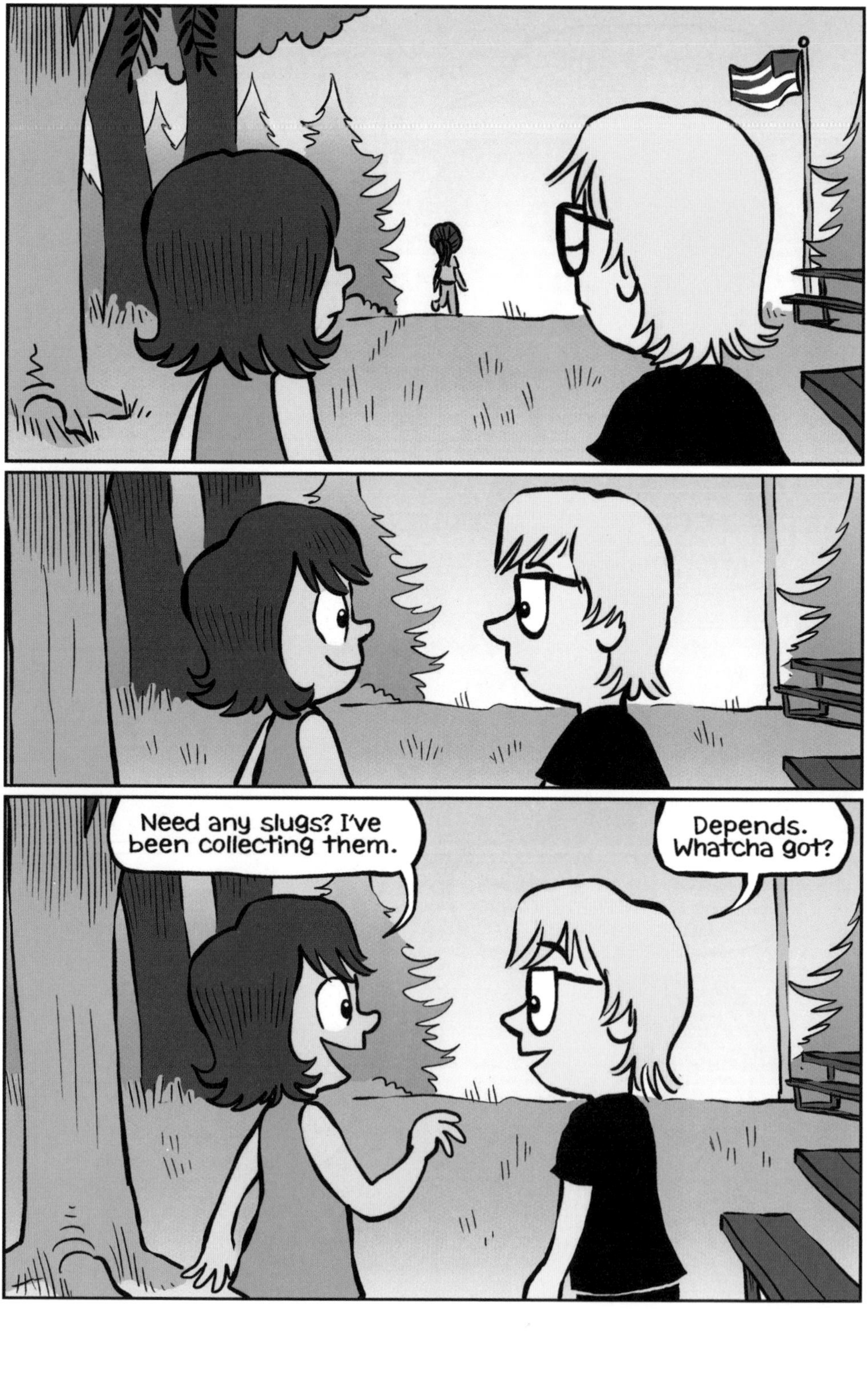
Need any slugs? I've been collecting them.
Depends. Whatcha got?

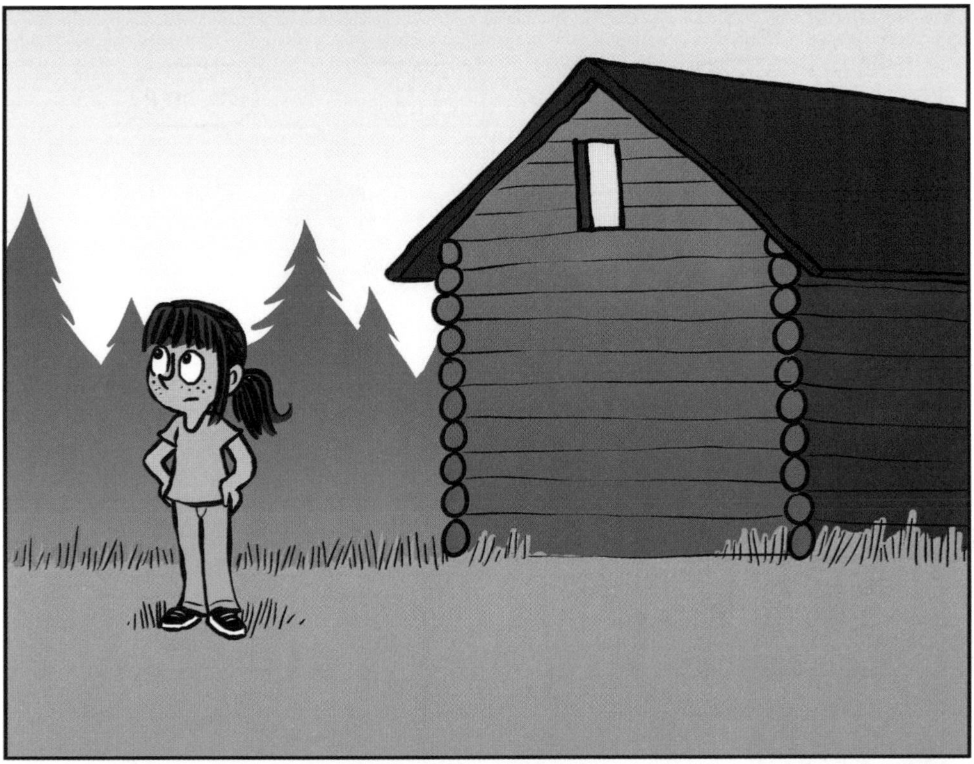

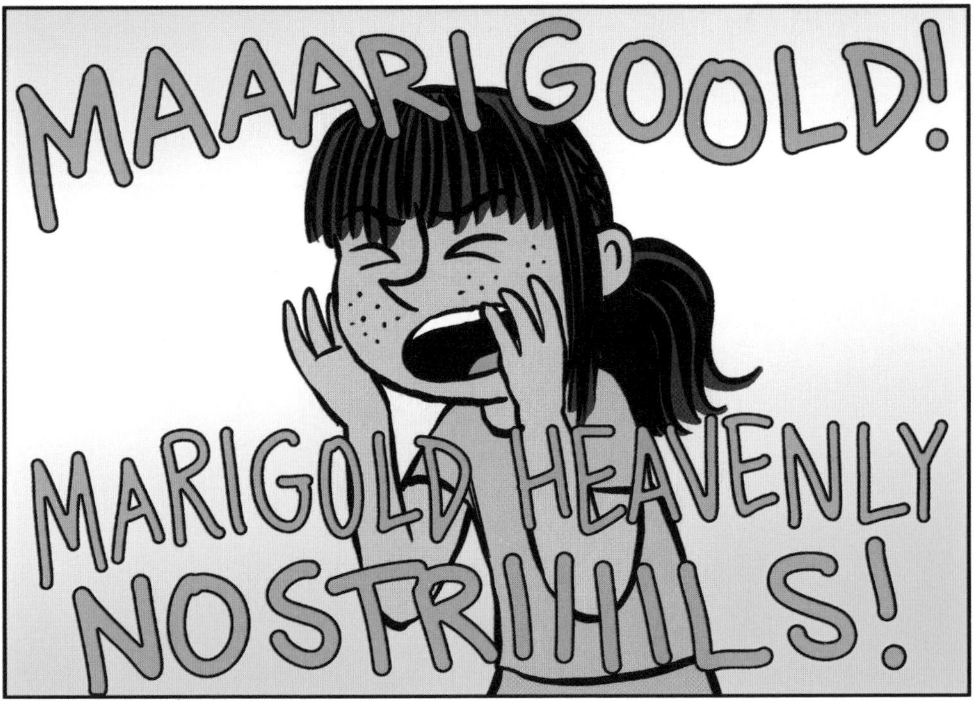
MAAARIGOOLD!
MARIGOLD HEAVENLY NOSTRIIILS!

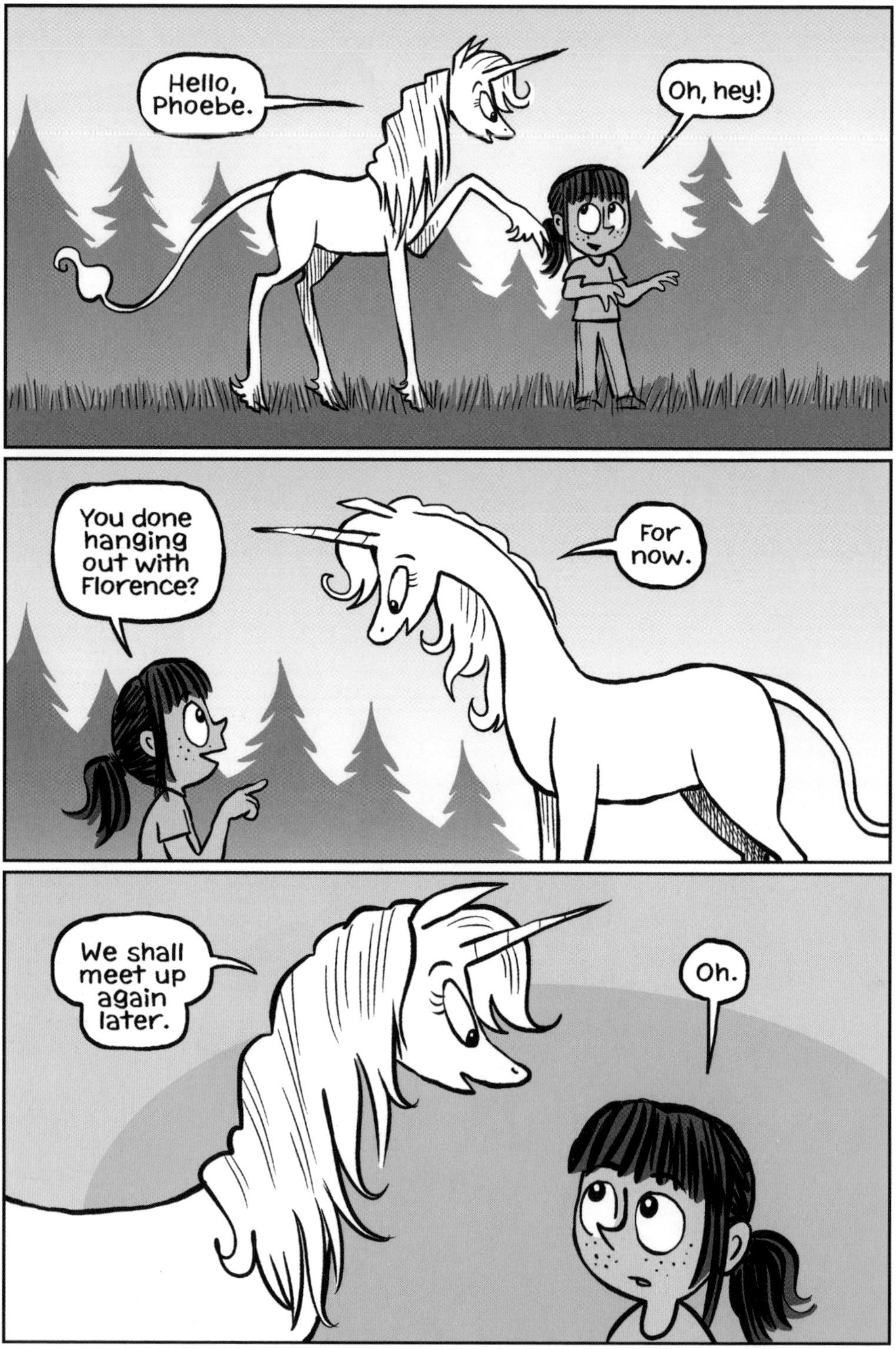
Hello, Phoebe.
Oh, hey!
You done hanging out with Florence?
For now.
We shall meet up again later.
Oh.

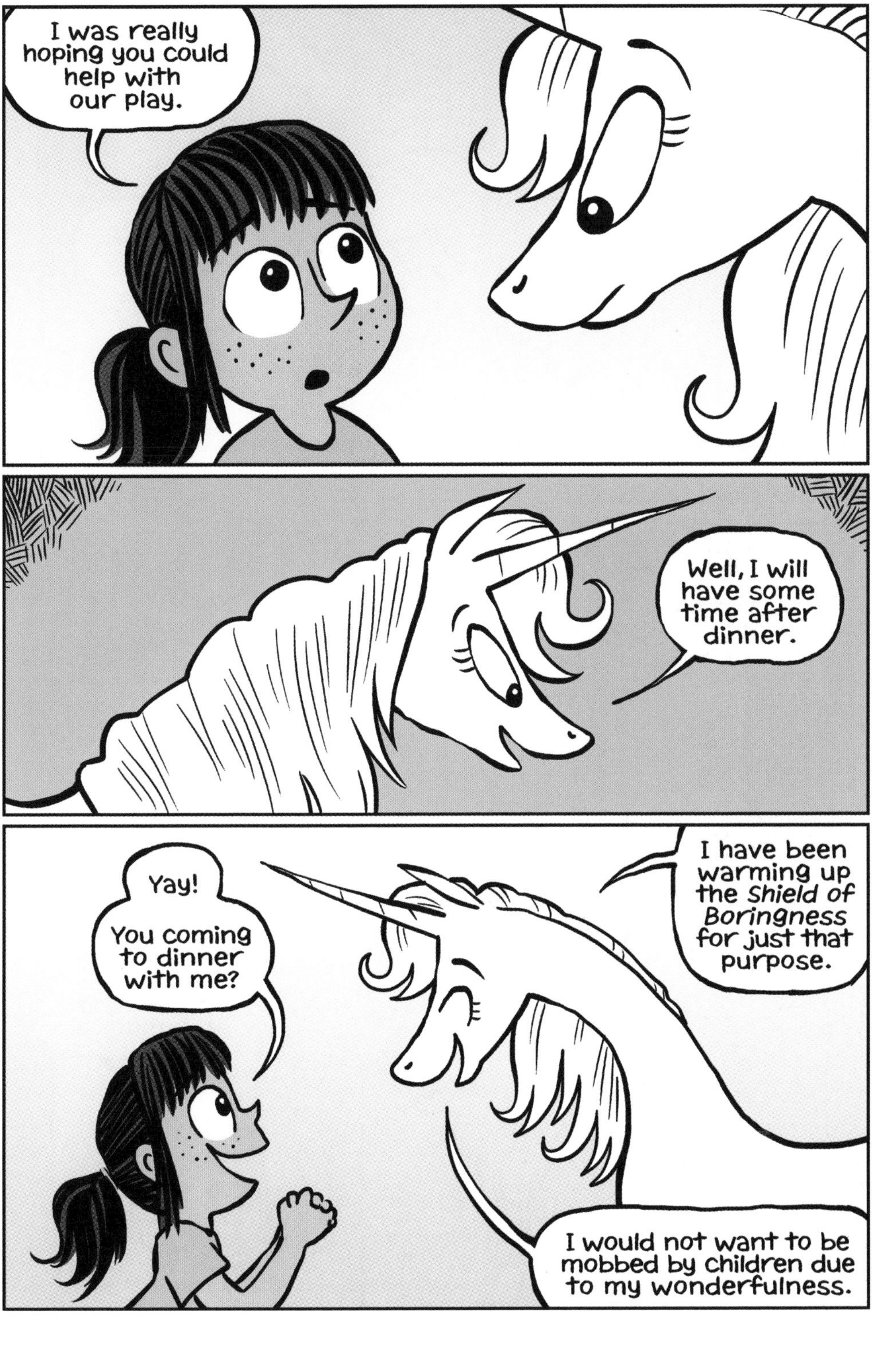
I was really hoping you could help with our play.
Well, I will have some time after dinner.
Yay!
You coming to dinner with me?
I have been warming up the *Shield of Boringness* for just that purpose.
I would not want to be mobbed by children due to my wonderfulness.

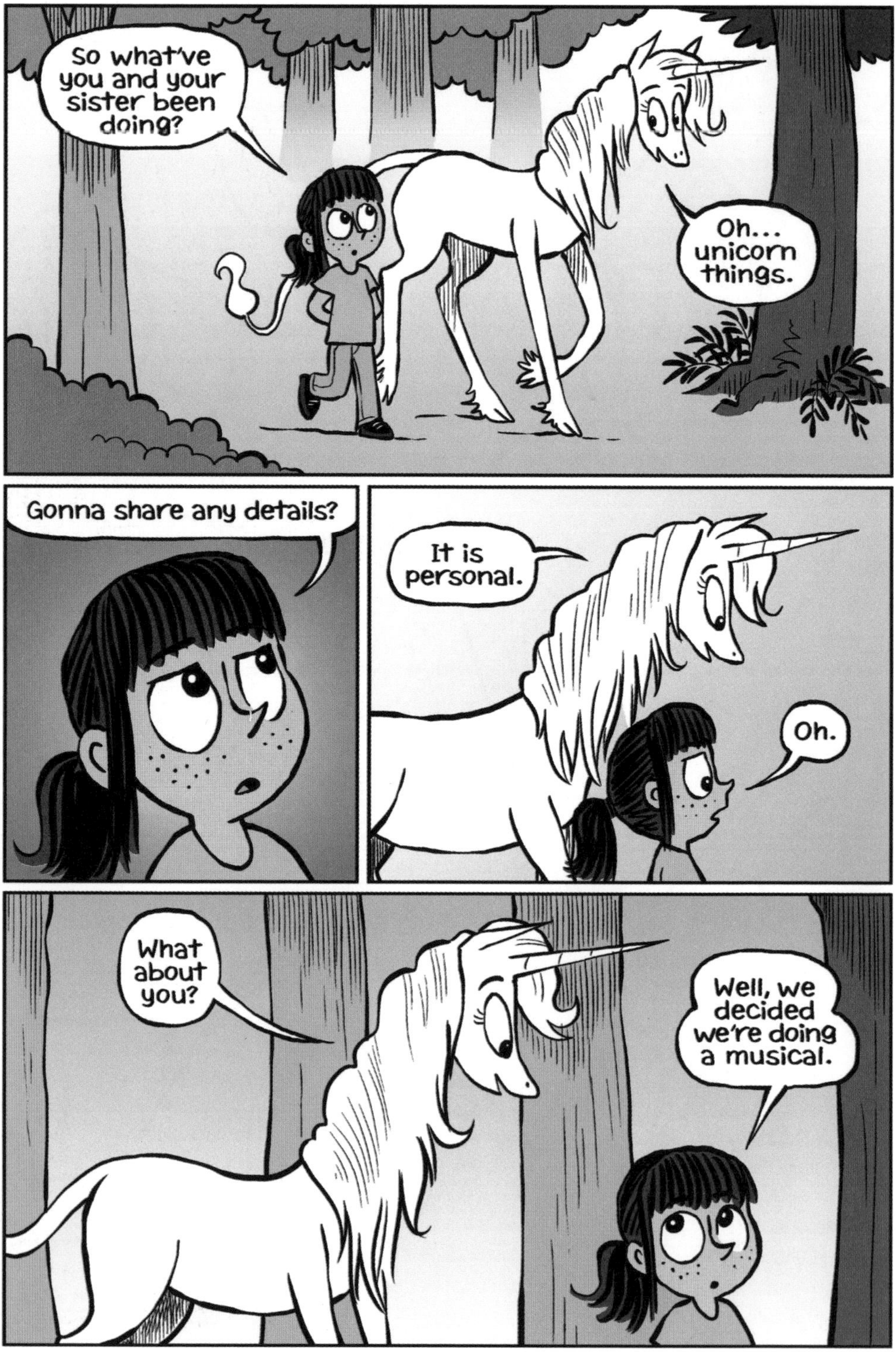
So what've you and your sister been doing?
Oh... unicorn things.
Gonna share any details?
It is personal.
Oh.
What about you?
Well, we decided we're doing a musical.

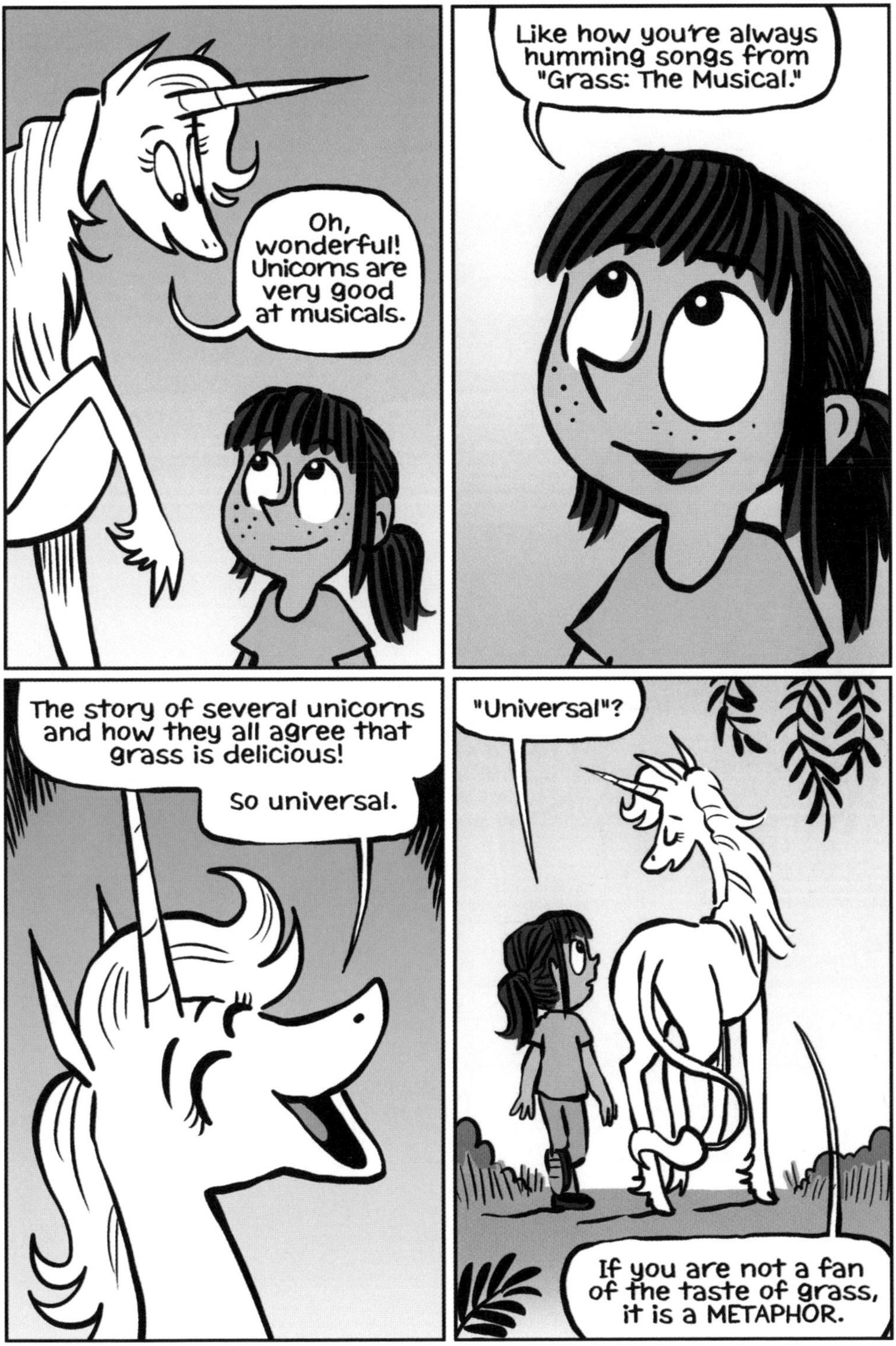
Oh, wonderful! Unicorns are very good at musicals.
Like how you're always humming songs from "Grass: The Musical."
The story of several unicorns and how they all agree that grass is delicious!
So universal.
"Universal"?
If you are not a fan of the taste of grass, it is a METAPHOR.

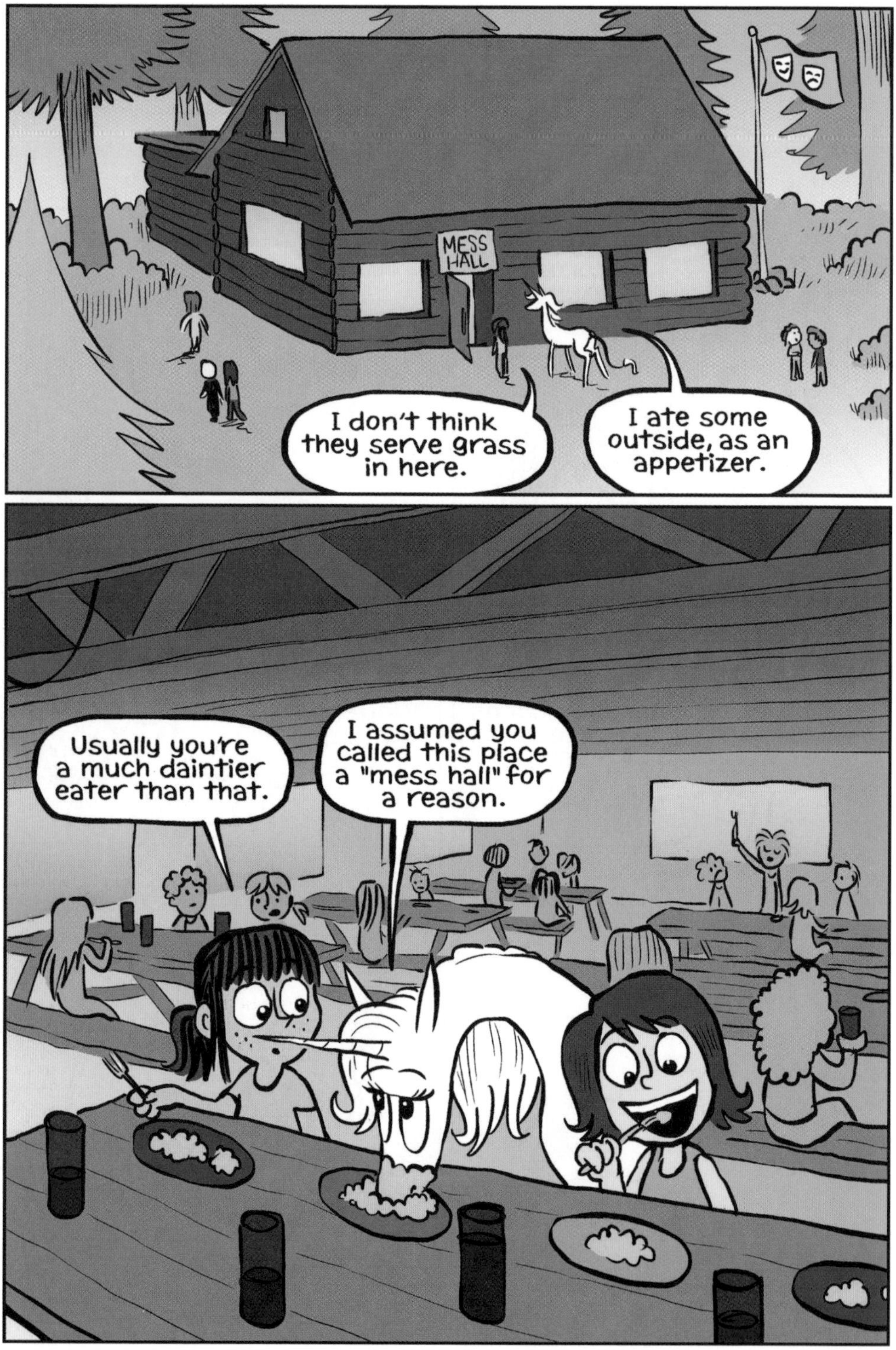
MESS HALL
I don't think they serve grass in here.
I ate some outside, as an appetizer.
Usually you're a much daintier eater than that.
I assumed you called this place a "mess hall" for a reason.

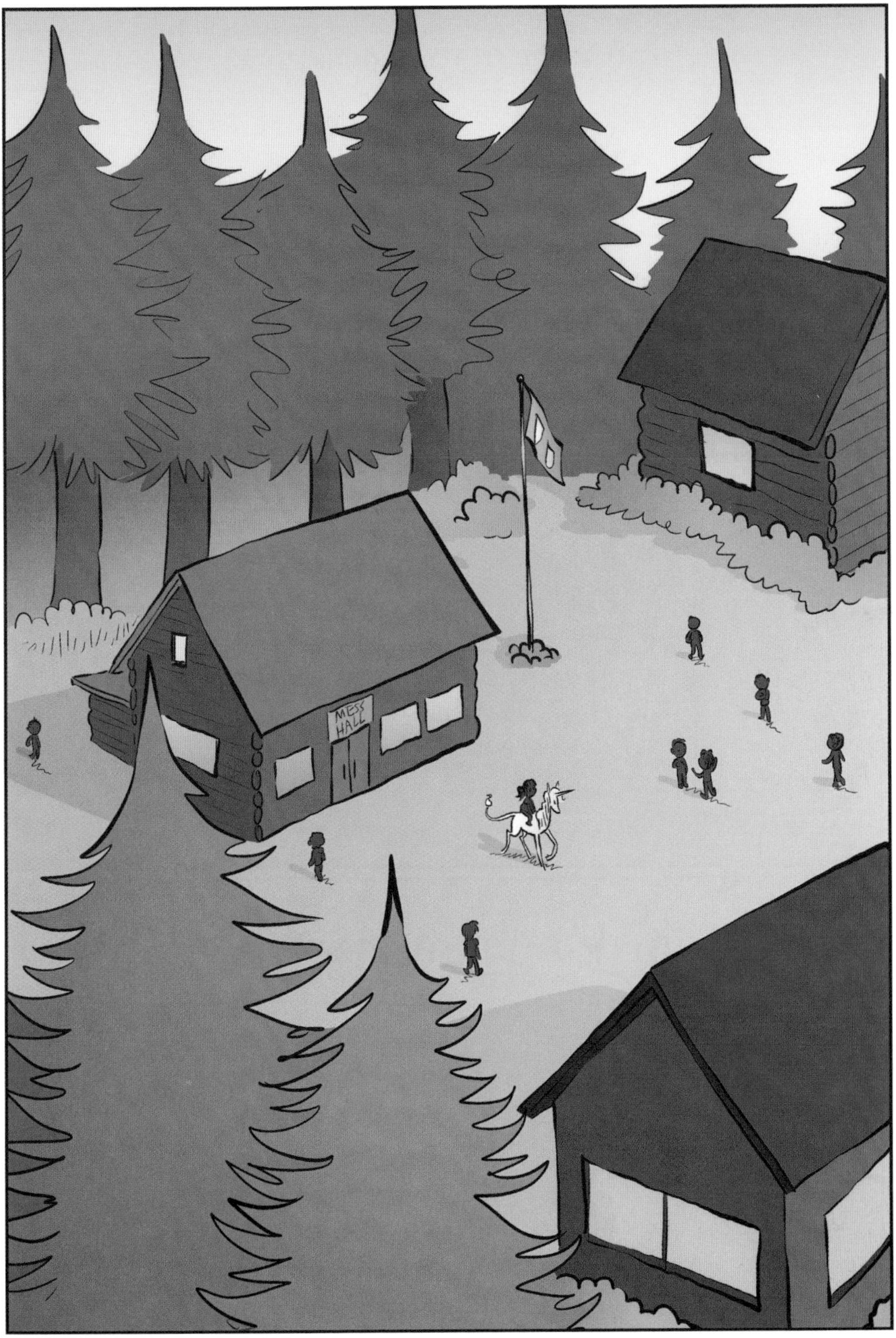
MESS HALL

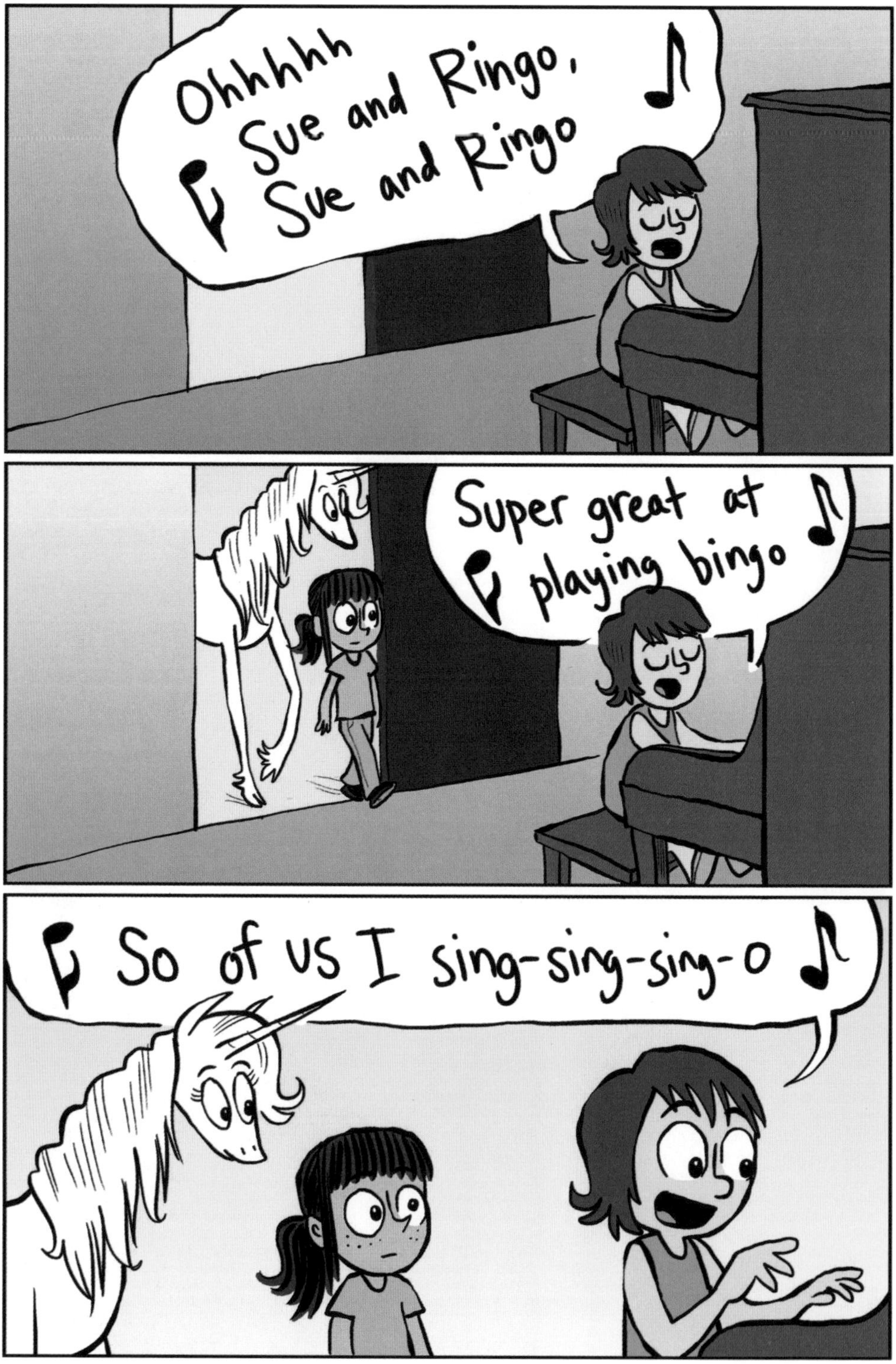
Ohhhhh Sue and Ringo, Sue and Ringo
Super great at playing bingo
So of us I sing-sing-sing-o

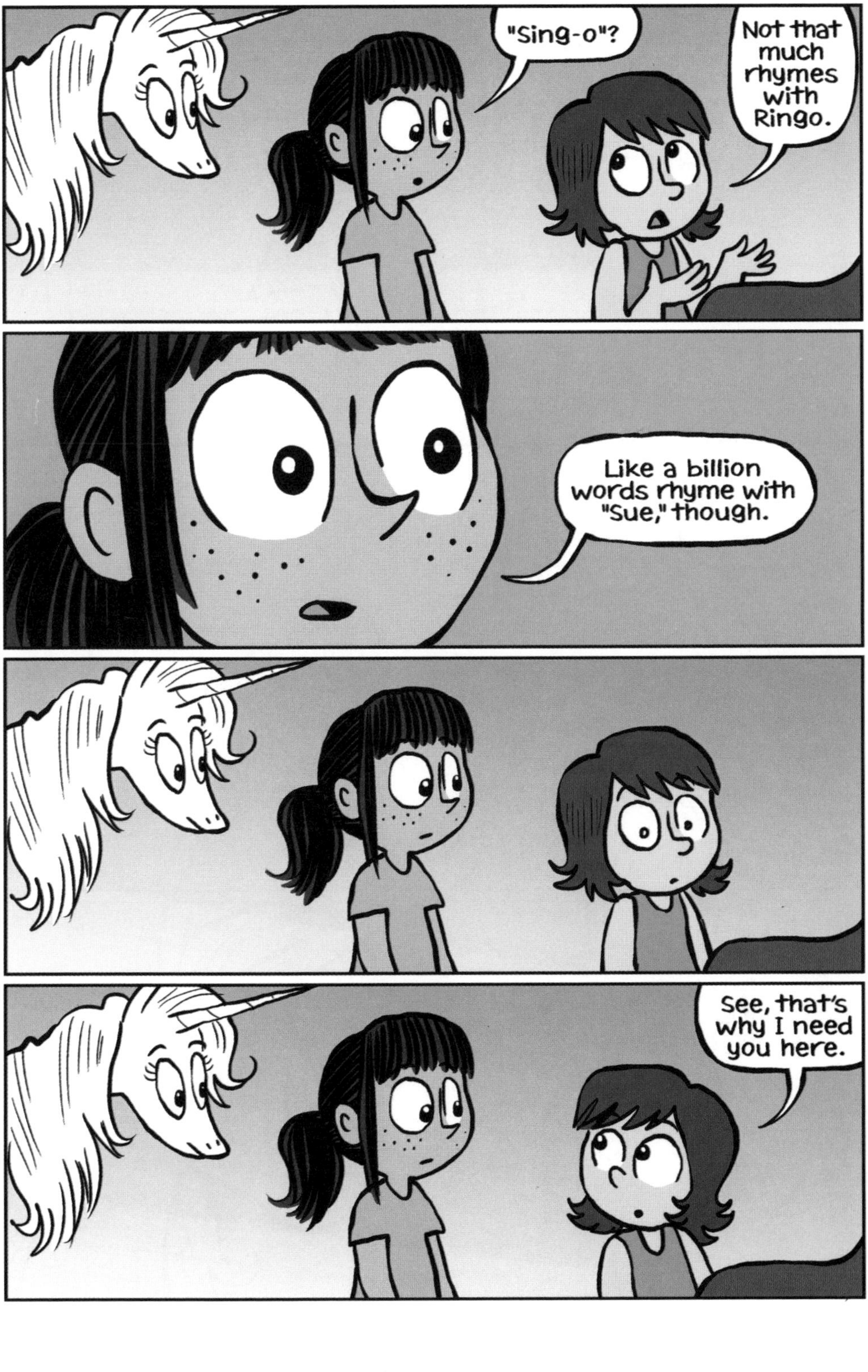
"Sing-o"?
Not that much rhymes with Ringo.
Like a billion words rhyme with "Sue," though.
See, that's why I need you here.

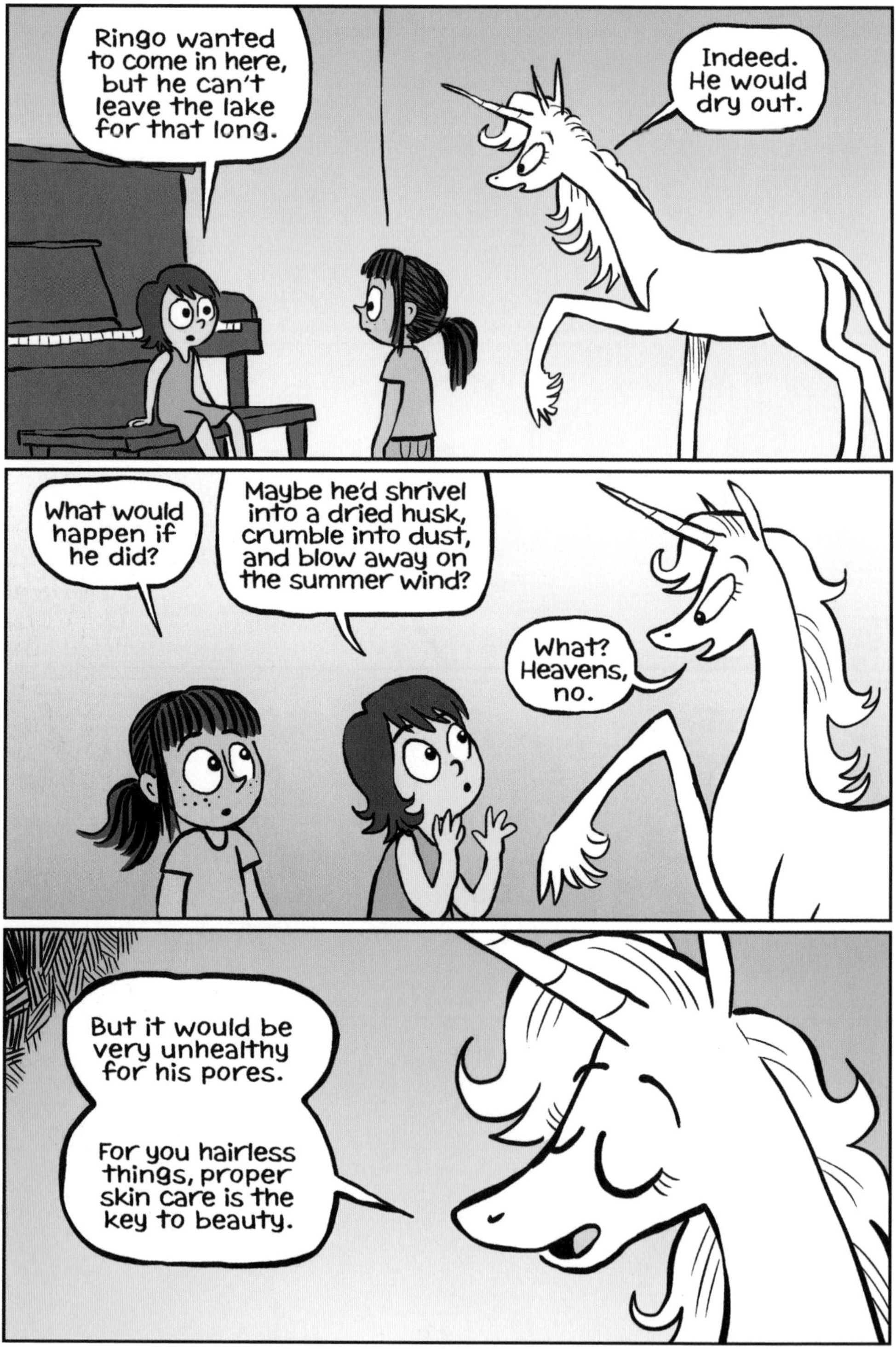
Ringo wanted to come in here, but he can't leave the lake for that long.
Indeed. He would dry out.
What would happen if he did?
Maybe he'd shrivel into a dried husk, crumble into dust, and blow away on the summer wind?
What? Heavens, no.
But it would be very unhealthy for his pores.
For you hairless things, proper skin care is the key to beauty.

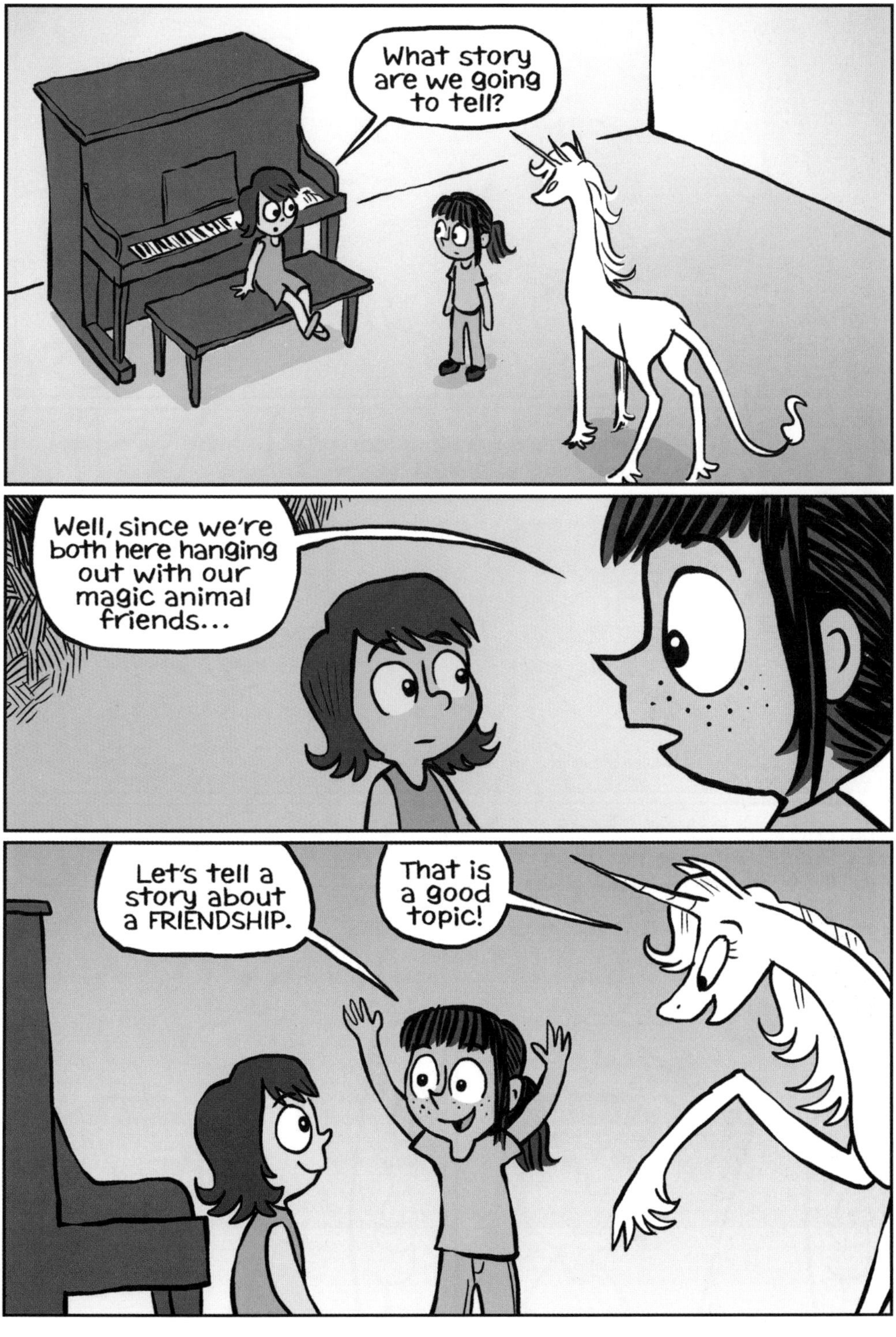
What story are we going to tell?
Well, since we're both here hanging out with our magic animal friends...
Let's tell a story about a FRIENDSHIP.
That is a good topic!

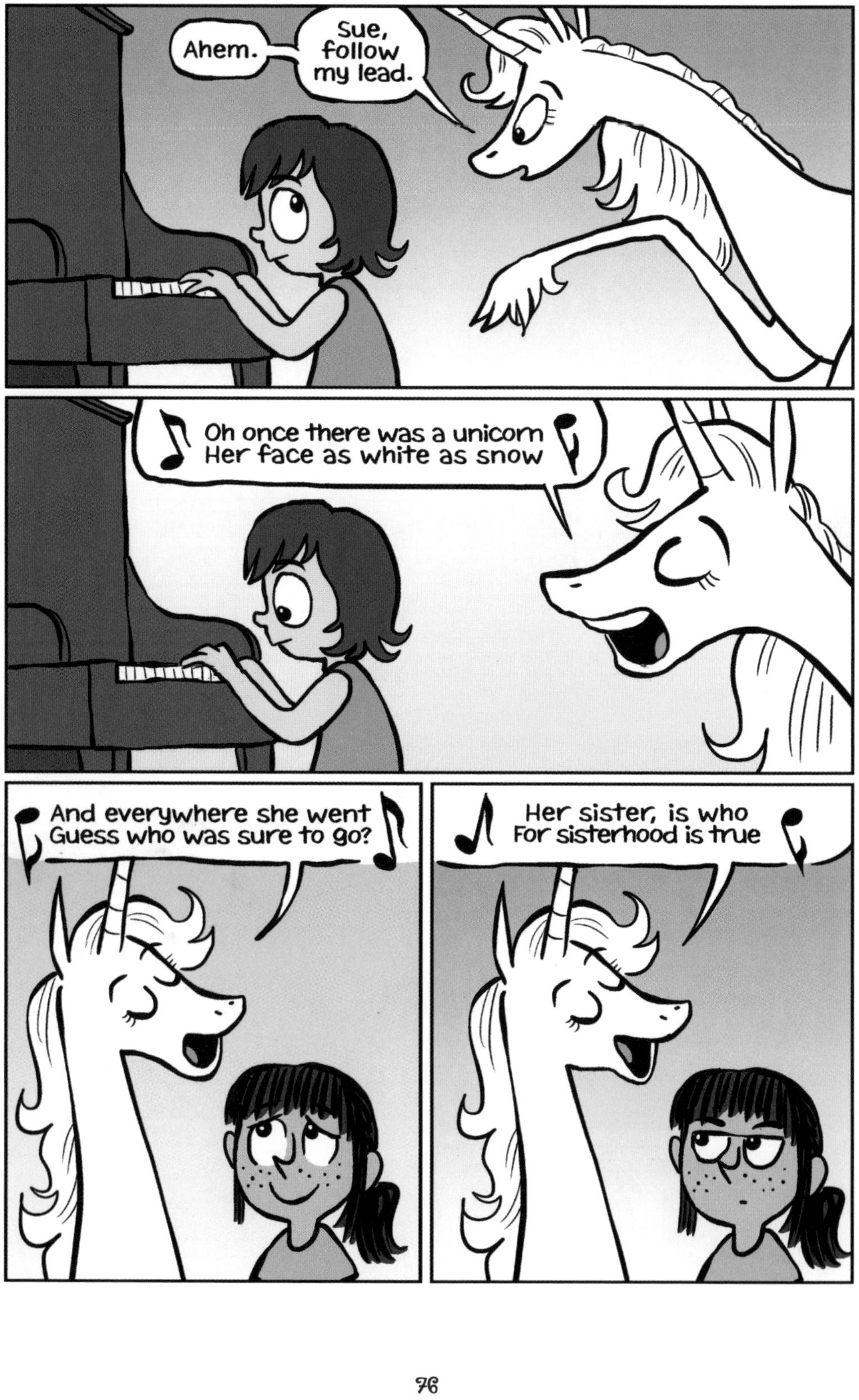
Ahem.
Sue, follow my lead.
Oh once there was a unicorn
Her face as white as snow
And everywhere she went
Guess who was sure to go?
Her sister, is who
For sisterhood is true

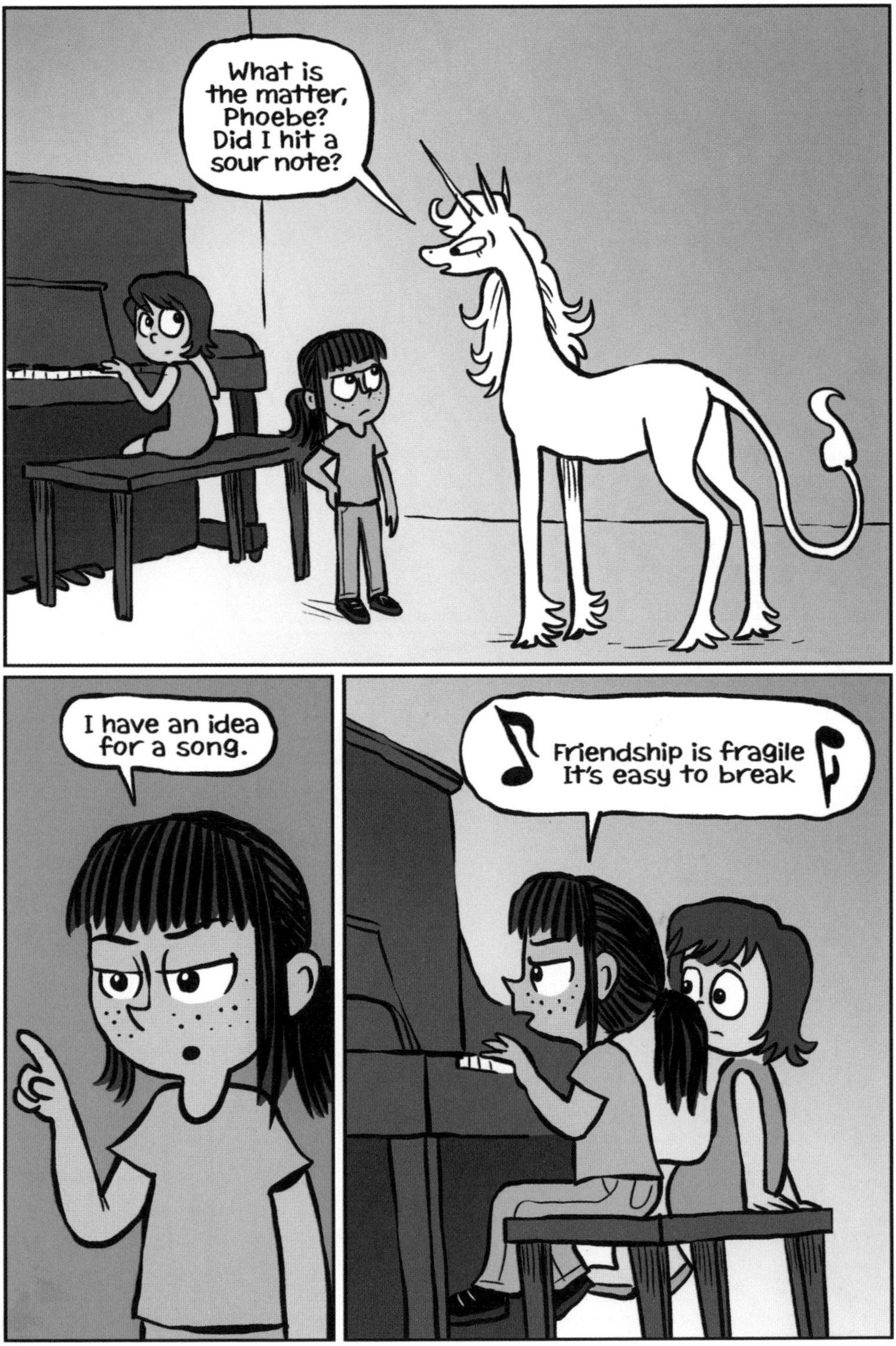
What is the matter, Phoebe? Did I hit a sour note?
I have an idea for a song.
Friendship is fragile
It's easy to break

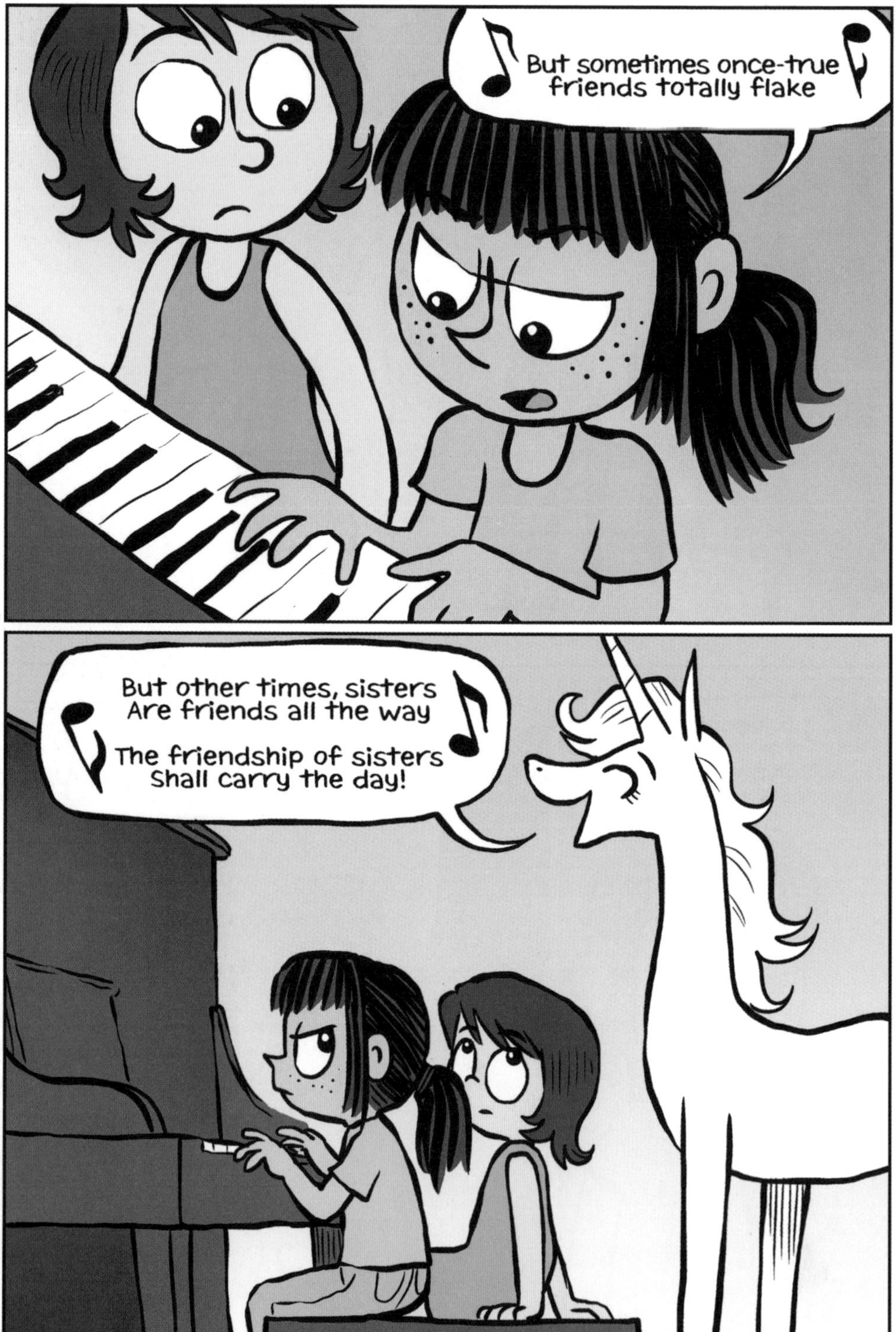

But sometimes once-true friends totally flake
But other times, sisters Are friends all the way
The friendship of sisters Shall carry the day!

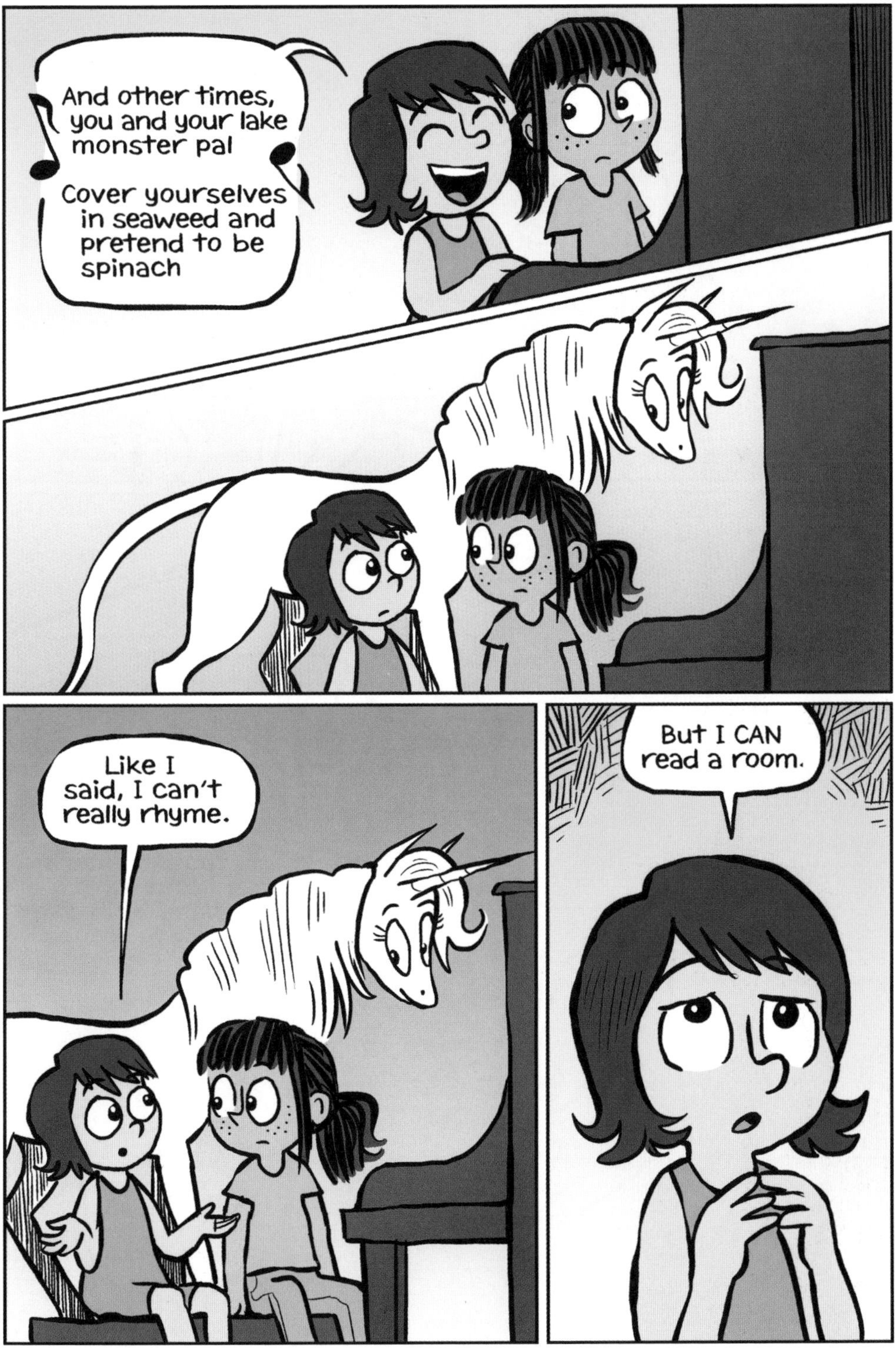

And other times, you and your lake monster pal
Cover yourselves in seaweed and pretend to be spinach
Like I said, I can't really rhyme.
But I CAN read a room.

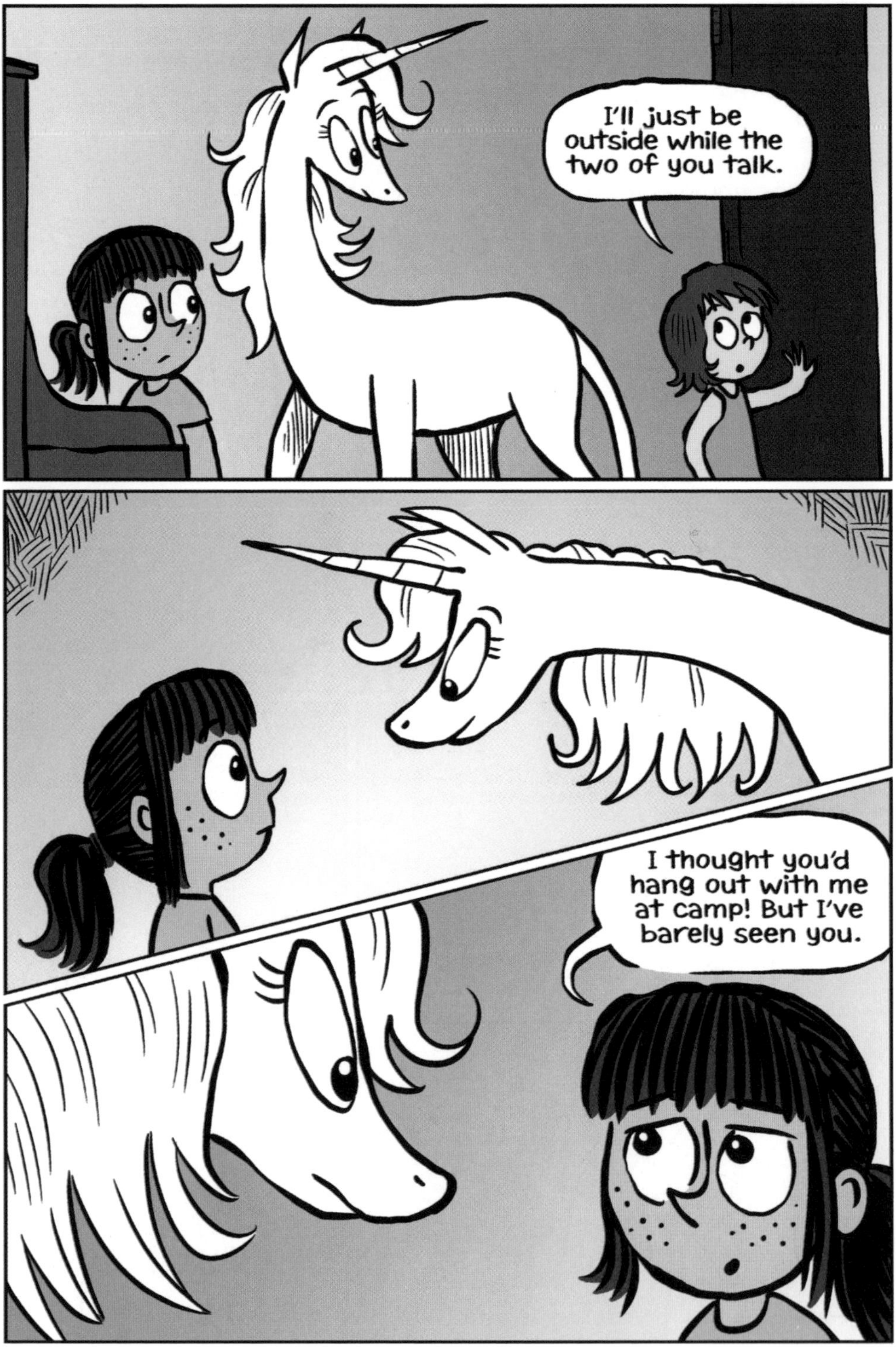
I'll just be outside while the two of you talk.
I thought you'd hang out with me at camp! But I've barely seen you.

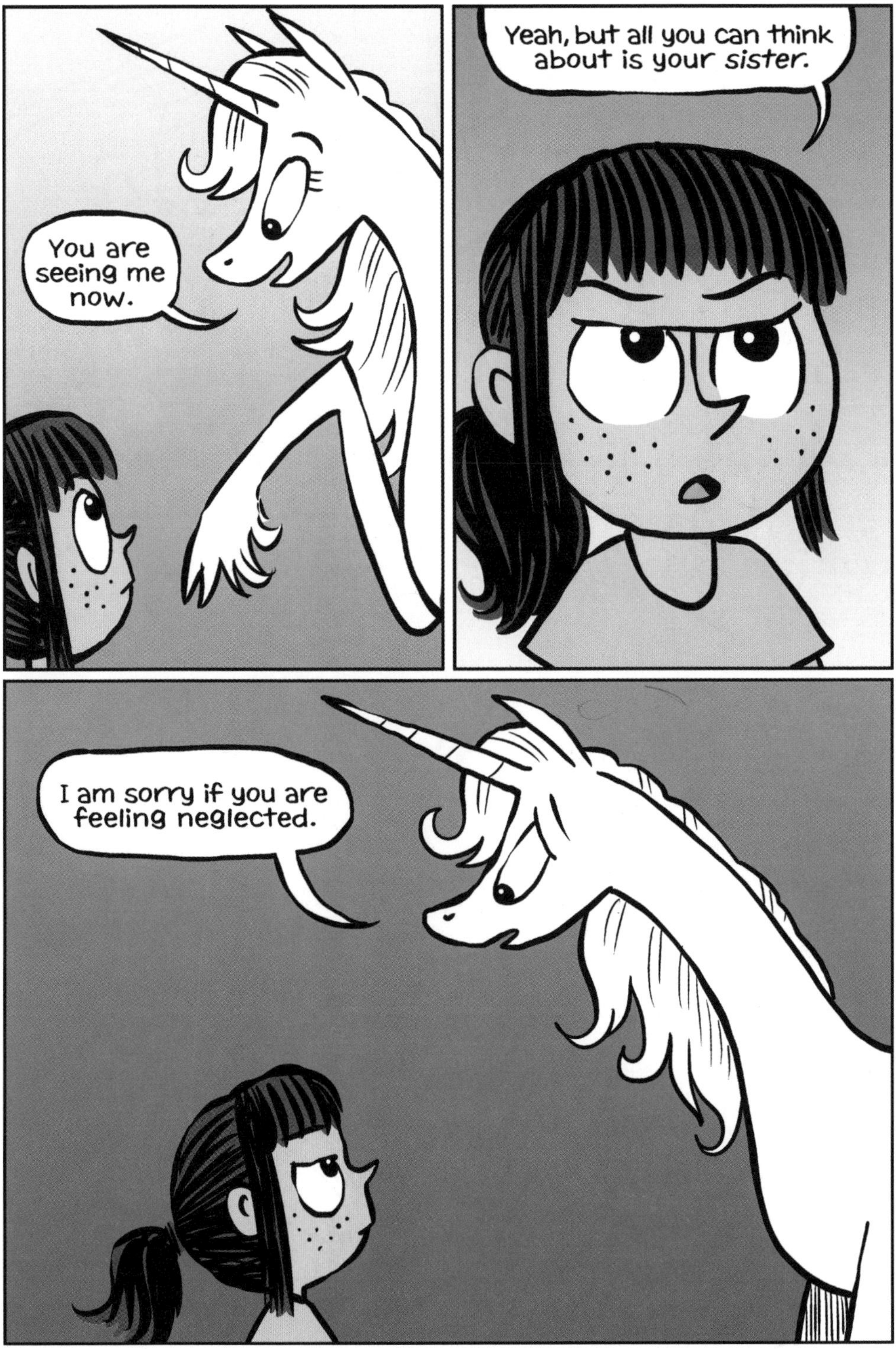
You are seeing me now.
Yeah, but all you can think about is your *sister*.
I am sorry if you are feeling neglected.

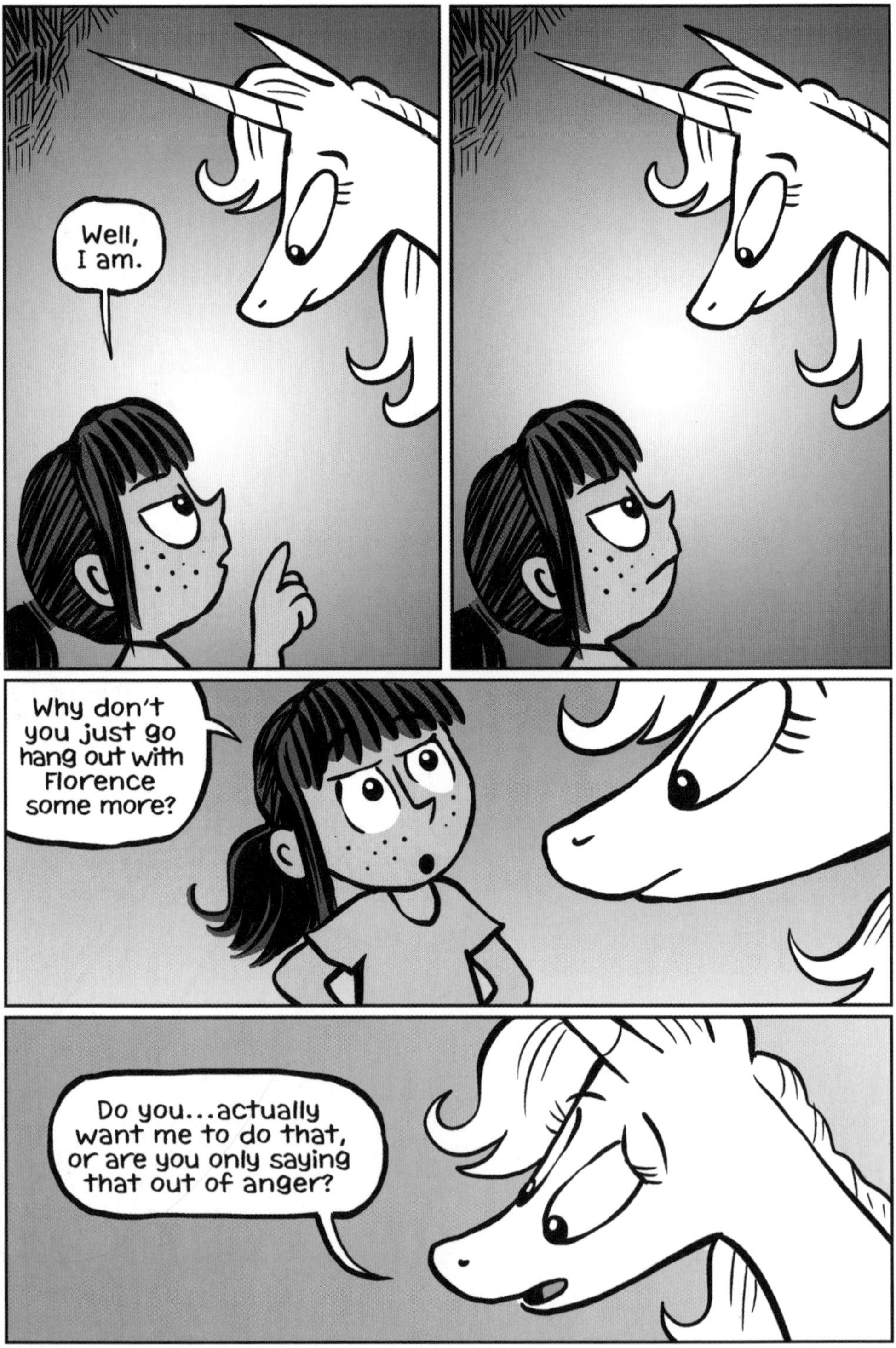
Well, I am.
Why don't you just go hang out with Florence some more?
Do you...actually want me to do that, or are you only saying that out of anger?

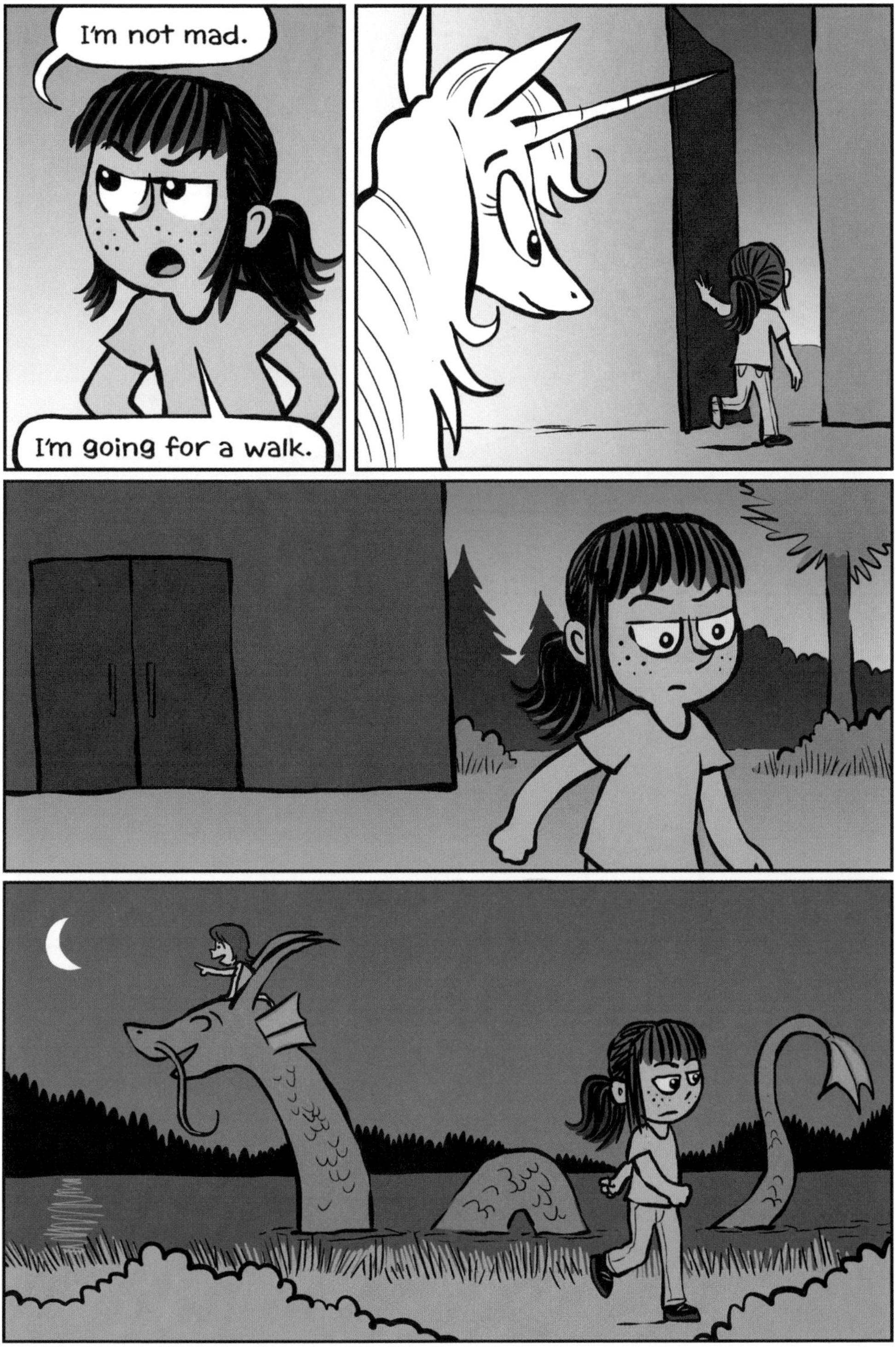
I'm not mad.
I'm going for a walk.

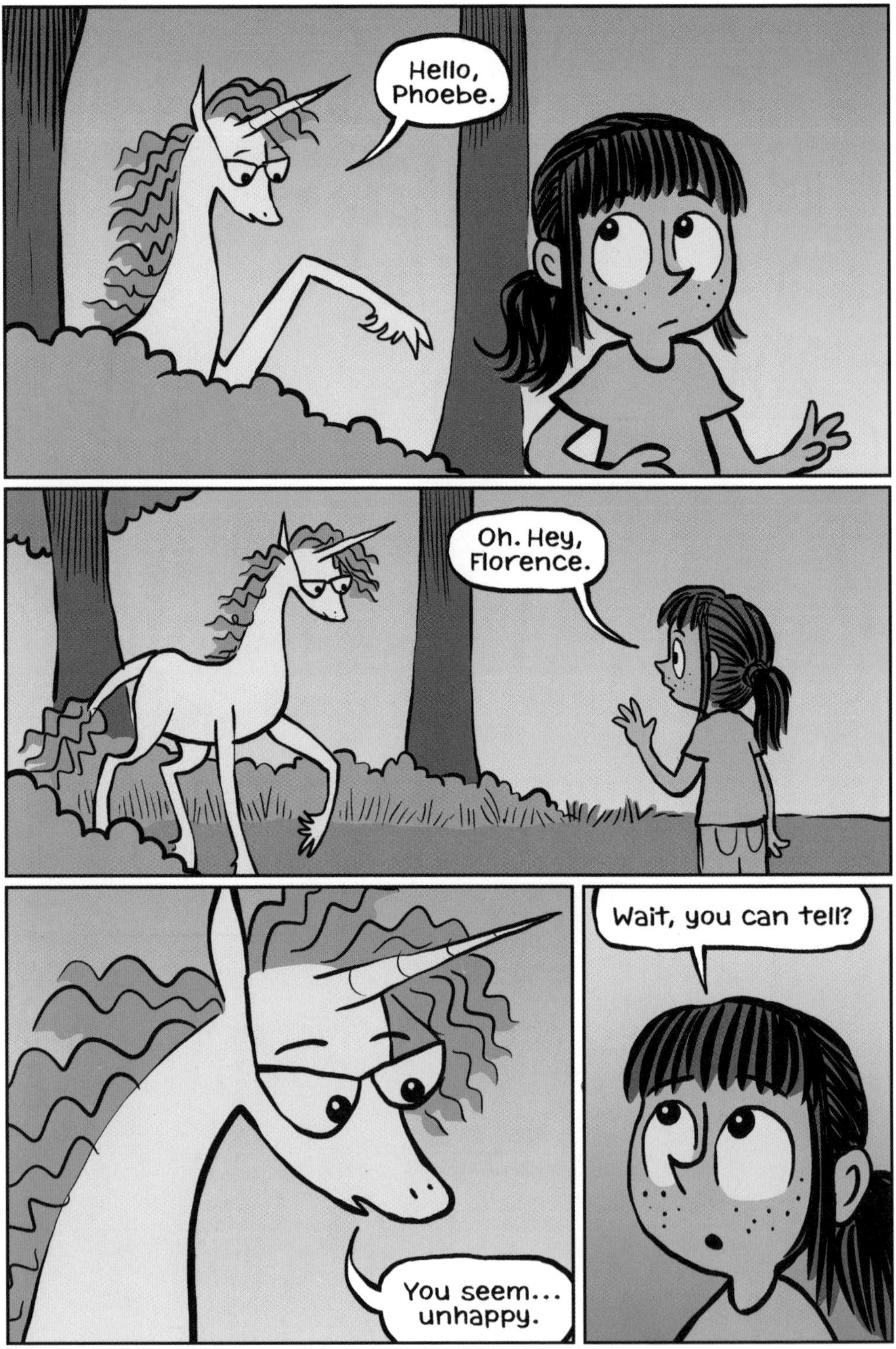
Hello, Phoebe.
Oh. Hey, Florence.
You seem... unhappy.
Wait, you can tell?

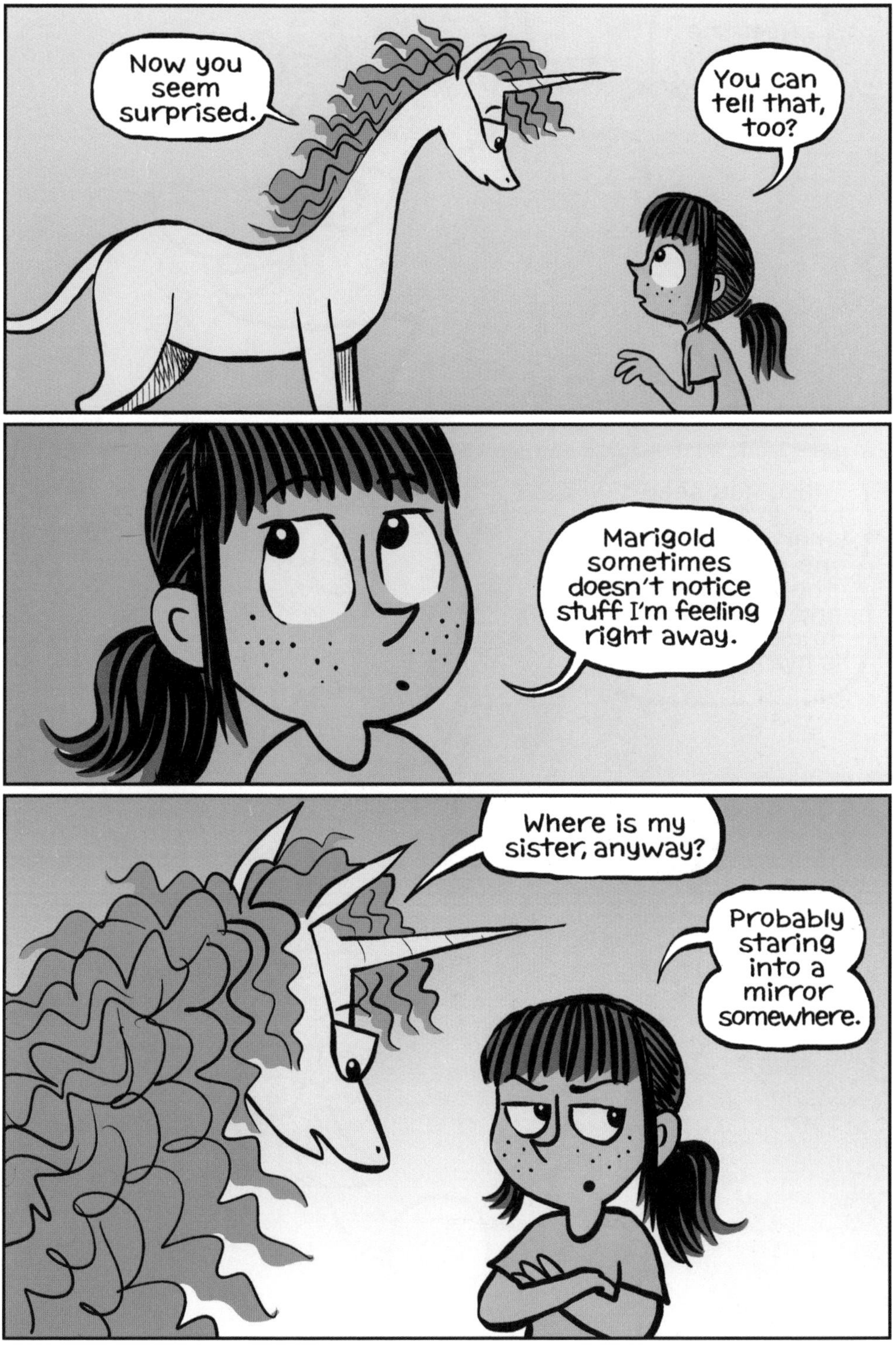
Now you seem surprised.
You can tell that, too?
Marigold sometimes doesn't notice stuff I'm feeling right away.
Where is my sister, anyway?
Probably staring into a mirror somewhere.

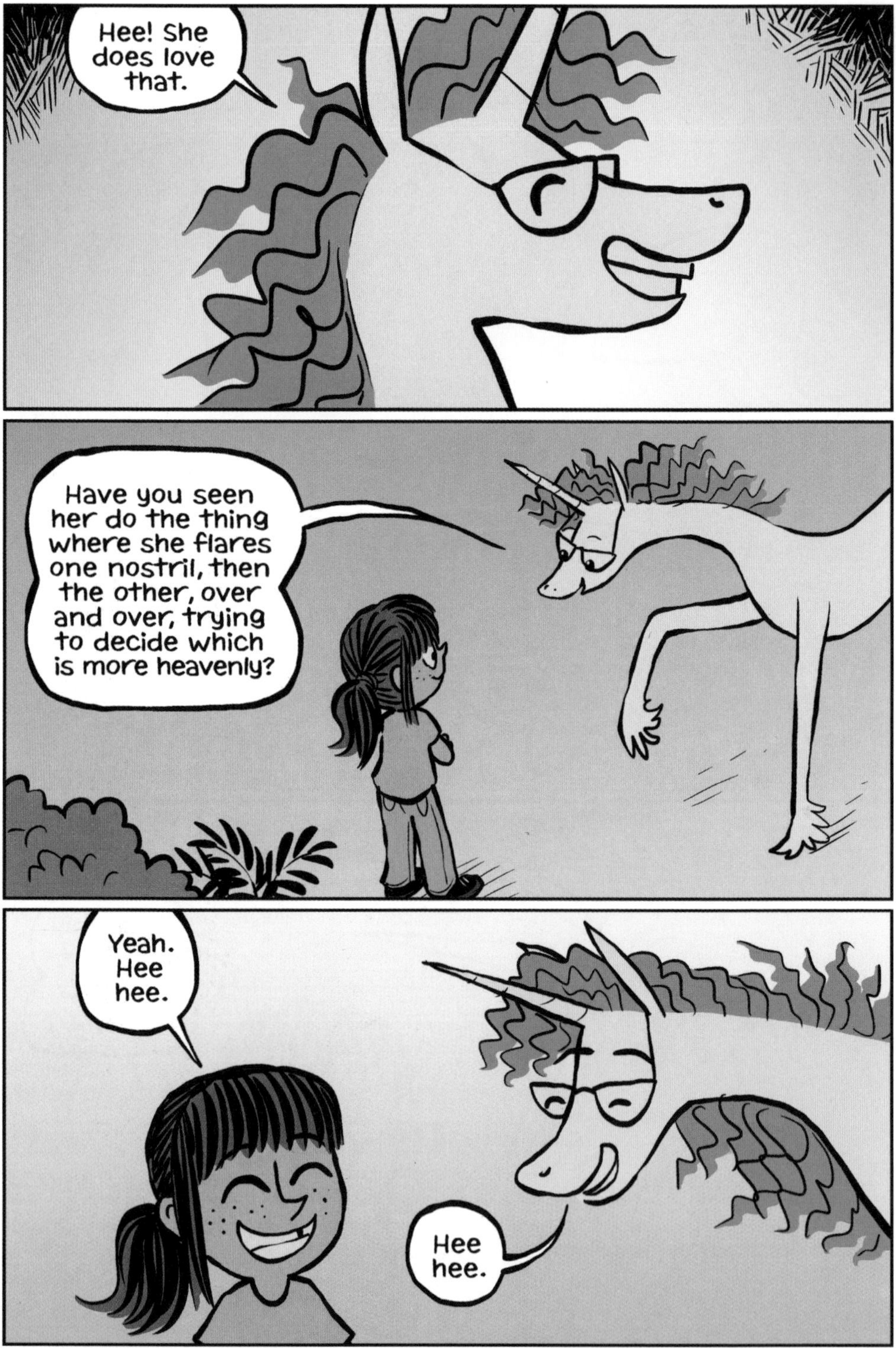
Hee! She does love that.
Have you seen her do the thing where she flares one nostril, then the other, over and over, trying to decide which is more heavenly?
Yeah. Hee hee.
Hee hee.

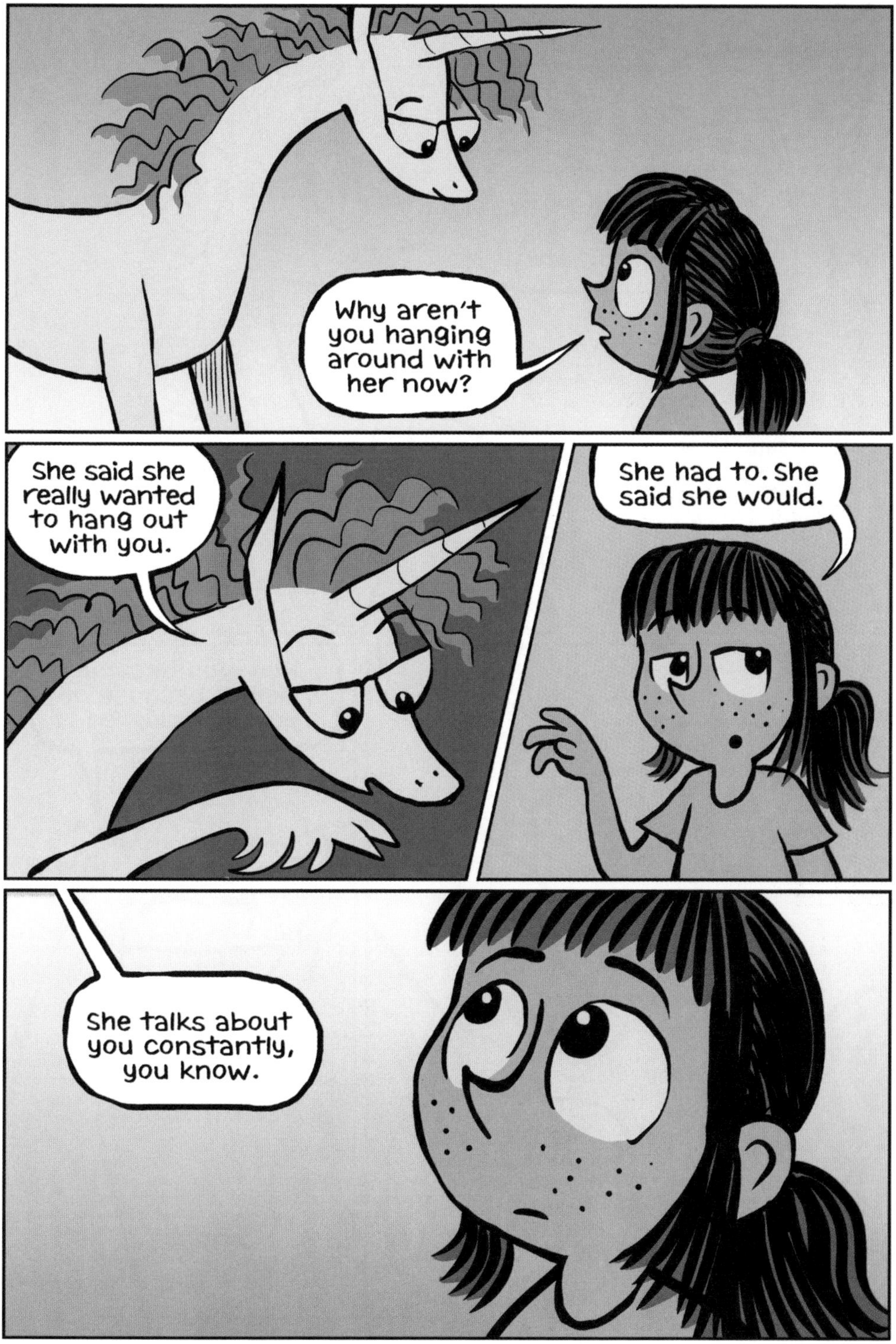
Why aren't you hanging around with her now?
She said she really wanted to hang out with you.
She had to. She said she would.
She talks about you constantly, you know.

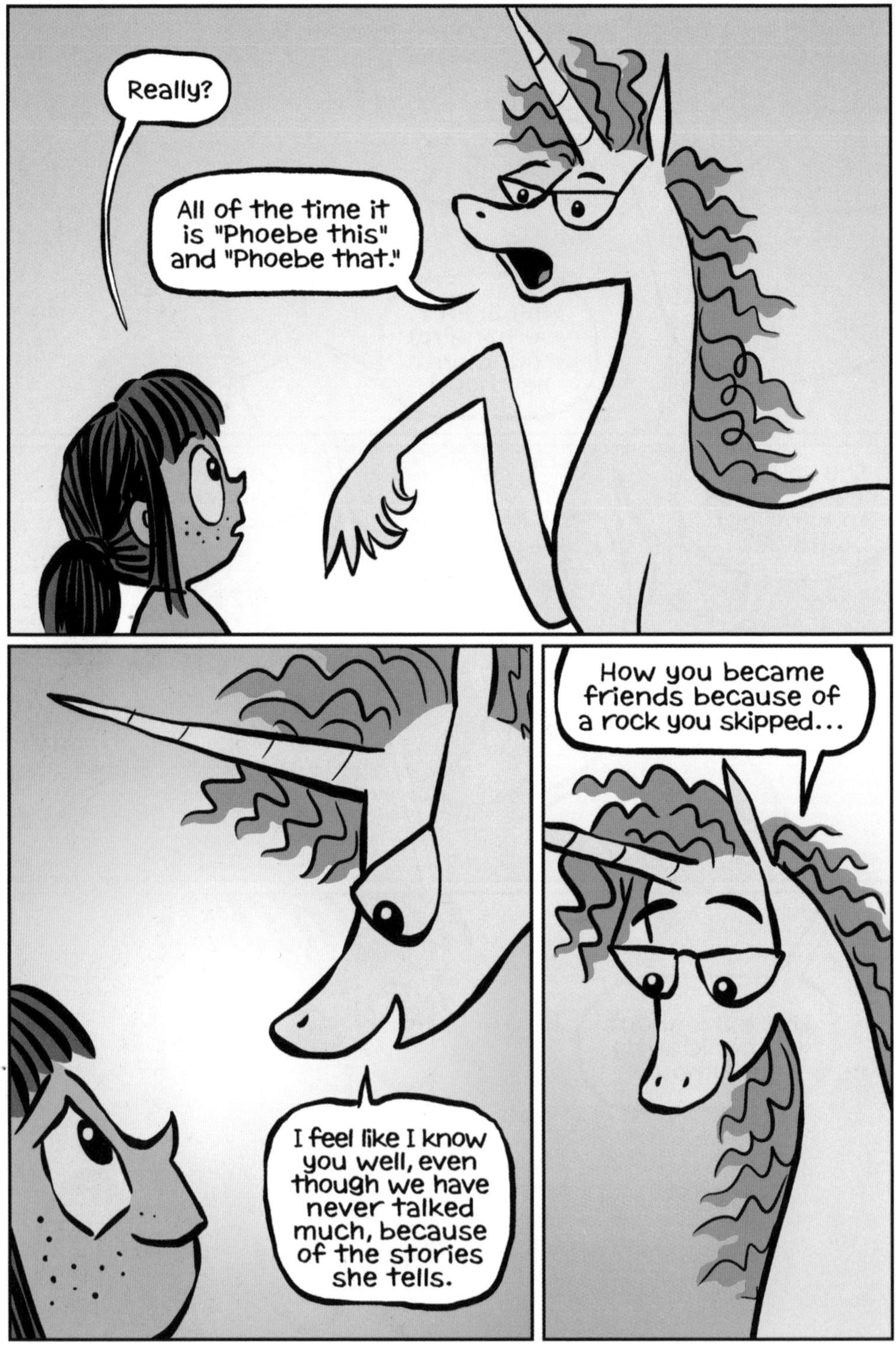
Really?
All of the time it is "Phoebe this" and "Phoebe that."
I feel like I know you well, even though we have never talked much, because of the stories she tells.
How you became friends because of a rock you skipped...

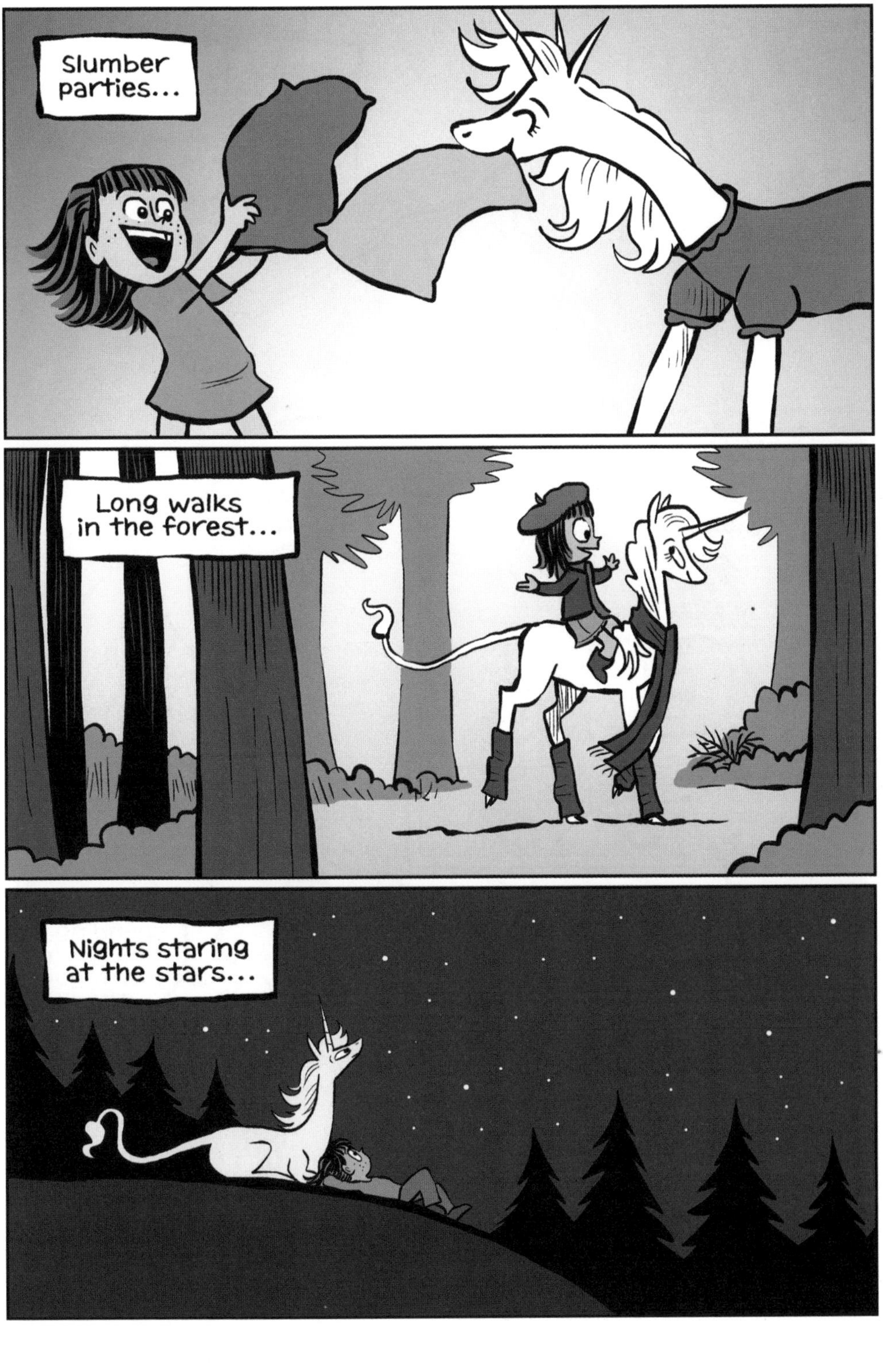
Slumber parties...
Long walks in the forest...
Nights staring at the stars...

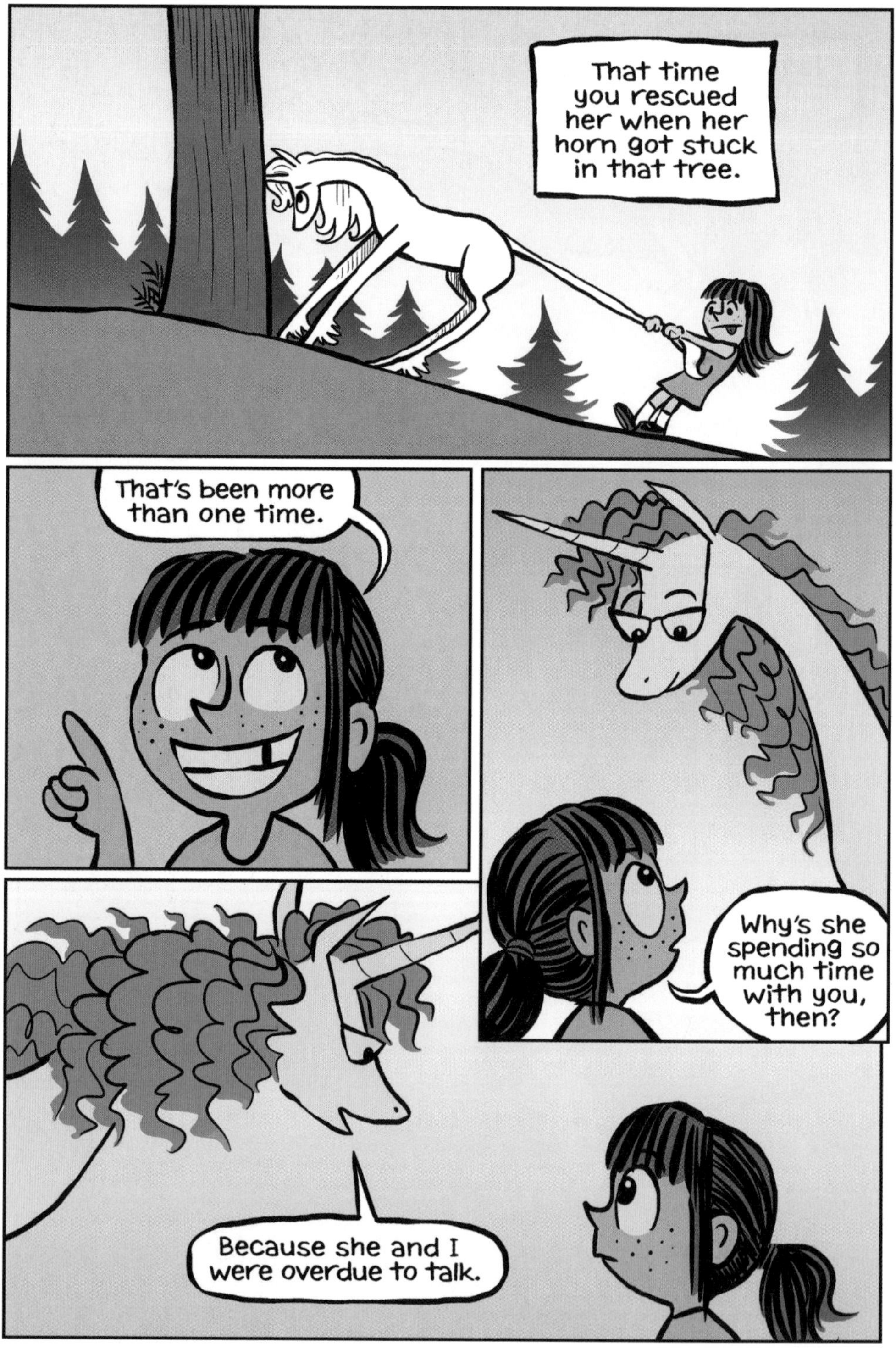
That time you rescued her when her horn got stuck in that tree.
That's been more than one time.
Why's she spending so much time with you, then?
Because she and I were overdue to talk.

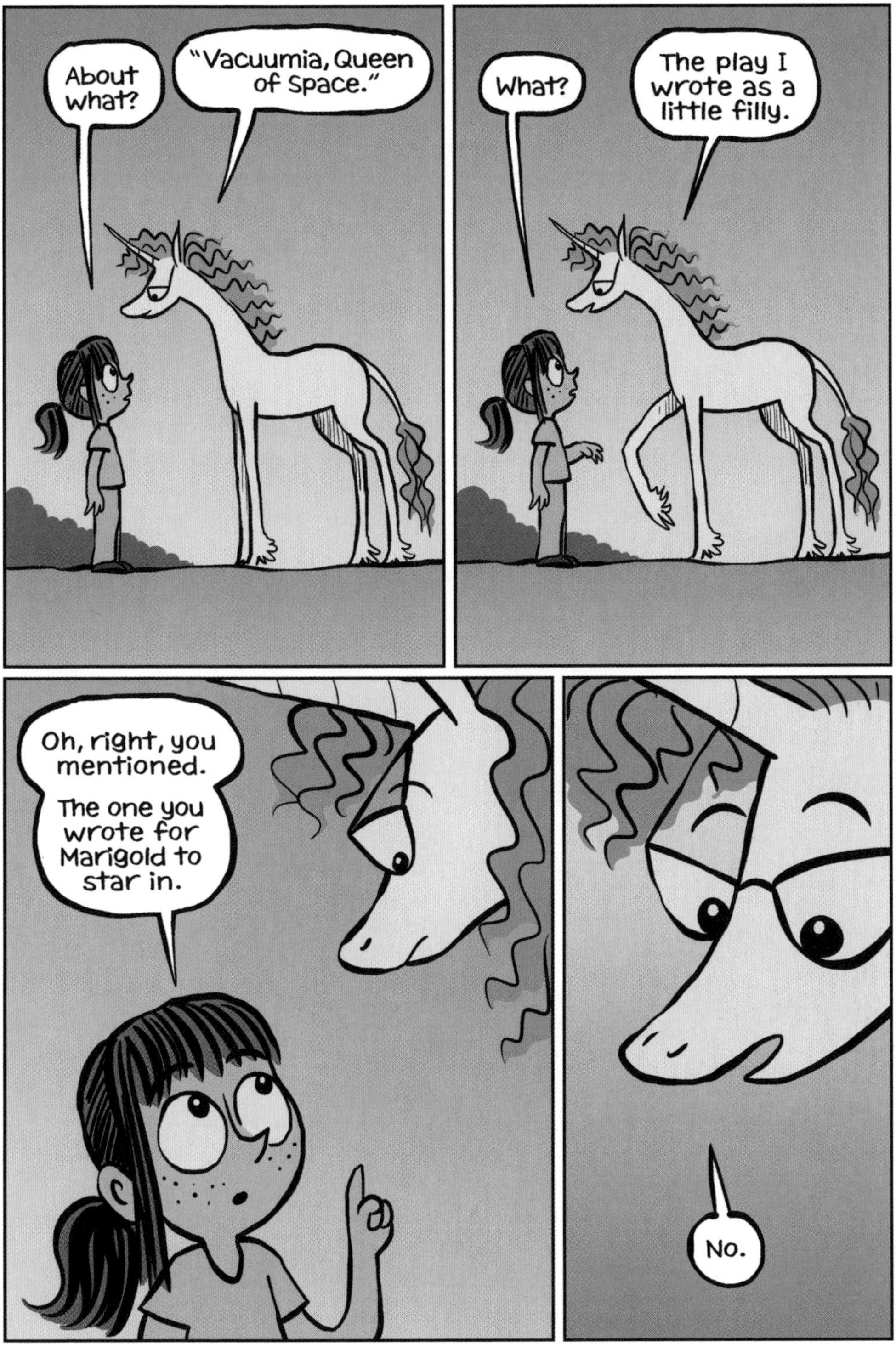
About what?
"Vacuumia, Queen of Space."
What?
The play I wrote as a little filly.
Oh, right, you mentioned.
The one you wrote for Marigold to star in.
No.

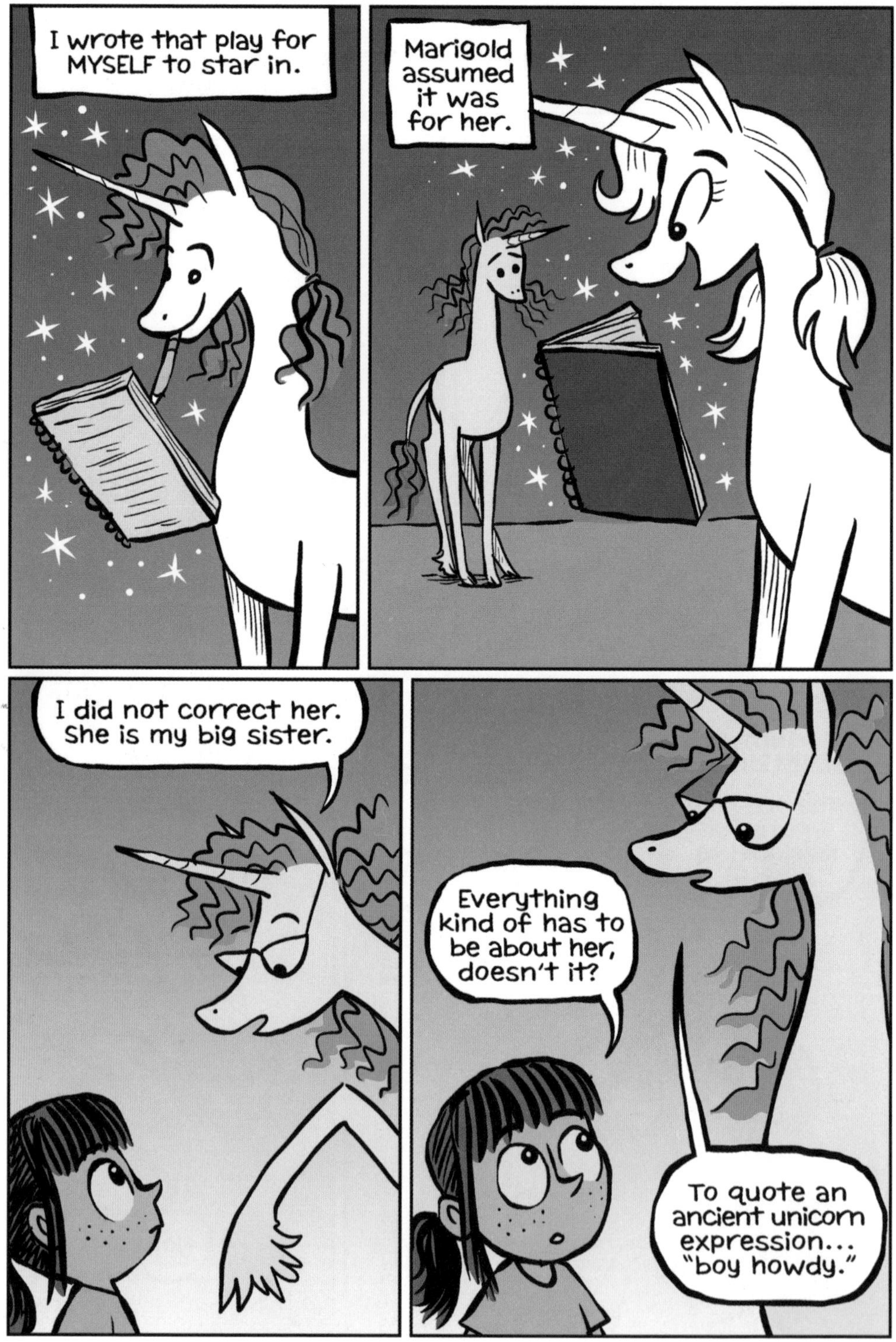
I wrote that play for MYSELF to star in.
Marigold assumed it was for her.
I did not correct her. She is my big sister.
Everything kind of has to be about her, doesn't it?
To quote an ancient unicorn expression... "boy howdy."

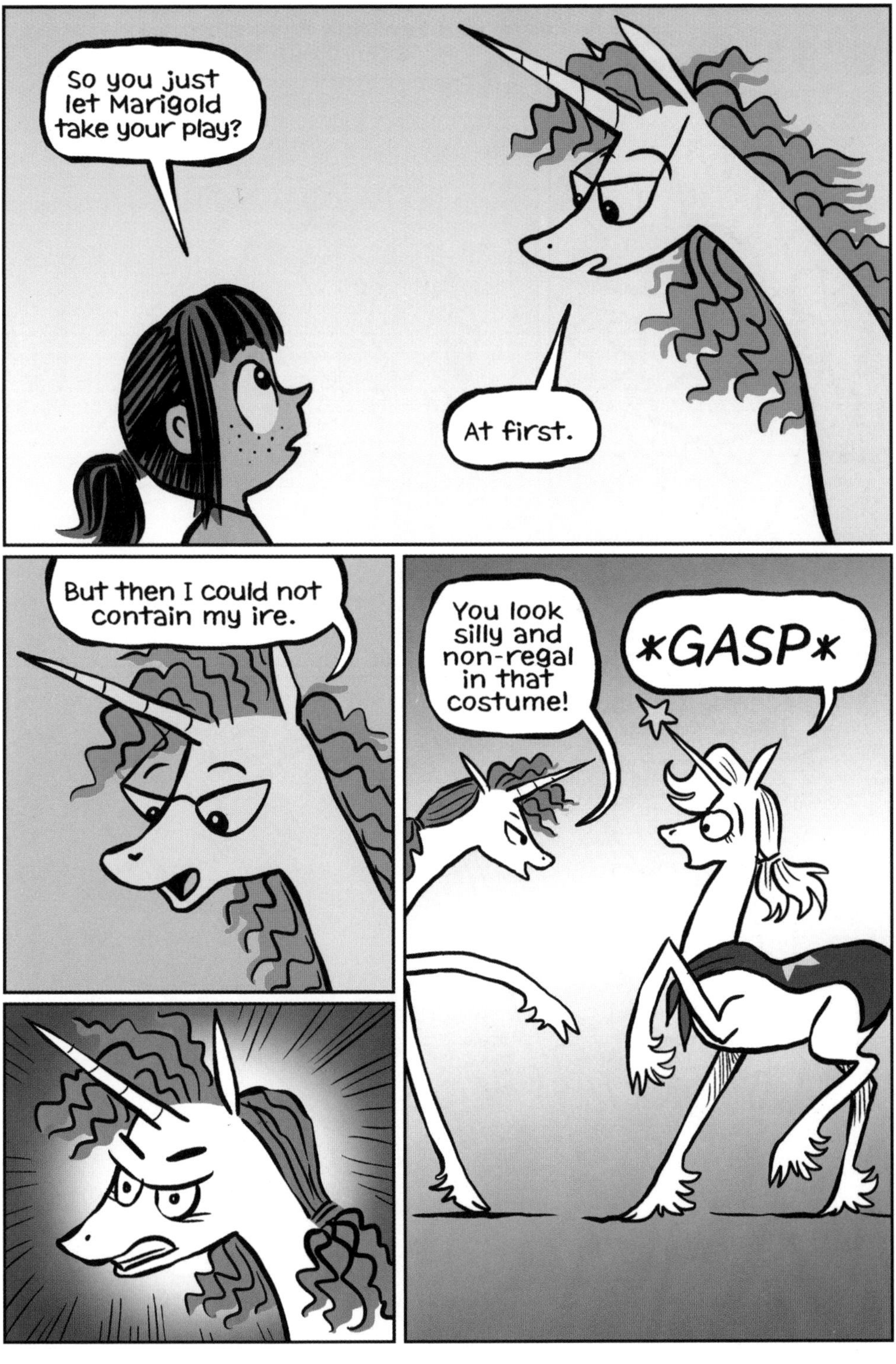
So you just let Marigold take your play?
At first.
But then I could not contain my ire.
You look silly and non-regal in that costume!
GASP

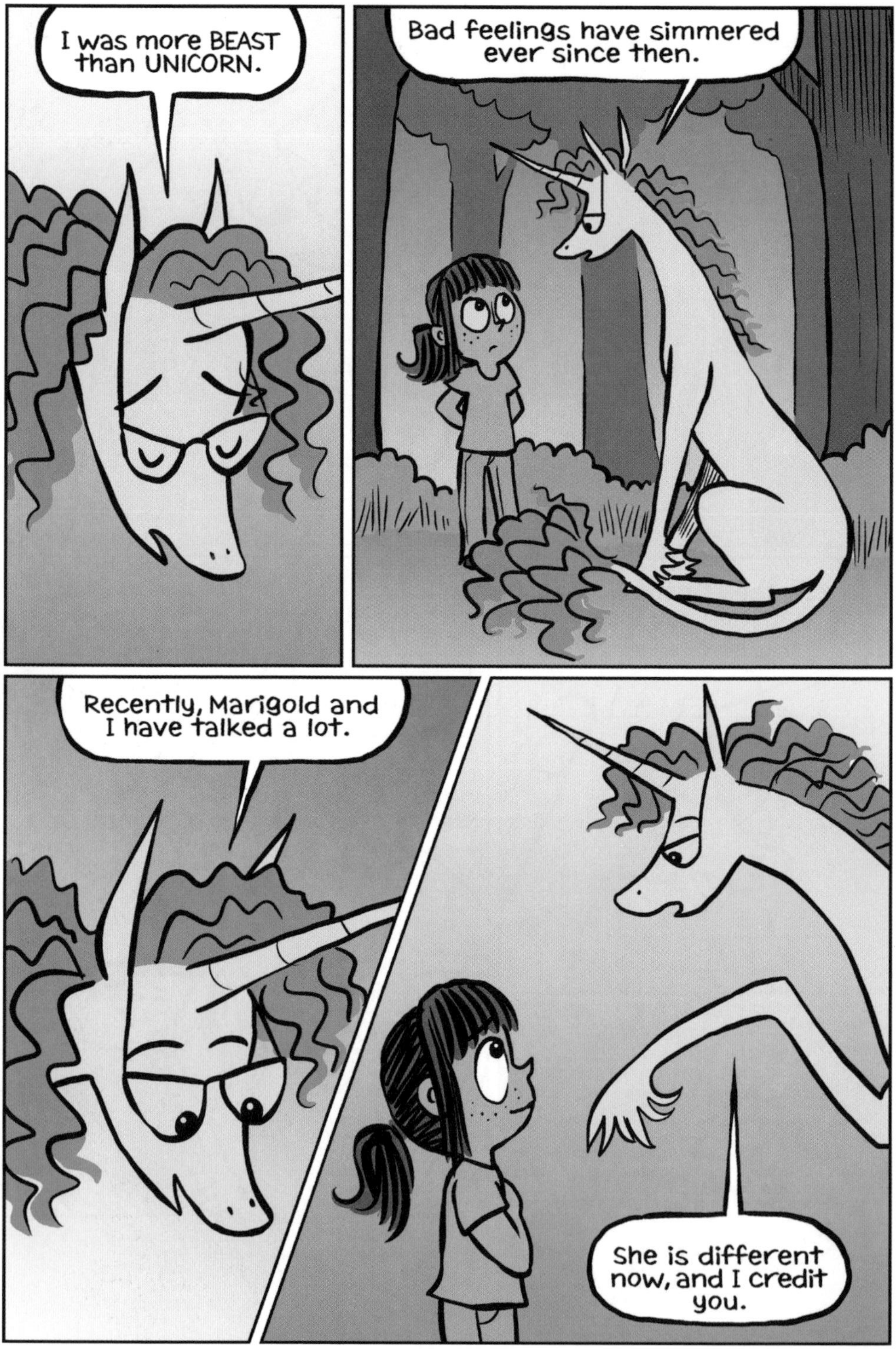
I was more BEAST than UNICORN.
Bad feelings have simmered ever since then.
Recently, Marigold and I have talked a lot.
She is different now, and I credit you.

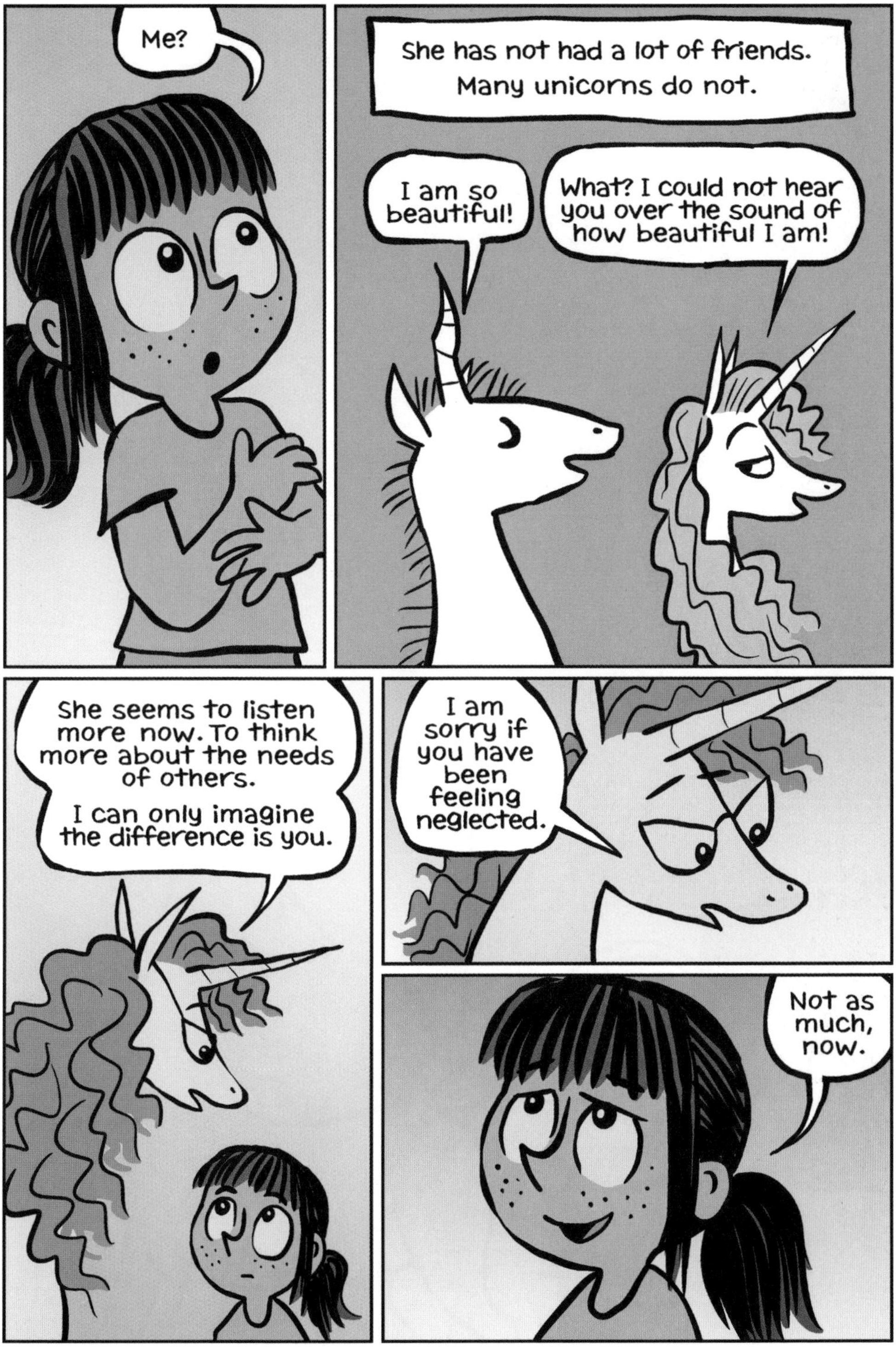
Me?
She has not had a lot of friends. Many unicorns do not.
I am so beautiful!
What? I could not hear you over the sound of how beautiful I am!
She seems to listen more now. To think more about the needs of others.
I can only imagine the difference is you.
I am sorry if you have been feeling neglected.
Not as much, now.

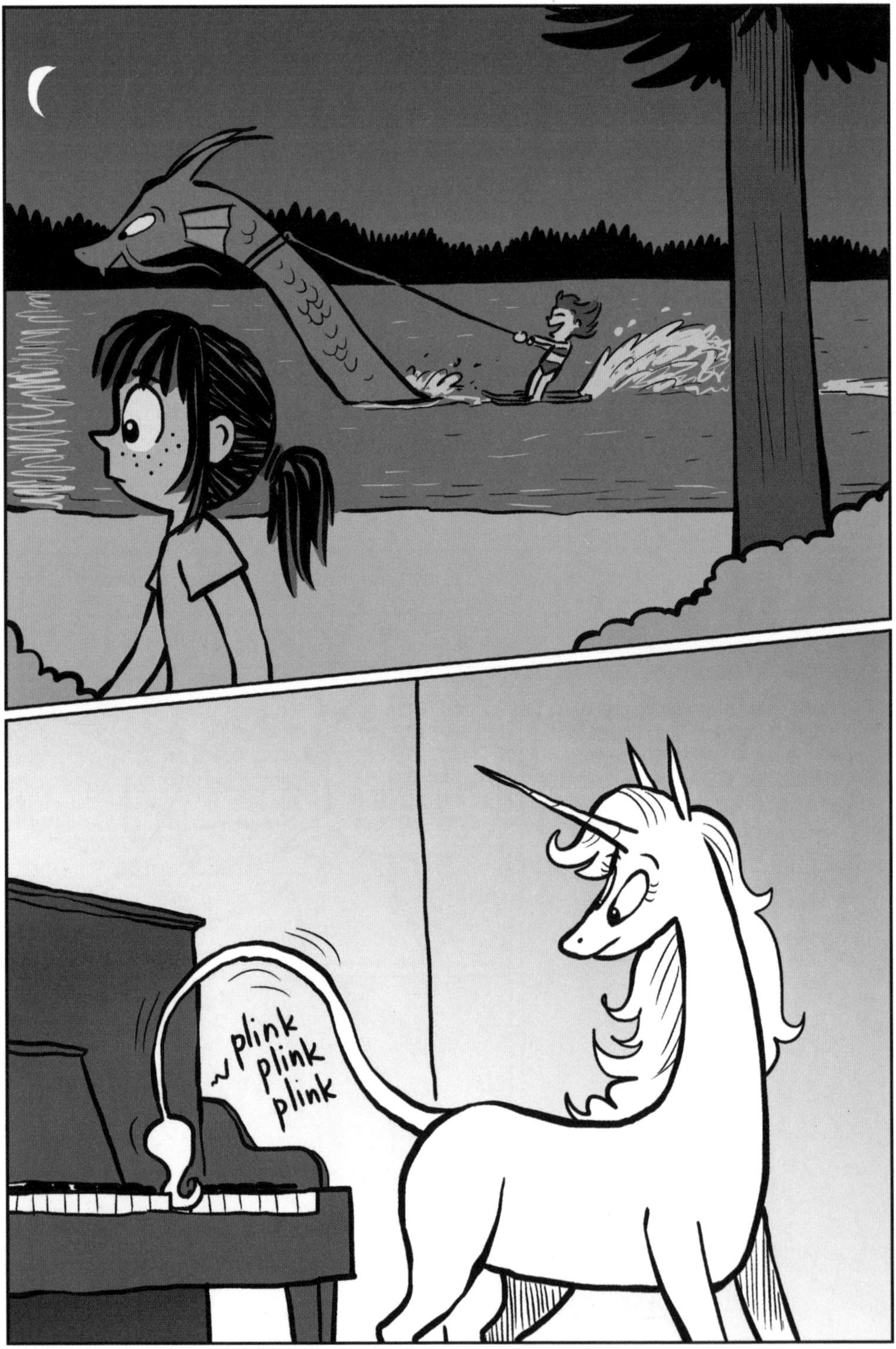
~plink
plink
plink

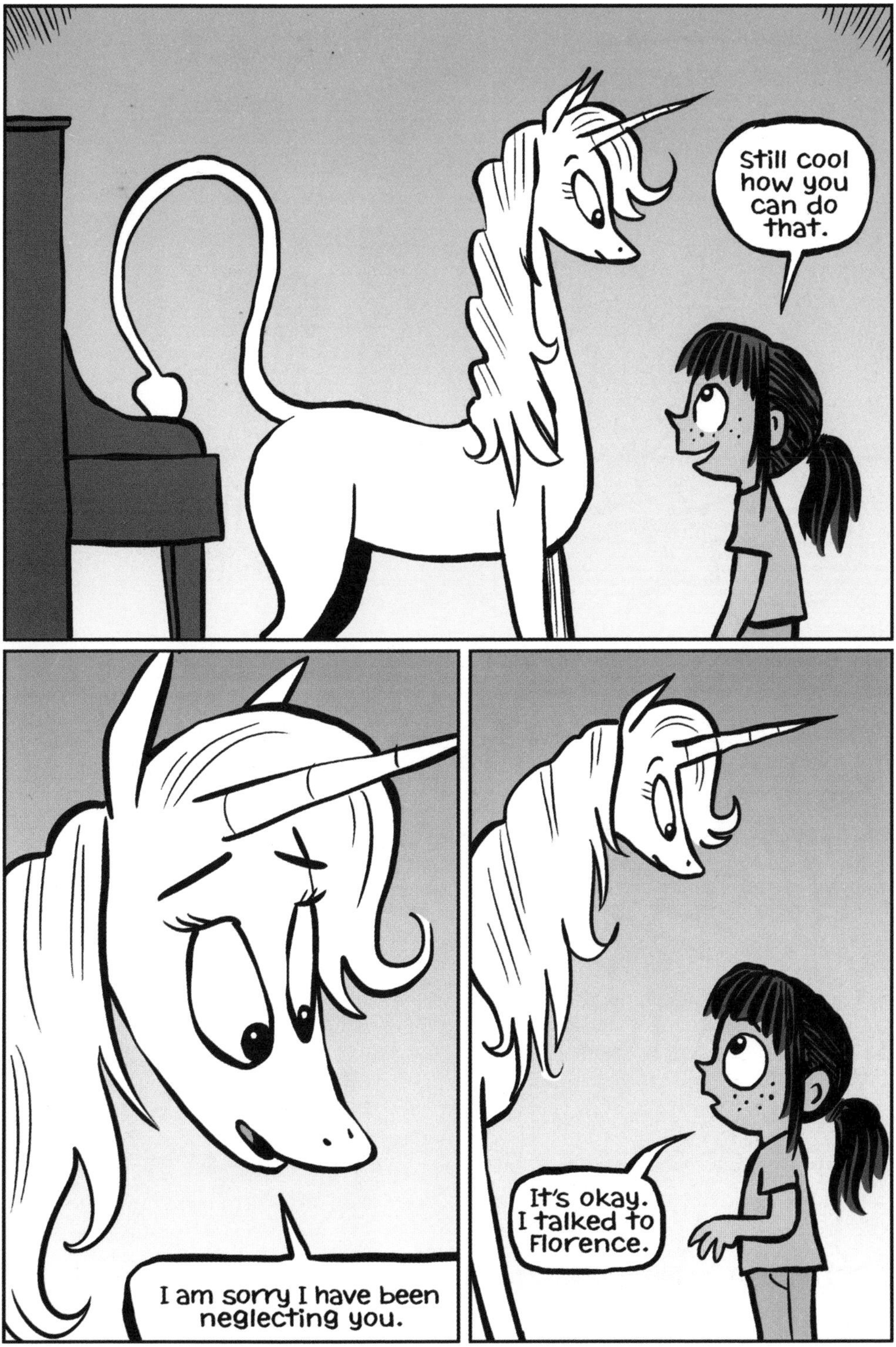
Still cool how you can do that.
I am sorry I have been neglecting you.
It's okay. I talked to Florence.

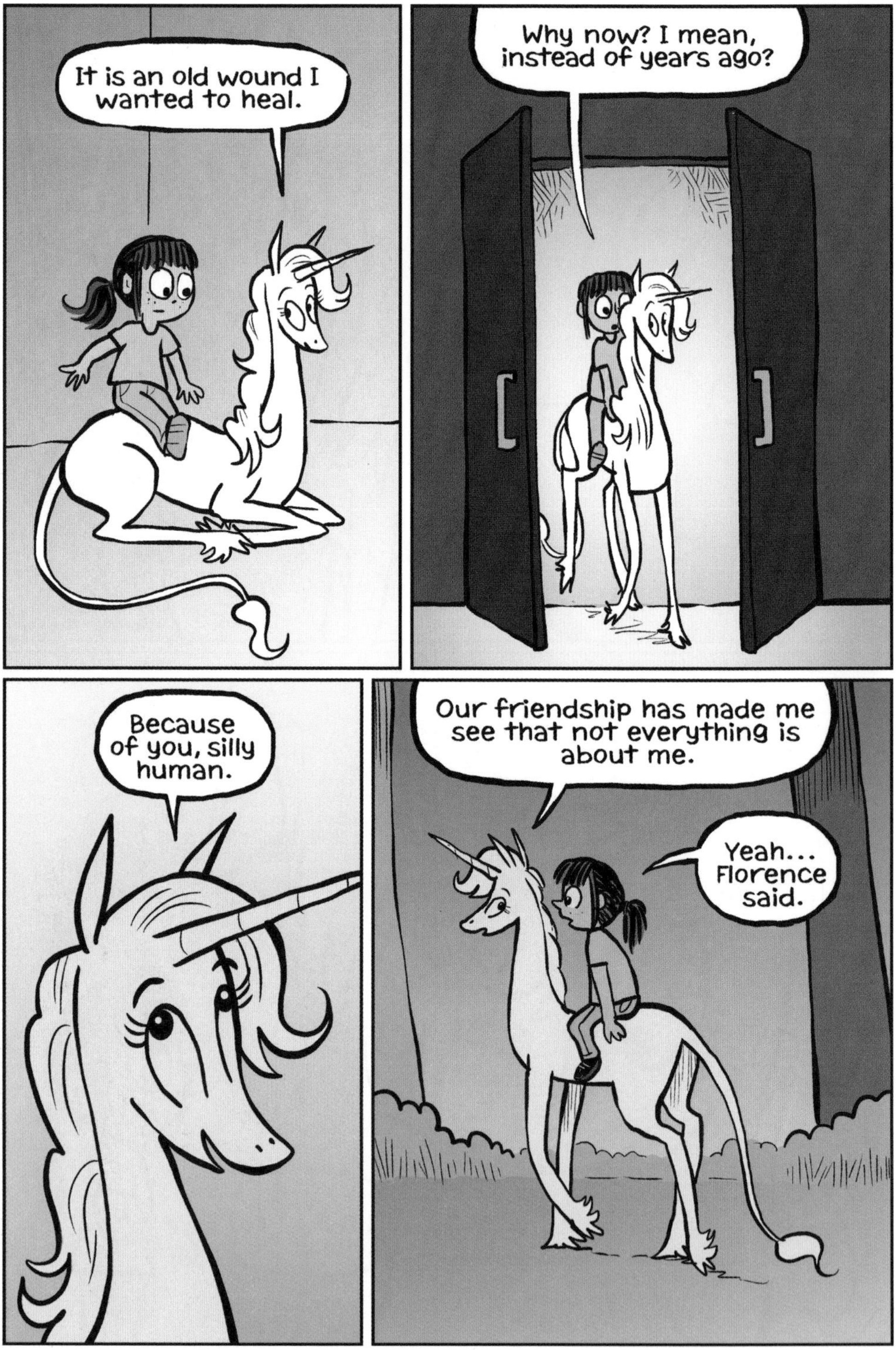
It is an old wound I wanted to heal.
Why now? I mean, instead of years ago?
Because of you, silly human.
Our friendship has made me see that not everything is about me.
Yeah... Florence said.

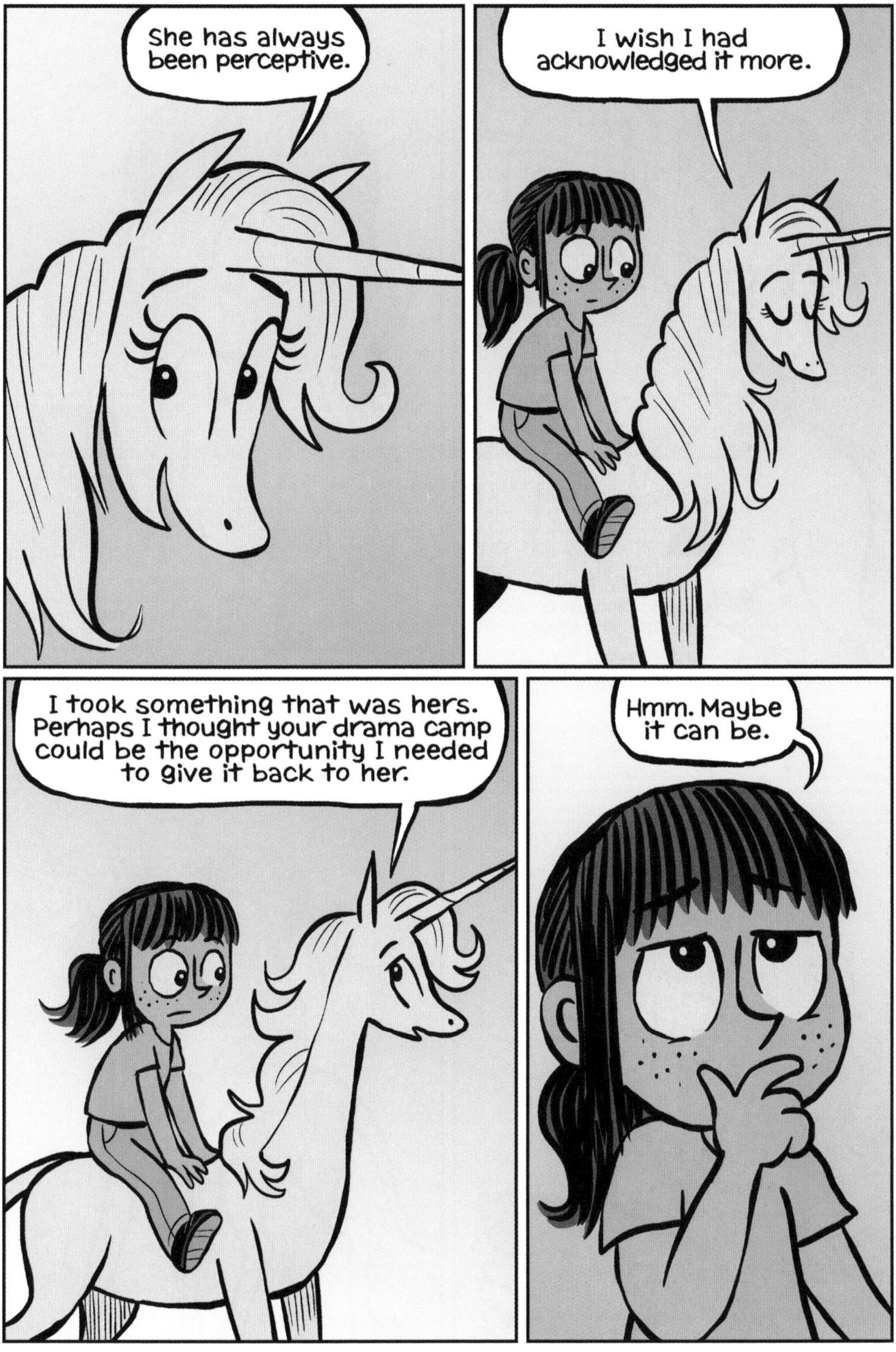
She has always been perceptive.
I wish I had acknowledged it more.
I took something that was hers. Perhaps I thought your drama camp could be the opportunity I needed to give it back to her.
Hmm. Maybe it can be.

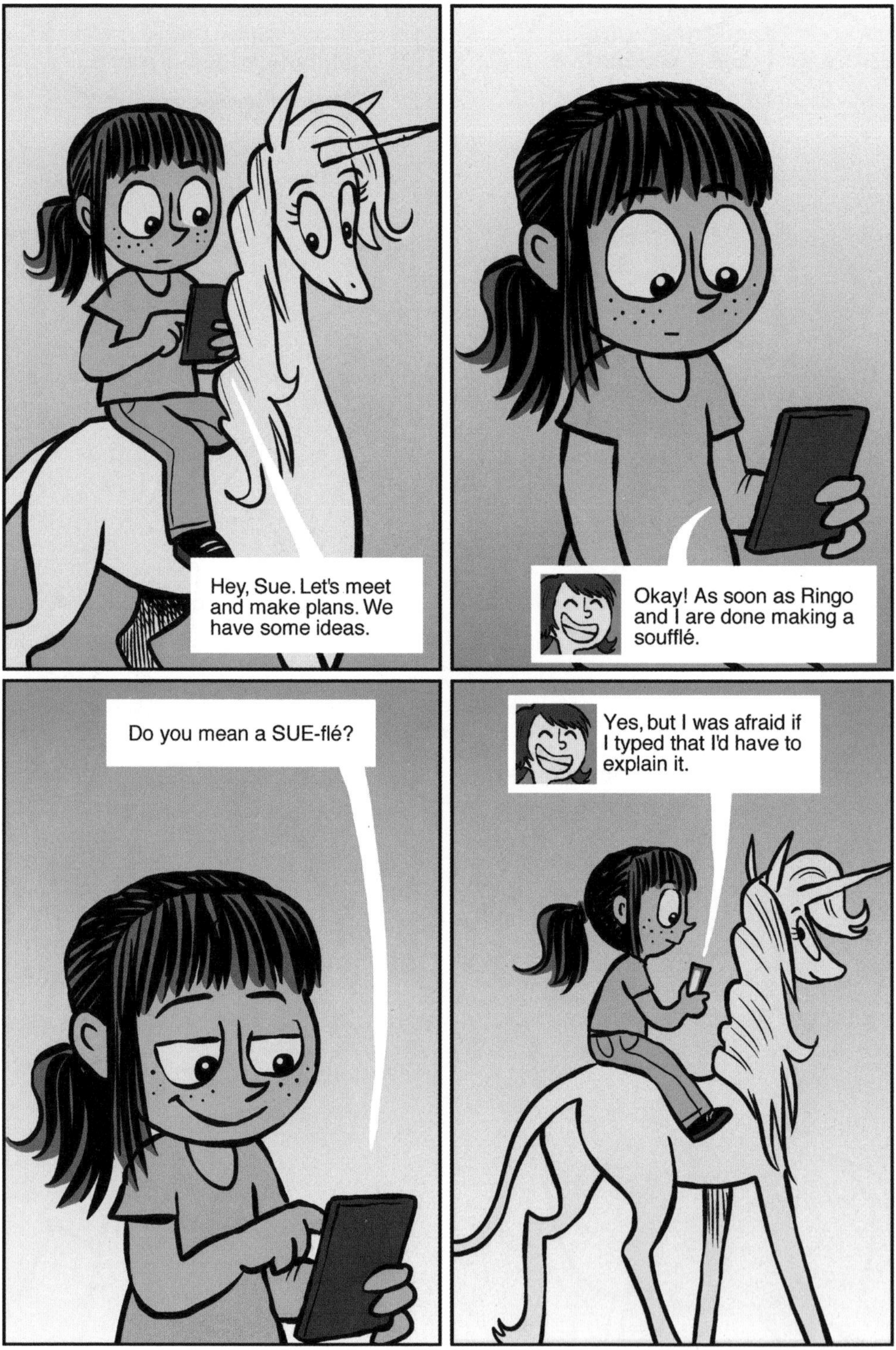
Hey, Sue. Let's meet and make plans. We have some ideas.
Okay! As soon as Ringo and I are done making a soufflé.
Do you mean a SUE-flé?
Yes, but I was afraid if I typed that I'd have to explain it.

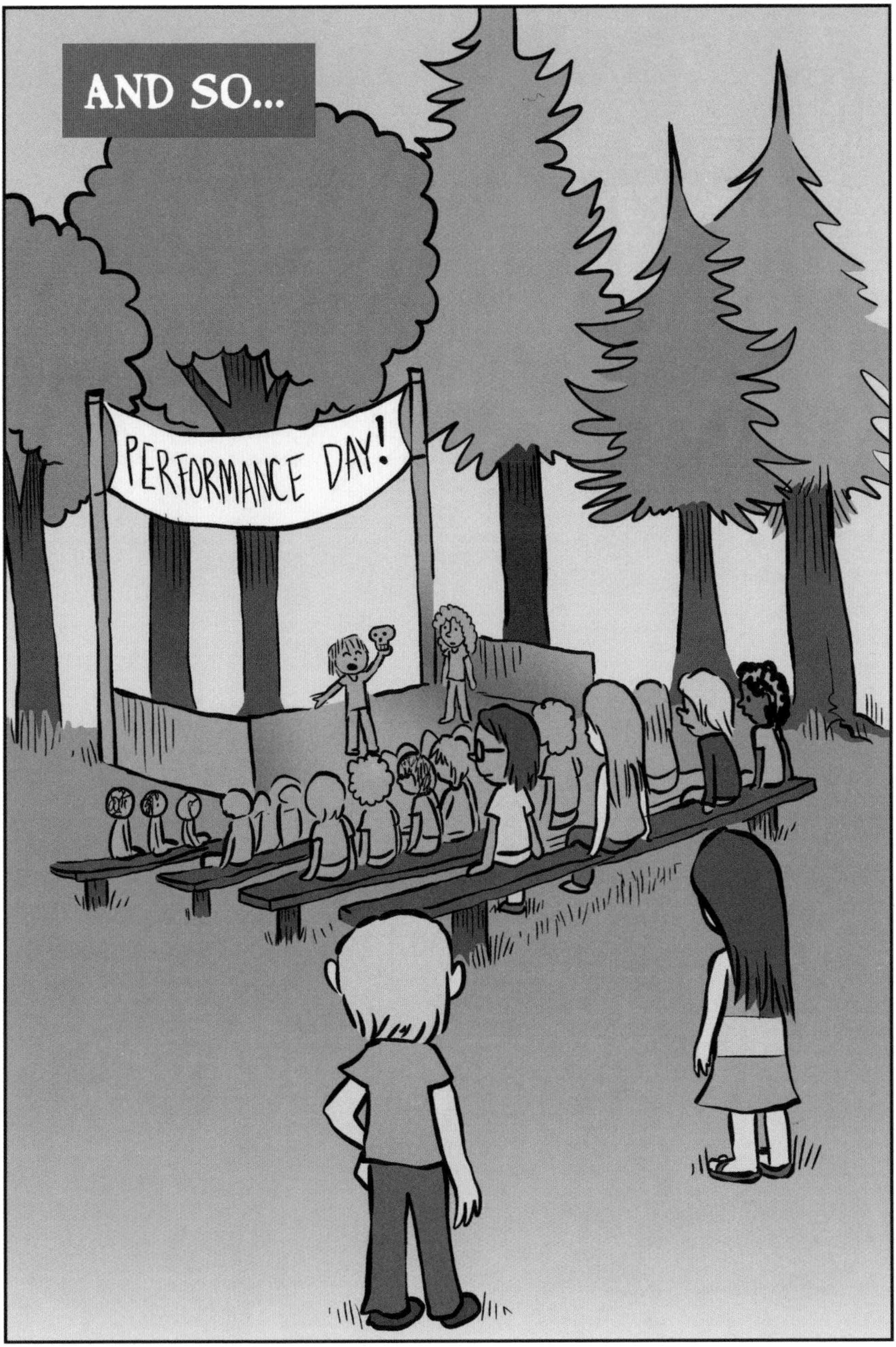
AND SO...
PERFORMANCE DAY!

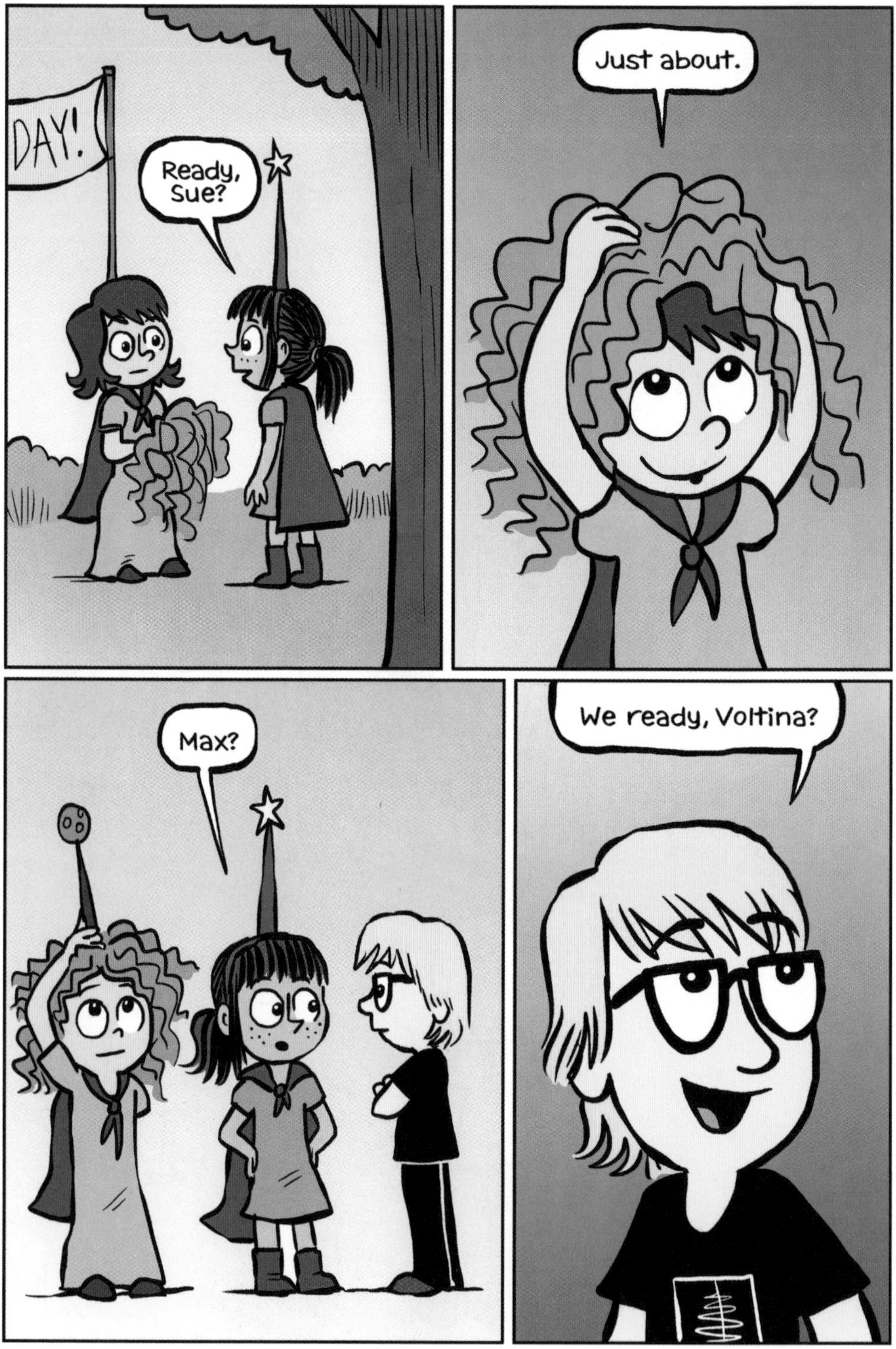
DAY!
Ready, Sue?
Just about.
Max?
We ready, Voltina?

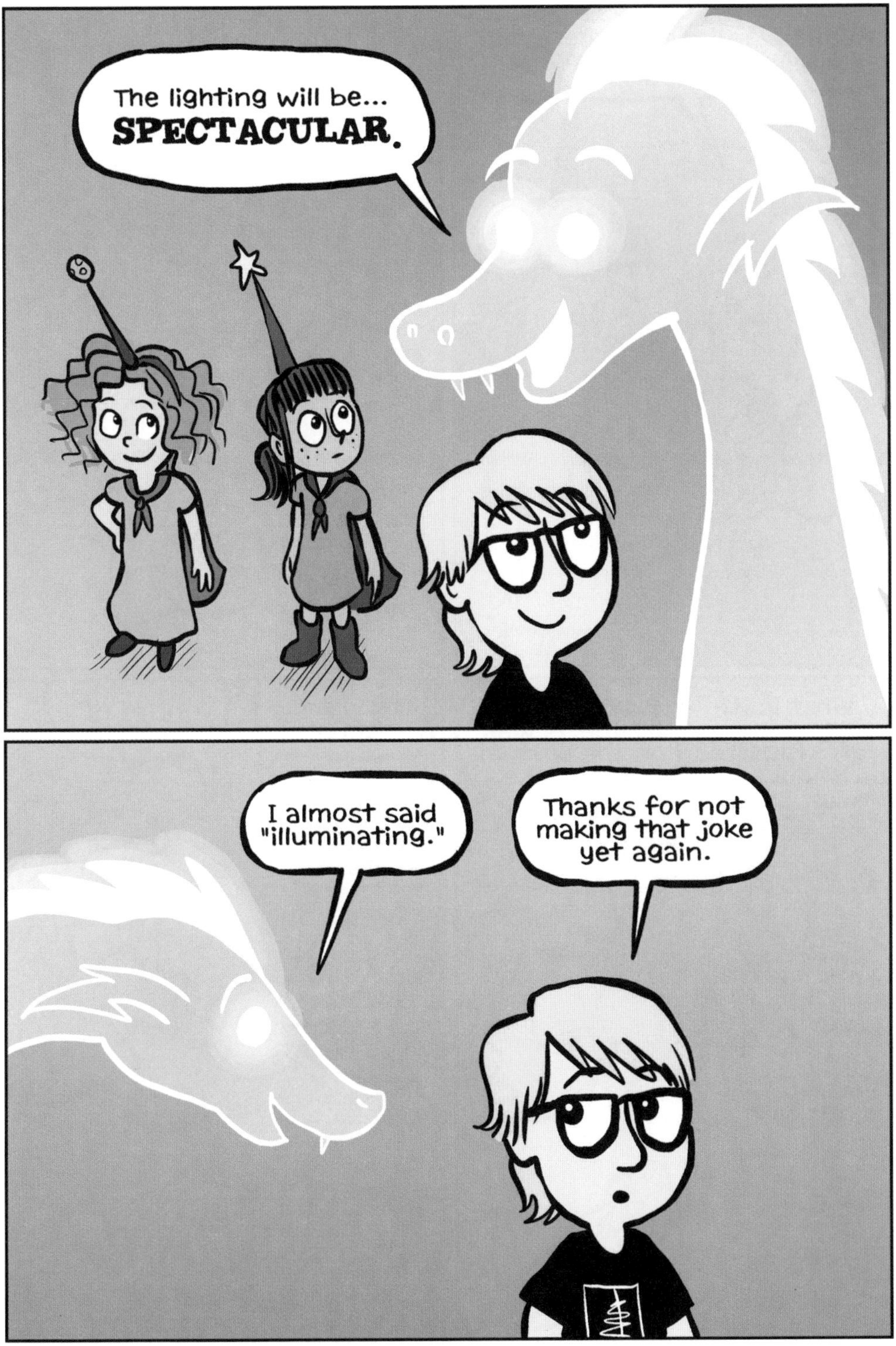
The lighting will be...
SPECTACULAR.
I almost said "illuminating."
Thanks for not making that joke yet again.

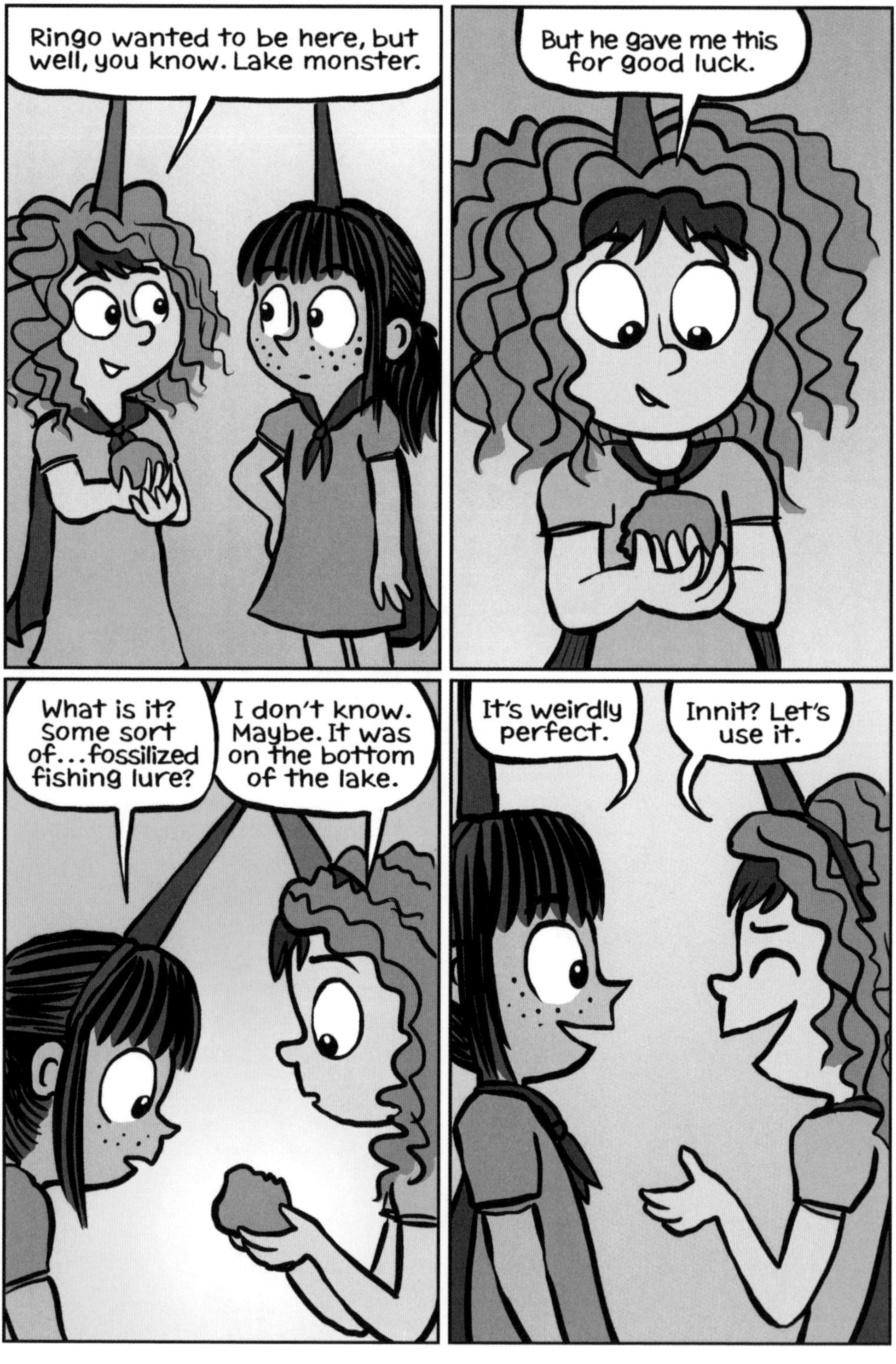
Ringo wanted to be here, but well, you know. Lake monster.
But he gave me this for good luck.
What is it? Some sort of...fossilized fishing lure?
I don't know. Maybe. It was on the bottom of the lake.
It's weirdly perfect.
Innit? Let's use it.

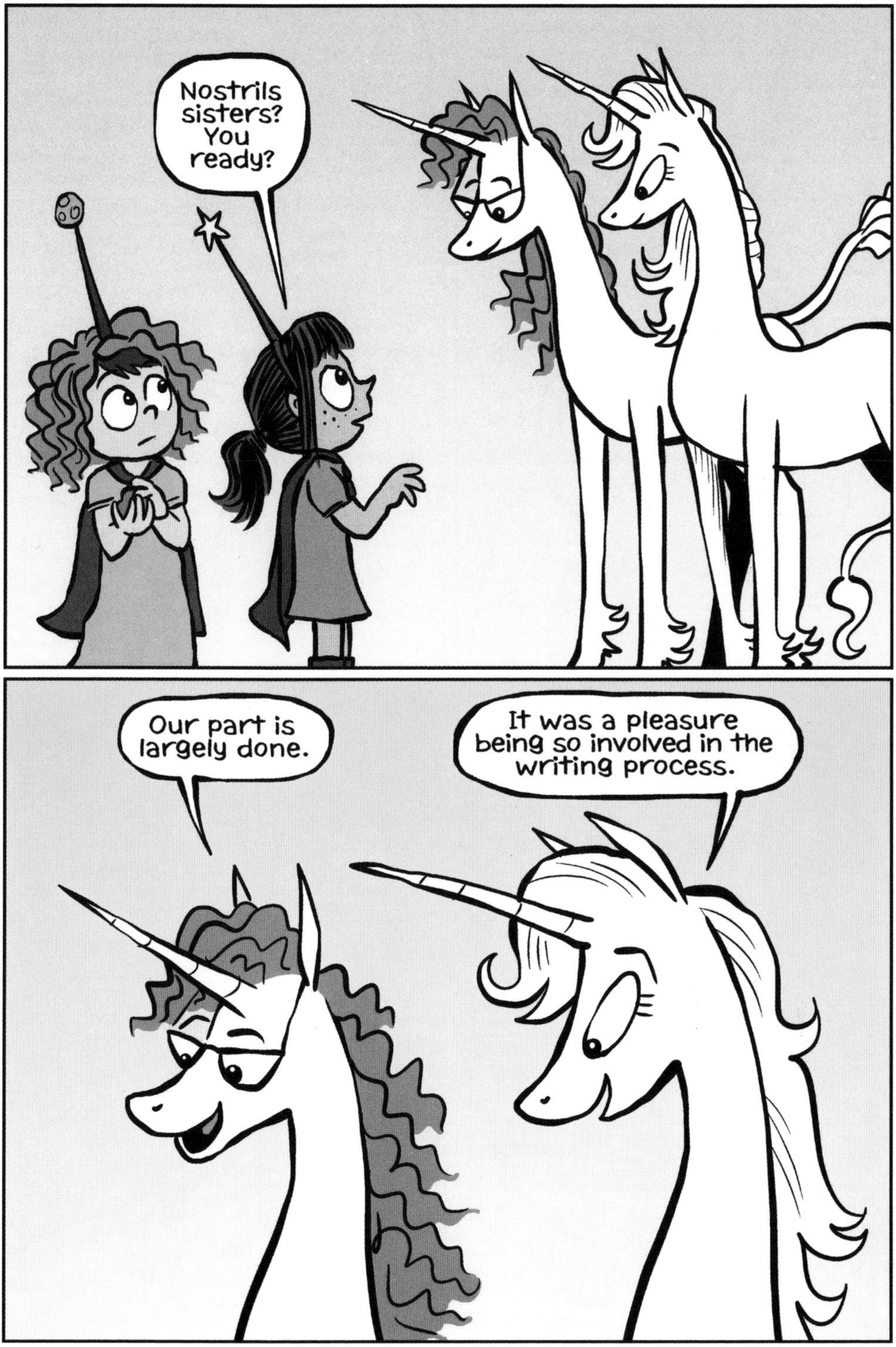
Nostrils sisters? You ready?
Our part is largely done.
It was a pleasure being so involved in the writing process.

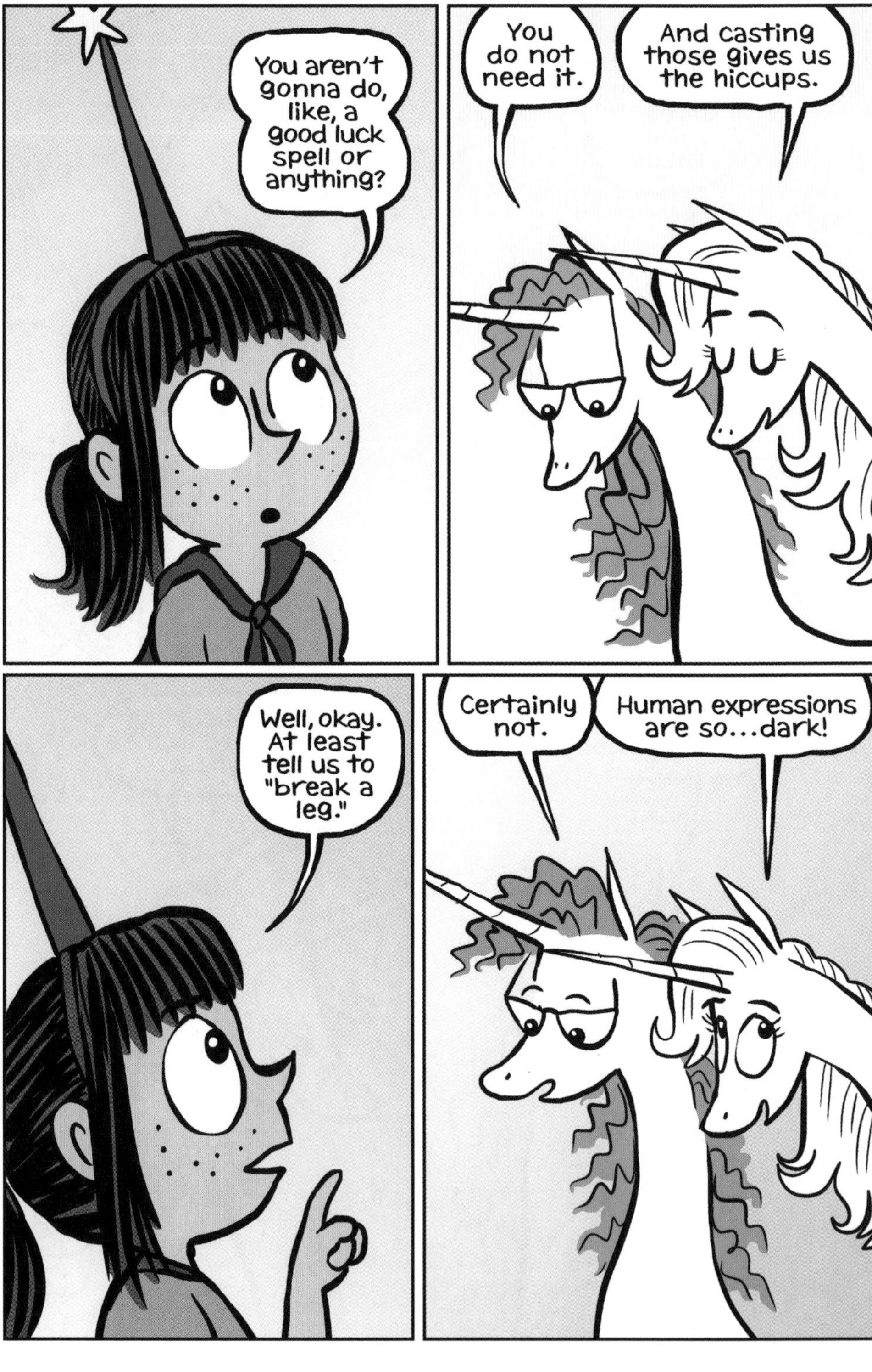

You aren't gonna do, like, a good luck spell or anything?
You do not need it.
And casting those gives us the hiccups.
Well, okay. At least tell us to "break a leg."
Certainly not.
Human expressions are so...dark!

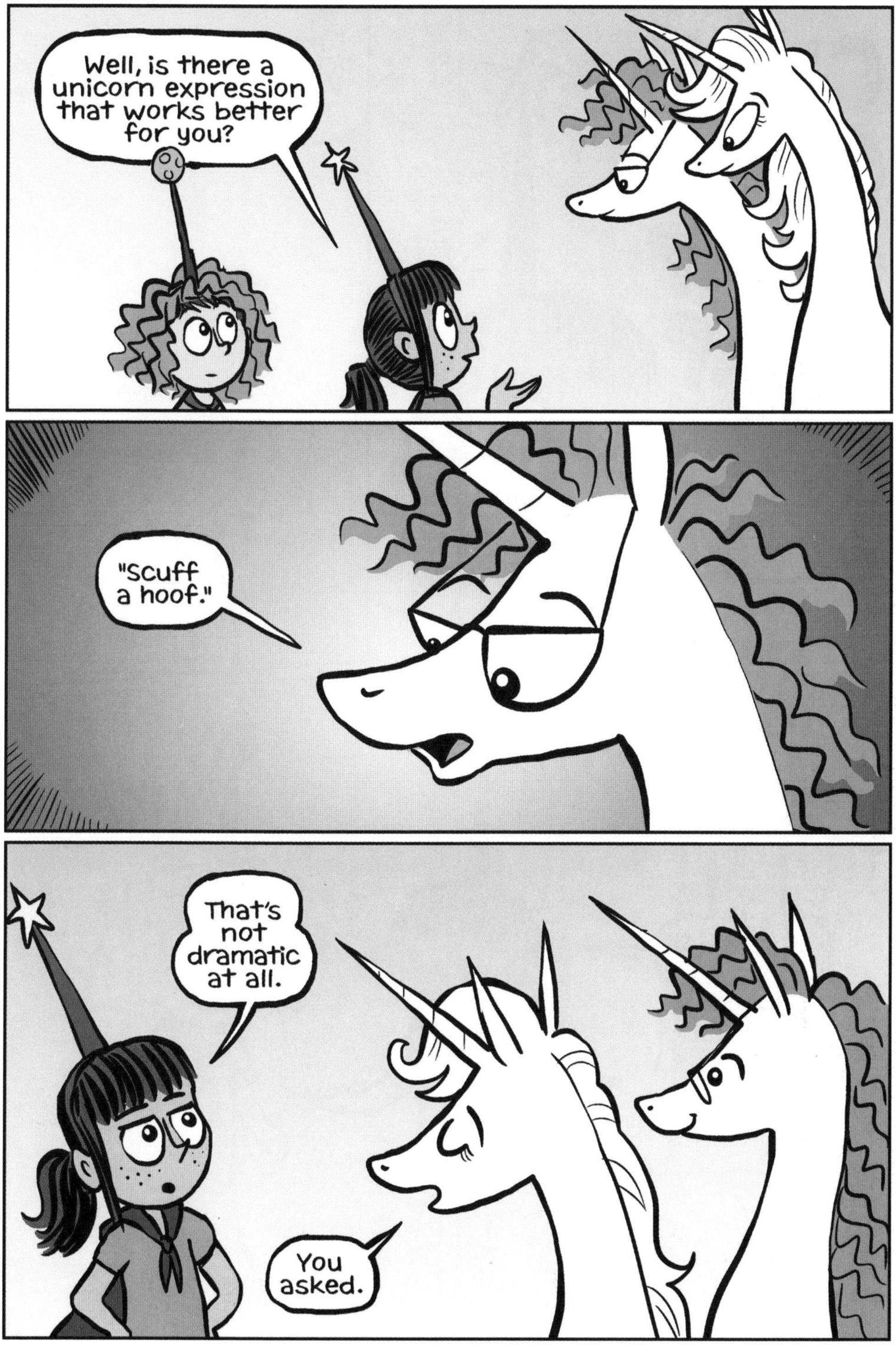
Well, is there a unicorn expression that works better for you?
"Scuff a hoof."
That's not dramatic at all.
You asked.

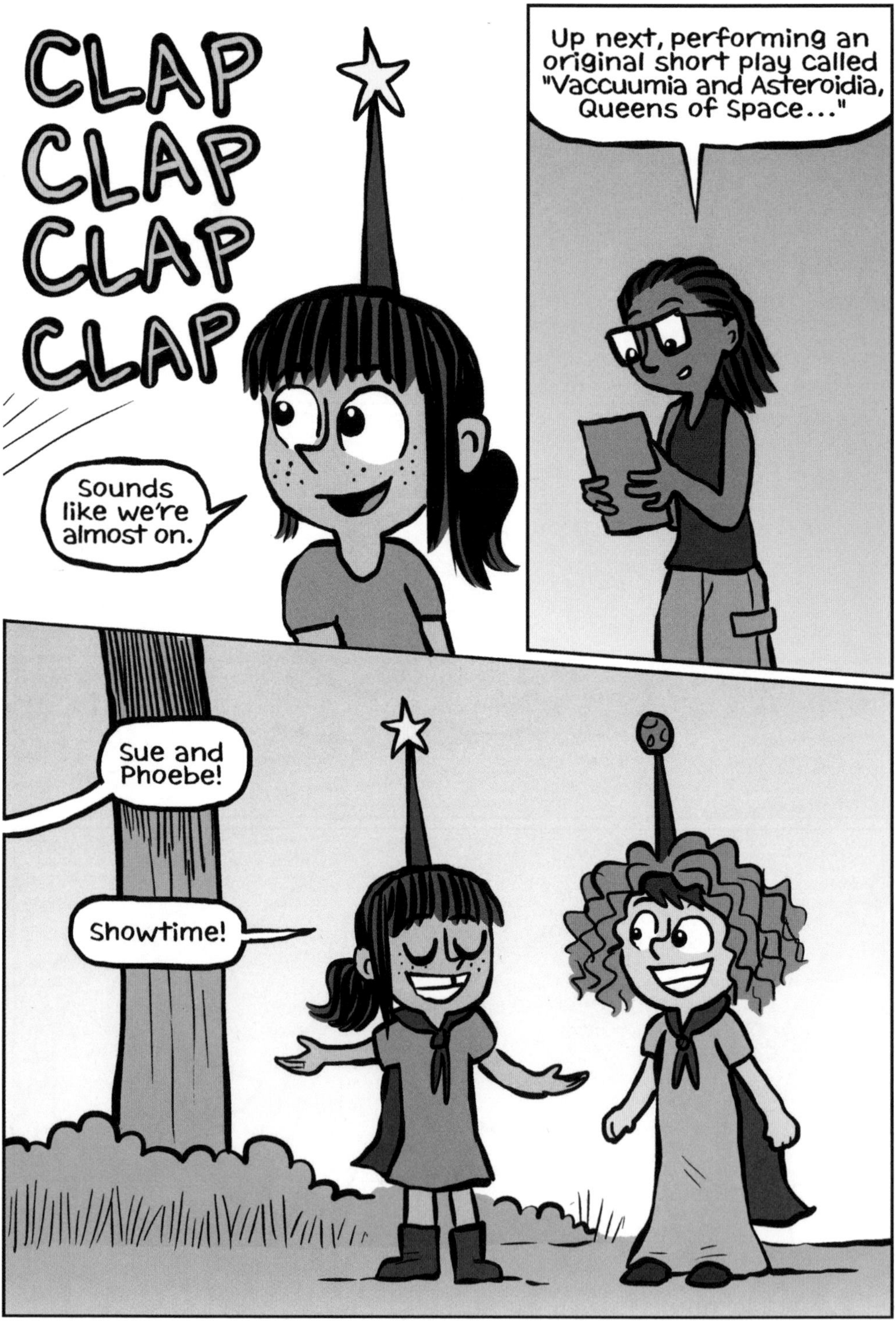
CLAP CLAP CLAP CLAP
Sounds like we're almost on.
Up next, performing an original short play called "Vaccuumia and Asteroidia, Queens of Space..."
Sue and Phoebe!
Showtime!

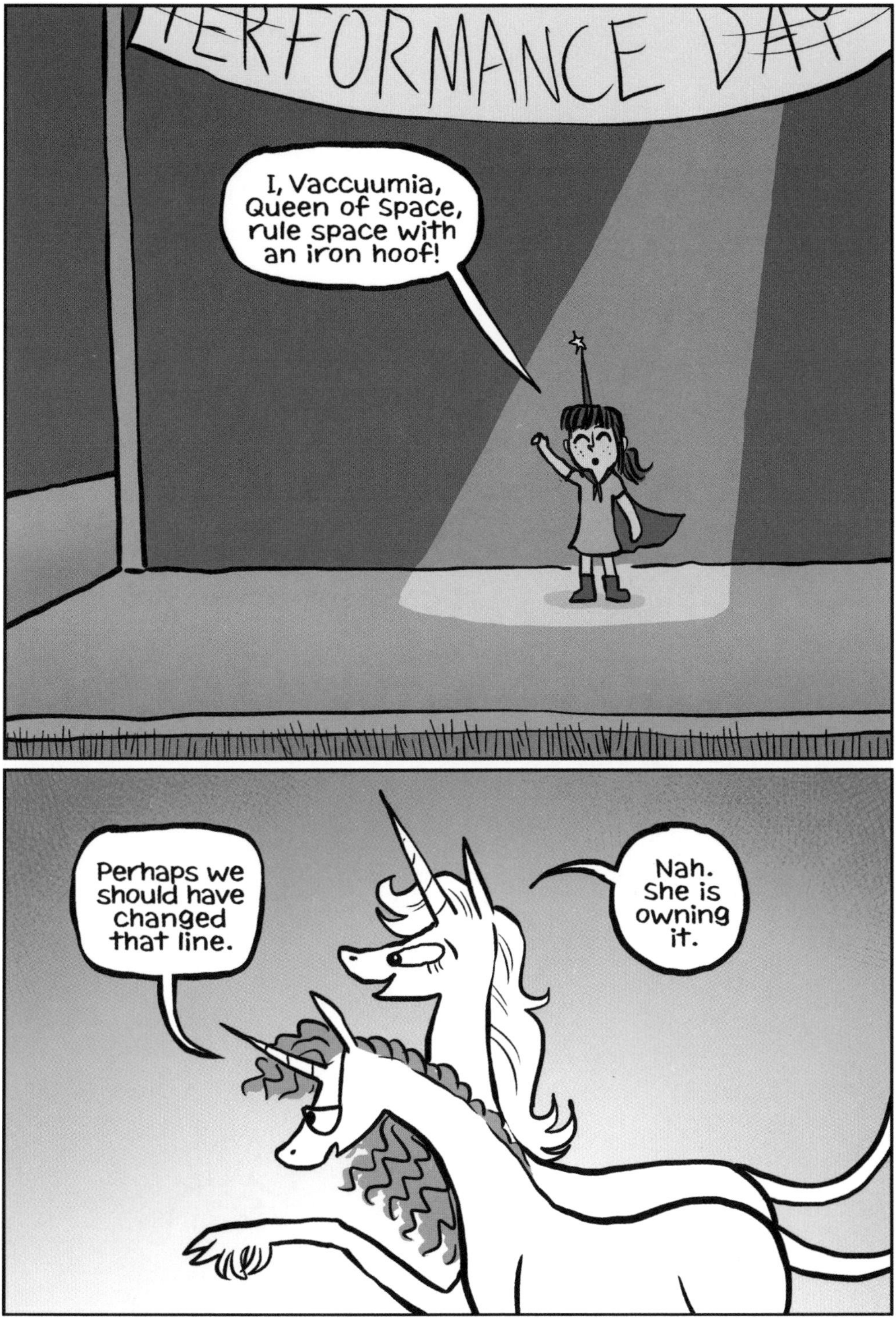
ERFORMANCE DAY
I, Vaccuumia, Queen of Space, rule space with an iron hoof!
Perhaps we should have changed that line.
Nah. She is owning it.

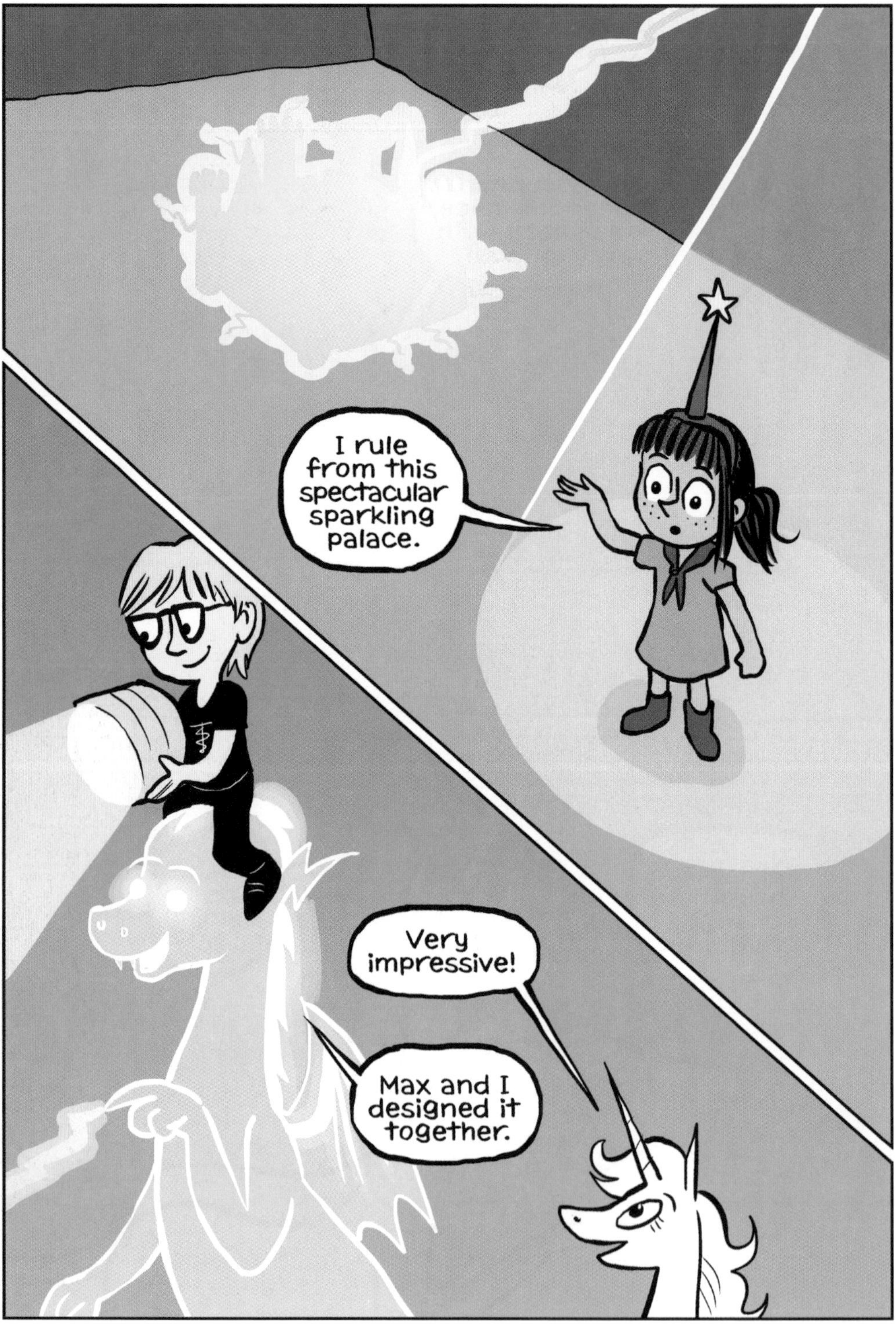
I rule from this spectacular sparkling palace.
Very impressive!
Max and I designed it together.

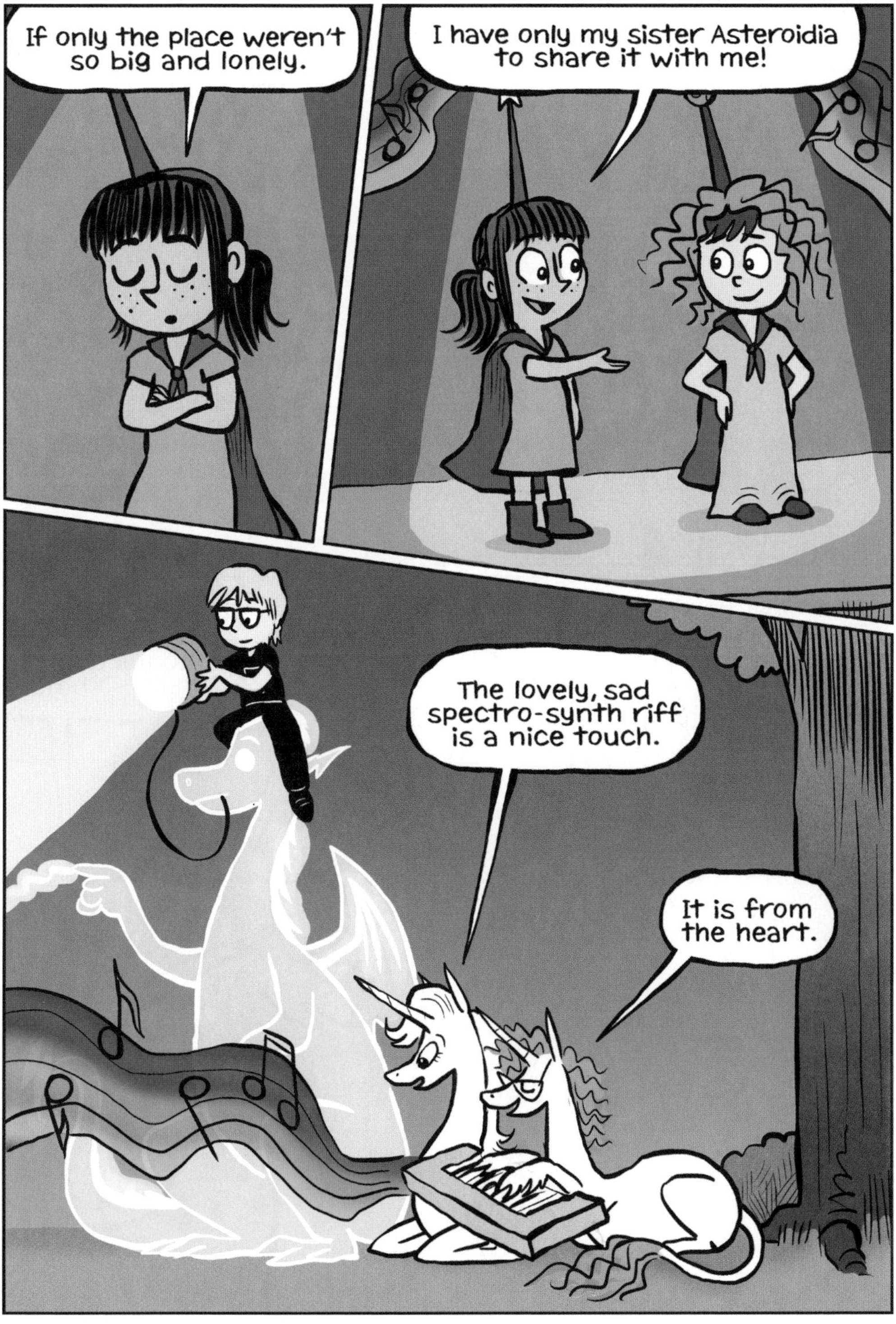
If only the place weren't so big and lonely.
I have only my sister Asteroidia to share it with me!
The lovely, sad spectro-synth riff is a nice touch.
It is from the heart.

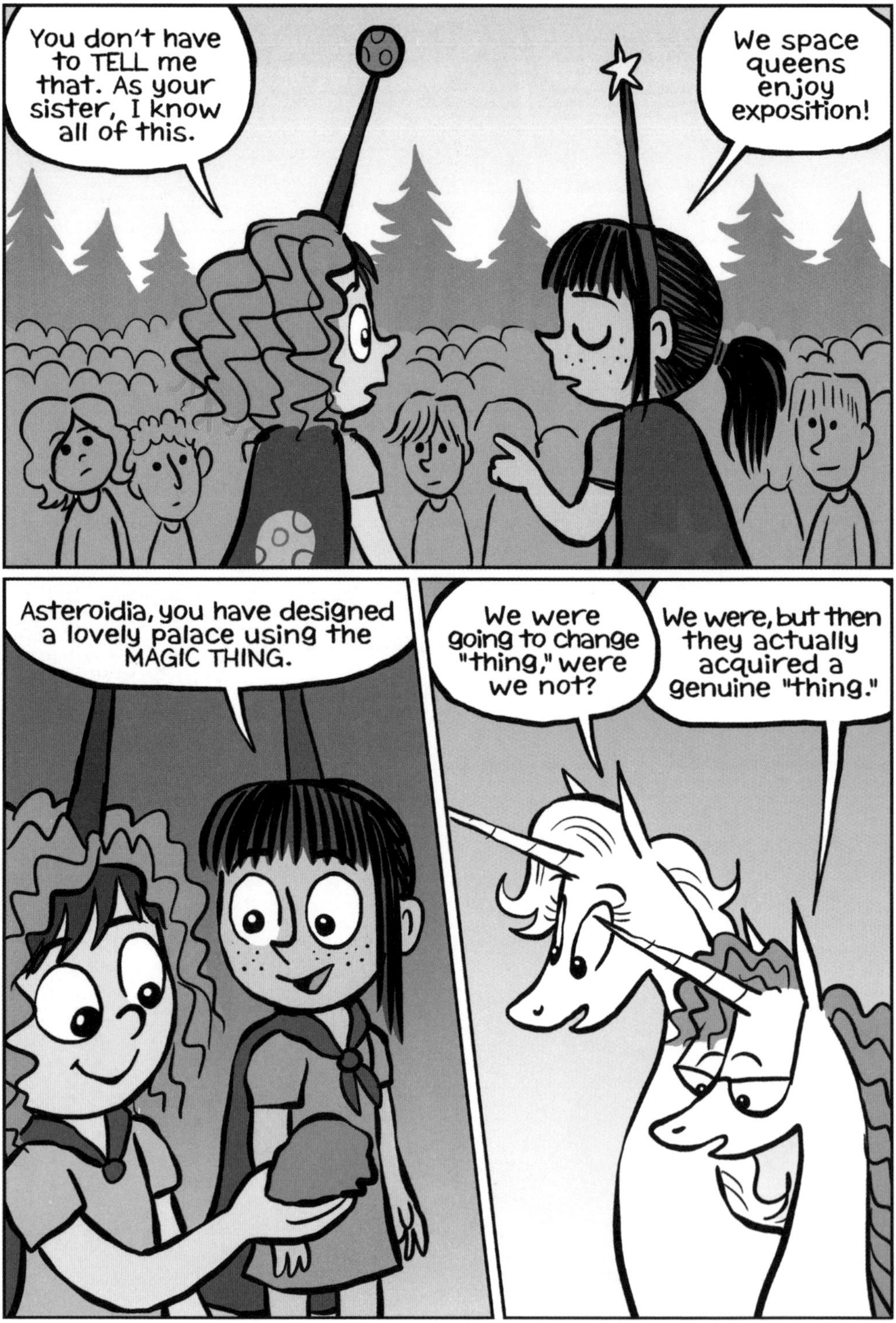
You don't have to TELL me that. As your sister, I know all of this.
We space queens enjoy exposition!
Asteroidia, you have designed a lovely palace using the MAGIC THING.
We were going to change "thing," were we not?
We were, but then they actually acquired a genuine "thing."

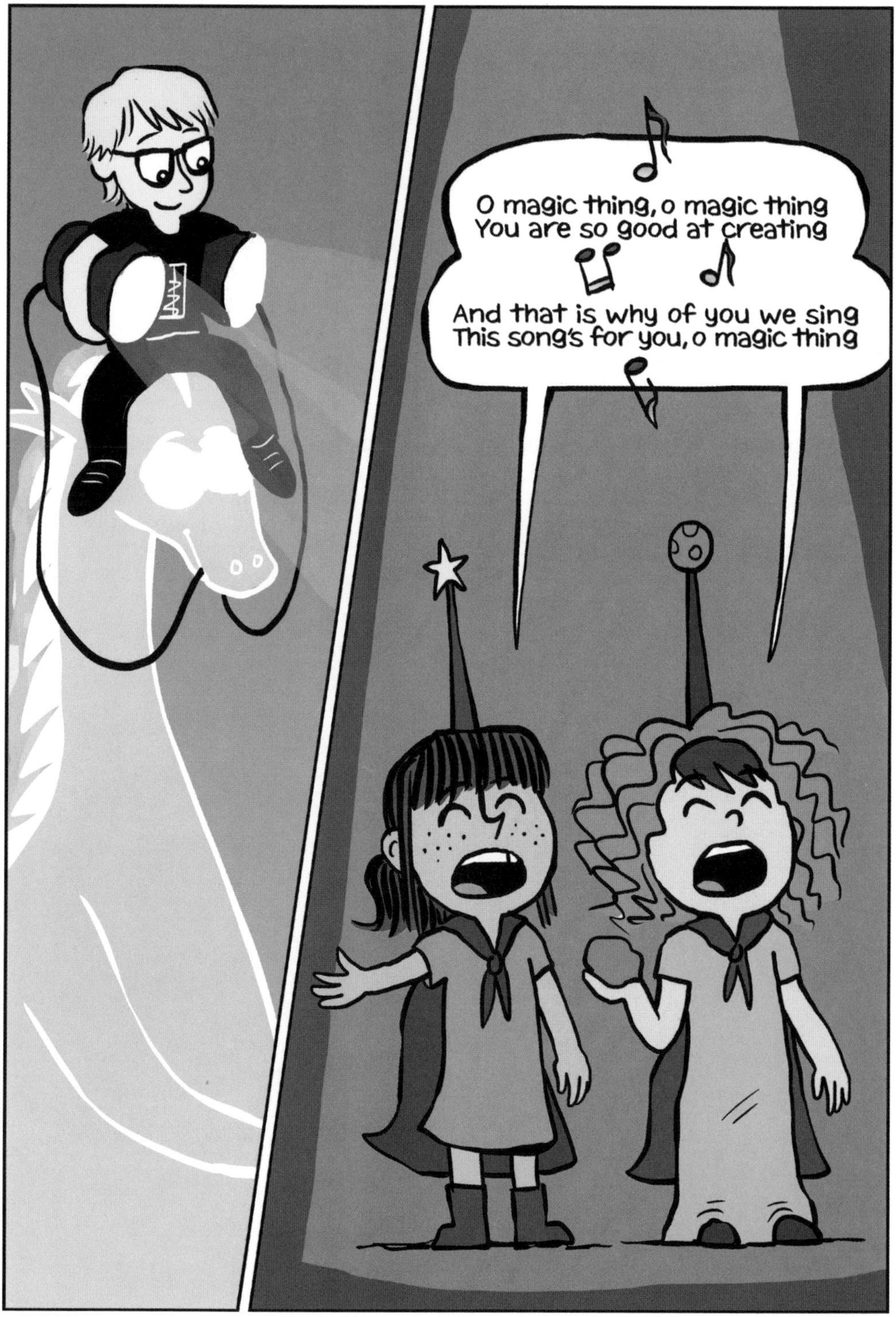
O magic thing, o magic thing
You are so good at creating
And that is why of you we sing
This song's for you, o magic thing

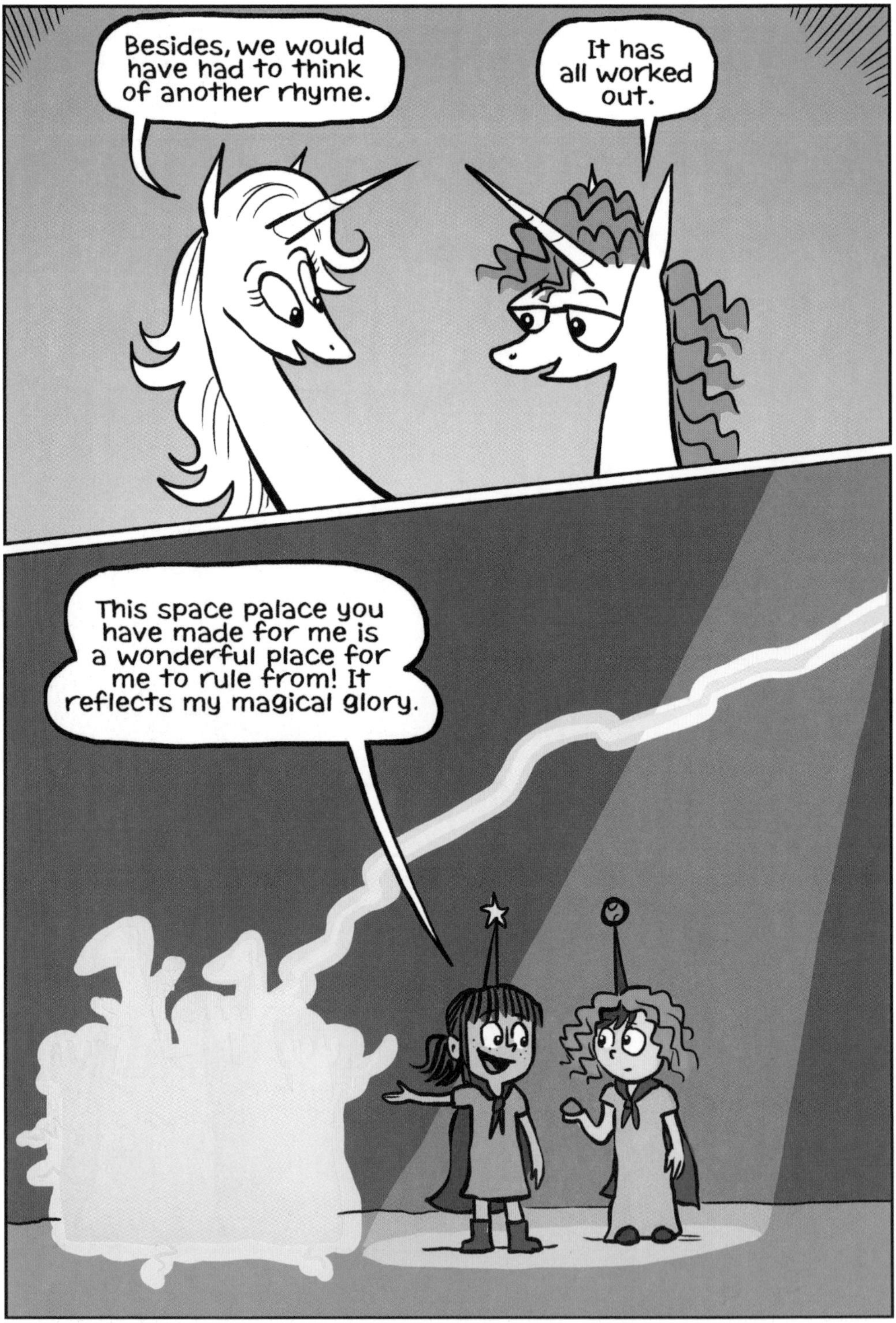
Besides, we would have had to think of another rhyme.
It has all worked out.
This space palace you have made for me is a wonderful place for me to rule from! It reflects my magical glory.

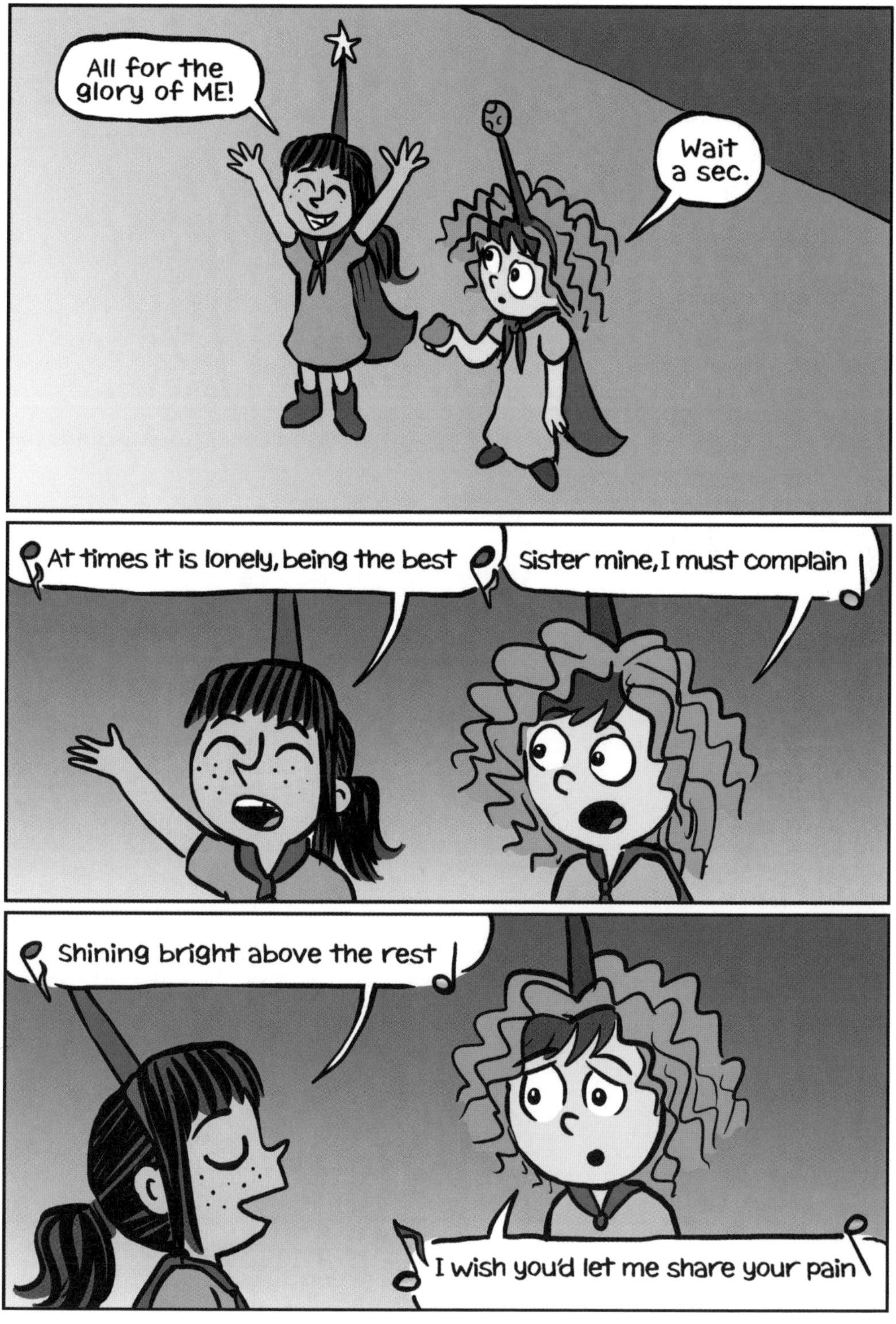
All for the glory of ME!
Wait a sec.
At times it is lonely, being the best
Sister mine, I must complain
Shining bright above the rest
I wish you'd let me share your pain

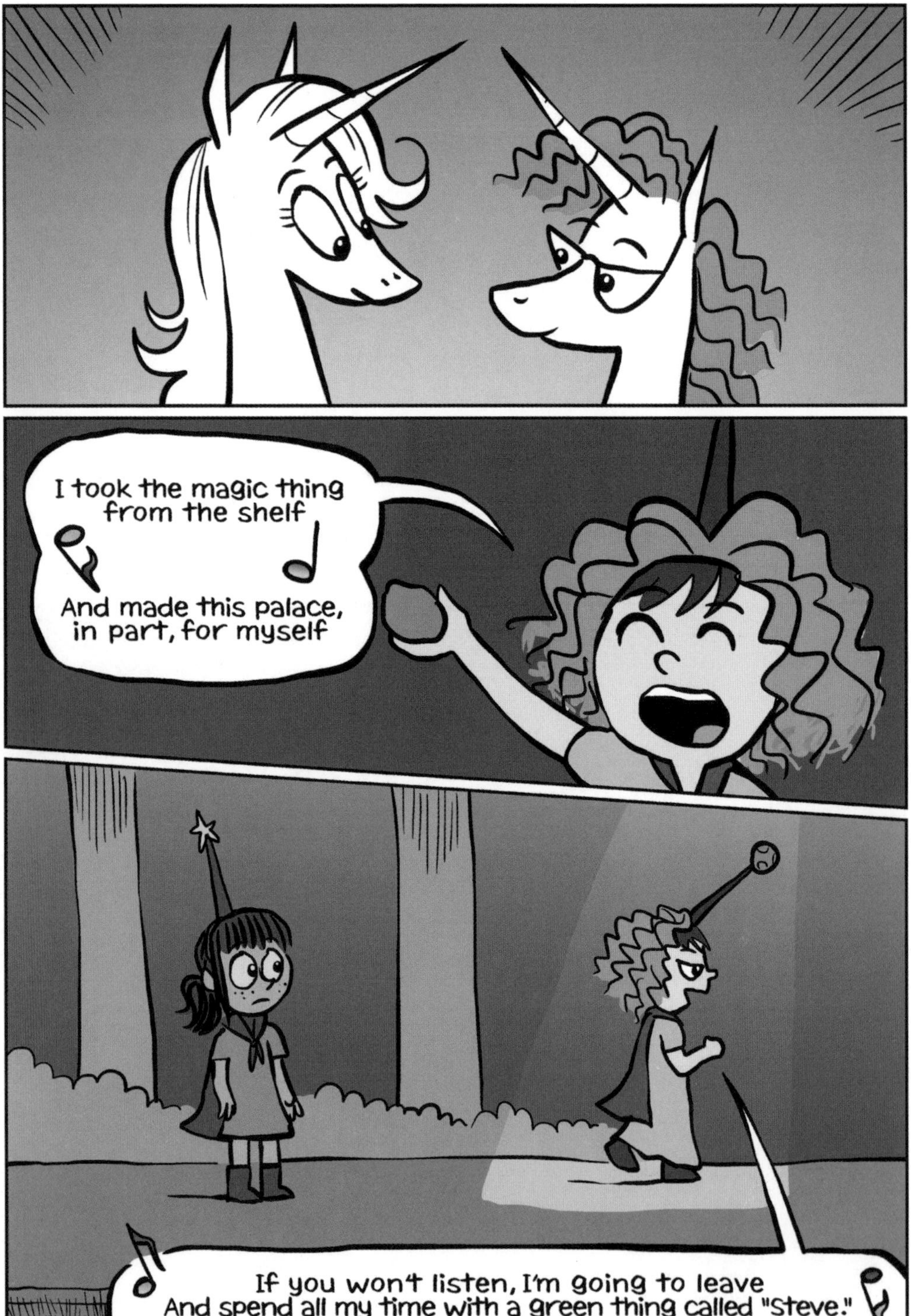
I took the magic thing from the shelf
And made this palace, in part, for myself
If you won't listen, I'm going to leave
And spend all my time with a green thing called "Steve."

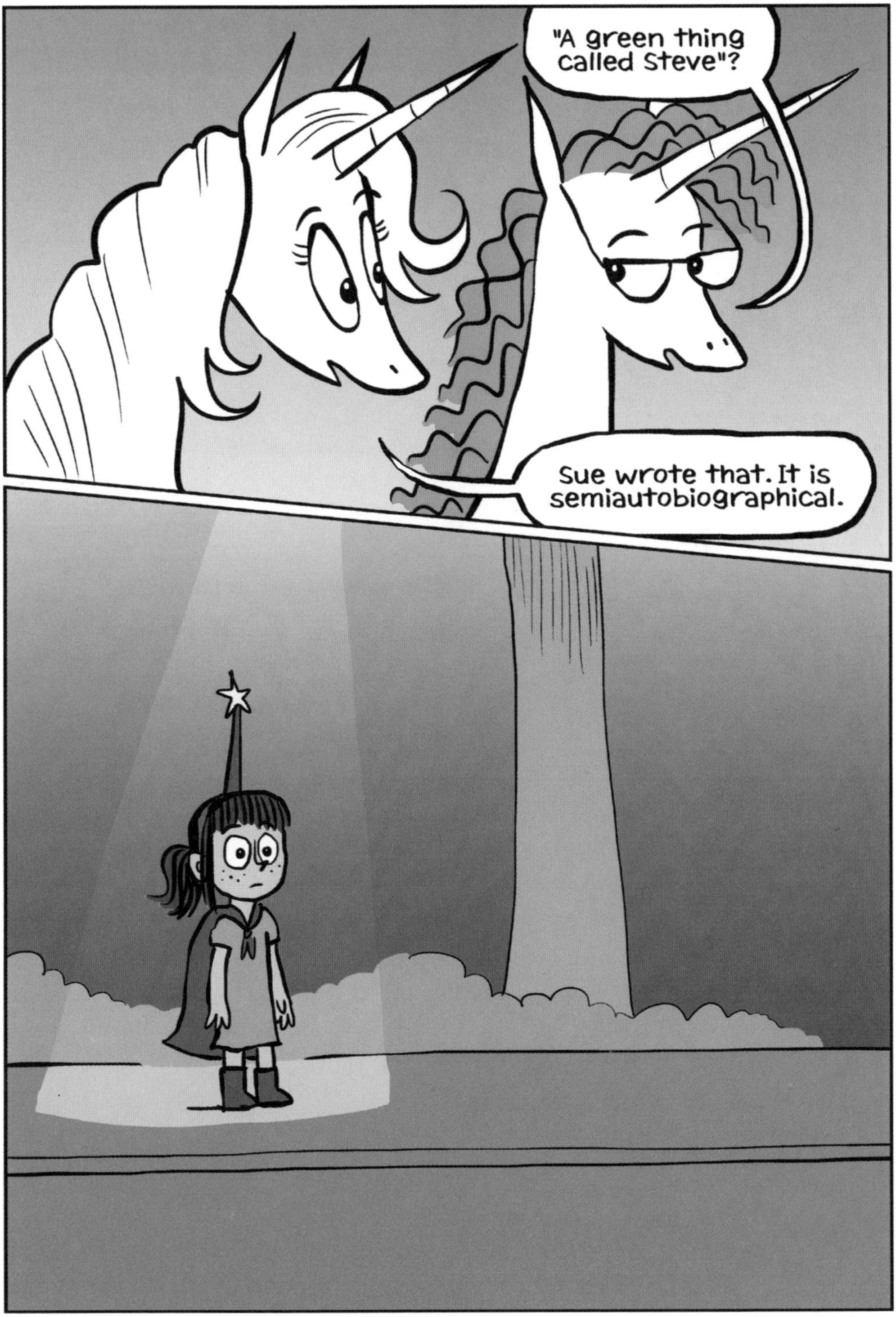
"A green thing called Steve"?
Sue wrote that. It is semiautobiographical.

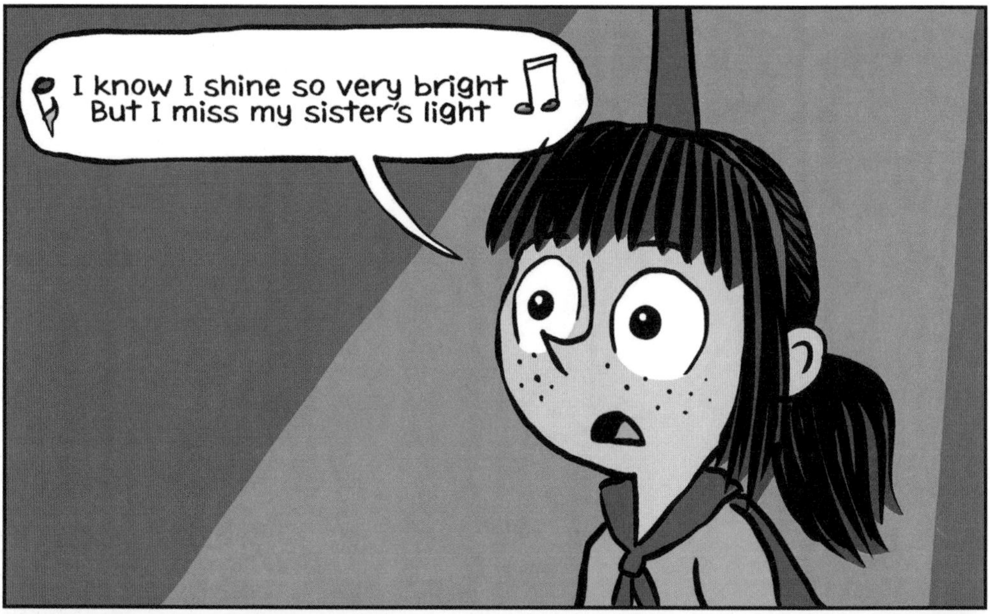
I know I shine so very bright
But I miss my sister's light

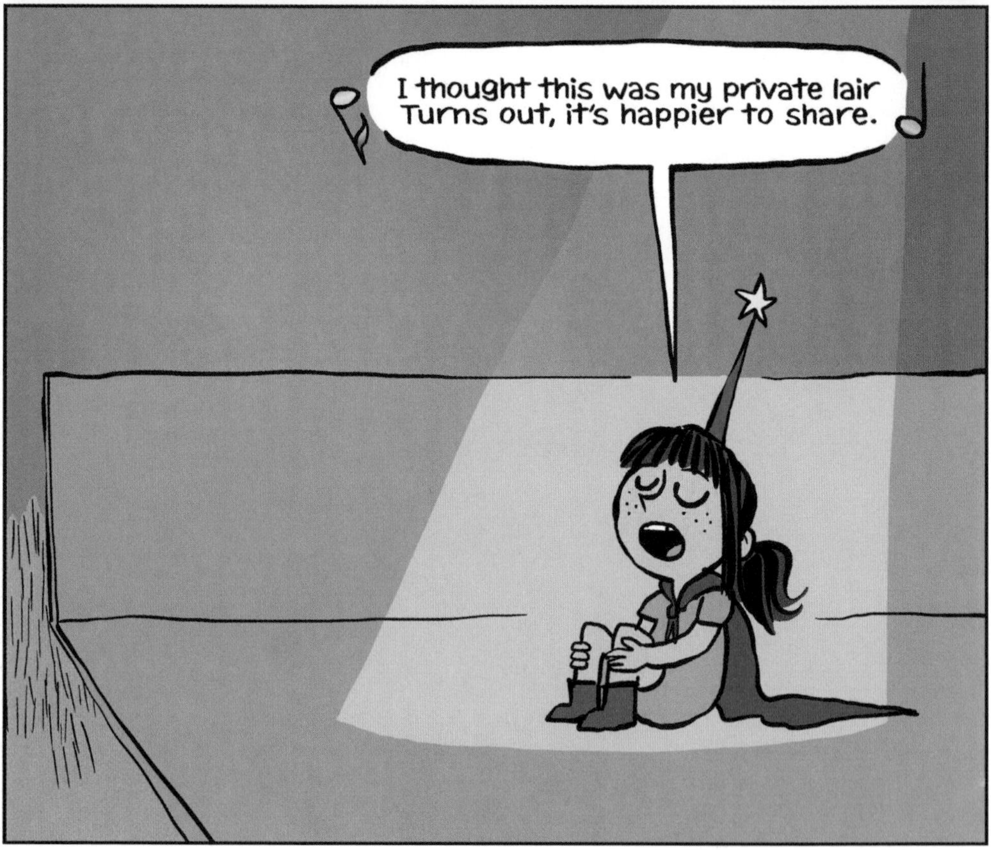
I thought this was my private lair
Turns out, it's happier to share.

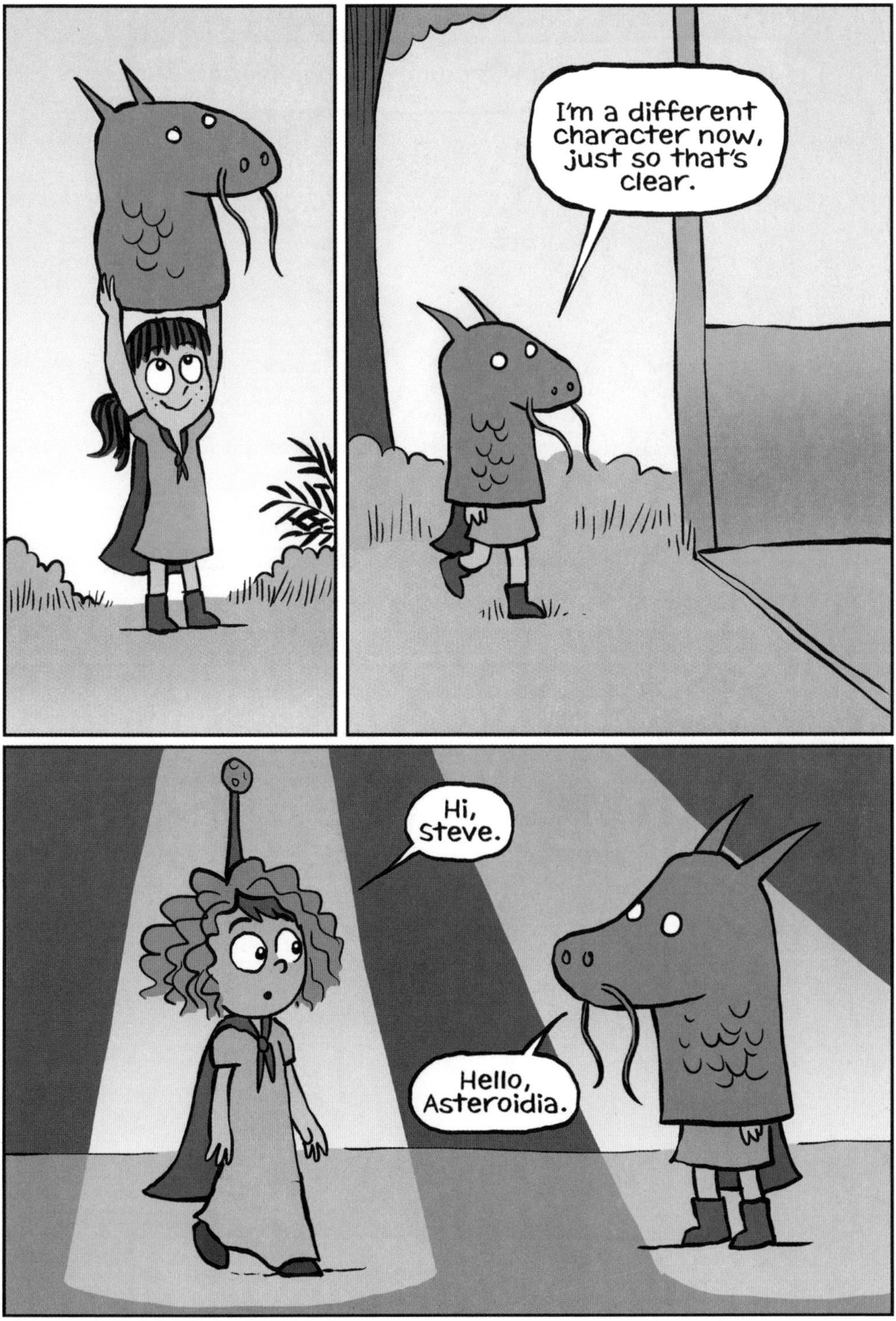
I'm a different character now, just so that's clear.
Hi, Steve.
Hello, Asteroidia.

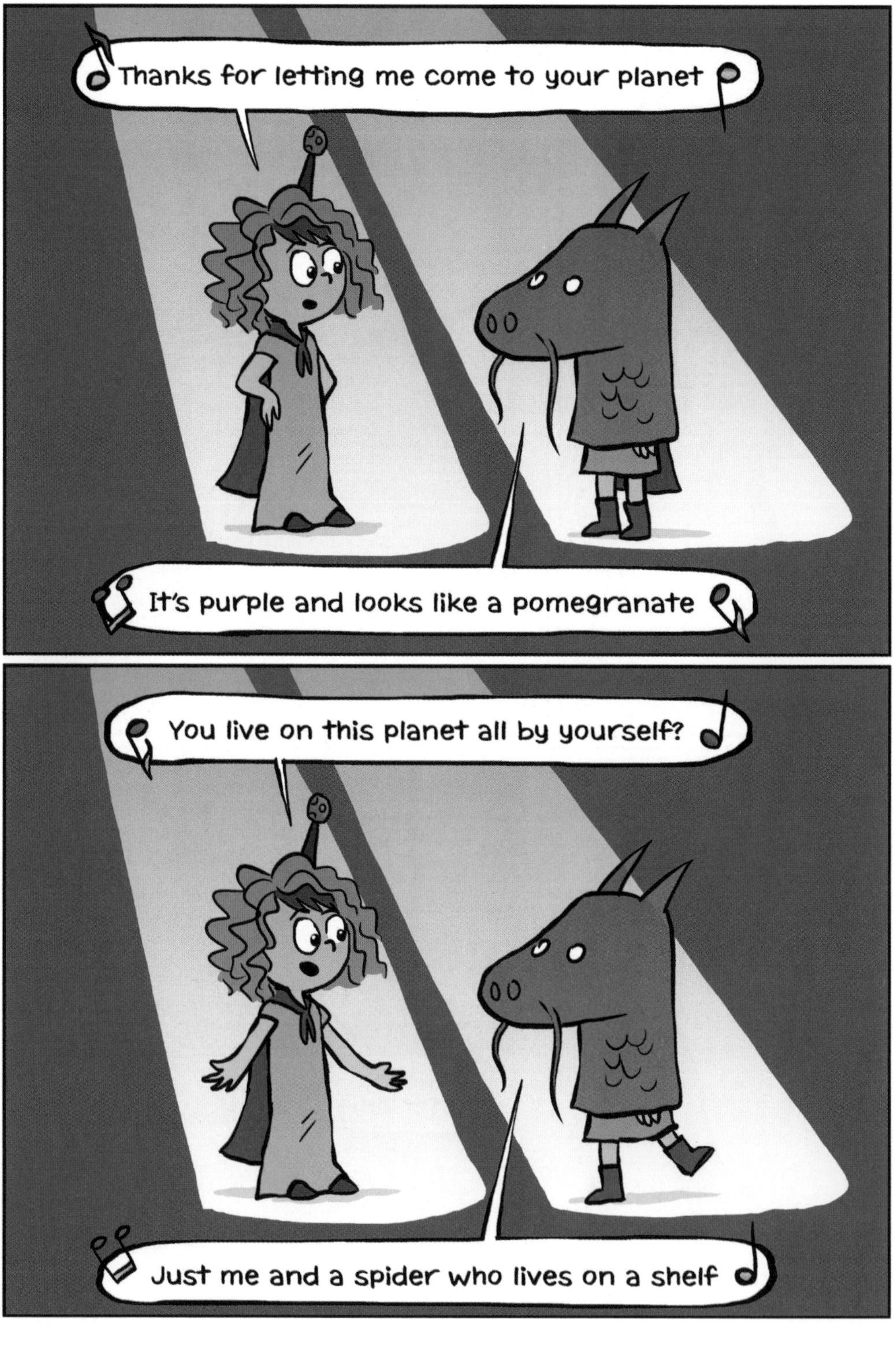
Thanks for letting me come to your planet
It's purple and looks like a pomegranate
You live on this planet all by yourself?
Just me and a spider who lives on a shelf

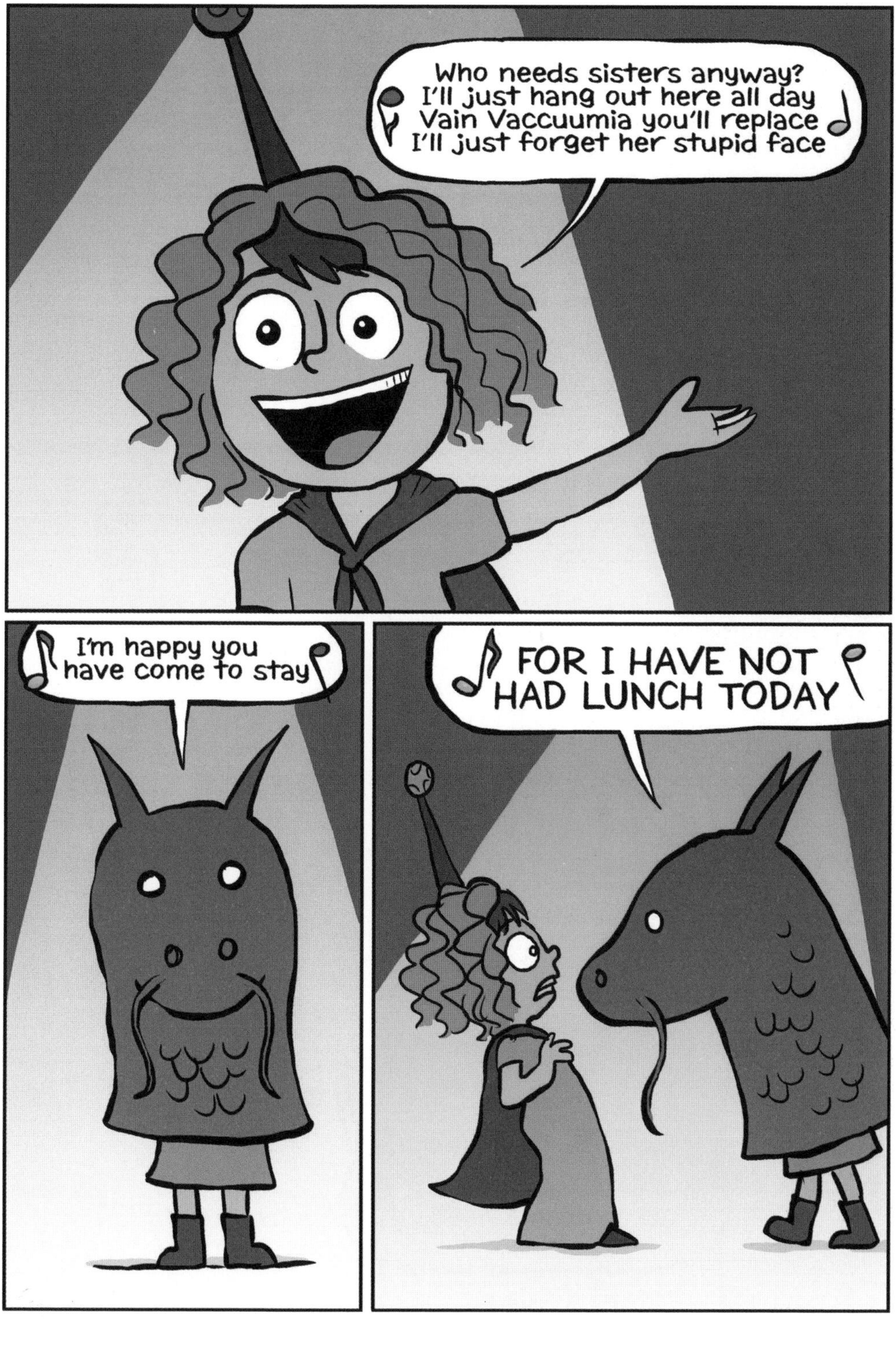
Who needs sisters anyway? I'll just hang out here all day Vain Vaccuumia you'll replace I'll just forget her stupid face
I'm happy you have come to stay
FOR I HAVE NOT HAD LUNCH TODAY

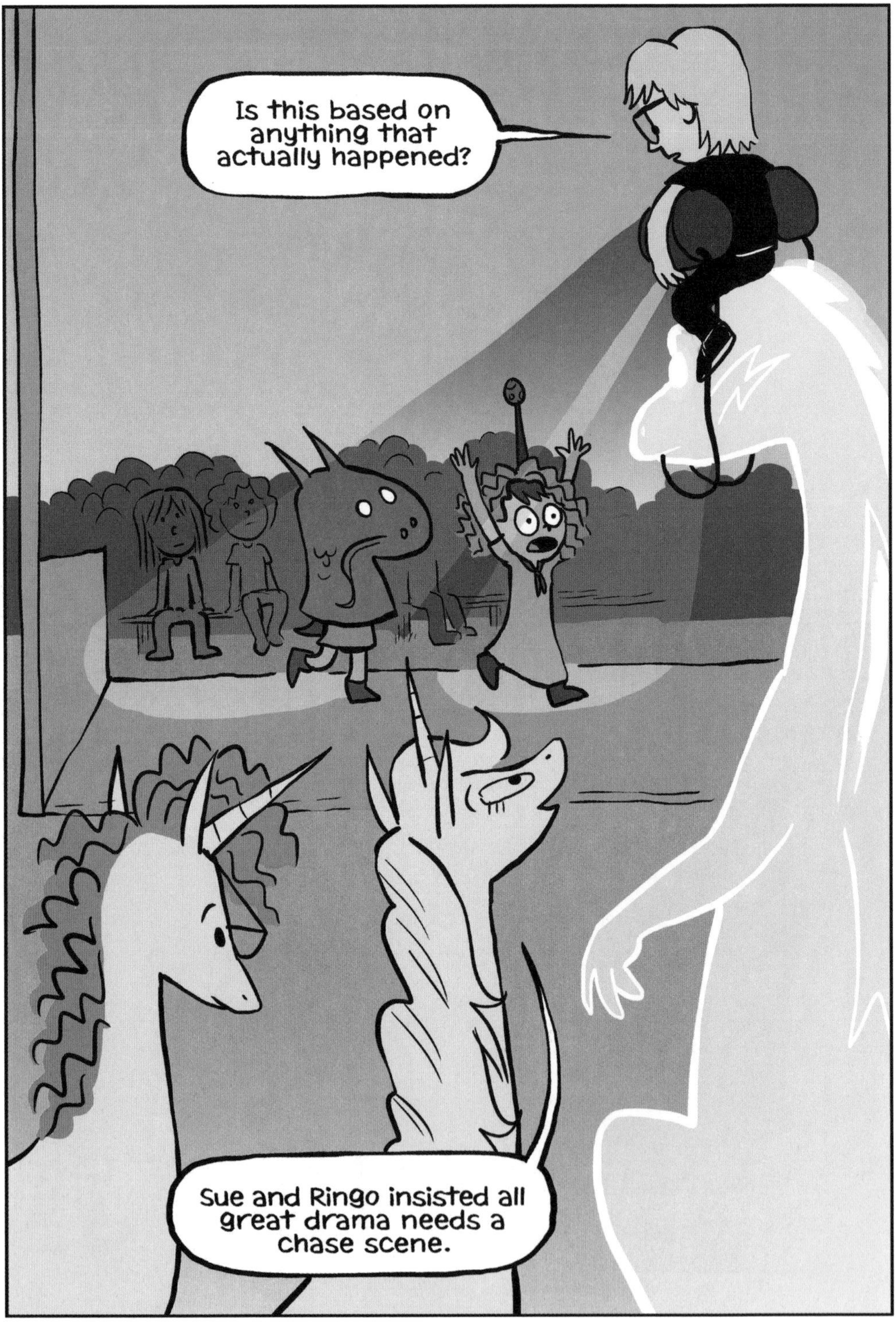
Is this based on anything that actually happened?
Sue and Ringo insisted all great drama needs a chase scene.

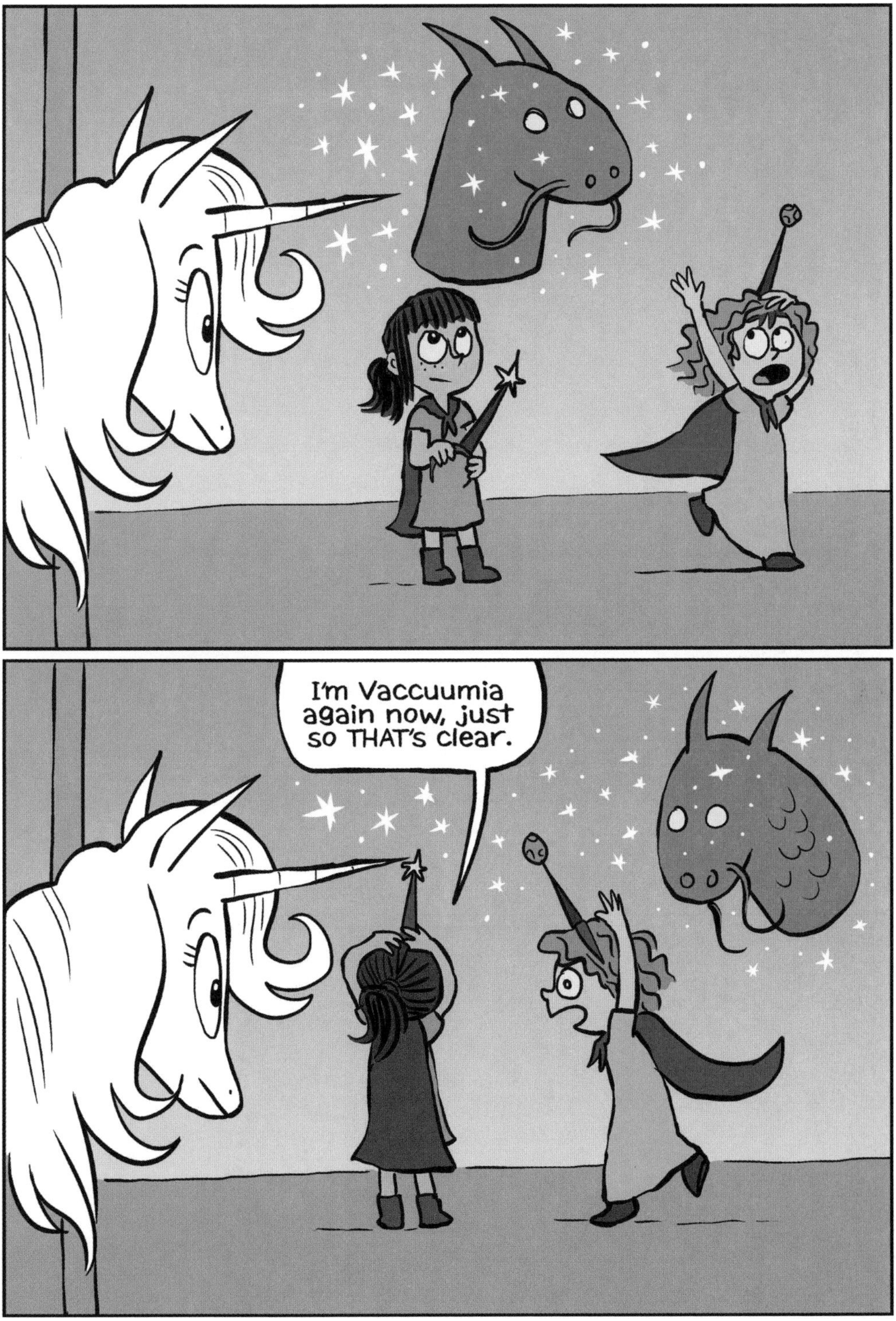
I'm Vaccuumia again now, just so THAT's clear.

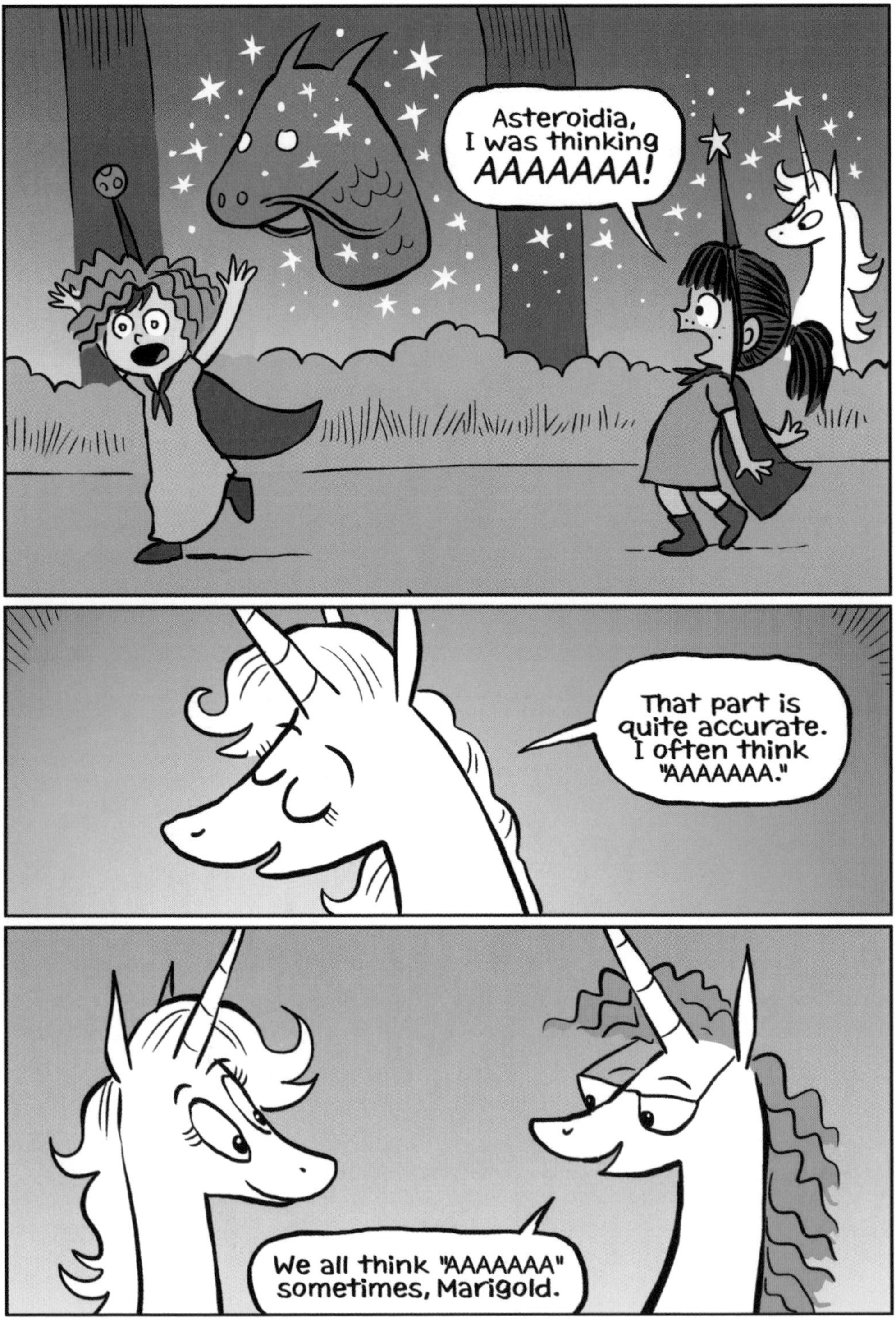

Asteroidia, I was thinking AAAAAAA!
That part is quite accurate. I often think "AAAAAAA."
We all think "AAAAAAA" sometimes, Marigold.

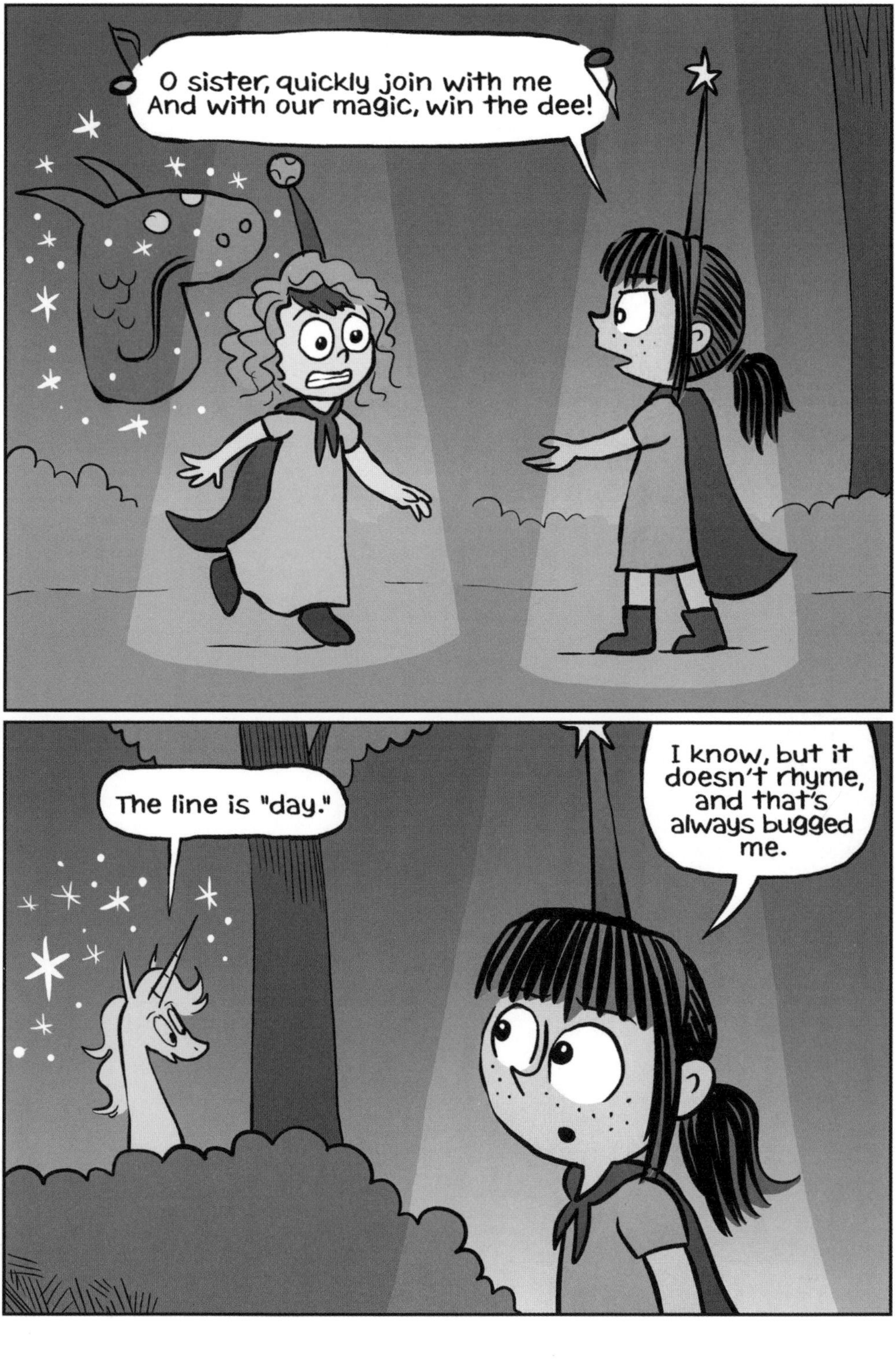
O sister, quickly join with me
And with our magic, win the dee!
The line is "day."
I know, but it doesn't rhyme, and that's always bugged me.

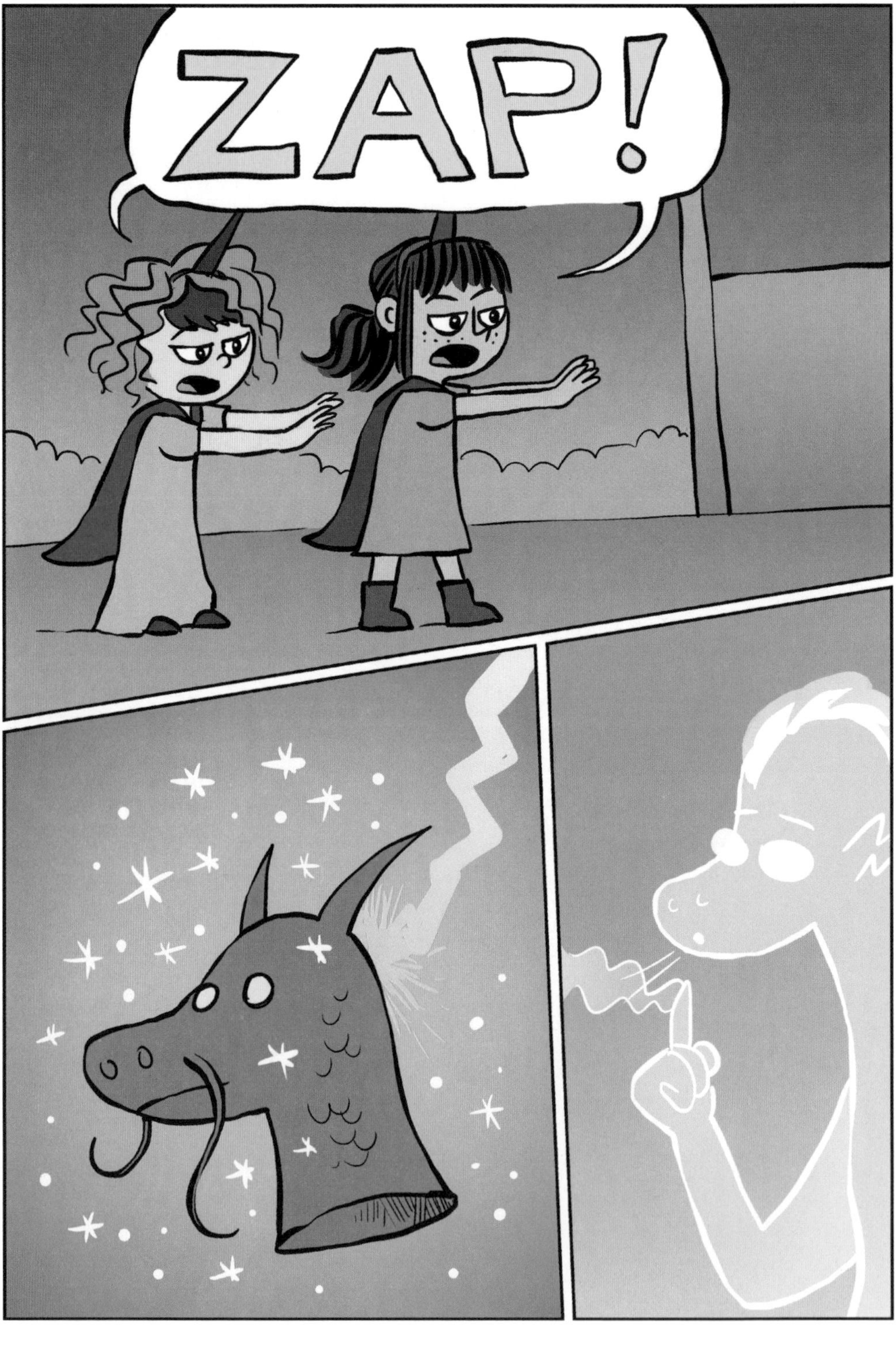
ZAP!

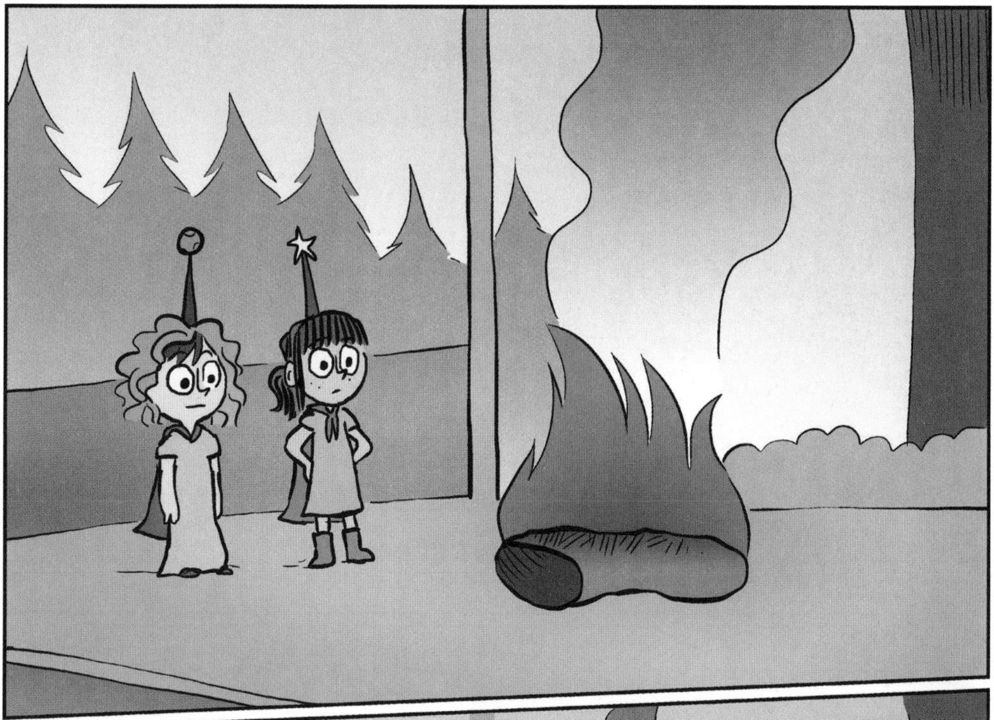

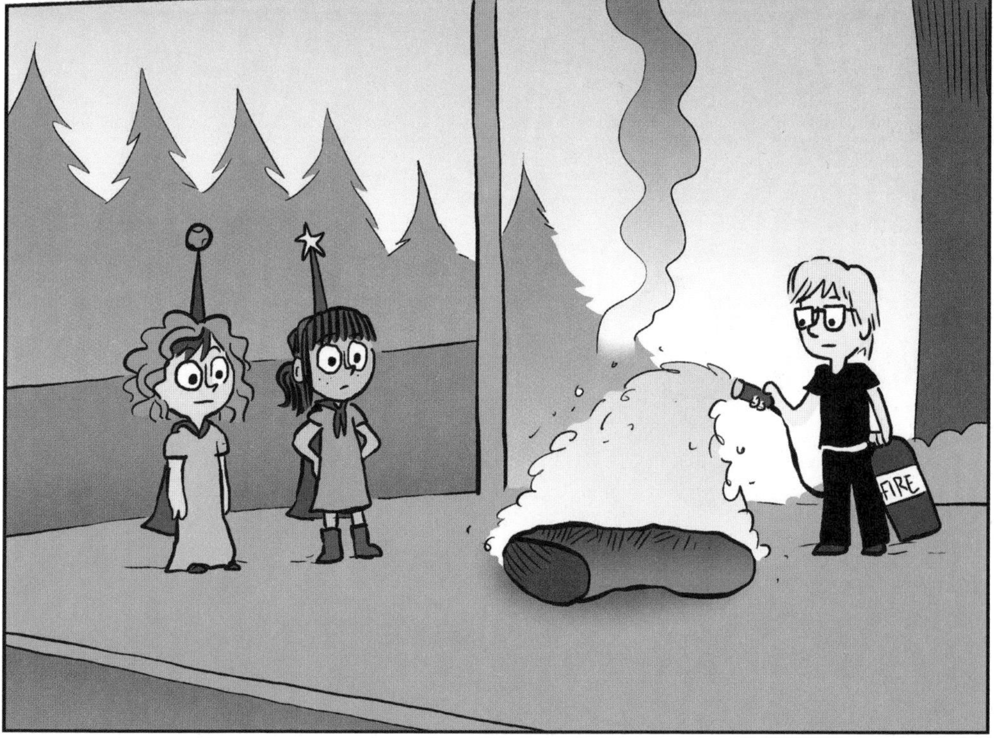

FIRE

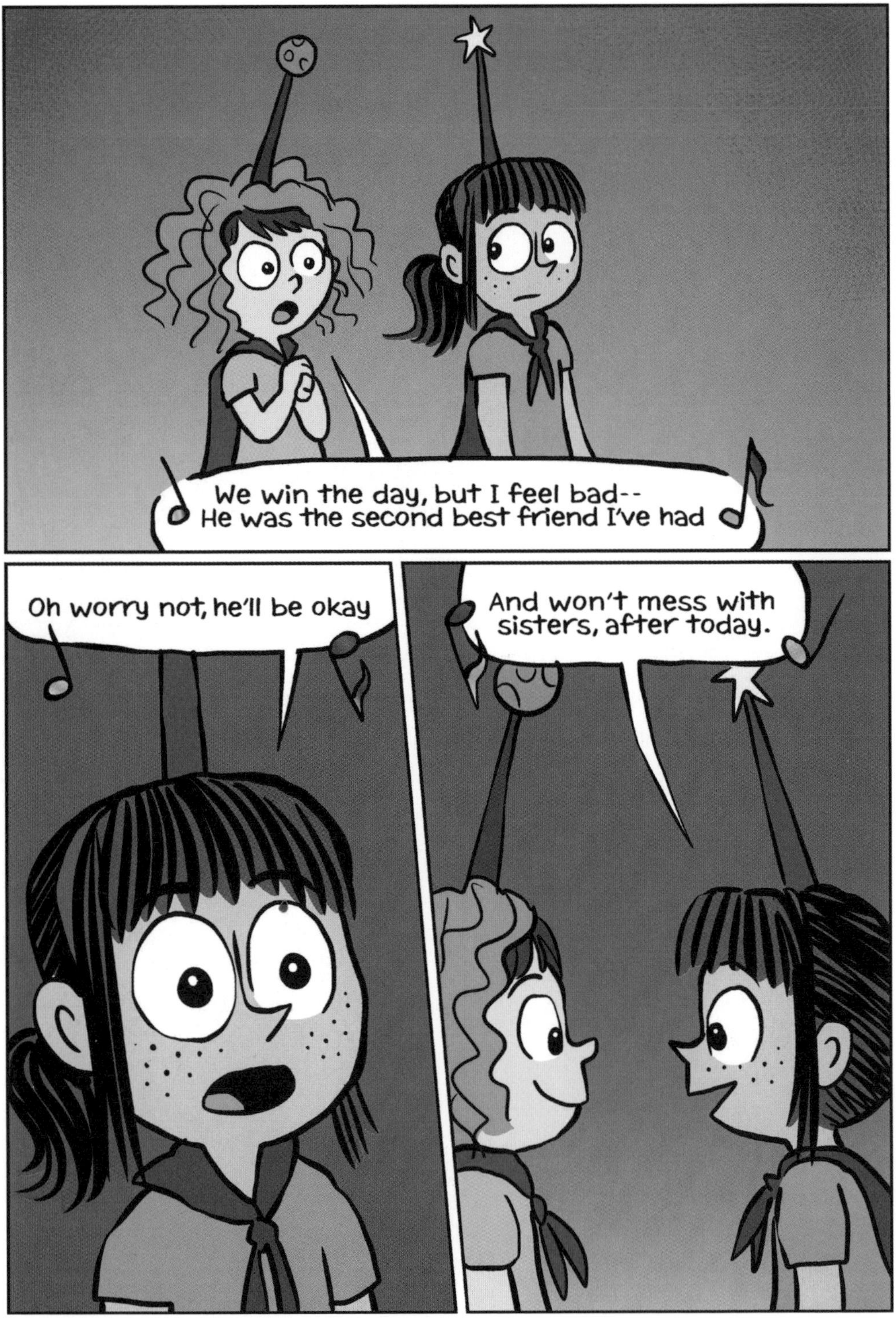
We win the day, but I feel bad--
He was the second best friend I've had
Oh worry not, he'll be okay
And won't mess with sisters, after today.

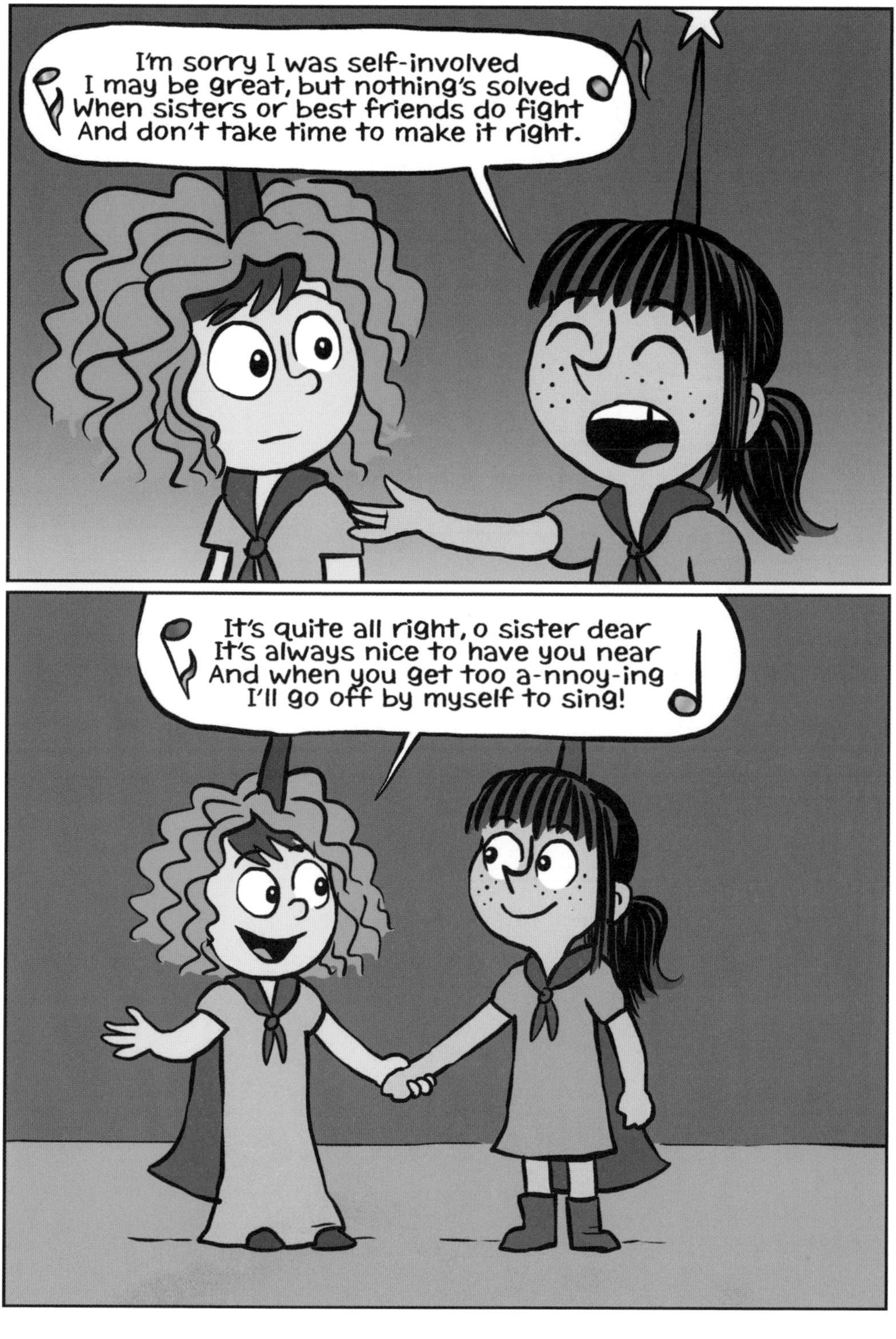
I'm sorry I was self-involved I may be great, but nothing's solved When sisters or best friends do fight And don't take time to make it right.
It's quite all right, o sister dear It's always nice to have you near And when you get too a-nnoy-ing I'll go off by myself to sing!

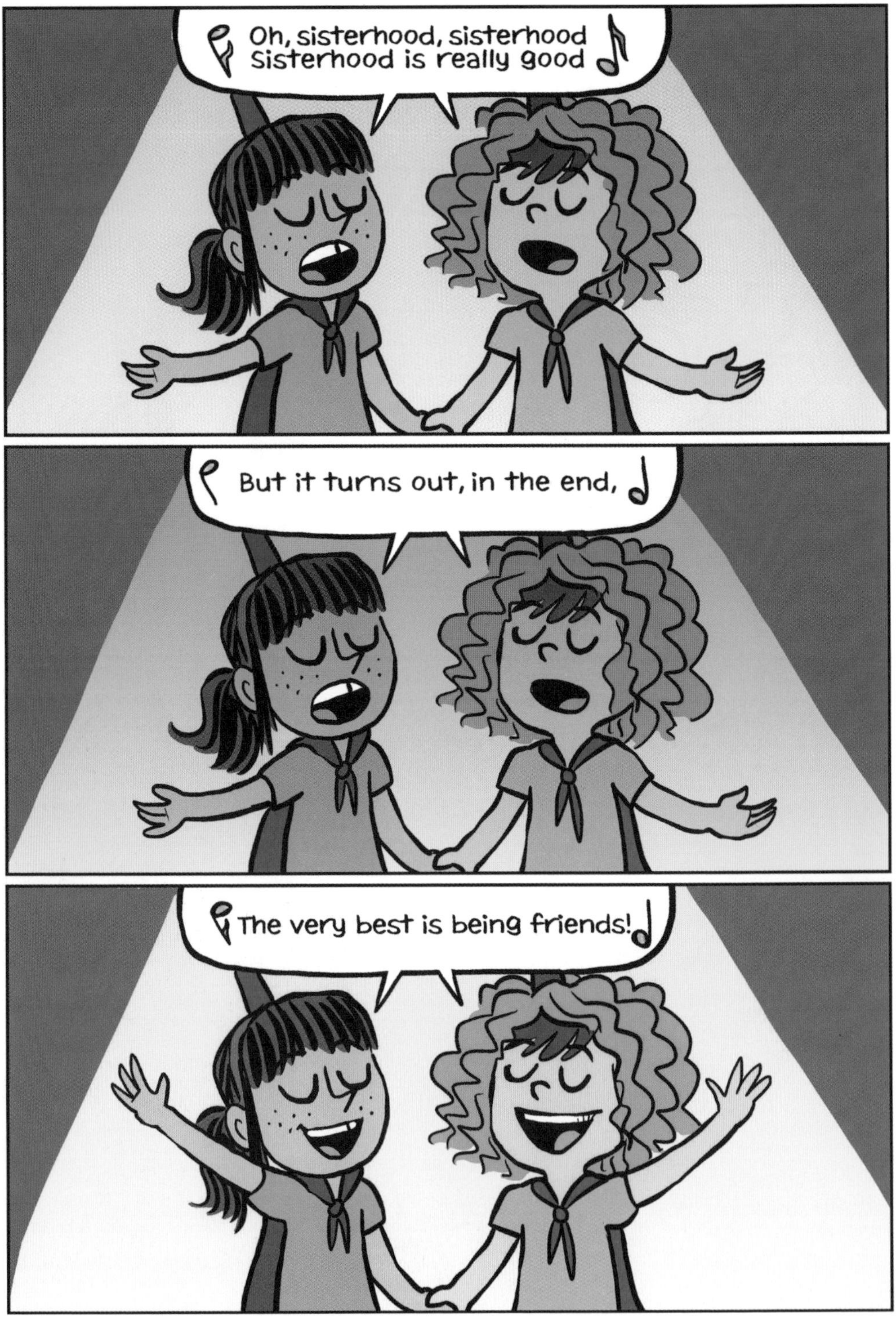
Oh, sisterhood, sisterhood
Sisterhood is really good
But it turns out, in the end,
The very best is being friends!

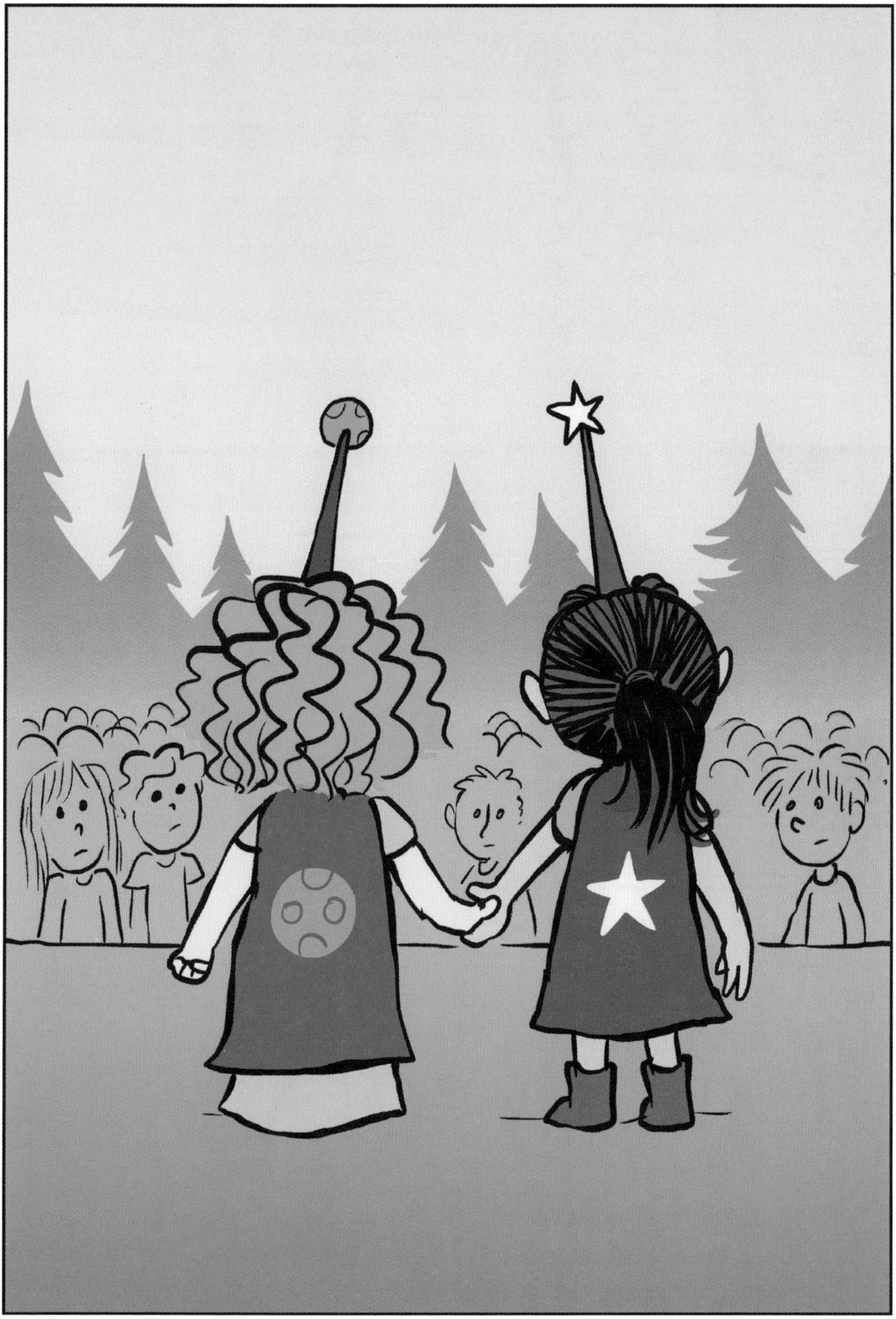

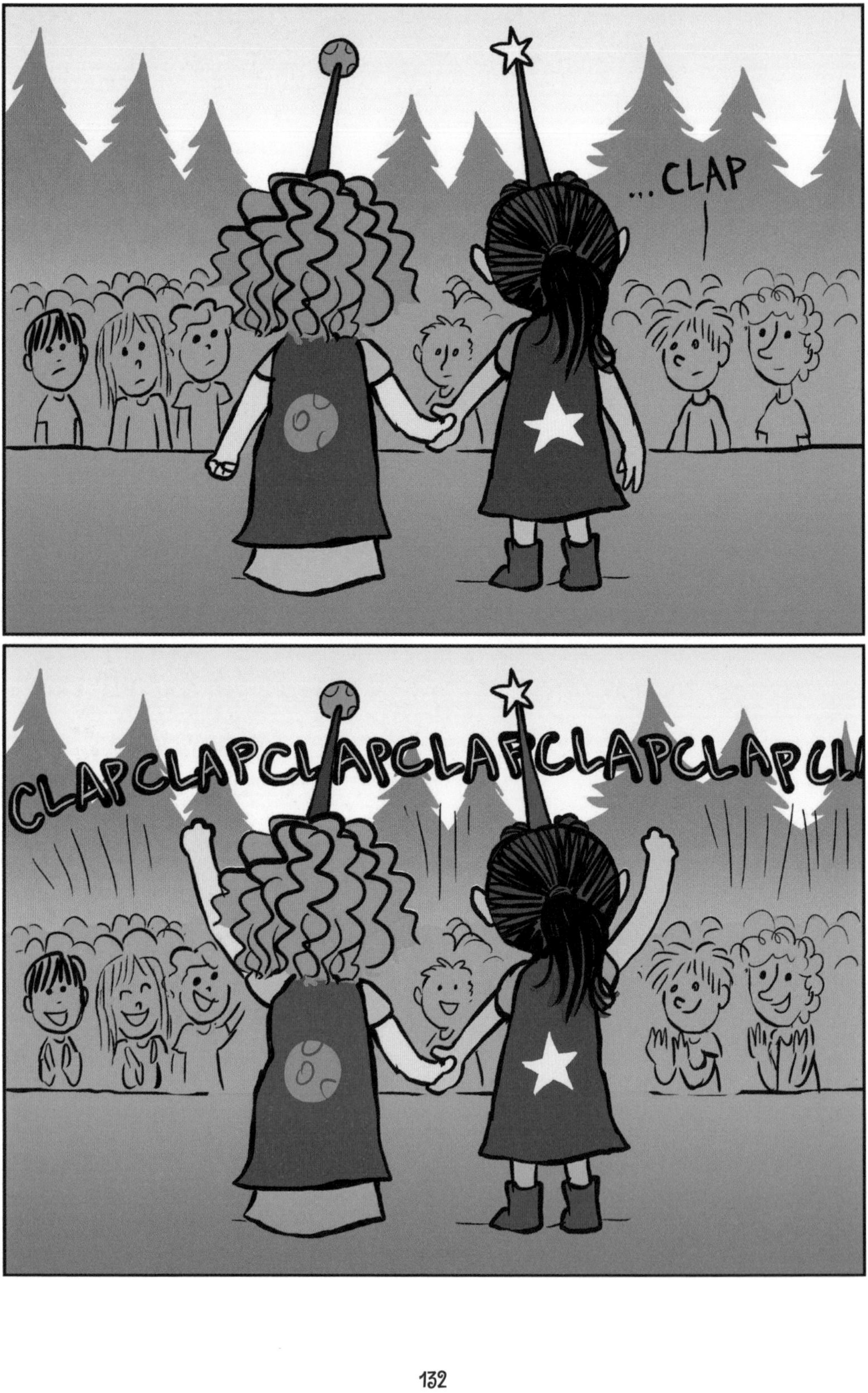
...CLAP
CLAPCLAPCLAPCLAPCLAPCLAPCL

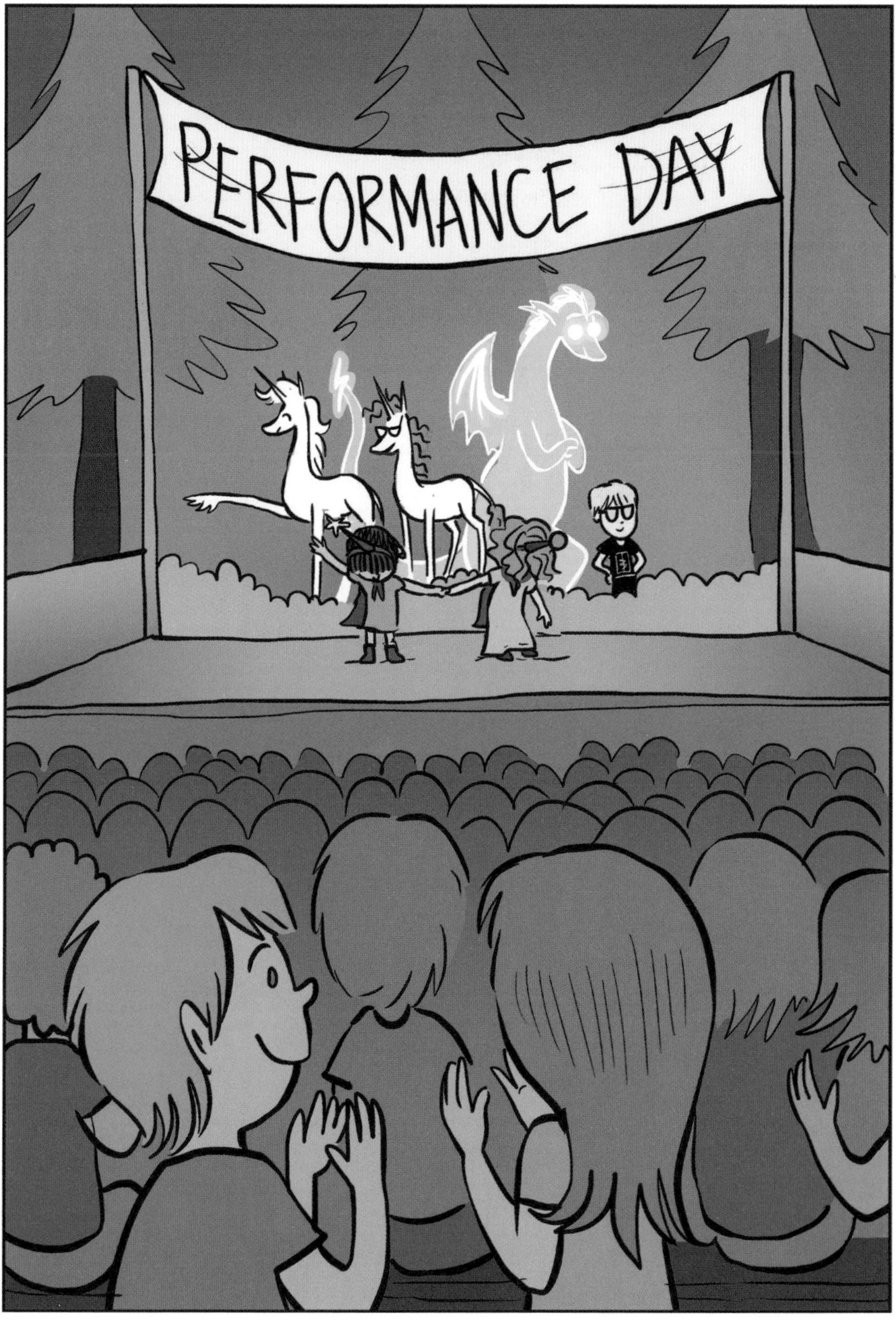
PERFORMANCE DAY

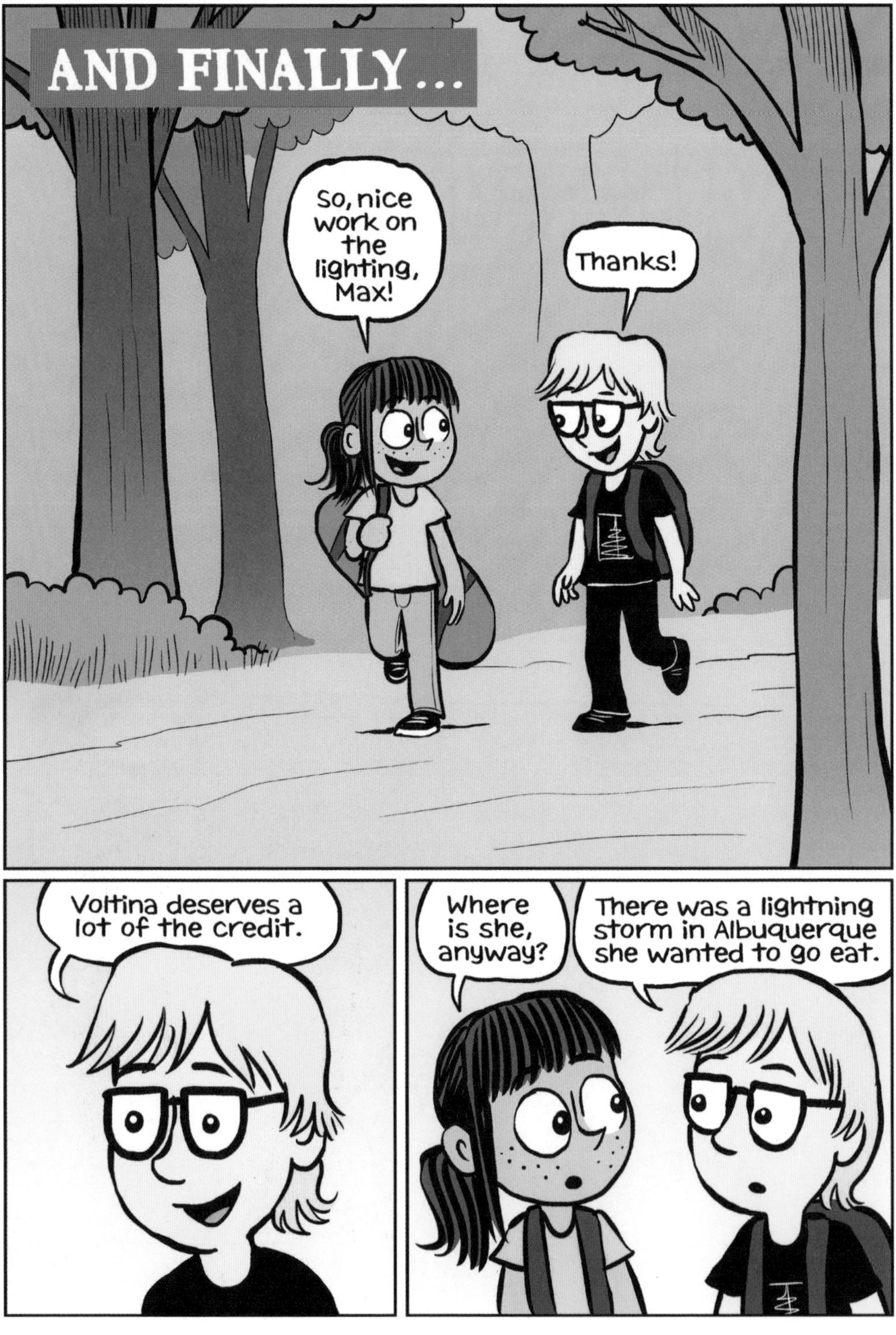
AND FINALLY...
So, nice work on the lighting, Max!
Thanks!
Voltina deserves a lot of the credit.
Where is she, anyway?
There was a lightning storm in Albuquerque she wanted to go eat.

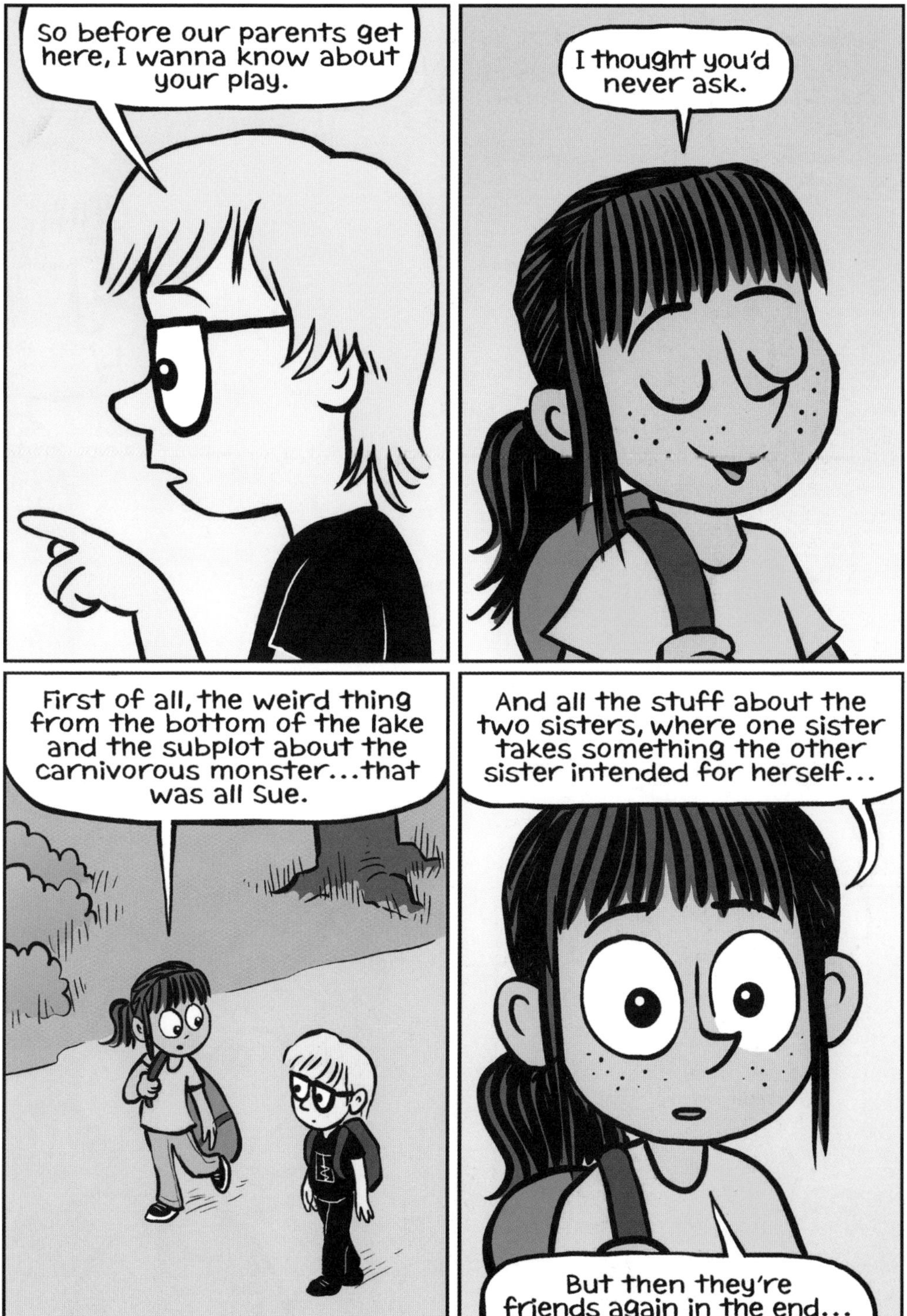
So before our parents get here, I wanna know about your play.
I thought you'd never ask.
First of all, the weird thing from the bottom of the lake and the subplot about the carnivorous monster...that was all Sue.
And all the stuff about the two sisters, where one sister takes something the other sister intended for herself...
But then they're friends again in the end...

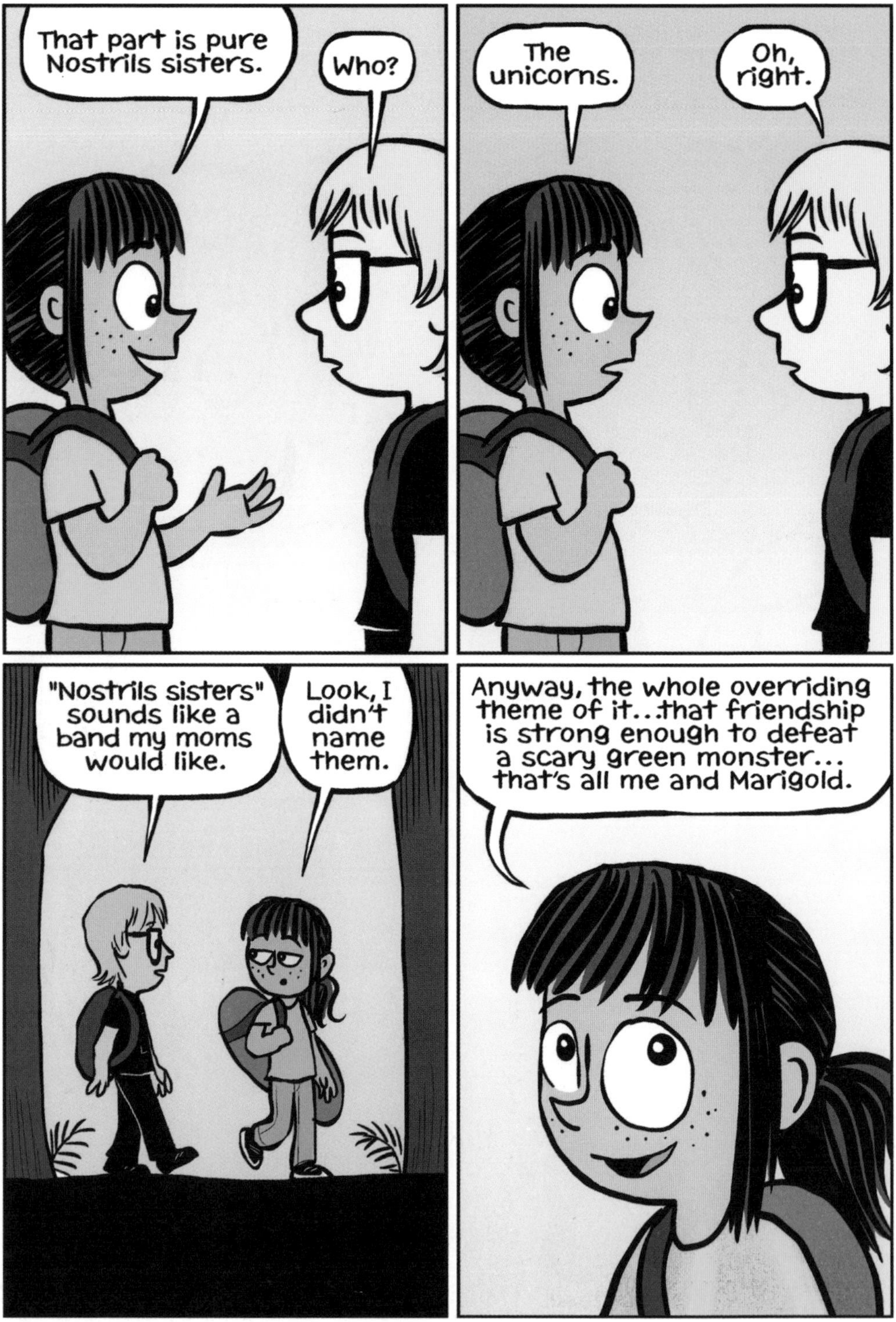
That part is pure Nostrils sisters.
Who?
The unicorns.
Oh, right.
"Nostrils sisters" sounds like a band my moms would like.
Look, I didn't name them.
Anyway, the whole overriding theme of it...that friendship is strong enough to defeat a scary green monster... that's all me and Marigold.

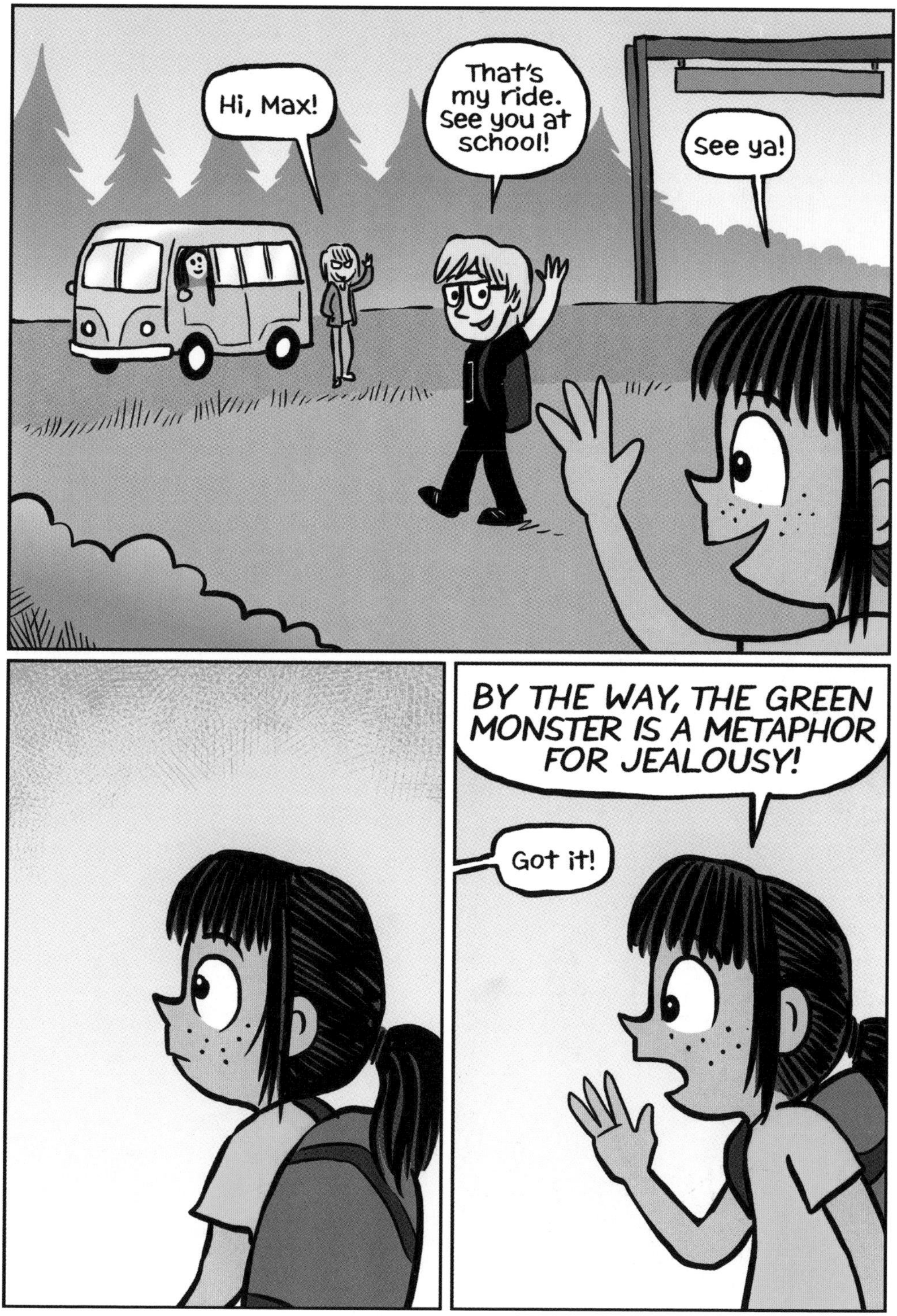
Hi, Max!
That's my ride. See you at school!
See ya!
BY THE WAY, THE GREEN MONSTER IS A METAPHOR FOR JEALOUSY!
Got it!

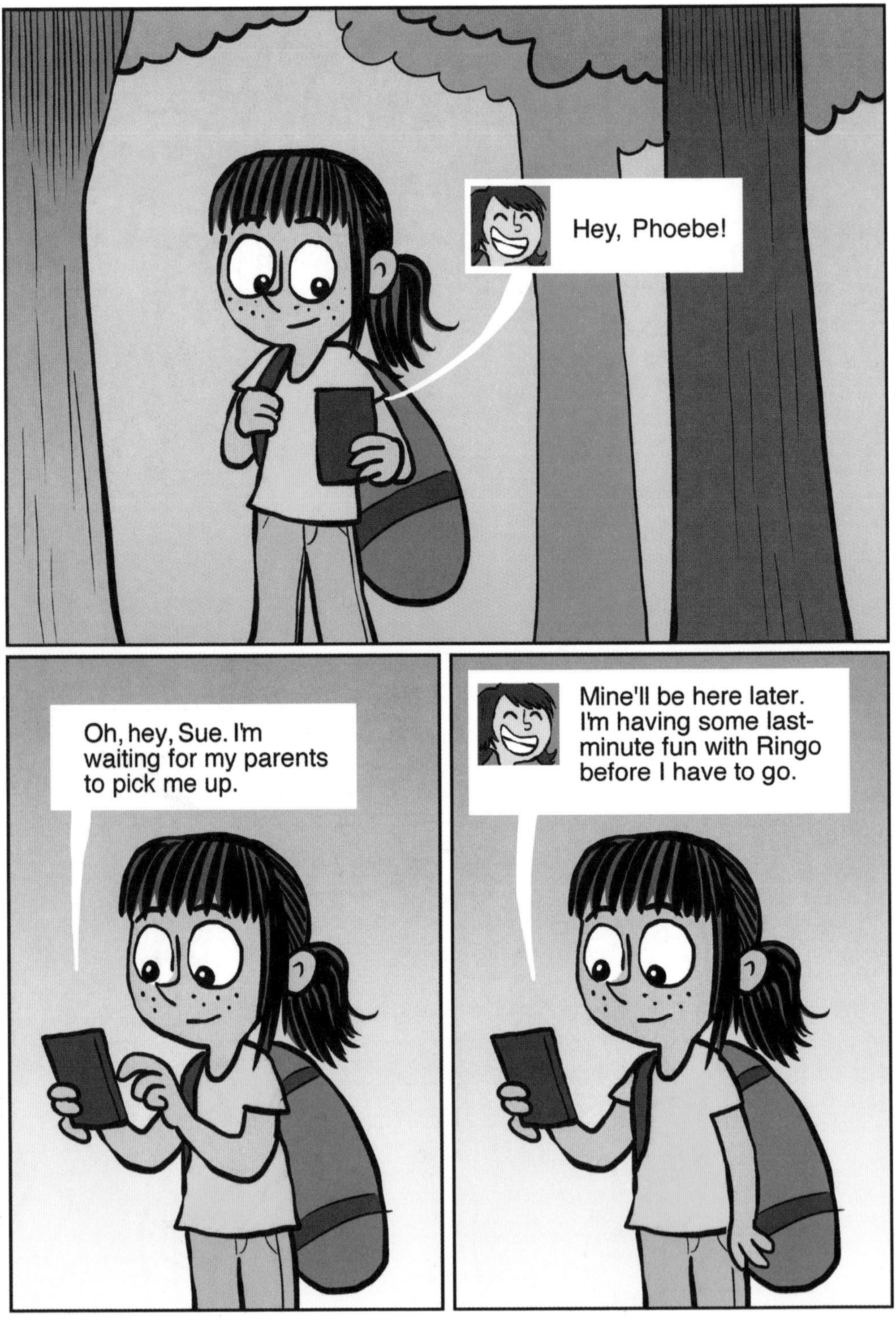
Hey, Phoebe!
Oh, hey, Sue. I'm waiting for my parents to pick me up.
Mine'll be here later. I'm having some last-minute fun with Ringo before I have to go.

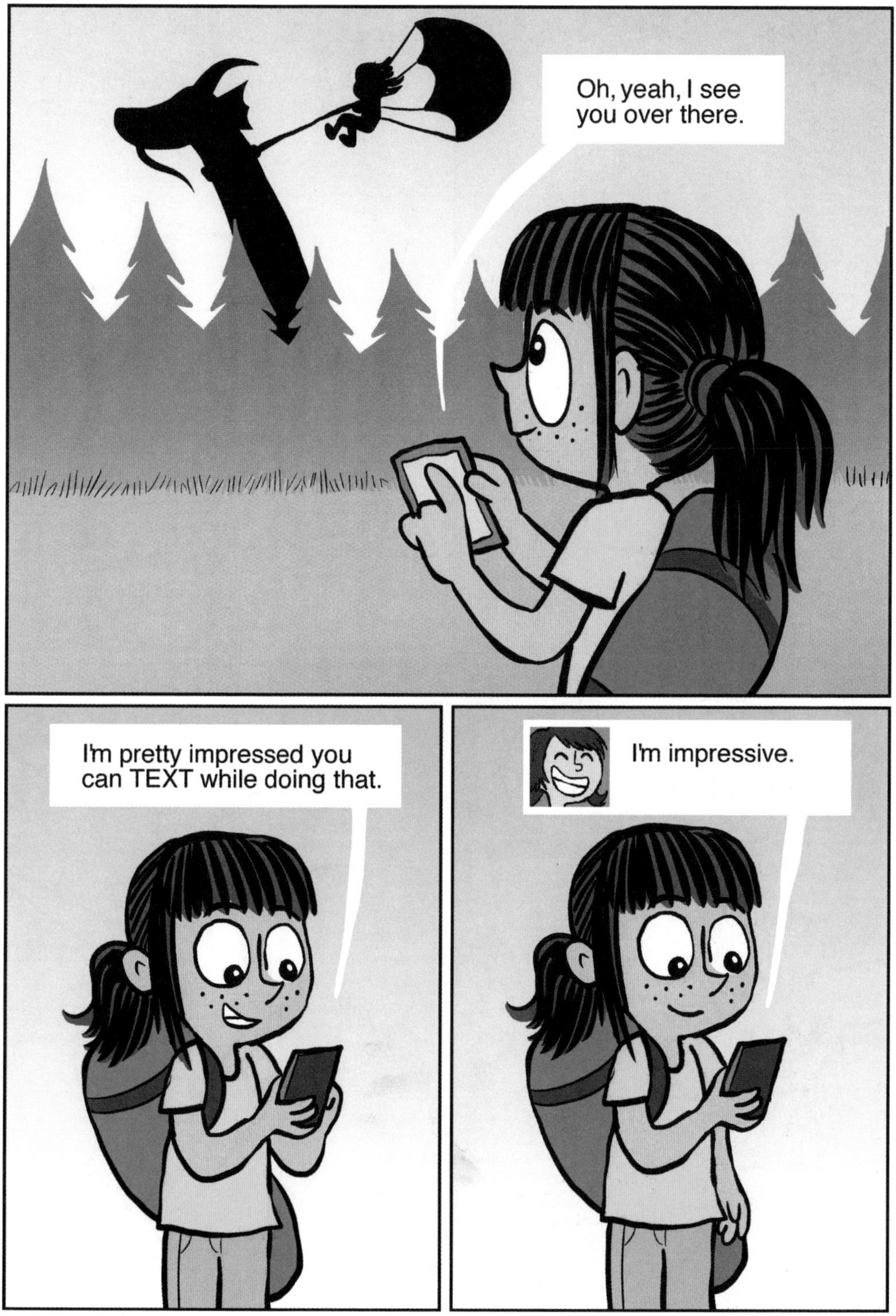
Oh, yeah, I see you over there.
I'm pretty impressed you can TEXT while doing that.
I'm impressive.

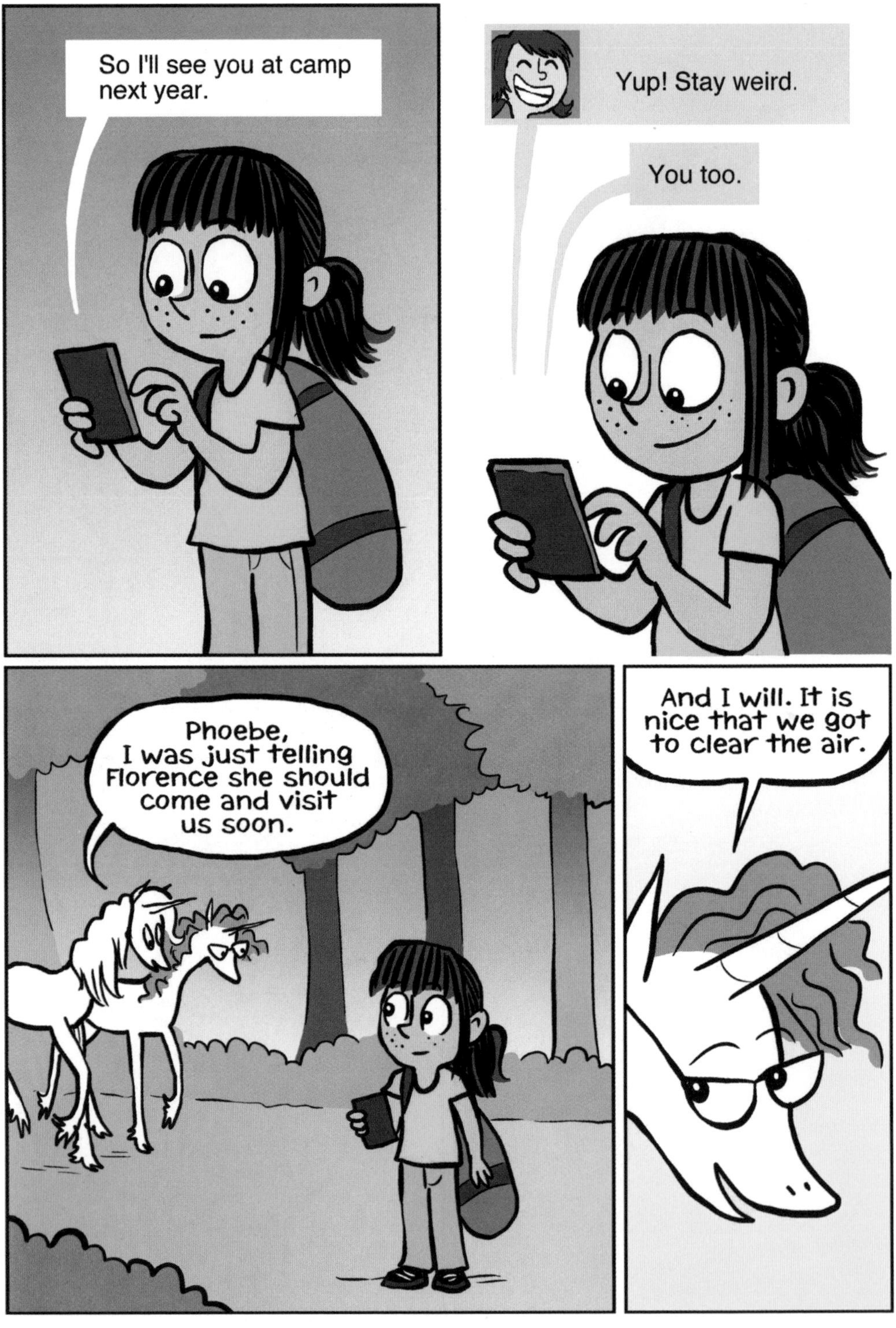
So I'll see you at camp next year.
Yup! Stay weird.
You too.
Phoebe, I was just telling Florence she should come and visit us soon.
And I will. It is nice that we got to clear the air.

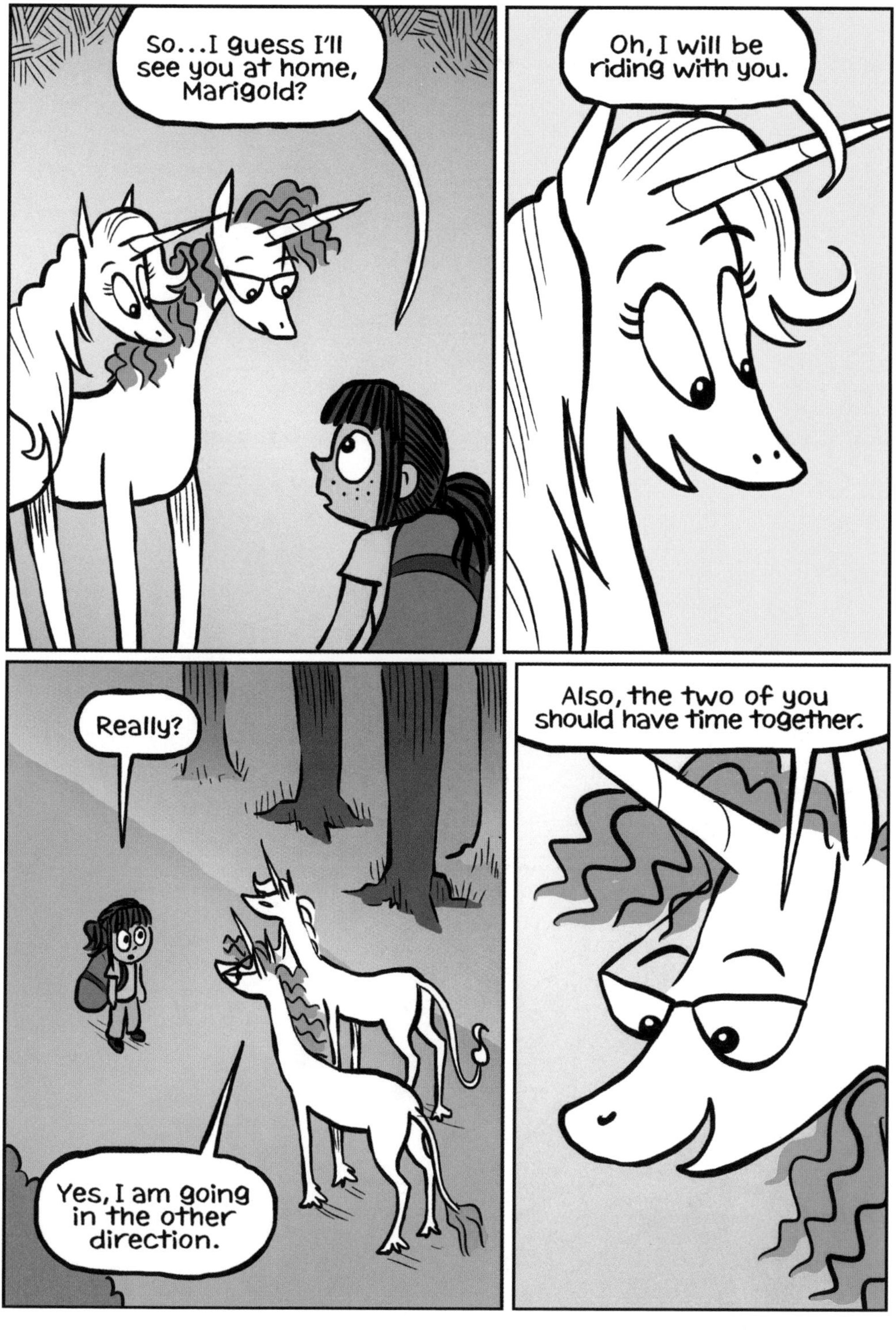

So...I guess I'll see you at home, Marigold?
Oh, I will be riding with you.
Really?
Yes, I am going in the other direction.
Also, the two of you should have time together.

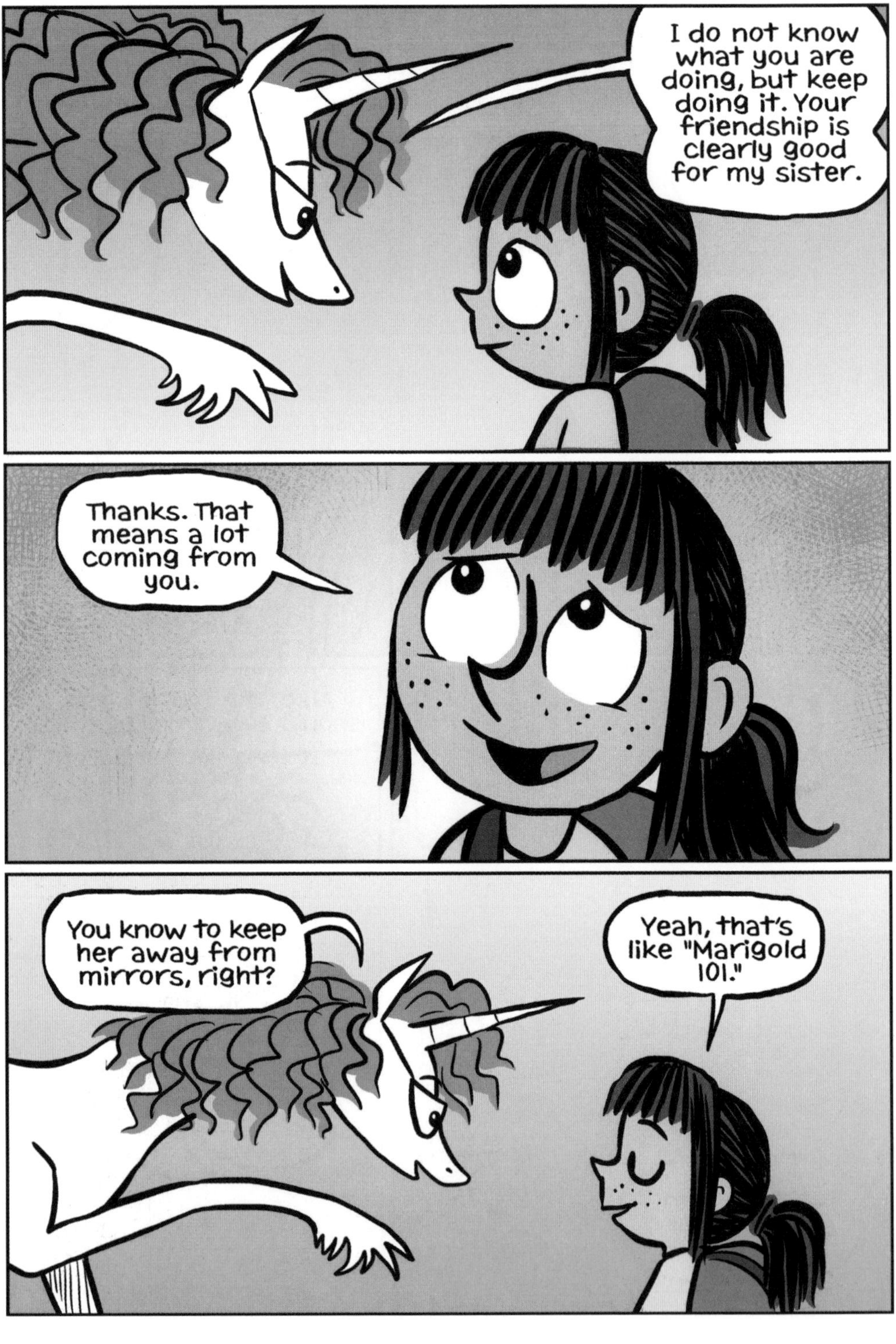
I do not know what you are doing, but keep doing it. Your friendship is clearly good for my sister.
Thanks. That means a lot coming from you.
You know to keep her away from mirrors, right?
Yeah, that's like "Marigold 101."

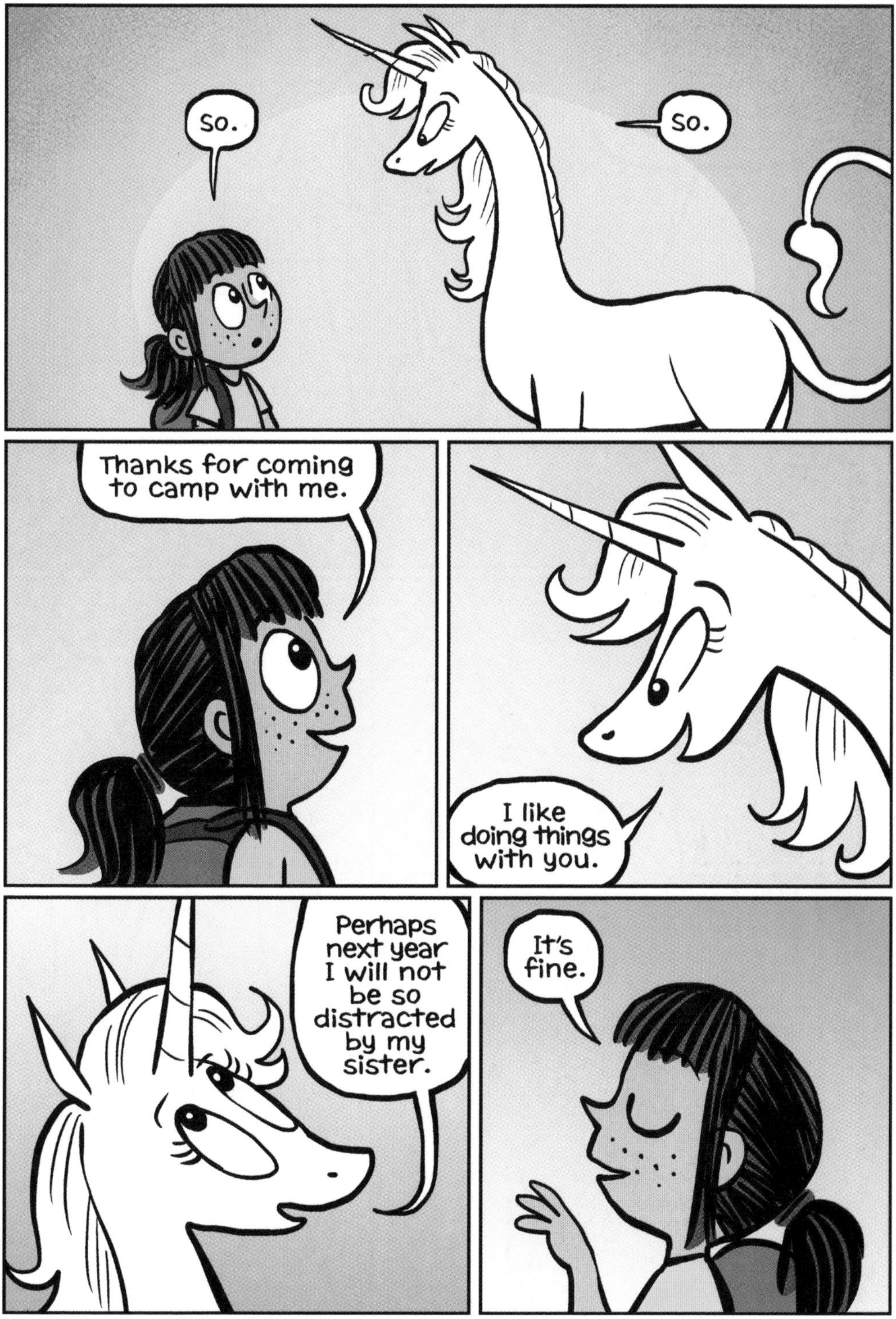
SO.
SO.
Thanks for coming to camp with me.
I like doing things with you.
Perhaps next year I will not be so distracted by my sister.
It's fine.

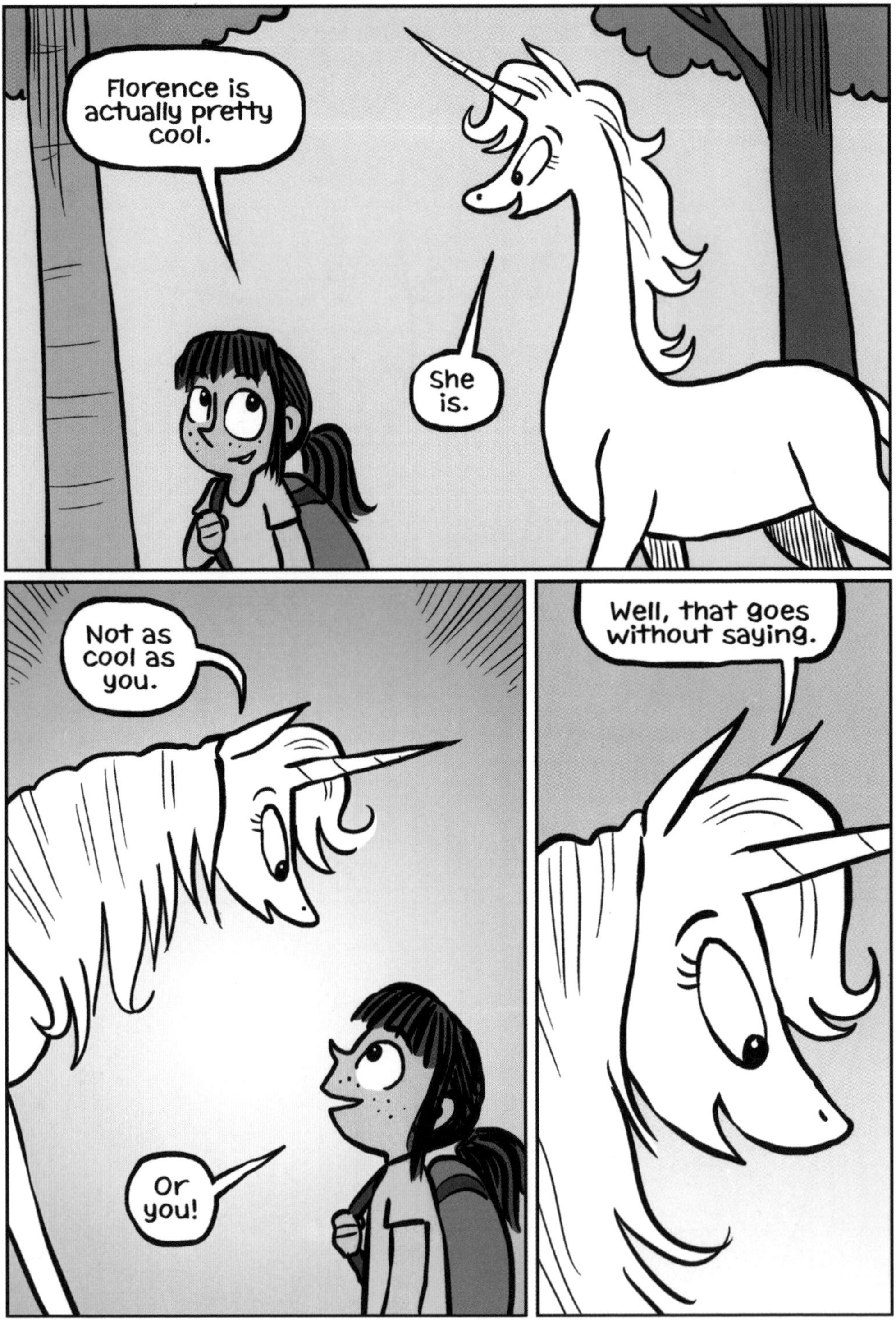
Florence is actually pretty cool.
She is.
Not as cool as you.
Or you!
Well, that goes without saying.

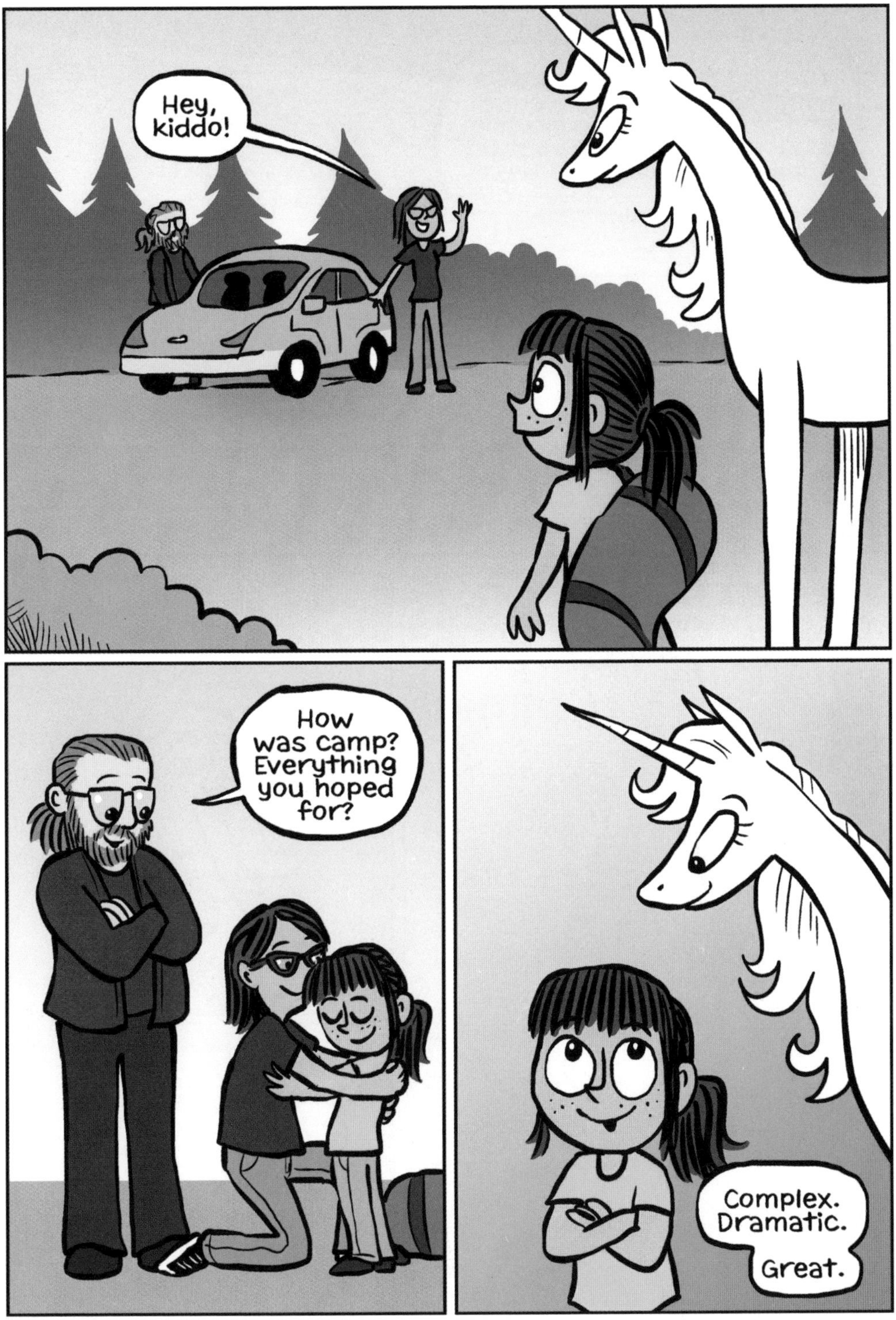
Hey, kiddo!
How was camp? Everything you hoped for?
Complex. Dramatic.
Great.

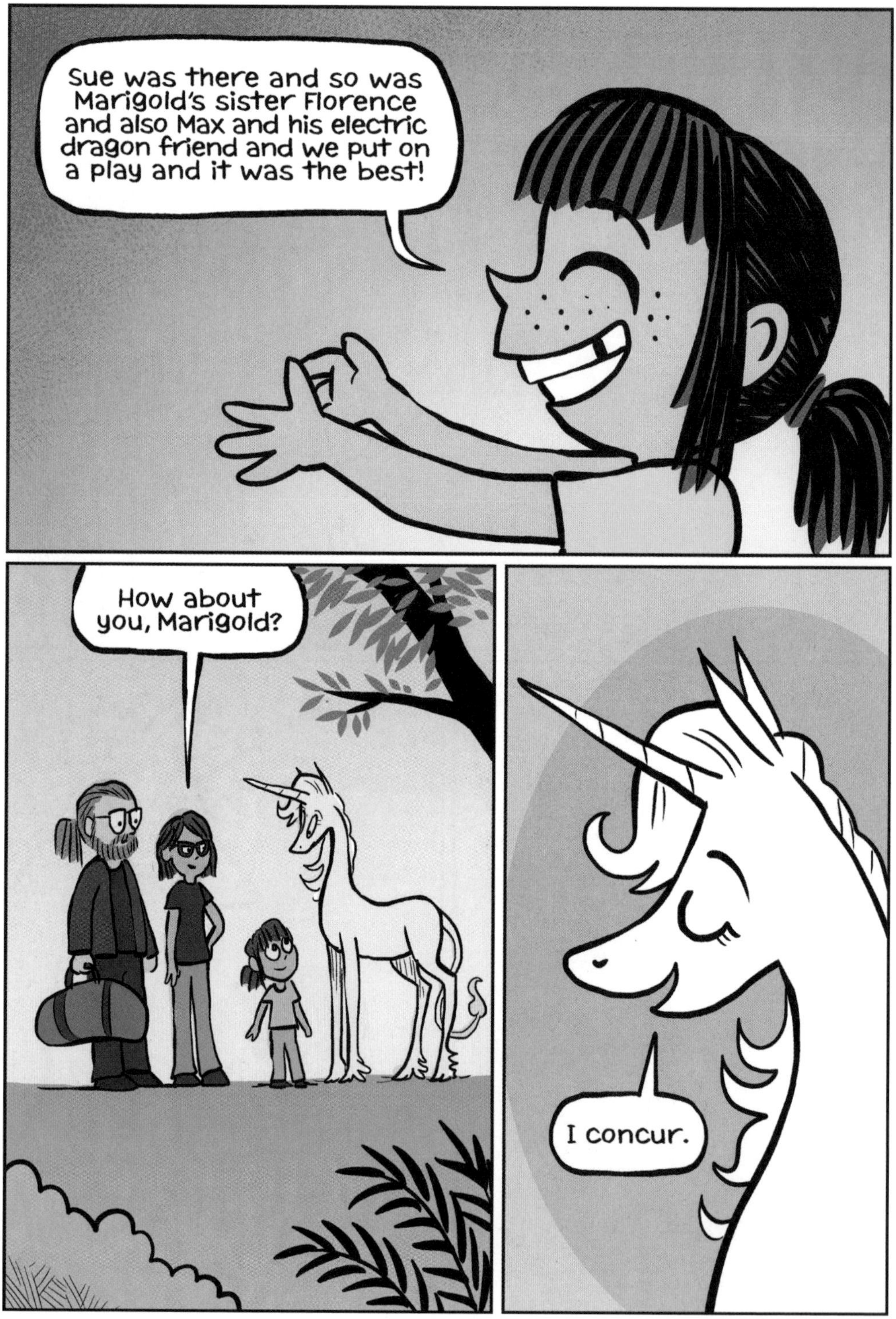
Sue was there and so was Marigold's sister Florence and also Max and his electric dragon friend and we put on a play and it was the best!
How about you, Marigold?
I concur.

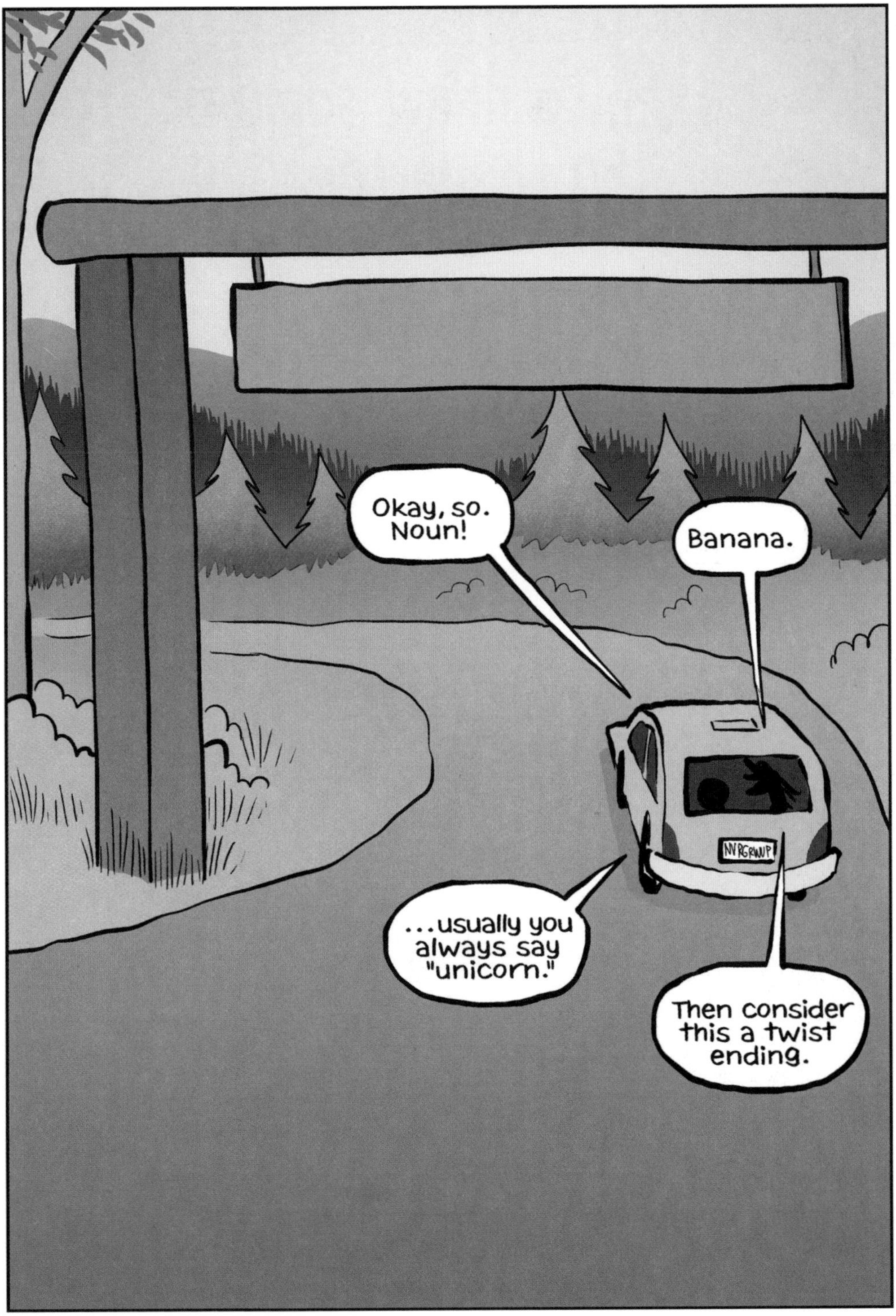
Okay, so. Noun!
Banana.
...usually you always say "unicorn."
Then consider this a twist ending.
NVRGRWUP

MORE TO EXPLORE! A special section featuring fun activities!

Learn to draw some of the characters!

Sue and Max

Like Phoebe's, Sue's head is based on a circle.

Max's is more of an oval.

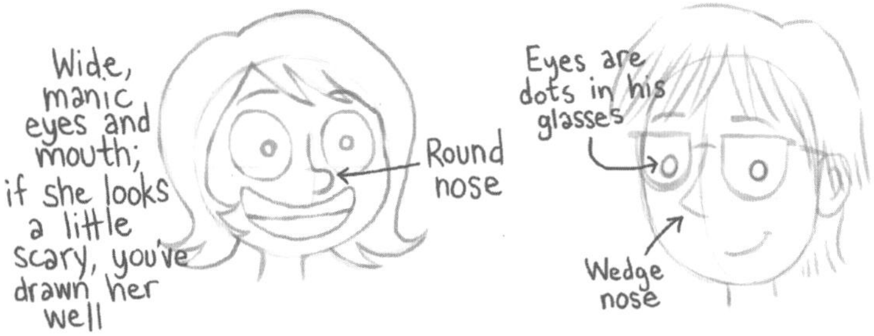

Wide, manic eyes and mouth; if she looks a little scary, you've drawn her well
Round nose
Eyes are dots in his glasses
Wedge nose

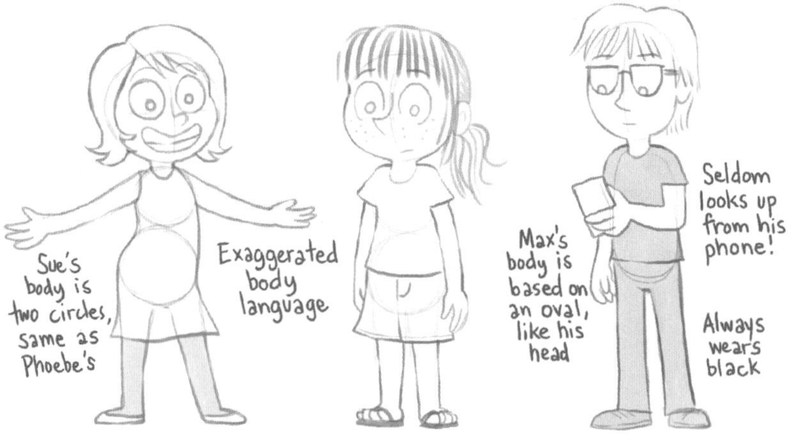

Sue's body is two circles, same as Phoebe's
Exaggerated body language
Max's body is based on an oval, like his head
Seldom looks up from his phone!
Always wears black

Ringo the Lake Monster

(For no particular reason, he's named after the drummer from the Beatles.)

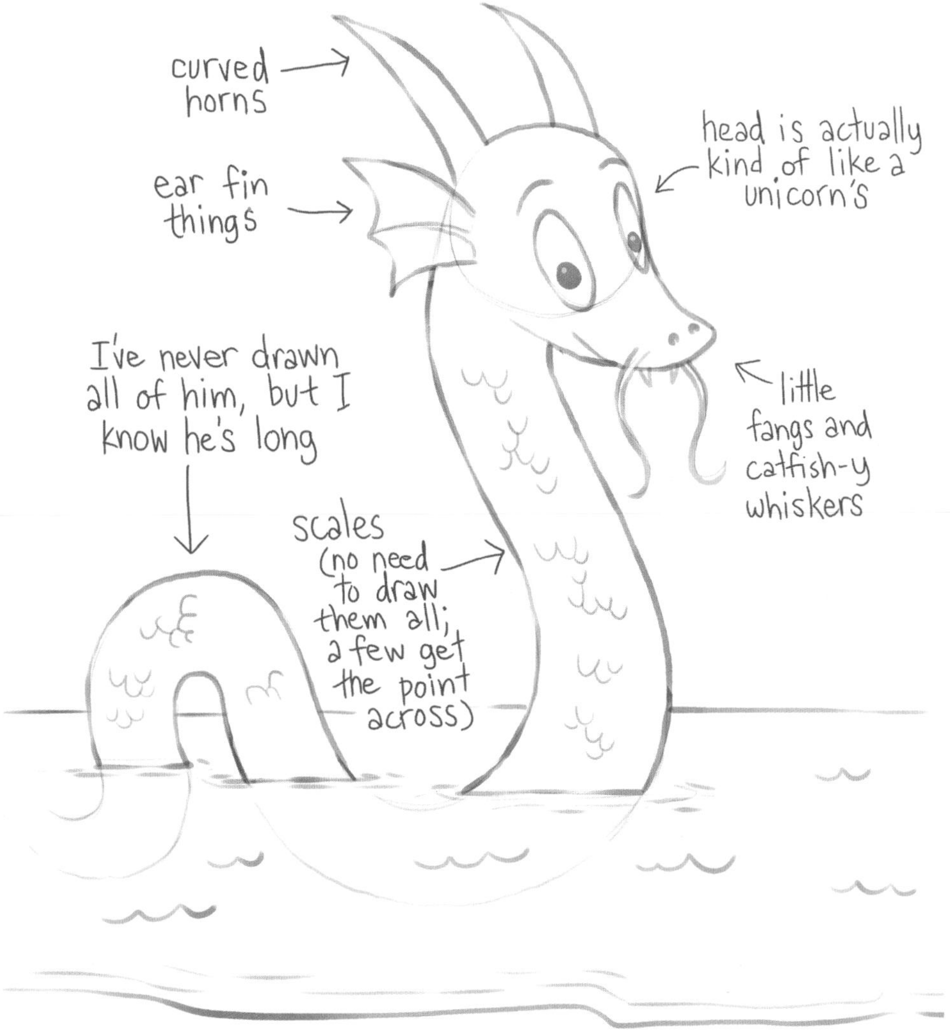

curved horns
head is actually kind of like a unicorn's
ear fin things
I've never drawn all of him, but I know he's long
little fangs and catfish-y whiskers
scales (no need to draw them all; a few get the point across)

Voltina

She's hard, because unlike any of the other characters, I draw her using all white lines. I do all my art on a computer, and it would be pretty hard to draw Voltina on paper. (But she'd look great as, say, chalk on a sidewalk.)

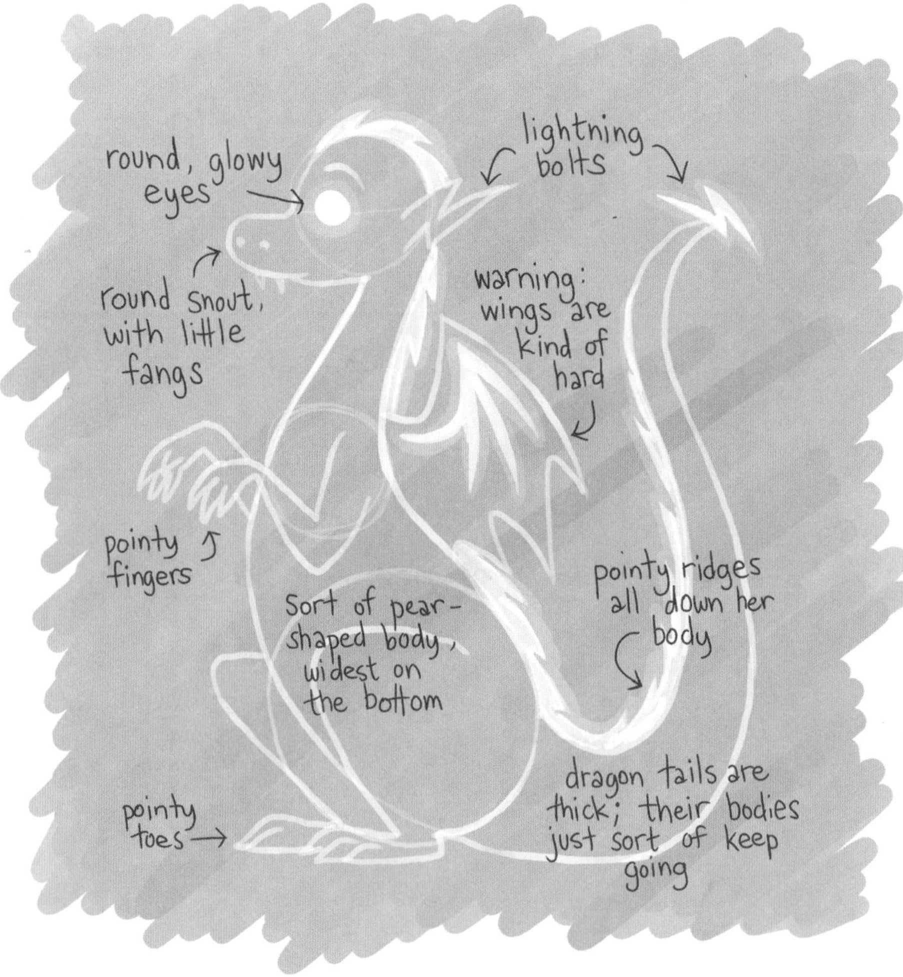

round, glowy eyes
lightning bolts
round snout, with little fangs
warning: wings are kind of hard
pointy fingers
pointy ridges all down her body
Sort of pear-shaped body, widest on the bottom
dragon tails are thick; their bodies just sort of keep going
pointy toes

Andrews McMeel Publishing
a division of Andrews McMeel Universal
1130 Walnut Street, Kansas City, Missouri 64106

www.andrewsmcmeel.com

18 19 20 21 22 SDB 10 9 8 7 6 5 4 3 2 1

ISBN: 978-1-4494-8981-6

Library of Congress Control Number: 2018930849

Made by:
Shenzhen Donnelley Printing Company Ltd.
Address and location of manufacturer:
No. 47, Wuhe Nan Road, Bantian Ind. Zone,
Shenzhen China, 518129
1st Printing—7/30/18

ATTENTION: SCHOOLS AND BUSINESSES

Andrews McMeel books are available at quantity discounts with bulk purchase for educational, business, or sales promotional use. For information, please e-mail the Andrews McMeel Publishing Special Sales Department: specialsales@amuniversal.com.

Check out more *Phoebe and Her Unicorn*

Unicorn vs. Goblins
Another Phoebe and Her Unicorn Adventure
Dana Simpson

Razzle Dazzle Unicorn
Another Phoebe and Her Unicorn Adventure
Dana Simpson

Unicorn Crossing
Another Phoebe and Her Unicorn Adventure
Dana Simpson

Phoebe and Her Unicorn in
The Magic Storm
Dana Simpson

Rainy Day Unicorn Fun
A Phoebe and Her Unicorn Activity Book
140 Magical Puzzles
Dana Simpson

Unicorn of Many Hats
Another Phoebe and Her Unicorn Adventure
Dana Simpson

If you like Phoebe, look for these books!

Anne of Green Gables
a graphic novel

OZY AND MILLIE
Dana Simpson

WALLACE the BRAVE
Will Henry

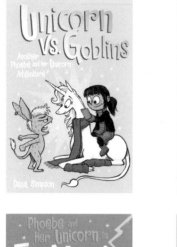

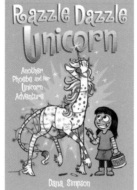

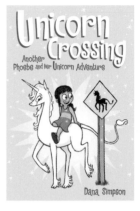

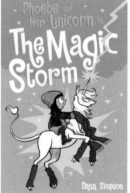

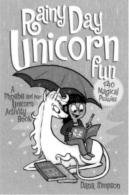

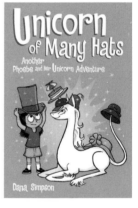

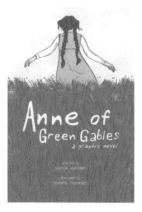

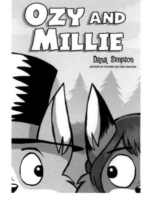

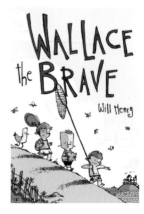